For every girl or woman
who ever stood her ground,
regardless of the outcome.

AM
G
TRADING
POST
GUARD
OUTPOS
ETONIA
PRISON
T
HUT
CATORI'S
PARENT'S
VILLAGE
FOREST

Blending of the Sands

BOOK TWO

R. M. MULLER

WILLOW HOUSE Publishing

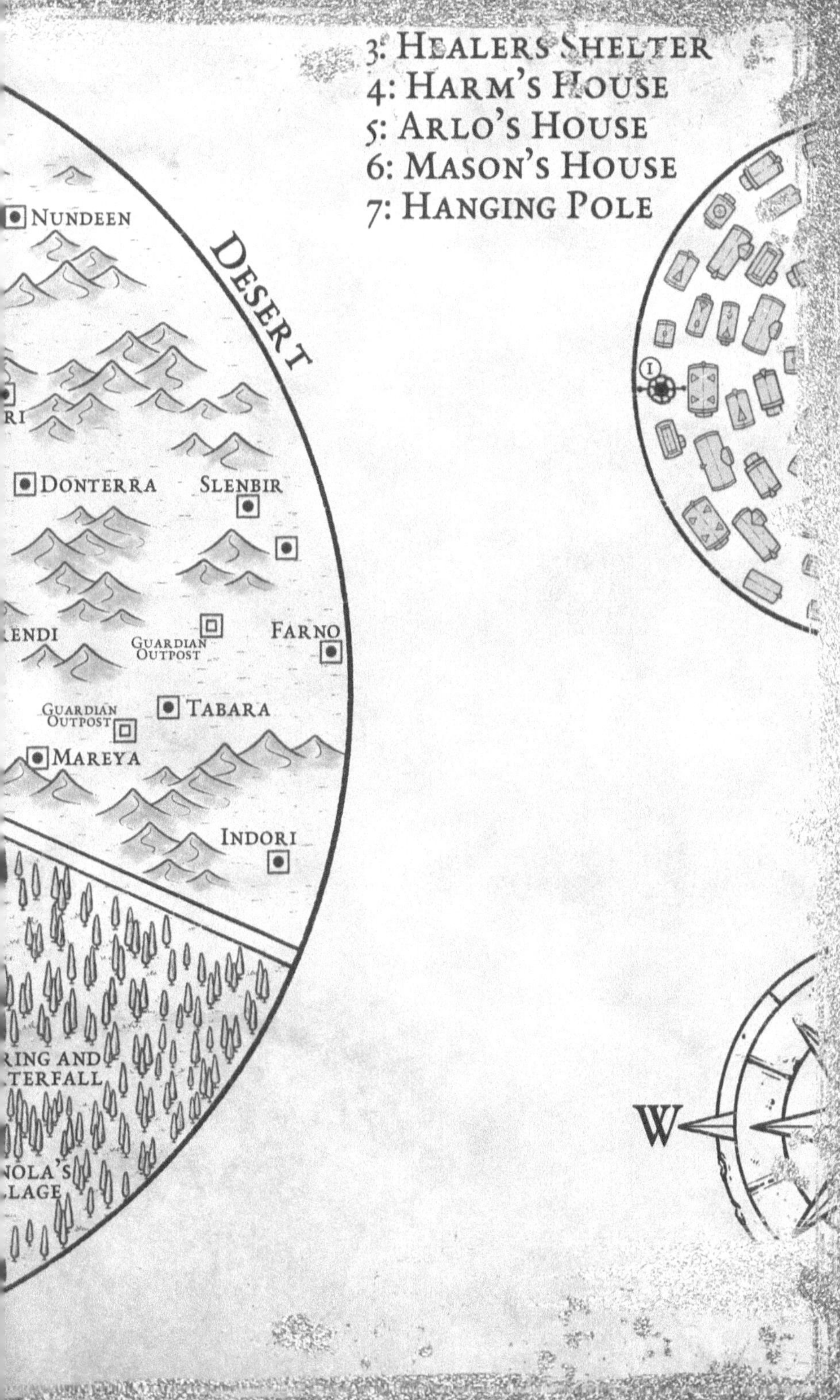

3: HEALERS SHELTER
4: HARM'S HOUSE
5: ARLO'S HOUSE
6: MASON'S HOUSE
7: HANGING POLE
NUNDEEN
DESERT
DONTERRA
SLENBIR
RENDI
GUARDIAN OUTPOST
FARNO
GUARDIAN OUTPOST
TABARA
MAREYA
INDORI
RING AND TERFALL
NOLA'S LAGE
W

Through darkness and light, my heart is still yours, our path still the same, our world slowly changing.

Blending
of the
Sands

CHAPTER I
HARM

Rattling chains wake me from a restless sleep. Warm blood seeps from beneath the metal bonds around my wrists. I pull against the short chains tethering me, trying to stretch out my aching body, before hunching over on trembling legs. Through the small window near the ceiling, splinters of light pierce through the dark.

"Thirty-seven," I whisper, shaking my head. "I can't see them. I can't see the stars, Imani."

Thirty-seven, the number of days since I last saw Imani. It feels like a lifetime. No one will tell me anything about her.

"Please be there when I get out."

I close my eyes and wince at the sting that lances through my face. Unable to fully close, my left eye is infiltrated by slits of light. *I know you can hear me, Imani.*

My heart hammers, pushing a lump into my throat. I know she's alive. I can feel it.

Scuffing echoes through the darkness toward me. I push my eyes open and shuffle to my feet. Mason stands on the other side of the cell door, arms folded over his chest, eyes burning into mine, his mouth a thin line. His uniform is dirty, shirt untucked and hair tousled. He swallows, his gaze covering every inch of my battered body and face. He grunts, spinning on his heel and mumbling something as he stalks back into the darkness. Screams break through the dim light of the half-open door, echoing through the emptiness of my isolation chamber before he slams it shut. I sink onto the grimy stone floor. This is the first time Mason has come to see me since the gallows.

By the time the light hits halfway up the stone wall in front of me, footsteps come again. It's always three of them, one for each side and one for the locks and chains, always the same ones. Heavy steps rhythmically close in on me. Three Guardians stand at my cell door, just like each of the thirty-six days before. Their expressions are flat, as if this routine is as tiresome to them as it is to me. I stand as they enter, having learned on the first day that it doesn't pay to be sitting. The shackles on my wrists weigh down my arms and legs, scraping against busted skin.

They remove my metal castings with swift fingers and shove me through the door. I falter every few steps, and hard hands jerk me up and along. The stone floor is cool under my feet, relieving some of the discomfort from yesterday. Every day is different. Every day is the same. Surely, they will run out of new ways to hurt me soon and put me out of my misery altogether.

In the darkness, I wish for that. In the darkness, I wish for Imani's face, her touch, her voice. I linger in that daydream for as long as possible. She rolls her eyes at me, smiles, and stares up at me with her dark hair framing her face, the most heavenly thing I have ever seen. Being with her is the darkest, deepest place I go. The last thread I hold onto is the hope that I will see her again. I will hold her again. I will hear her voice, see her smile.

A sharp shove onto a wooden chair brings me back to reality. Rope burns my wrists as my hands are tied behind me, my ankles tied to the chair legs. Mason sits backward on a chair in front of me, arms draped over the top. He rolls a short piece of rope between his fingers, watching its strands fling around as it twirls in his grip. Suddenly, he stands, tossing the rope to the floor.

"Leave us," he grunts.

The three officers slip out the door, pulling it shut. I watch him move around the room. He paces with a controlled gait, as if processing the best way to approach what comes next. Maybe he's trying to invent a better way to extract what he wants from me. I wish he would get it over and done with. Curiosity has me wondering why Mason is here this time and not Fletcher, or the usual three with their standard questions and stony faces?

"What do you know about the dial, Harm?" he asks.

I am slightly disappointed that he asks the same routine thing. He faces me and waits for an answer.

"Not a lot. Only that it's controlled by a man with a special ability." I relay the same answer I have given to every other Guardian that has stood in that spot for the last thirty-six days.

"Do you possess that ability?"

"No."

His eyes glaze over, and his hand lands across the side of my face. Heat rises, bringing with it the burn. The corner of my mouth stings and starts to bleed, a split that is never allowed to heal. I turn and spit blood on the floor. The pain pushes away the darkness of my mind temporarily. The burning is a relief from the weighted ache in my chest.

Mason turns away and bends over the back of the chair, as if trying to muster the strength for what comes next.

"Why did you turn yourself in?" The chair creaks as his grip on the back of it tightens.

Well, that's different.

"Why does it matter, Mason? You got what you wanted." His focus clears, and for a moment, he studies my face.

He shakes his head, as if ridding it of whatever is plaguing his thoughts. "You are a wanted felon. Turning yourself in was suicide." He's quieter than I anticipated as his eyes lock onto mine. "Harm, you're not going to get out of this one. So, either tell me what you know, or I'll have to pull it out of you."

I hold my gaze on his. "Do what you have to, Rayner. You've already betrayed everyone. It doesn't get much worse than that."

Mason moves into my space, his jaw clenching, hands gripping the top of the chair behind my shoulders. His focus wavers again, pupils dilating. He stands back and cracks his neck to one side. Without warning, his fist smashes into my nose. Instantly, blood pours over my mouth and chin. I groan and look back up to his face. A snarl rips from his twisted mouth, and he stands tall, rooted to the spot with his hands at his sides, shaking with anger.

"Tell me what you know about the ability. Do you have it?" he hollers.

I chuckle maniacally, knowing this is going to hurt.

Mason leans back and kicks a boot into my chest. I topple backward with the chair, and my head cracks against the stone. Black spots cloud my vision, and a splitting ache grows at the back of my head. My hands are crushed under the weight of me and the chair, sending shooting pains up my arms. I turn my head and gasp for air, spitting up bile and blood.

Mason stands over me, a foot on either side. He drags me back upright, chair and all. "One last time. Tell me what you know," he growls.

"Nothing. I know nothing, Mason."

I wait for the next blow.

It doesn't come.

I find his gaze again, and it is clear, regret twisting his features like a sour, rotted desert fruit. Mason turns back to his chair, then hurtles it into the corner of the room. It busts apart the second it impacts the stone. He lingers with one last look before opening the door and storming out.

Moments later, the three Guardians return and untie me from the chair. I am tugged back to my feet and dragged back down the passageway to my cell. Once I am secured to the wall again, they leave.

Not a word is spoken.

With the heat of the sun outside, the stone around me radiates warmth, and like every other day, Toby comes with my meal tray. He lays it on the ground beside me and sits on the floor, keeping an eye out for Guardians. I sit against the stone wall, so my chains will allow me to eat. Leaning against the stone is a comfort. Toby watches me with sorrowful eyes as I eat the bread and soup.

"Harm, I can't help you this time," he finally says.

I swallow a mouthful of bread. "I know."

"Also, there's something else."

I look up from the food. His face is twisted with pain. I meet his gaze, and my stomach drops.

"It's about Imani," he starts, fingers fiddling with the hem of his trousers. "I saw her clothes and possessions with the pile of things that belonged to the executed prisoners."

I swallow hard and force air to fill my lungs. "Are you sure?"

"She's the only female prisoner we've had, so yeah. Pretty sure."

"What happened to her after Fletcher took me?"

"All I saw was Mason dragging her off in the opposite direction. She was still screaming your name even after you went through that door. I haven't seen her since. Just her clothes," he says.

"Imani would not go down without a fight. If she's not here in the prison, maybe there's a chance she escaped in all the commotion."

"She was pretty beat up, Harm. They strung her up for two days, trying to get information about you. I don't know if she would have been up to escaping by that point. Plus, there were orders." Toby stands with the empty tray.

"What orders? What are you talking about?"

"From the Chancellor. He ordered her execution, Harm."

My breathing turns shallow, heart racing like the winds over the glittering dunes.

No. Please, no.

"But she's the commander's daughter!"

"It doesn't matter. She's committed too many infractions to go unpunished. Then she paired up with you. Her years of wandering around interfering with regime orders had to get noticed eventually. Even Fletcher knew that."

A combination of sadness, guilt, and anger rage through my ragged body. I lie on my side as Toby makes his way out of the barred gate and locks it behind him.

I close my battered eyes, and for what feels like the thousandth time, I replay a vision of what Imani looked like the last time I saw her. Rags hung from her thin body, stained with old blood, thanks to similar treatment to what I have endured at the hands of the Guardians. Her eyes were clouded by a grey lining that had never been there before. Her long, dark, wavy hair, once as bold as her soul, was gone, like a part of her had been removed. It was just another way to hurt her, taking away what made her elegant and strong, leaving behind a tattered and tormented version of who she once was.

Only, that is what they saw. That is what the Guardians think they have done. Imani would never succumb to that, and in her heart and mind, it would only make her even more dangerous. I believe that. I have to believe that.

The few unwavering truths I cling to are interrupted by the sound of the cell gate. Black boots stop only inches from my face. This must be a hallucination; I have been to the interrogation room already today. I close my eyes again.

"Stand!"

Fletcher.

I push up from the floor and struggle to my feet, our faces only inches apart.

"Aren't you a sight?" he mutters.

I sway on my feet, heat spreading from my chest, flooding my veins.

"Without the information we need from you, you're good as dead, Travesci."

"I already told your officers, I don't know anything. No more than anyone else. Why would I?"

"Why would you? A very good question," Fletcher mocks, but doesn't lose his focus. "Maybe because there is low-life scum, such as yourself, who come from the south and are connected to the ability. I assume you've figured out that Barlow had it."

"You didn't need to kill him," I hiss. "He never would have used it."

Fletcher laughs. "Really? And you think we would trust a man who couldn't even hold up his end of a bargain? He may not have named you specifically, but I have my sources, and they say you were in that village when his wife sent her message. I don't believe in coincidences, boy."

"How is it that you knew about his ability, but you let him live all this time?" I ask, daring to be direct, even though I mostly know the answer.

"He was useful—unlike you, Harmen. You are proving to be a liability. You should have died in that well, saved everyone a lot of trouble."

Does he mean Imani?

If Fletcher knows I have the ability, he is not letting on, but trying to drag it out of me. I am not going to offer it up to him. He walks away from me, lost in thought. Immediately, I think of Imani.

"What happened to her?" I call after him.

Fletcher spins on his heel and faces me. "She is dead." His eyes narrow as his jaw clenches.

I stare hard at him, digesting his words one at a time.

She. Is. Dead.

"No," I rasp.

Fletcher's face splits into a smirk. I drop to my knees, my head sinking into my hands. The breath that leaves my lungs doesn't return. As I gasp amidst uncontrollable sobs, my fists hit the floor to support my weight. Screams pour from my constricted throat. Fletcher stands motionless, witnessing my descent.

After a time, my screams peter out to a low growl, my voice hoarse. My chest aches, keeping my trembling body alive, only just. A snicker comes from Fletcher. I raise my head to look at him. His smug expression is laced with hate. Heat shoots through my body. My arms stiffen with tension, and I push myself up, lunging at him in one fierce movement. Metal bites into my wrists and ankles as I slam to the end of my chains. Fletcher is motionless, his face unchanging. Warmth trickles down each of my hands. I push to stand as tall as the chains will allow.

"When I get out of here, Fletcher, you're a dead man." I spit at his feet.

"Oh, you won't be getting out of here, Travesci. We are waiting for you to provide information about the dial. If you don't, well... You're coming to the tower. The Chancellor wants to meet the last person with the ability before he is dispatched."

That's it. He knows every part of me now.

Imani.

The ability.

I have nothing left to hide from him.

He has it all.

"You knew all along?" My words are so quiet, I'm not sure he heard me.

"I wasn't sure if there were any people left with it, actually. It was just a hunch. But then, you revealed yourself to save that gutter rat. How touching. The only way you could save her is if you had something of value to trade for her life. I'll take that as confirmation."

"How can you speak of your own daughter like that?!"

Surprise shows in his eyes. He thought I wouldn't know. His eyes wander to the wall behind me.

"I have no daughter."

The last thread I have been grasping onto slips through my fingers.

He turns and leaves.

CHAPTER 2
IMANI

Stale air surrounds the makeshift bed against the stone wall of the cage that holds me. Every inch of me is filthy. I run my hands through my nonexistent hair for what feels like the hundredth time since it was severed off with a dull blade. No sharp scissors or neat cut; it was hacked off in a show of intimidation and power, by my own father. Fletcher. And Mason just stood there and watched, his expression flickering between horror and pleasure as they tried to break me in a thousand different ways.

The last glimpse I had of Harm still haunts me, his eyes lined with desperation and pain. In my dreams, he just stands in front of me, staring. My heart almost lurches out of my chest every time I wake up and remember that he's gone. At least, that's what Mason told me. I don't believe him. Mason is the only person I have seen since the gallows, and I am locked up in his house like a rabid house pet.

Yesterday, he removed the chains from my wrists and ankles. Apparently, I have been good enough for that little luxury. But the scraps he feeds me are barely enough for a small child. I try not to let him see me cry; if he knew why, he would only get angry. He keeps telling me to move on from Harm, that *he* is my best match and my only hope. His words are disgusting and arrogant. He watches me every night before he asks to come into my space. Every night, he tries. Every night, I refuse. I am partly scared of him, and partly loathe him in every way. He is the complete opposite of Harm.

I lie on my bedding of rags and study the beams of the ceiling to pass the time. Mason is on duty. It's better when he's not here, but incredibly boring. I roll over and scratch marks into the wall to entertain myself. I hover the small stick close to the wall. Did I count yesterday? I don't remember. The days before that...?

Tears prickle behind my eyes, and I scrub out the marks, blurring the tallies, and loose a moan. I fling the stick from my fingers, and it hits the floor and snaps. There is no point in marking the days anymore.

I rise to my knees, sinking onto my heels, and double over, forehead meeting the stone floor, hands gripping my hair that is slowly growing back thicker, eyes squeezed shut. I let out another moan. The wounds from the beatings I got in prison have faded now, and my body is healing, but I am skin and bone.

The sound of the door's metal latch interrupts my thoughts, and Mason strides through it, his uniform drenched in sweat from the heat outside. He throws his hat, wrap, and goggles on the small wooden table in the center of the room. He removes his belt and shoes and slumps into his only chair. I study his movements, trying to work out which mood he's in today. He leans back and sighs, closing his eyes. Spinning around onto my bed, sitting with legs and arms crossed as I lean against the wall, I watch him.

"Imani, how long are you going to stay in there? If you let me in, you can come out." His eyes are still closed.

I swallow down the disgust at the thought of him touching me. His overbearing stature and menacing pale blue eyes make my skin crawl. His muscled body moves under his uniform as he stretches on the chair. I'm sure it's only a matter of time before I don't have a choice.

"Won't you be punished for stealing a prisoner? Especially a high-ranking Guardian's daughter?"

"Fletcher does not claim you as his own anymore, Imani. You made sure of that when you paired up with that filthy traitor," he mutters.

My blood races through my veins. How dare he talk about Harm that way! "Harm is *not* a filthy traitor!"

"*Was*, Imani. He *was* a filthy traitor; now he's dead. I've told you this already."

I scoff at his effort to make me believe Harm is really dead, but it hurts enough to tear a hole right through me.

"I need another blanket. The nights are too cold," I say.

"I can think of another way to keep you warm," he says, a smirk growing over his face as his gaze meets mine.

"There is no way I will ever let you touch me."

He stands and walks over to the metal bars that make me his prisoner. He grabs the gate, shaking it, anger flooding his face. "You will be mine, or you will never see daylight again, Fletcher!"

"I will never let you lay a finger on me. You disgust me on every level."

He rattles the metal door and growls at me before walking away, back to the table. He plants his fists on it and hangs his head, breathing out fiercely.

"As long as it takes, Imani," he says, then disappears into the washroom.

I curl up against the wall, immensely grateful for the barrier of iron bars between me and him. His size alone frightens me enough, let alone his short fuse. He is a stark contrast to Harm, who is quiet and almost painfully slow to react, his fire kept more restrained than mine. The Mason who was my friend so long ago is unrecognisable. That boy grew cold and mean. By my father's hand.

An hour later, he emerges from his room. Washed and in civilian clothes, he announces that he is going out. A smirk crosses his face as he leaves, reminding me of his freedom and my captivity. I pick up a small stone that has been rattling around the cold floor for days and scratch it along the wall, feigning disinterest.

I try to draw the lines of Harm's face, but I can't. So, I just add another mark to the wall for another day passed in this cell, starting the tally again. Night comes, and Mason still hasn't returned. I swaddle myself up in my worn sheet and set in for another cold night.

The sound of my own cries wakes me, his name on my lips. *Harm.* My face is wet from crying. Shuffling comes from behind me, keys jangling before one turns in the lock, then the barred door opens. I freeze. Mason steps into the cell. My heart thunders out of my chest. As I stare at the wall, panic clutches my entire body while my mind reels.

A blanket drops onto my body. I flinch, forcing myself to breathe, eyes still wide open. A strong hand lands on my shoulder. I can smell him. He smells wrong.

"Imani."

"What?" I whimper.

"You were crying out his name in your sleep." He sits on the floor beside me.

"Sorry to be such an inconvenience," I hiss, sounding braver than I feel right now.

"Harm is gone, Imani," he says quietly. His kindness surprises me, but I don't trust it. Not for a second.

"I don't believe you." A single tear streaks down my face and soaks into the rags beneath me, the lack of air squeezing my heart tighter.

Mason crosses his arms over his chest, mouth tugging up at the corner. "When will you get over that scrawny traitor?" His demeanor is back to normal.

I tuck the blanket more tightly around my shoulders. "Leave me alone, Mason."

He doesn't leave. His hands lift my shoulders, and he pulls me up to sit in front of him. Cold air hangs between us, mixing with his hot breath. Mason moves in to hug me, and I recoil, hitting the wall.

A fierce sting swallows my cheek. I breathe out, and my hand instantly reaches for my burning skin. Heat prickles through my chest. His face warps as he rubs the palm he smashed across my face. I remember seeing his father flog him for losing a goat once, back in Amondo, just before he practically volunteered to join the regime. Behind the fire that laces his eyes is a glimmer of hurt. He pushes up and gets to his feet before walking out and closing the cell gate.

"Where does Fletcher think I am, Mason?"

He stills and turns back to me. "He knows exactly where you are, Imani. He put you here."

He crosses to his bedroom door. I flinch as he slams the door. I fall back down on the floor. My father did this? Stuck me in a cage to be thrown scraps by Mason, taking away the last bit of freedom I had? Every memory of my childhood with my father, every hug and moment I treasured but had pushed down come flooding up, like a spout of water from a broken well pump, as uncontrollable and rapid as the winds of a raging sandstorm. His hands on my face, his laugh, his embrace when I was hurt, the look of love and pride in his eyes when I started school ... I slap a hand over my mouth to hold in a cry. Why, after everything, do I care?

But I do. I do, more than I want to, more than I ever realized I would.

Before the sun lights up the desert sky, I hear the familiar shuffling of Mason's feet as he organizes himself for his shift. I don't dare look at him after last night. The loathing I have for him has only multiplied after his hand damaged my face. I trace my fingers over the welt he left, snuggling down into the blanket and feigning sleep, keeping my eyes cracked so I can see what he does.

After gathering his work gear, he throws on his belt and shoes and heads for the door. His hand lands on the doorknob. He hesitates and turns, his stare is cold and cruel. His hand drops from the door, and he stalks over to the cell. He pulls the keys out of his pocket, shoving one into the lock. The cell gate swings open, and in a few strides, he is standing over me. I pretend to be woken by his sudden entrance, and he leans down and rips the blanket away from me.

My head hits the cold floor, and a snort escapes his mouth. He leaves the cell, locking the door, shoving the keys in his pants pocket. I want to spit on him, but he's too far away, so I throw him a deathly glare and hope that hurts just as much. Prick. A growl leaves his mouth before he barrels through the front door and slams it behind him.

I sit up, distancing my body from the cold floor, shivering as I readjust the thin sheet I am left with. I can't stay here. I would rather die than be touched by Mason. I will not stay in this cell, locked up like an animal. I would rather take my chances in the middle of the desert, looking for Harm, even if I'm chasing a ghost.

I stand and look around Mason's small home, searching for anything to help me escape. My hands grip the iron bars that seal my enclosure, and I notice for the first time since I was brought here how thin I have become. My muscles are probably next to useless unless I start using them. I need more food.

I run a hand over one arm, then the other. I lift the ragged tunic that I've been wearing since the prison. My knees are knobby, and the bones of my shins are visible through my grubby skin. My hand traces a path over my torso, and my ribs bump rhythmically under my fingers, in stark contrast to the body I had before the prison.

A tear falls down my face, and heat rises through my chest as my breath quickens. This is not happening. Harm or no Harm, I am getting out of here.

I return to my bed and close my eyes, running through possible ways to escape. Moments later, I am curled up on the floor, tangled in my sheet, eyes drifting shut from hunger, cold, and hopelessness.

CHAPTER 3
HARM

Imani lies on the green grass beside me in Charlie's oasis. Her hair frames her pretty face, resting over her shoulders. I touch her face, tracing the bones of her cheeks, and her eyes are closed, but she is smiling. Her breathing fills the space between us, and I watch the rise and fall of her chest. I trace from her shoulder to her breastbone, and her eyes open, piercing mine, her soft smile still there.

One of the small birds flitters past, and I look up and chuckle. After a moment, I look back at Imani—but her eyes are red, her neck sliced open, and her skin is fading to grey. She gasps for breath. I freeze, choking out her name, begging her not to leave me. She fades away until all that is left is the flattened grass where she had been.

I wake with a start, hitting the ends of my chains. Splinters of light penetrate the small opening that is the only window in my cell, signaling another night gone. I told Imani about her father last night. She would want to know. I mentioned seeing Mason too, although I know she doesn't like him. I certainly don't like him around her. Talking to her makes me feel a little less insane. My words are still swallowed by the darkness, but imagining her listening and talking with me is the one sliver of hope I have left.

A flood of heaviness rolls into my chest as I remember Fletcher's words. She is dead. Sobs pour from my feeble body. I cry for hours, the pain never easing, no matter how many tears I shed. Waves of sorrow wash in, and I struggle to breathe. Finally, I fall into the darkness of sleep, just as I imagine twilight descends on the desert sands outside.

The sound of metal on metal wakes me, my eyes burning from my heartbroken sleep. Mason enters my cell with two other Guardians. It is early, not time for my daily treatment, and I search Mason's expression for a sign of what's happening. His face is blank, bored, like nothing that happens in here matters. I rise to meet them. Mason's stature dwarfs my hunched-over skin-and-bone frame. We stare at each other while the shackles are removed. Then he spins on his heel and walks out of the cell. A hand grips each of my arms, and I am shoved through the door after him.

No one speaks as we walk down the passageway that leads from the isolation cell back to the main part of the prison. As I walk the hall between the cells, the inmates pause in their deliberations, their gazes fixed on me. Mason, oblivious to their stares, walks on undisturbed. At the last cell, a man rises at the gate, his hands on the bars, eyes searching. I turn my head to get a better look at him while I am escorted past. Charlie...? A slight smile curves his lips, but does not reach the sorrow in his eyes. His face is not right. It's not Charlie. My stomach plummets.

A scraping noise swings my focus back to the large wooden doors ahead of us. Mason makes light work of the enormous metal bar across the twin doors, opening one, and we walk through. He closes the door behind us, and the space dives into darkness. The hands that hold my arms grip tighter.

"Where are we going?" I ask.

No response.

Three knocks sound in front of me. Seconds later, a stone door pivots on its hinges, and we are inundated with sunlight. I squint, the swelling from last night aching through my face. My mind wanders to images of Imani as we stand there, waiting for something to happen.

A Guardian appears in the doorway. His uniform is immaculate, nearly identical to Mason's, but he has golden epaulets, where Mason's and Fletcher's are silver. He signals for Mason to enter. His face is freshly shaven, and he leaves behind him a pleasant scent, nothing like the sweat and dirt we smell of living in the desert. Mason is almost rigid as he walks behind the Guardian in front of him. The passageway has a high ceiling and echoes with our footsteps. Light slips in, blue sky with white clouds floating beyond the high windows.

Something flies past one of the windows—a bird, like those in Charlie's haven, but much larger. My attention turns back to the men in front of me. The hall seems to go on forever. Doors are scattered sparingly on the right-hand wall. Concealing what? Where do they lead?

We stop at the next door on the right, and the Guardian leading us opens the door. He glances back at me with a hesitant look before turning and walking through. Reaching the threshold, we are immersed in sunlight and open sky. Stretching out beyond the door is a stone bridge, its sides flanked by half walls topped with ornate brickwork every few paces.

With one step, we are on the bridge. The prison falls away, with a vast distance between us and the ground below. The wind dances around us, playing with our hair and tugging at our clothes. The four men with me walk on, as if our environment has not just changed dramatically. I watch their faces. Nothing. We stop halfway along the bridge to let three Guardians pass, all wearing the golden epaulets.

Held with my back pressed against the wall of the bridge, I turn to look behind me. An expanse of trees fills the space below us—thousands of them. A forest! Déjà vu creeps in. They are the trees from my dream—the one with Imani. Air tries to escape my chest like a fleeing animal, the blood in my veins pounding in time with my quickening heartbeat. Warmth rises from the trees, carrying a woody scent, and every breath feels like a cleansing. Sounds of animals and birds resound in bursts from all around. I can't see through the trees, but I can imagine them scurrying around like the ones Charlie had.

The Guardians pass by, and we continue to travel across the bridge. It turns a corner, and rising up in front of us is a tower. We can't see any of this from the desert side. As we move closer, with wide eyes, I study the tower that stands above us, covered in sky-blue tiles, reflecting its surroundings as if it doesn't exist. Beneath the tower and its enormous metal doors lies a stone building that looks like the prison, but much larger, stretching out for hundreds of yards, forming an enormous rectangle with an empty space in the center. A training ground? Everything is surrounded by trees.

The metal doors swing open as we approach. My bare feet ache from walking on the stone, but I am reminded by the firm grip on my arms to move forward, and we enter the tower. The room is made of stone, but decorated like a home. A long carpet runs through the center of the huge chamber. Adorning the walls are tall arched windows, dressed with thin curtains that dance in the constant breeze. The room smells of flowers—at least, that's what I think it is.

Two large wooden chairs sit at either end of a long wooden table. The wood is dark, like nothing I have ever seen before. Perhaps it comes from the trees below? A woven basket sits in the center of the table, holding plump rounded fruits. There is no one else here, just us. The Guardian tells us to wait by the door, then disappears. I take a quick glance at Mason. He is standing tall, his face like stone, the same as before.

A moan from behind us grabs everyone's attention. Through the metal doors steps Fletcher. Behind him are two more Guardians of the silver rank, and between them, they are holding up Charlie. I suck in a sharp breath, curling my hands into fists. His clothes are torn, his face greyed, and his usual hunched posture seems even deeper. His eyes meet mine, and torment contorts his face. He releases a ragged cry as he studies me, running his gaze over my body. Then he closes his eyes and shakes his head.

"Charlie," I rasp over the lump that has formed in my throat. A hand lands across the back of my head, and I stumble forward slightly. Charlie is fidgeting, moving about on the spot, his eyes darting around. He appears to know where we are. Footsteps close in, coming from a door on the left at the back of the room. He shoots me a look of reassurance. I steady my breathing and track my gaze back to the approaching footsteps.

The Guardian leads two people toward us. I glance over at Charlie. His head is down, eyes fixed on the floor. I look at the man behind the Guardian: Arthur, the Chancellor, Charlie's younger brother. He is followed by a woman of the same age. They come to a halt in front of us. The Chancellor is dressed in robes, a light cream fabric with gold trim on the long sleeves and bottom hem. A sash is tied around his oversized waist. This is nothing like the uniform he wore in the prison when Charlie and I first encountered him, before the gallows. The woman wears a matching ensemble that covers her thin, aged, but still elegant frame. Her grey hair is pulled up and kept in place with a jeweled pin set in gold. Her eyes are a stunning golden brown, and she wears a slight smile on her face, probably trying to make us feel more welcome. She holds a ceramic bowl and spoon, as if she was interrupted when we arrived.

Fletcher steps forward and rattles off our status and crimes. The Chancellor inspects me slowly, and his expression doesn't change, except for a slight narrowing of his glare.

"Hello," the lady says.

The Chancellor throws her a vile look, and she drops her head in submission.

"This one here is the traitor that escaped execution," Fletcher says, indicating me. "He is also the last non-relation of yours to hold the ability, sir."

"Tell me, Fletcher, how incompetent must one man be to let this bag-of-bones commoner escape him multiple times?" the Chancellor responds. Fletcher's jaw tenses, and he swallows before setting his shoulders back and stepping back.

The Chancellor steps into my space, huffing an indignant laugh. "So, you are the last person with the ability to manipulate the dial. Look at you. Pathetic. I suppose you had some idea that you could change things back to how they were before. Your type always does." He turns and paces the room in front of his wife. "And now there is only one of you left. Not for long, boy. I'm afraid your time to draw breath is up." He stops on the spot, turning to face me with a smirk.

He stands staring at me for a moment before shifting his gaze to Charlie, frowning. "Why is this other piece of filth wasting my time again?" He directs his question at Fletcher while examining Charlie, who still hangs his head, reluctant to raise it.

"Another of the traitors, sir. He was aiding the boy," Fletcher says.

"Bit old for that kind of adventure, aren't you?" he says to his older brother. "Or was this all part of your ridiculous scam of claiming to be the true Chancellor?"

Charlie does not respond.

Fletcher shifts on his feet.

"I asked you a question, filth. Answer me!"

Charlie's body shakes, his bony fingers curl into fists, and a small growl leaves his chest. "Never too old for the important things."

A smirk appears across the Chancellor's face, followed by the shadow of realization. His gaze alternates between Charlie and me, his face pinched.

"What is your name?" he asks as he turns to me.

"Harm."

"Harm what?" he spits.

"Harmen Travesci."

"Hmmmm…" The Chancellor rubs his chin with one hand. "There will be no more Travescis left shortly. You are the last of your line. And you, old man? What is your name?"

Charlie slowly raises his head, his tortured face now calm and determined."You tell me, brother." He holds the Chancellor's gaze and waits.

The ceramic bowl hits the floor, the crash echoing off the stone walls. The woman's face goes from pained to shocked. Her eyes widen as her breathing quickens.

The Chancellor freezes, his smirk gone. He gasps. The sound of his wife behind him, whispering Charlie's name in exasperation, entices him to stand tall once again.

"My brother is dead," he replies firmly.

"Is that what you told everyone, Artie?" Charlie responds, his voice brimming with anger.

Arthur spins on his heel and paces behind his wife, who is now trembling where she stands.

"It has been almost forty years," he says, as if to himself, rubbing his hands over his face.

Arthur's wife steps toward Charlie, her hands reaching for him. Her shoulders shudder with sobs, but she holds her head high as tears run down her creased ivory cheeks. With every step, Charlie takes her in. She touches his face, and her eyes close as she looses a ragged breath. "Charlie...?" she whimpers. Her palm molds to his face. Charlie stands wide eyed, breathing shallow and quick, his gaze locked on her face. He takes her hand and wraps it in both of his.

Arthur jerks, stiffening before lunging toward his wife with a low growl. "Don't you touch her!" He tries to put himself between his wife and Charlie.

"Emmie?" Charlie chokes out, ignoring his brother.

My stomach flips as it sinks in. She is Charlie's Emmaline, his betrothed. All this time he believed she had been killed. I watch as he reels with the realization that she is alive—and now Blended with his brother. The agony distorting his face hits me in the chest like a stone.

"Arthur told me you were dead! Oh, my Charlie!" Emmie cries, her breaths coming heavy and fast as she rediscovers Charlie's face with her hands for the first time in decades.

Charlie steps closer to her. The Guardian beside him pounds his fist into Charlie's ribs, and he doubles over, breaking from Emmie's hold.

"No!" Emmie screams. "Stop this immediately!"

Arthur steps between them, breaking their contact.

Her eyes burn into Arthur's. "What have you done?! What did you do to..." She closes her eyes briefly, pulling in a breath, steadying herself. "*You* did this, to your own brother, and to me. How could you, Arthur?!"

"Get her out of here!" Arthur shouts.

A Guardian grips Emmie by the arm and leads her away. She calls for Charlie, unable to turn away even as she retreats, pleading with her eyes for him to recover from the blow. Her protests fall on deaf ears.

"Emmie," Charlie whispers, struggling to breathe.

Arthur moves closer and stands over him. "You were dead to us the day you refused to join our cause. You didn't deserve Emmaline then, and you will not have her now!" The fire in his voice turns to a vicious snarl.

"You stole the lands and took anything of value from the people, and betrayed your own brother. What kind of a man does that?!" Charlie spits, slowly rising with no assistance from the Guardians.

"One who gets whatever he wants, big brother. I got your life, I got your position, and best of all, I got your wife," Arthur snaps. With a quick gesture to the Guardians, he turns to leave. Their grip on us tightens, and we walk toward the metal doors.

"Charlie," Arthur tosses out, turning on his heel. The Guardians pause just beyond the door, hands clasped on Charlie's arms. "At least I have been around for *all* of the important things." A smirk grows across his face that makes my stomach plummet.

Charlie's thin arms strain against the Guardians holding him, and he lets out a pained moan. They push us back along the bridge. Tears flow down Charlie's face, and he shakes his head continuously, whispering Emmie's name.

CHAPTER 4
HARM

Different cell, same routine. Fletcher arrives just after dawn to haul me into a separate room. Mason is not there; another Guardian stands in his place. The ropes that bind my wrists to the chair cut into my raw wounds, and I wince at even the slightest movement. Fletcher stands over me with his cane in hand. All business today, his face is stone, eyes vacant as usual.

"I will ask you one more time, Travesci: what do you know about the dial?"

I contemplate mocking him, but my body is weary of pain. "Nothing, like I told you before, Fletcher." My words are bolder than the courage I can barely grasp. I hold his stare, as if what he sees there will prove I am not lying.

The cane lands across the side of my face before I have time to react. Searing pain rips across my jaw, and blood dribbles from the corner of my mouth. I close my eyes and wait for another blow.

Footsteps, moving away, and then back. Only when they come to a halt do I open my eyes. A new Guardian now stands in front of me, his gaze less maleficent than Fletcher's. He transfers his weight from foot to foot before repeating the question.

"I told you, I know nothing. Why would I? We have limited education. Nobody learns about the dial, so why would I know anything about it? You probably know more than I do."

The Guardian looks back at Fletcher, who simply nods. The cane meets the other side of my face. Spit and blood fly out of my mouth, and I growl through a long groan. The Guardian's face struggles to stay stony. I look up through the tears that fill my eyes from the pain. His facade falters, and his jaw clenches.

"How many days are we going to do this? It is not going to change what I don't know," I say dryly.

His face turns to stone, matching his commander behind him. But instead of another blow, like I expect, he drops the cane and walks out. Fletcher flings an irate look at the Guardian and storms out after him, barking over his shoulder that we are done for the day.

The remaining Guardian stands over me while he cuts the ropes. He hauls me to my feet and drags me back to my cell, shoving me through the door and onto the floor.

Charlie gives me a wry look before checking my face with shaking hands. The cold touch on the sides of my face offers a little relief, and he forces a weak smile. "Could have been worse, boy." He lies back on the floor, hands under his head.

I lie back on the cold floor with him, hands under my head, fingers intertwined. I close my eyes and pull up my favorite memories of Imani. Her face, her smile, her laughter. Her hair and her shape. I breathe out slowly. Water running over her skin. Moonlight piercing the night air around her half-submerged body in the water of the oasis. My thoughts slide back to the time we were in the desert shack, after running from Barlow. I remember her warmth as she slept beside me on the hard floor. My body craves it now. An ache curls up around my heart at the thought that I may never see her again. It consumes me, like water lapping over stones, like it did in Charlie's oasis. It trickles over me, covering every inch of me. I can't breathe.

I sit up, trying to suck in air. Gasps rattle out of my chest. Charlie sits up next to me with a groan. A bony hand rests on my back. Tears stream down my face. I choke on my sobs, and Charlie pats my back gently. I suck in deep breaths, trying not to suffocate under the feeling of having lost her.

Charlie starts humming a slow tune. My heartbeat and breathing slow to match his melancholy melody. I shove my head between my knees. Tears slide down my nose and hit the grimy floor, forming a puddle of despair.

"Harm, you mustn't give up." Charlie's words are a soft whisper.

"I... I..." I steady my breathing so I can talk. "It feels like I'm falling apart. How do I stop the pain? It's everywhere," I sob. The rubbing on my back quickens, and he blows out a breath.

"How did you live without her, Charlie?"

"You're asking the wrong man, Harm. You saw what happened to me after I lost my Emmie." He blinks and a tear falls down his bony cheek. "I didn't."

I blow out another deep breath before wiping away my tears with the backs of my hands. The salt stings my broken face. I look into Charlie's eyes. Brows pulled down and mouth twisted, he shakes his head. And I realize right then, it doesn't go away. Ever.

Our cell door rattles, and a tray bearing the slop they pass off as food and two chunks of stale bread slides through the small opening at the bottom. I get to my feet and retrieve it before giving Charlie his. We eat in silence. He watches me while he picks at his food with filthy fingers.

"What?" I finally ask.

"You have to keep going, even without Imani. You must," he leans in to speak more quietly, "you need to escape from here and do what you were born to do."

The weight of his words flickers in his eyes as he waits for me to respond. I stare at the grey blobs in my bowl and pop the last of my bread into my mouth.

"Anything you know about the dial, you keep it to yourself. Don't tell them a damn thing. The minute you do, you're as good as dead," he whispers.

I meet his gaze and swallow. I know that, very well.

"Any suggestions as to how we get out of this dump?" I ask.

"Not really. But I'm hoping the others will have a plan of sorts." He stops talking and lies back down as he stares at the high ceiling above us.

The sunlight has just started its retreat from our cell floor when the door rattles open and three Guardians appear: Fletcher and two others. They haul us from the cell and back toward Arthur's tower again. On the bridge, the wind is up, whipping around us like an approaching sandstorm. But all there is for miles is forest. No sand here; not a grain. The scent of pine drifts up to the bridge, the forest below still so fragrant, even as the day cools down. The sun recedes in the sky, heading toward twilight. To the east, a handful of stars reveal their shimmering points.

Charlie walks in front of me, one Guardian holding his thin arm so tightly that he groans intermittently as we walk. Fletcher and the other Guardian flank me, each holding an arm, their canes dangling from their hips. The click of their black shoes along the stone bridge counts down the steps until we reach the tower. Birds call out in the forest, settling in for the night ahead. I breathe in the deep forest air, so different from the dry air of the desert. No dusty, sandy breaths; just pure air, almost damp.

We reach the entrance to the tower and are pushed inside until we reach Arthur's meeting room. In the fading light, it looks almost cozy. Arthur and Emmie sit side by side on two grand wooden chairs on the opposite side of the large room.

We halt a few steps past the threshold. Charlie and I are pushed to our knees. Arthur sits on his chair, elbows propped up on the arms, his fingers steepled and tapping. Emmie sits as rigid as stone and sucks in a deep breath. Arthur throws her a sideways glare. None of the Guardians speak, not even Fletcher. For a time, it feels like we all just stare at each other, waiting.

Finally, Arthur stands, clasping his hands behind his back as he makes his way over to us. Emmie grips the arms of her chair until her knuckles turn white. Her frightened eyes, like a prey animal that knows what happens next, stay on Charlie.

My gut drops like a rock.

"Emmie," Charlie chokes.

Arthur's furious expression is followed by Fletcher slapping Charlie upside the head. Emmie closes her eyes, her chest heaving, fingers trembling around a white handkerchief.

"Do not speak to her," Arthur growls.

"I can't be here," Emmie suddenly declares and gets up to leave. The side of her face catches the last of the setting sunlight, illuminating a number of bruises.

"Sit down, woman!" Arthur hollers.

Emmie anxiously sits, tears lining her eyes, her face contorted. She pulls the handkerchief to her face, its golden trim shimmering, and weeps in her seat. My heart flings against my ribs, chased by the pulsing blood in my veins.

"Tell me about the rebel group," Arthur barks at Charlie.

"What rebel group?" Charlie's gaze stays on Emmie.

A cane lands across his back, and he falls forward, gasping for air.

"Again, brother. The rebels: how many, and where?"

Charlie rises again, looking Arthur in the eyes. His face is hard now, something I have never seen from him before. "Go to hell, brother." He spits at his feet.

Three canes flog down on him. Emmie's screams rise above the nauseating thuds that land on Charlie's scrawny frame, curled up on the floor. Blood gushes from his face and head as blow after blow rains down. His eyes open briefly, staring right into mine: one last plea for me to survive, to get out.

Fletcher hauls him to his knees. Arthur stands over him, eyes burning into his brother's, and he gestures to Fletcher with his right hand. Fletcher moves in to stand behind Charlie, hands frozen on either side of the old man's face. Charlie pushes his shoulders back, recognizing the command.

Oh no... Please, no. Stop!

I strain against the grip holding me. Charlie's gaze stays steady on Emmie's.

"You really should have made better choices, brother," Arthur croons, flicking his wrist.

Fletcher's jaw clenches. He hesitates briefly, meeting Arthur's dark gaze, and then his arms whip to the side, taking Charlie's head with them. The snap of his neck resounds through the otherwise silent room.

Charlie falls limp to the floor.

My body trembles, and bile rises in my throat. I can't breathe. Emmie's screams reverberate through the large room. Arthur doesn't even look at her, standing over Charlie with a smug expression as he gestures for Fletcher to remove Emmie from the room. He obeys and leads her out by the elbow, returning moments later.

Arthur's focus now turns to me, and his eyes are vicious. I

return the glare, holding in my grief for Charlie. I cannot break now. I owe that much to Charlie. To the people of the sands. My people. The rebels. Imani.

"Fletcher tells me you may also know of the rebellion." He walks away, as if his words need space to form. "Is this true?"

"I don't know anything about it."

He spins and faces me. In two strides, he is standing over me, hands still behind his back, as if he can torment me with only his words. "But you escaped the prison, not to mention, you were supposed to be executed months ago, along with the rest of your grubby family. I don't believe in coincidences, boy. You are either extremely lucky, or people have been helping you. For what reason?"

"Like I told you, I don't know anything about that dial thing, or about any rebels. I have no idea how I've stayed alive all this time—possibly luck, but most likely just the kindness of others."

The grip on my arms tighten as Arthur bends down to meet me at eye level.

"A delightful sentiment, but I doubt it, boy. People are never kind for no reason. There is always some kind of personal gain involved," he snarls.

In that moment, I remember his story as Charlie told it to me. And for a slim second, I pity him.

"What do you know? Why are you still alive? Who is helping you?" he spits.

"I don't know why I'm still alive," I say quietly, staring at Charlie's body lying still on the floor in front of me.

"As of right now, you're the very last person with the ability, apart from myself. You have three days to remember what you know about the dial and the rebels—or you will hang. I have no use for you if you won't talk." He stalks back to his chair and sits down without breaking eye contact. "Get him out of my sight. Do whatever you like with him until the three days are up."

He studies my face, as if gauging my reaction. I mask my face to that of indifference as I am hauled to my feet. Fletcher shoves me back through the doorway, and the others drag Charlie's body away in the opposite direction.

"At least I get the pleasure of finally killing you now, Travesci," Fletcher grates, his words laced with a guttural tone, and I know he means it. In his mind, I am as good as dead. I take in the forest below the bridge one last time as we walk back to the cell. The breeze plays with my hair, and I imagine for a moment that it is Imani's hands, very aware that her sadistic father walks alongside me, holding me in place. It is my last act of defiance, even if he is completely unaware of it.

We pass the cell that Charlie and I have been held in these past few days and down the hall toward a closed iron door. Fletcher says nothing as we walk. My hands are still bound, and the light is fading fast. He unbolts the large door, and we walk through it. Steps spiral downward. He pushes me down them first, gripping the ropes that bind my wrists, knowing that I can't get past him with him a step above me. When we reach the bottom, he lights a wad of cloth wrapped around a metal pole. Fumes fill the space from the oil-soaked rag. As it roars to life, rows of bars brighten before me. Fletcher comes around my left side and unlocks a cell gate, the iron bars notably grimy. This part of the tower prison must be rarely used.

He walks me to the back wall, pulls a knife from his pocket, and flicks it open. He hesitates as he takes in my face. I hold his stare in the dim light. Shadows flicker over his weathered face, making him appear pure evil with every contour. I realize right then that Guardians like Fletcher are made, and part of me wonders what he has been through to make him this callous. Not even as the Chancellor's highest-ranking officer does he get respect from his leader.

A tug, and the ropes around my wrists hit the floor with a soft thud. He pulls one arm up, knife in his teeth now, and claps a shackle around my wrist, then the other. He gives me a passing glance before squatting down to shackle each ankle. I stand before him like a man strung up and ready for slaughter. And the thought must have run through his head as well, as his eyes dance with something like satisfaction, seeing me at his mercy. He pulls the knife from his mouth and folds it back up before slipping it into his neatly pressed pants.

The cell gate clangs shut, followed by the jangle of keys before Fletcher's footsteps retreat up the winding stairs. The flame hisses, snuffed out in a vessel of water, and more steps echo and fade. Blackness swallows me. I slam my eyes shut over and over, trying to coax some light into my vision, but none comes. Before I have time to feel fear, my mind starts replaying the images of Charlie, the look he gave me just before he died, and the sight of his limp body lying next to me on the floor, all life drained from his face.

Heat rises from my chest and rips through my body, my chained hands balling into fists, and I let out a thunderous scream from the depths of the belly of this stone prison.

My warning to all.

CHAPTER 5
IMANI

Fierce knocks rattle the front door, waking me up and sending Mason hurtling toward it in the dawn's meek light, his hands dragging his pants up his muscular thighs. He runs a hand through his scattered dark blond hair before flinging the door open. A Guardian stands there, shuffling from foot to foot, his nervous hands gripping his hat in front of him, like just the thought of disturbing his superior officer is completely terrifying. Hurried words fall out of his mouth, and Mason rushes into his bedroom. A cupboard door slams before he reappears, his shirt only half done up, his belt hanging from his teeth as he dons his socks and boots. He tucks his shirt into his pants before throwing on his hat and heading for the door.

Mason hesitates at the threshold, looking at me for a moment, then he bolts out and slams the door behind him. He left me with the extra blanket from last night. In his rush, he forgot to take it back before he went. I scramble to my feet and look up, inspecting the rafters, judging the height of them. I grab the sheet and start ripping it into strips before tying each piece together. My shaking hands make the knots more difficult than they should be. But

Harm taught me, and I still remember the simplest of them. As long as they work and don't send me slamming back into the cold stone floor, I don't care.

I wrap the smaller, thicker blanket around my waist, not wanting to leave it behind, since I have no other shelter against the cold desert nights. Then I toss the long makeshift rope, and it flies over my head toward a rafter. It hits the side and falls to the floor. I let out an anxious breath, eyes flicking from the rafter to the door, heart hammering. It leaves my hands again and flies up to the rafter, this time sagging over the wooden beam briefly before plummeting back to the floor.

A grunt vibrates through my chest. Again!

The sheet rope sinks to the floor before making it to the rafter. I let out a muffled scream. Warmth rises in my shaking body, and my chest heaves at the hopelessness above me.

One more time. I toss it with both arms. It sails over the beam, dropping halfway to the ground. A whoop leaves my mouth as I clutch onto the sheet rope and pull it toward me. I tie it off on the metal bars of the cell and start heaving my weight up the cotton length, grateful for my leaner condition now as my hands burn under my tight grip around the material. I wrap the knotted sheet between my feet and push up with my legs. Before long, I fall into an easy rhythm, inching closer to the beam.

I release my hold on the rope with one hand, slap it over the beam, and pull myself up over it. The next beam over hovers above the bars of my cell door. I steady my limbs and launch toward it. For a moment, I am weightless, flying toward the solid wooden beam. Sickness surges up my throat, and I glance briefly at the unforgiving surface below. I collide with the second beam, wrapping both arms around the rough wood, my hips and legs swinging forward. Splinters rip into my upper arms, and a whimper escapes my mouth. Legs flailing, I force my torso upward and finally hug the beam with my legs.

I must get through the gap between the ceiling and the beam. The sloped roof steals the space I need to move freely, but I push my body through. I get to my chest before the squeeze starts to ache. Kicking against nothing, I wrestle with the small space, gasping for air, my lungs crushed. Nothing; no movement. My hands shake, and tears prick my eyes as I clench my teeth before one last push with my arms.

A cry leaves my lips as I slip through the gap with scathed ribs and manage to swing my legs over the top of the bars, shimmying down the vertical iron. Feet firmly on the floor and head between my knees, I suck in deep breaths, fighting down the nausea that curls its way up through my insides.

Suddenly, men outside start yelling. Fear claws up my spine, and I hunt for somewhere to hide or some way out. The men approach the door, and I race to Mason's bedroom, praying it has a window. I close the door behind me and stand in his room on shaking legs. Apart from a bunk, a chair, and a small closet, the room is bare.

The front door opens. My blood surges through my veins.

Just beyond the closet is a window, its thin white curtains flicking around in the desert breeze. I dash to the window and peer outside. Nothing, just a back lane. I haul myself onto the ledge. Climbing through the window frame, I hold my breath, trying to stay quiet. A triangle of bright blue catches my eye from underneath the neatly folded uniform on Mason's chair.

It's my scarf—the one Harm gave me. I scramble back to the floor and run over to the scarf, plucking it out from under his grey clothes. Footsteps draw closer, and my heart thunders in my chest. I wrap the scarf around my neck and jump back onto the windowsill.

My feet land on the sands outside just as Mason's roar rips through the house. I grab the blanket from my waist and throw it over my head and shoulders, covering the bright blue of the scarf. I make my way rapidly down the narrow lane, stopping in the shadows of the last building. I can still hear him hollering, and the sounds of furniture being overturned. Then for a moment, it goes quiet.

I can't stay here. With nothing but a tunic and no robe, I can't even risk finding out if Harm is still here. I need to get away and get sorted, find Jonah, then return.

"Where are you?!" Mason screams.

My heart jumps into my throat. I peer around the corner of the building into the village center and see him running around erratically, turning over anything that is not nailed down, screaming my name.

"I will find you, Imani!"

A chill snakes its way up my spine. I lean against the building to save my trembling legs. The people in the village are frozen, staring at him. Some push their children behind them as he nears. He runs to where stalls stand in the sand, and grabs a merchant by his collar, screaming at him, demanding to know where I have gone. The pale-faced man shakes his head before being dropped to the sand. Women retreat into their homes as he stalks back to his house. The door slams.

I run.

With the sun as my guide, I fly across the hot sand, the soles of my feet not touching it long enough to burn. From the outskirts of the village, I head for the rocky outcrop. Fear and adrenaline pump fire through my limbs. As the sun reaches its apex, I reach another rocky outcrop. The heat is too severe for my bare feet, and I pick my way through the stony formations, hoping to find one large enough to shelter under.

A stone towers ahead of me. I crawl to its base and spread out the blanket, lying down and pulling half of it over my body, trying to keep the cruel sun off my skin.

Long exhales trail their way out of my chest, and my body starts to relax. A whimper laced with tears turns into an ugly sob. I cover my face and just lie there, releasing the pain, sorrow, and aches from these past weeks. And I realize it's the first time I have been alone since the day I met Harm.

Harm...

Thoughts of him swell in my chest as memories play through my head. The look on his face and his laugh the time we found him after he escaped the prison, and I pummeled him down the side of a dune. How the sound of him shook through my body, and I had never hated him and needed him so much at the same time. His arms enveloping me as I fought to escape the nightmare that has haunted me ever since his family was executed. The pain in his eyes when he saw me standing on the gallows, like it was ripping him apart from the inside in a thousand places.

My breaths come too shallow, choked by every cry that leaves my heaving chest. The crushing pain in my heart makes me draw my knees up, and I pull at my hair. The air is too thin.

I wait for the pain to suffocate me. Rocking myself onto my side, I lie wrapped in the blanket until the stars appear and cool air whispers around me. I search the darkness above me for our stars, the constellation we made ours, our Harmony stars. My gut sinks. They all look the same. Without Harm, I can't find them. Heat burns my eyes, my heart aching in my chest. A heartbeat later, tears soak into the sand, and I can't stop the deluge of sobs.

My whole body aches. My eyes open to see a brownish-grey rock rat sniffing around my head. I let out a breath, and it startles, running back behind the surrounding rocks for cover. Pushing myself up from the ground, I take in the dark rocks clustered in a wide span around me. These are the eastern outcrops, from what I remember of the map. It would be a day's walk to the nearest village. I grab some velvety leaves from a plant wedged between the rocks closest to me, chewing on the watery leaves before swallowing. It's the only plant that grows out here that is edible, or so Enid told me.

I tear pieces from the hem of my tunic. Wrapping the strips around my feet, I tie them off on the tops. The hot sands will blister my soles quickly if they are not covered. My legs and midriff are now exposed; only the worn undergarments I have had for years cover me now. But at least my feet are protected. I can wrap the blanket around me when I reach the village. The sun is going to ravage my bare middle, but if I stay here, I will die in a few days.

I head out, blanket over my head and draped down my back. The wind and sands are warm but gentle on my bare skin. I like it. The feet coverings are working well so far.

A few hours into the trek, one of my knots loosens, and the rags slip from my left foot. Sand burns along the underside of my foot, and I grab the fabric, hopping on one foot to tie it back on. I look up to get a feel for my position. Dunes in every direction. I keep moving. The sun soon reaches its apex, and I come to rest under a small group of spindly bushes. My throat is so dry now. My head thumps, like my brain is rattling around inside my skull. I need to drink something.

My stomach rumbles, and I brush my hands around in the undergrowth to see if anything squirms that's worth eating. Nothing presents itself, and I start digging for the roots of the plant. My lessons with Enid flash through my mind as I try to remember what she taught me about edible roots and leaves in the short time I had with her. The warm dirt embeds itself under my nails. Another stroke, and a soft, wiggling white grub flips to the top of the broken earth. I shove it in my mouth before I have time to look at it or think about it. The small, writhing grub bursts in my mouth, and when I don't gag, I start digging for another. I find three more and almost swallow them whole before leaning back on the bush's flimsy branches and closing my eyes. Water would be so good right now. I doze off.

The screech of a bird overhead jerks me awake. Panicking, I look to the sky to see how much time I have wasted sleeping, but the sun is still high. I push myself off the hot sand and brush down my legs. Fixing the blanket back over my head, I make my way through the dunes again, with the sand almost burning its way through the layers, and I am thankful for the fabric covering my feet. The hot wind buffets my back, pushing me along. I slip inside my mind as I cover the distance. I can't help it. Memories of Harm squeeze my heart like a desert viper constricting around its prey. I catalogue every smile, every laugh, and every touch. I muse over the times when I hated him, and every time the looks he gave me hurt so bad that I thought I would stop breathing. I relive the kiss we shared in the middle of the dunes. I think of our Harmony stars. I couldn't even find them. Tears line my eyes with that memory, and I switch from memories of just Harm to memories of others.

Some memories have Jonah in them. He is the only family I have left now. If I survive this desert and can find clothes and the bare essentials at the next village, I will find him. He has been the only father figure I've had for the last five years, always grounded and practical, but willing to fight for the important things. Harm was one of those things; he was important to me.

Is.

He *is* important to me.

So very important. Hot tears cascade down my face that I don't bother wiping away.

When the sun finally starts its descent, I see the glimmering outline of a village up ahead. I pick up the pace immediately. Just as the sun slips over the horizon, I reach the outskirts. Aware of my lack of clothing, I wrap the blanket around me to cover my waist and legs. My face feels tight and hot, and I scan the village for a place to stop and rest. Hopefully, I will find a kind soul willing to give me clothes, a meal, and water.

I knock on the door of the first house I come to in the outermost ring of homes. I hold my breath. *Please let somebody kind live here...*

CHAPTER 6
HARM

Dripping. The blurry pool of blood under me means I am the one bleeding. My head sways on my shoulders, my mind and strength failing to hold it up. The blows keep coming. Pain thunders through my head and rattles around, forcing more blood and spit from my mouth and nose. The shape of my face feels wrong. Parts of it are numb, and my cheekbone feels shattered, bone grating on bone with every blow. The air I drag through my wrecked nose only comes in on one side, and every breath comes with a stream of blood that I choke back.

My shackled wrists run a consistent stream of warm blood down my shaking arms, soaking my chest and back, adding to the pool of red below me. A grunt from Fletcher is the only warning another blow is coming. With his arm raised back, cane gripped in white knuckles, the air hisses at me just before pain splits through me again, this time radiating around my ribs.

Crack!

Instant burning fills my lungs, and I cough, gasping for a sliver of the stale air down here. A heartbeat later, air rattles back down my airway. The labored breaths of Fletcher whisper past my ears.

The tang of salt and blood seeps through my one good nostril, making my stomach lurch.

The heavy door at the top of the stairs opens. My vision fills with stars, the ringing in my ears half drowning out the sound around me. Voices slip through the bars, followed by a loud sigh from Fletcher.

I try to reposition my feet to take some of the weight off my wrists, but they slip on the bloody floor. Fletcher's cane pokes my dangling head, pushing my head up. I try to focus on what he is saying, but I can't. Everything is a blur. The cane disappears, and my head drops. The cell door clangs shut, and the keys jangle as he secures the lock. Two Guardians make their way up the stairs, then the light is doused again and the heavy door slams.

I am thankful for the cool and quiet as I dangle, waiting here in the darkness.

Waiting for death.

There is no light, only a small flicker that bobs around outside the cell gate. Two figures huddle together, as if something frightens them as they draw closer to the gate of my cell.The jingle of metal echoes as one of them fumbles, releasing sharp, breathy words. A woman. The other gasps—another woman, younger. One of them looses a breath as she closes the cell gate and they come to stand in front of me. Their sweet, clean scent barely penetrates my damaged senses.

"I am so sorry, Harmen," Emmie whispers, her words thick.

Next to her is a girl around my age and Imani's size, who steps into my space to work on the shackles on my wrists. Blonde curly hair bounces around her shoulders as she works. Her breathing is quick and ragged. Emmie's bony hands rest on either side of my chest, holding me up, taking some of my weight off the shackles. One hand falls free, and I try to take more weight on my feet so I don't fall into her. The second hand falls free moments later, and I topple forward. The girl grabs me under the arms to stop me from falling onto Emmie's thin frame.

They lower me to the blood-stained floor before the girl releases my ankles from the shackles. I lie limp, too ruined to move. Emmie tries to roll me over. Her companion helps, and they put me on my back. A wet cloth wipes over my face, the swelling preventing me from feeling much. I groan in appreciation, but stay stuck to the floor. My eyelids drift down, and I choke through a shallow breath.

Hands grab my shoulders, shaking me. "You need to get up," Emmie commands.

Her companion tugs at me under my arms, her small hands stronger than Emmie's. Two more hands pull from the other side, and I am sitting up. Emmie's thin hands trace over my arms and legs, as if assessing what's broken.

"Harmen, can you hear me?" Emmie asks.

I focus on each breath. My body is sluggish. I move my hands to my face, trying to feel what is left.

"Harmen?" the girl says.

"Yes." I pull in a breath. "I can hear you."

"It's Emmie. This is Nirri, my granddaughter." She clears her throat, as if grounding herself. "The Guardians are gone for a couple of hours—something about an incident to the north."

I try to offer her my thanks with a smile, but my face can't make the movements.

"Harmen," Nirri says, placing a hand on my arm, and I turn to where she sits beside me. "We're getting you out of here. But you need to help us. We don't have much time before the others come for you."

"The others?" I choke.

Emmie confirms this.

I grunt in response to her request. It's the best I can do as dizziness claws its way up through me. Emmie places her thin hand on my chin, and I meet her gaze.

"I know who you are. I know your family," she starts, drawing in a breath, like the memories affect her still, and the realization of how I am connected to the people she once knew. "Arthur will stop at nothing to keep these lands the way he has made them. You need to live. You need to stop him. For decades, I have watched as the man I married slowly turned into a monster. But killing Charlie was unforgivable." Her voice breaks, and a moment passes before she continues. "You can fix what he has broken, Harmen. You can change things for the better. Please do this for our people. Please, you must try." She lifts my hand into hers. Nirri blows out a breath.

I turn my head to Nirri and then back to Emmie. "I will try," I choke out through my desecrated mouth.

"Good. Right, let's get you up." She nods to Nirri, who stands and bends to haul me up. Their small arms heave under my deadweight, and I try to engage my legs to help. After minutes of me scrambling, I am finally standing, but I am swaying with sickness on the weak, leaden legs that have been dangling below me for days.

"Can you walk?" Nirri asks.

"I think so," I rasp and try to take a step. Nausea rolls up my throat, and I only make it slightly forward before bile spews from my mouth. Neither reacts, only reassuring me as we make for the cell gate.

I lift my head and see the stairs.

"I can't," I pant. "The stairs..."

"No, we'll go through the wall," Emmie says mysteriously. They turn me in the opposite direction toward what appears to be a solid stone wall. Once we are mere steps away from it, she holds out a hand, her palm flat against the stone, searching for something in the dim light. Her hand stops on a certain stone, and she presses hard. There is a grating sound as a small opening is revealed to our left, and we duck through and into a passageway.

The stone slides shut slowly behind us. With the dull thud of the door closing, Emmie lets out a sigh, and Nirri a nervous laugh. She grabs a small stick with oily cloth wrapped around one end from a carved-out shelf in the wall and lights it with flint. Flames crackle to life, lighting up the small space.

"Well, that was the hard part. Now we walk through this wall. It's connected to that tower cell you were in, but it leads to the farthest part of the wall, east of the forest. Your people should be waiting on your side," Emmie says matter-of-factly.

Something like hope ripples through my body.

"How far is it, Grandmother?" Nirri asks.

"Last time I traveled this passageway, it took around three hours, but my companions were not hurt this badly," Emmie says softly.

"You've done this before?" I force out.

"Once. It was a long time ago."

"So, you've helped others?"

"Just one other," she replies, but doesn't offer anything further.

After an hour of walking through the dim passageway, guided only by the flickering flame of Nirri's torch, we stop. Emmie hands me a canteen, and I drink the water down like I have been without it for weeks. Nirri chatters away about village life, asking me questions about our daily lives, and I gradually realize that she has never been past the wall to our side before. With slurred words, I try to tell her about the things that matter most, like our families, the trade, and the work it takes to survive in the desert. She listens to every word. Emmie remains silent.

My legs are like lead. My body is shaking from the exhaustion of the constant pain. Nirri readjusts under my shoulder, and Emmie does the same before we continue on.

Emmie breaks the silence after what feels like miles of walking in this confined tunnel. "Do you know about the dial, Harmen?"

I grunt in acknowledgment.

"Good," she says, before throwing Nirri a look of concern as my legs falter under me. "It's in the top tier of the tower, and it is guarded. You will need to get to it to change the weather back to a normal pattern of seasons."

I breathe out, trying to steady my pain, trying to make sure I remember what she is telling me.

"It's been a long time since it has been altered, but it should recognize you. You have the ability," Nirri offers.

We are silent for a long time before I start shaking so hard that Nirri stops, her small body tensing to stop me from plummeting to the stone floor. I groan as I try to shift my feet before I collapse.

"You're shaking. Is it the pain?" Nirri asks.

I breathe out an assent.

"Sorry," she says before making to continue. But my feet don't follow, and I stagger toward the wall, doing my best to lean on it before I crush her with my weight. My hand finds the cool stone, and I turn to lean my back against it. For a minute, I am relieved that I'm still upright. But shooting pains up my legs have me sliding to the floor seconds later. Emmie yelps, and Nirri lunges out from under my shoulder to assist her grandmother, who is half trapped under my left side.

"Sorry, Emmie," I breathe, every shallow breath a burst of pain in my broken ribs.

"Don't apologize, Harmen. None of this is your fault." She gets to her feet with Nirri's help. "Please know that."

I try another haphazard attempt at a smile, but my contorted face just protests with painful aches. Emmie's hand gently lands on my face as she leans down to me, her gaze racked with guilt and pain. She gives me a small smile. I can see decades of regrets that fill her wounded heart, and for a moment, I see my mother's face—the elegant and gentle face that I loved, that always held me steady, in her strength and in her soul. Warmth rises through my chest, and I push hard on the floor with my hands, determined to stand.

Nirri jumps back to my side and helps me up. I stand tall before Emmie, every muscle in my body protesting, pain shooting out like stars from my wrists and ankles. "I will give it everything I have, Emmie."

She grabs my hands and squeezes them before nodding toward the passageway before us. It takes another couple of hours before we reach the stone door that leads to the exit east of the forest, into the dunes on my side of the wall. My feet and legs are numb at this point, my breathing so labored that Emmie and Nirri share concerned glances. Emmie instructs Nirri to feel for the smooth stone, and she sweeps her hand over the wall for a minute before finding what she is looking for. She hesitates.

"How do we know if the right people are on the other side?" Nirri asks.

"We don't." Emmie's gaze remains on her granddaughter, whose hand is frozen on the stone. Fear shines in her eyes, and I pull in a deep breath, my mind rebelling at the realization of what will happen to me if the Guardians are on the other side of this door. What will happen to Emmie and Nirri? Clearly, Arthur has no qualms about executing family. What will befall Emmie and Nirri if we are caught? I fight to breathe past the lump in my throat, heart hammering in my chest.

"You two go back," I say. "If there are Guardians on the other side, let it just be me standing here for them to find. You've done enough to help me already."

Nirri stands taller and grounds her feet, and her eyes meet mine with fire and commitment. "No."

Emmie takes the same stance, the two of them letting the fire in their eyes pierce through as Nirri slams a hand down on the smooth stone. For seconds, nothing happens. Nirri raises her hand to slam it again, when the first crack of heady sunlight slithers through the opening. We all instantly slap our hands over our eyes to stave off the blinding light after being in darkness for hours.

Gritty winds tunnel past us, sand whirling around our feet. I smell the glittering dust from the second the winds fill the space. The desert is right in front of us. Simultaneously, we lower our hands to see who is waiting for us. A small cry catches in Emmie's throat, and Nirri tenses up beside me.

CHAPTER 7
IMANI

A plump middle-aged woman in a worn dress and apron frowns from just beyond the threshold. Her tied-back blonde hair is coated with dustings of flour, as are her thick hands. Her hazel eyes scan me from head to toe and back up again before she raises a brow and gestures for me to enter. Her home, small and dim, is lit with scant candles, and the smell of baking bread fills her front room. Judging by the sounds coming from the heart of the home, she has two small helpers.

"You look like you've fended off the devil himself, girl," she says.

I hold the blanket around me and study her home. Sensing my hesitation, she points to the wood box under the hooks by the door. I obey and sit. She heads down the hall, but turns back to scan me once again, then disappears.

A few moments pass, and a harsh word rings out at the two helpers in her kitchen, followed by giggles, and I can only imagine what they are up to with her flour. She reappears and hands me clothes, nodding for me to put them on. "This ought to fit you. You can change in the back room. Follow me."

Trusting the only person who has been kind enough to open their door to me after trying six, I wander after her down the narrow hallway, passing the door to the kitchen. Two little girls stand on wooden stools, flour up to their elbows. They stare at me, and one whispers to the other as I walk past. At the end of the hall, she points to the room on the left. I walk in, and she closes the door.

Judging by the possessions, it's the room of a young woman. The bunk is perfectly made, with an old striped pillow and a thick grey blanket adorned with a small bundle of dried desert flowers, a white ribbon holding them together. A simple three-drawer dresser bearing a fine layer of dust flanks the left wall. I step over to it. A tarnished silver brush and a mirror lay neatly on top. By the window is a small tin trunk with a white ribbon tied in a bow on the latch.

I slip my blanket off, sitting on the bed. Slowly I untie the cloths from my feet, trying to gather the sand into the material while I go, to save the floor. I rip off my torn shirt and slip on the clothes she gave me, tucking the tunic into the pants. Carrying the sand-filled cloth to the window, I release all but the ends and let the sand empty outside. I twist my hair and tie it up with the scarf Harm gave me, wrapping the cloth around and around. Pieces of hair stick out where they never have before, my hair now too short for a proper updo. I head for the door, wishing I had a belt to hold up the pants on my emaciated hips.

A soft knock comes from the other side. I open it and find thin socks and some boots, and I pull them on. They fit perfectly. A few steps back through the hallway to the kitchen, and my presence in the doorway gets another giggle from the two little girls as the woman bends over the oven door, organizing her bread loaves.

"Do they fit you, girl?"

"Yes, yes it all fits, thank you."

She dumps a hot loaf pan on the wooden table, swatting the two hungry girls' fingers away from the bread. Steam rises from the swollen mound in the hot tin as she walks around the table toward me. Swift little hands pinch at the bread before the two girls dart from the kitchen, laughing and shoving each other through the wooden door frame, pushing their stolen loot into their mouths. Their quick, happy feet thud down the hall. Her eyes meet mine.

"The clothes were my daughter's. They look good on you. Keep them." She scuffs her way to a wooden rocking chair, plopping down on the protesting seat before taking up a sock dangling with a needle and thread, and she starts to darn one of the many holes. Intent on her work, she doesn't look back at me when I pull out a kitchen chair and sit. Not knowing if I am welcome to stay, I rest in the chair and trace the battered wooden tabletop with my finger, hoping she will speak.

"Where is your daughter now?" I ask after moments of silence drag out between us.

Her needle stops, and her gaze meets mine. "Gone. She died." Sorrow hijacks her face in every way.

"Oh, I'm sorry," I whisper. My hands go still on the tabletop. "I'll get out of your way, then."

I stand and take in her small but well-stocked kitchen. Utensils are neatly contained in metal canisters. The stone sink overflows with bread tins from a previous batch. She must cook a lot. Most likely, it's her trade.

"Stay for supper if you like. Perhaps a decent night's sleep in a bed will help."

I swallow, imagining sleeping in her dead daughter's bed, in her room, surrounded by things she held dear, that her mother has to see again and again, revisiting heartbreak every time.

"I don't want to be a bother, and you have already been more than generous to me." I move toward the door.

"Nonsense, it's no bother, and it will do the twins good to have some company other than mine for a night." She smiles briefly. I return the gesture.

"Do you need help with anything?" I ask, feeling out of place just hanging around watching her work the thread.

"There's wood for chopping just out the back door, or you can help the girls with their chores. Suit yourself." She points toward the hall that I assume leads to the back door. I nod and amble down the hall. It has been so long since I have been in a home such as this, and I take my time, surveying each bedroom. There are three. One has a few toys scattered on the floor, and the muffled sounds of the two cheeky girls float up from under the bed. I bend down and meet their stare. Squeals follow, and I move on. Next, a smaller room with a bed for two. So neat, but mostly bare, with only the bed and a small dresser supporting a crazed mirror, dust lining the surface of it also.

I reach the back door, a flimsy frame with thin cloth secured over it, more for keeping things in than keeping things out. I push it open with a long squeak. To my left is a pile of wood and a chopping block, an axe buried in its face. I tug the axe out of the block and select the first log, with a glance down at the already finished pile to the right. Split logs and smaller kindling sit neatly waiting. My exhausted frame wavers under the weight of the axe in my hand.

With the log centered on the block, I swing the axe over my head and haul it down into the log. The axe buries halfway down. I wiggle it free and turn the log on its head, swinging down in the same spot. The log flies apart, each half landing on opposite sides of the block. I pick up one half and hold it steady as I throw a more cautious blow into its center. Rotating it on its head, I repeat the action until it is quartered. I shove it onto the pile of like pieces and do the same to the next half. The satisfying sound of the wood splintering under the sharp and heavy axe fuels every swing. I ignore the trembling in my forearms, determined to earn my keep.

Once my arms are all but useless, I pick up a few of the quartered timbers. I sit on the ground, the timber between my legs, and my hand closes around the axe-head. I carefully splinter them. As I'm tossing the kindling into the pile, shard after shard, it is only then that I notice the cool air pushing in from the approaching night.

The back door creaks, and two small heads poke around the door. I poke my tongue out at them, sending them back inside roaring with laughter. The night winds carry the sands on a glittering ride under the sinking sun. I plunge my hand into the sand and pull it up. It cascades through my fingers and blows away on the wind, illuminated by the receding golden light, the dying embers of the day. Then a voice from inside calls me to supper. I stand and dust off my clothes, taking one last look at the sun setting behind me before I sink the axe back into the block. I gather up a handful of split logs and pile on as much kindling as I can manage before I make for the door. It opens as I reach it, and the woman looks at her wood pile with wide eyes.

"You cut every last log!"

"Sorry, I didn't know how many you wanted done." I turn to the pile and back to her.

"Not at all, thank you! I hate that job down to my very bones." She holds the door open for me. I hover in the hall as she squeezes past and leads me to the iron wood rack inside. I kneel with my load, and she helps pack away the kindling before I start on the split logs. The room is warm from the oven, the table set for the four of us. No man of the house, then. She calls the girls to the table, and we sit down to eat.

"My name is Gwyn," she says. "You have a name also, I suppose."

I half choke on my food at the amusement in her face. Stares come from the girls.

"Imani," I say after swallowing. I take a drink of water from the tin cup at my place.

"Well, Imani, can you tell me why you were out in the desert, dressed in rags?" She raises a brow, and the girls go still, their food suspended in their cheeky mouths.

"I was traveling," I say, not sure how much information is warranted or smart, after all that has happened.

"I see," she says and gives me a small smile. "Where are you traveling to?"

"I'm trying to find my father." It's not a complete lie; Jonah has been a father to me ever since I ran away from home five years ago. I don't want to offer up Harm's name, or the fact that I'm tracking down a wanted traitor of whom I am an accomplice.

"Oh, is he in these parts? What's his name? Perhaps I can help," she offers, lifting another morsel to her mouth.

"Jonah. He travels with the gypsies."

"Oh my! I didn't know there were any gypsies left,"she quips.

I nod. "He's one of the last of his kind. My cousin travels with him too." I hover over my next mouthful. "We got separated a few months back."

"Where is your mother, girl? Surely, she's worried sick. I know I would be if you were mine." She looks down at her food.

"What happened to her—your daughter?" I ask, half not wanting to share about my own mother, and half wanting to know what happened to the girl Gwyn loved so much.

She pokes at her food for a moment before meeting my gaze. "She was almost of the age to be Blended. She was a stunning girl." She trails off, lost in thoughts of her daughter. "But it was because of her looks that she's not here now. Three boys attacked her. They took her womanhood from her and left her badly beaten. She recovered from the injuries, but never from the scars in her mind. We tried to get those boys hung for their actions, but the Guardians were not interested. She left us on her own accord, not long after. She is at peace now." Chin trembling, she sucks in a long breath and wipes the moisture from her face before darting a quick look at the girls, whose heads are down. My heart sinks into my stomach as I witness the torment on their faces, and on Gwyn's.

"It was a year ago now. My daughter was not the only girl they attacked; there have been many others," she says, straightening her tunic, as if it will smooth out the pain along with the wrinkles. I stare at her face, heat rising in my own.

"What are their names?" I keep my voice steady as fire grows in my core. They should have hanged for that.

"Only two of them still live in the village. I keep the twins far away from them. Thomas and Timothy, brothers. Their family is a mean bunch. They came here from Trindari."

Of course they did.

"Last name?"

"Randle." She pauses before meeting my stare, which now feels like I'm in a trance. "They live on the other side of the village. Their home sits directly in front of the well; you can't miss it. There's an iron bar right down the center of their door." She studies my face before her gaze falls back to her plate.

I take a piece of the warm bread and shove it mindlessly into my mouth. "What was your daughter's name?" I ask.

"Annalise. This is Audrey and Amber. They're five,"she offers.

"Pretty names," I say to the girls. They smile and continue eating. We finish our meals, and Gwyn stands to clear the table. I jump up and take her plate and the girls', stacking them on top of mine.

"Please, let me." I walk the plates over to the sink and plunge them into the hot, soapy water. Through rhythmic swirls with the cotton cloth, I mull over my thoughts and plans. I can't stay here. But I can help Gwyn—in a small way, at least—to keep her two beautiful little girls safe from those monsters. I can do what the Guardians refused to do.

I thank Gwyn for the meal, and she walks me down the hall. I turn to her and throw my arms around her. She lets out a small yelp, but her arms wrap around me briefly before she puts me back at arm's length.

"Wherever your mother is, Imani, she would be proud of you."

I doubt it; she and I have not seen eye to eye for a long time. I bid Gwyn good night and crawl into the bunk. Looking around the room in the dim light, I can see every treasure Annalise loved. I twirl the bunch of dried flowers in my fingers, fragile petals falling from the arrangement. I set them on the foot of the bed, not wanting to damage them.

I wait for Gwyn and her little girls to go quiet. Then I wait another hour, ensuring they are sleeping deeply before I slip out of the bunk. I rifle through the top drawer of Annalise's dresser, feeling terrible for the invasion, but needing to find something to write on. Soon, my fingers find the smooth surface of a stack of paper. I lift it from its place, and a small pencil rolls off. Grabbing both and sitting on the bunk, I try my best to scratch out a note for Gwyn. I can't read much, and writing is an even bigger challenge, so I sound out her name as best I can. I write, *For Annalees*.

I rip the page in half and return the remaining paper and pencil to the drawer. Then I make up the bunk and place the flowers back on the pillow. Wandering down the dim hallway of this unfamiliar house, I make a brief stop in the kitchen. My hands search along the kitchen bench until I feel the steel handle of a drawer. Slowly, I slide it open. I run a finger over the knives and select a small one, easy to conceal, as well as a larger one. The small knife slides easily into my right boot; the other I wedge between the waistband of my pants and my right hip. I place the note under the enamel water jug in the center of the table.

Two traveling robes hang in the front room. I grab the one that seems to be my size and throw it on, dropping the larger knife into the deep left pocket. A small canteen swings from the hook. I pluck it from its spot and throw it over my head, tucking it under one arm. It sounds almost full, so I don't waste time going back to the kitchen. Then I slide my blue scarf over my head, secure it in place, and throw up the robe's hood. With a quick glance back down the hall, I pry the front door open and slip outside into the moonlit village.

It only takes me a couple of minutes to cross the village center and find the Randle home. I creep up to the door. A hideous iron bar runs straight down the middle, just as Gwyn said. I make my way to the open front window. From this vantage point, the house looks to have the same layout as Gwyn's. I scurry along the side, finding the last window, a bedroom window. Also open. With one hand, I tuck my robe up behind me and jump up onto the windowsill.

In the dim light that fills the room, two adults are sleeping.

Parents.

Wrong room.

I fall back down to the sand with a light thud and scurry around to the other side of the house. This time, I get the right window. Sleeping side by side are two brothers around my age, skinny build, limbs sprawled over their too-small bunks. I drop down onto their stone floor without a sound. As I reach the first boy, I pluck the knife from my pocket. I only have seconds to do this, or I risk waking the second brother—or worse, their parents.

The swift motion of my hand stains the first boy's pillow red. Gasps rattle through them. I step over to the second brother. His eyes fly open, and I waste no time, swift and quick like I was with the first. I wait until the redness soaks his pillow too, then jump back through the window. Before my feet even hit the sand, I am running. I wipe the knife clean on the inside of my robe, my body numb.

By morning, Gwyn and her girls will be safe.

Vigilante.

That's what my father called people who take the law into their own hands. Add it to the list.

At least I did something.

CHAPTER 8
HARM

Nothing but sand, hot wind, and the distant sounds of desert life echo back to us.

Nobody came.

Emmie is fighting back tears. Nirri stands silently, her jaw working, anger seething from her quivering body. In the sunlight, I can see her more clearly now. Her blonde hair lies in wavy lengths past her shoulders. Her small frame holds more curves than Emmie's. She looks at my face in the light, and tears line her gold-brown eyes the same as her grandmothers. She is dressed in a flowing cream-and-gold dress that is now marked with my blood and bile and grime from the passageway.

She looks to Emmie, who is trying to remain neutral and failing. Something between anger and despair crumples her face as she takes in my damaged body and face in broad daylight. I have no idea what I look like, but I imagine it's not pleasant. Through my one good eye and nostril, I can see and smell the desert dunes in the distance, their shimmering golden halos calling me home.

Nirri removes garments she has tied around her waist: traveling robes and a wrap for me. They lean me against the wall, out of the sun, before readying the clothes for me. Nirri extends my arm and slides the robe over it, then supports me in leaning forward while she wraps it around me, and Emmie fixes the remaining arm. She shakes out the wrap before placing it around my head. Her fingers tremble as she pulls it around my face, wincing as she tugs it tight.

Footsteps crunch into the sand just outside the doorway, and her fingers freeze. In unison, the three of us draw a breath and stand rigid, waiting for whoever is outside to appear in the doorway. Emmie's eyes flick from mine to her granddaughter's, bearing silent sentiments of love and loyalty. I can see the bond they have like an unwavering ribbon of gold in front of me, starting at Emmie and ending at Nirri, intrinsically precious, but stronger than anything else on this earth.

Against the wall, we shield our eyes, straining as the footsteps approach our concealed position. Nirri grabs my hand, and I grab Emmie's. We stand together, and every step hits like a new threat.

A colorful robe sweeps around the doorway before I see her face. With a belt made from silver and adorned with trinkets, she comes to a halt, bangles jingling on both wrists. She runs an eye over what she finds. Her gaze finally lands on my face, my wrecked body; she takes it all in. I blow out a breath as Emmie and Nirri relax beside me. The kind face of Saraya stares back at me, hands by her sides. She tilts her head to one side, her face carefully neutral.

"Where are the others?" Emmie asks, her voice shaking with the uncertainty of whether the woman in front of us can be trusted.

"They're busy distracting the Guardians. Hello, Harm," Saraya says and holds out both of her hands. Sadness lingers in her eyes, and she tries to hide it, but fails.

Nirri and Emmie shuffle me forward. Saraya marks my immobility and braces herself to support me, replacing Nirri under my arm.

"We don't have to go far, just a few steps to the caravan," she assures me.

I grunt and stumble forward. The sand makes every step even harder, and I look back over my shoulder to where Nirri and Emmie stand, still hidden in the opening of the wall. I nod my head and mouth a thank you. Nirri waves in response before they turn and hurry back the way they came, the stone door thudding closed, as if no one was ever there.

A short shuffle brings me to the foot of the caravan steps. There are only four, but there may as well be four hundred. Saraya prods me up the first step, almost barreling me toward the cover of the shadows inside the caravan. I force my body upward and fumble my hands along the wooden rails before grabbing for the threshold of the steps above me. I pull hard to haul myself through the entrance and fall into the small space with a groan loud enough to wake the dead. Every part of my body is revolting against the agonizing hours of movement I have endured.

Shuffling feet and the hem of Saraya's skirt flow around me as she readies the bunk for my journey. She helps me crawl onto it. I lay still as stone with the realization that I am out—out of the prison and out of Fletcher's grasp... for now.

Rolling bumps drag me from the depths of unconsciousness over and over as we travel in the caravan—to where, I don't know. The blanket under my burning wrists and ankles is wet from my weeping sores. Through half-closed eyes, I study the ceiling of the caravan, noting every mark and angle of the shaped wood. My chest aches as I remember the day Imani lay in this spot, with me under the bunk. Her hand had dropped down to squeeze mine. If my body wasn't aching already, the center of my chest now twists in painful torment at the memory. I am in Jonah's caravan, surrounded by his swaying possessions. Tears slide down my cheeks, burning their way across my mangled face, awash with relief, almost like the feeling of coming home... wherever that may be now.

Without Imani.

Home feels lost to me, forever.

The tang of damp soil takes me by surprise. I force my eyes to open as wide as they can.

Nothing sways. I'm no longer in the caravan. The stillness of the ground below me makes my stomach rise into my throat again. The pain floods back in. Aching throbs through my face. I raise a shaking hand and trace the brokenness I find, the swelling still so taut that I can't make out what shape anything is anymore.

Soft words bounce between two familiar voices, and every muscle in my body relaxes. Warmth radiates from a short distance away, accompanied by a crackle and hiss. Smoke. A fire. Between the banter, thudding sounds reverberate rhythmically over and over. The pungent smell of plants and herbs fills the air. I move my fingers around to feel for what lies on the ground. A velvety covering greets my touch, and in my mind, I see moss.

A tender hand rests on my shoulder, and the pungent smell becomes unbearable. A metal cup presses to my lips, and a foul-smelling substance pours into my mouth. I gag. Instantly, large hands slide under my shoulders, lifting me into a sitting position. I open my eyes, almost forgetting that I still have control over them.

The fire blurs in front of me. The familiar voices belong to two figures, one on either side of me.

"Harm, can you hear me?"

Jonah.

I grunt a reply.

"Enid has had you sedated for the pain, but do you want to sit up for a while? I can sit with you."

I nod.

My back is already aching from being motionless on the ground for what must have been hours. My fingers rise to my face again, but soft, thin hands intercept mine.

Enid. Grandmother.

"Try not to touch your face, Harm. I have poultices smothering it to take away the swelling and reduce the pain."

I drop my hands back into my lap. My focus improves a little as I turn to look at her. Her eyes are sad, but she is trying to offer me a smile. Her head tilts to the side, and she chokes back a sob, covering her mouth with a shaking hand.

"Thank you, Enid," I choke through the tight, immovable features of my face. "Thank you, Jonah."

His strong hand gives my shoulder a light squeeze, and he clears his throat. They help reposition me, so my back is against a wall of stone. I realize we're in a cave. We must be in Charlie's old home. My heart lurches as I remember his lifeless eyes staring up at me from the floor of Arthur's tower. He will never come back here. His oasis will die, just like he did.

And it's all my fault.

"Charlie is gone," I rasp.

Jonah grumbles something like a curse. "That's too bad. He was a good man."

"What happened to him?" Enid asks, her voice soft.

"Arthur."

"That mongrel!" Jonah spits.

We sit in silence. I breathe, head resting on the wall behind me, hands in my lap, my body so exhausted, like I have run for days on end through the hot desert.

Jonah breaks the silence, his voice tight. "Harm, we don't know where Imani is."

I swallow hard, wringing my hands. "Fletcher told me she's dead." I breathe in, choking back sobs as they hit me one at a time.

"All we know is that she's not in the prison," Jonah continues in a calm voice, as if he didn't hear me, or didn't want to. "That leaves us with some hope."

"Or it just confirms she's dead." I wrap my arms around my chest, trying to hold in the hopeless sobs that fill the empty cavity. Enid comes and sits next to me. She lays a hand on my leg and puts her arm around my shoulder. Her strength and kindness are just like my mother's. She squeezes my shoulders and rests her head against mine.

Something in me cracks open. I can't stop the pain burning through me. Uncontrollable strangled sobs rip from my chest, reverberating in the cave. An iron grip around my heart sends aching through my whole body. Enid's hands sweep up to my head, and she pulls me closer. Her body rattles as she cries alongside me. Jonah walks away, into the dark passageway that leads to Charlie's old room, his shoulders shaking.

After the tremors and pain subside, leaving a dull ache in my center, Enid releases me and goes about putting together some food. Jonah returns, but sits by the now half-starved fire, not speaking. He draws in the dirt beside where he sits, his big hands making the stick look flimsy and small.

A small plate of something mashed appears on my lap, and I spoon it into my mouth with Enid's help. Chewing is painful, but swallowing is easier. I finish the entire plate, and Enid pats my hand after removing it. Jonah gets up and helps me settle onto the ground for the night. It is hard to tell how much time has passed in the dark cave.

"I have something to help you sleep," Enid offers.

I stare at her, gathering her meaning. Sleep is better than heartbreak. "Thank you."

She slips a small portion of a tincture into the side of my mouth. It tastes like dirt and dank water, but I swallow it down. She removes the tin cup and adjusts my head on the cloth underneath me before returning to the fire, sitting next to Jonah. She leans into him, and his arms wrap around her. It is a small silver lining in all that has happened to us: they found each other, despite the horrors that they face every day.

My eyes slide shut with a heaviness I have no power against. No dreams find me.

When I open my eyes again, Jonah lies on his side next to my grandmother, their hands entwined as they sleep.

CHAPTER 9

HARM

"We should start visiting the villages and talking to the people, gathering men to fight, as soon as possible," Jonah says over our small breakfast of roots and greens. Enid's knowledge of plants has kept us from starving. Warmth and light from the fire push away the cool dampness of the cavern around us, the crackle lulling me to a distant place, far from the talk that fills the space around me.

"Harm." Jonah's voice snaps me out of my haze. I turn to see both Enid and Jonah looking at me, their faces tight, waiting for a response.

"Sorry, I was miles away. What was the question?"

Jonah's brow lowers at my response.

"Are you ready to start making plans?" Enid asks softly.

"Maybe. I…" Hesitation thickens my throat. "I don't know what I want at the moment."

"Things need to start moving on our side of this rebellion if we're to stand a chance of winning back the dial," Jonah says, eyes scanning my face for a reaction.

"Whatever you think is best."

"Harm, you must help lead this. Now is not the time to be ambiguous about it," he snaps.

Enid shoots him a warning glare.

My breathing hitches as my heartbeat kicks up, my hands curling to fists. "Everything I do just ends with people getting hurt, or worse. Leave me out of it."

Jonah shakes his head. "Every person who has paid the price should be what fuels you to push forward, not to give up."

I have never seen him like this, and he has never spoken to me like this before. His face carries lines of sorrow, now permanently embedded, as if losing Imani was the last straw, and whatever darkness had been wandering around in his weary soul is now trapped on his face for all to see.

"Perhaps another couple days' rest here would be best," Enid interjects, her gaze alternating between Jonah and me. I shrug, and Jonah throws his hands up in the air, then he rises and wanders to the entrance of the cave. His hands rest on his hips, his head hangs, and his deep exhale echoes through the small space. Enid pats my hand and puts on an empathetic smile. I don't reciprocate. Pushing to my feet, I steady myself against the mossy wall of the cave and feel my way down the darkened passageway to Charlie's room.

In the almost black space, I see the light of our fire glinting off a small metallic object. I scramble in the dark for it. The cold metal touches my fingers, and I grab it. Holding it out into the passageway, I make out the shape of a lantern. I shuffle back to our fire and tentatively tug a lit piece of kindling from the side. It lights the lantern with a few puffs from me. I drop the kindling back into the fire and traipse back down the passageway.

It is a few minutes before I come to the entrance to Charlie's oasis. The scent of fresh running water finds me first. I linger in the opening, memories of my last visit here flashing through my mind. The soft grass calls my name. I can almost hear her here. My heartbeats turn into flutters as I step onto the grass. With the lantern unnecessary now, I place it on the ground and blow out the flame, conserving whatever fuel it runs on for later.

The soft green grass is cool under my bare feet, and I wander from place to place. Everything looks the same, the tree in the center of the oasis still home to small birds and butterflies alike. The clear water trickles around the round landmass in the center, creating a liquid shield for the lone evergreen and its inhabitants. The large rock that Imani sat on rests at the waterline, the stream swirling around it on its way past.

I haul myself onto its cold surface and pull my knees up to my chest. Scurrying small animals go busily about their pursuits. Their twitching and antics prize a chuckle from my chest, a splinter of happiness. A small, wriggling, finned creature darts through the water, and I jump off the rock, feet landing on the smooth pebbles just beyond the waterline. The current folds around my feet, and my body sways.

I kneel in the cool water and run my hands through the current. It ripples against my fingers, and a smile sweeps over my face for the first time in weeks. A small silver-and-blue-finned fingerling startles before thrashing its way back to my fingers and suckling them. Chuckles reverberate from low in my chest. I shake it off and move back to the grass to sit and soak in the beauty of this place that Charlie conserved for decades, listening to the life teeming around me.

My gaze drawn to the shimmering water's surface, I pull up the last memory I have of it. Imani, bare and happy, her body slipping into the water, hair bouncing around her elegant shoulders. The ache that burned in my core for her then. Water touching every inch of her, and me wishing I was the water so badly. I was pretending to sleep, but I wanted to dive into the water right next to her and find out what she would do next. The loss of her burns, releasing embers of agony.

She was always the leader.

I was the follower.

I miss her.

Sucking in breaths, hard and long, I push down the agony that threatens to suffocate me. Hands covering my twisted face, I let each sob rack through me. Fire crushes my heart, and my breathing quickens.

Imani... I am so sorry.

Every word tugs out another memory of her.

I'm sorry, Imani.

Her fierce look the day we met in the outpost. The pain in her eyes when she told me Fletcher was her father. Her taunting when we first met, a direct jab at my helplessness. Her willingness to help me, and the loyalty she showed through every tough moment.

I fist my hands in my hair, pulling hard. Breathless screams pour from my trembling body.

Imani.

The devotion she wore the day she stood on the gallows to save me. Her fire, melded with steel.

Dammit, Imani.

Dammit.

My scream rips through the oasis, echoing around me, sending birds into flight.

I'm so sorry. I am so, so sorry.

I don't deserve her.

... Didn't.

I pound the grass with both fists, screaming, fire raging in my head and heart, tears dripping from my jaw, breath shredding my lungs.

When the last of the fire ebbs from my wrecked body, I lie on the grass and roll onto my side, knees up to my chest, until the last whimper falls from my lips. Water running over stones is the only other sound in the cavern. Light pouring through the small opening in the cave ceiling slowly rotates as the day progresses. I lie unmoving on the grass for hours.

Everything we lived through, every sacrifice she made for me, will have been for nothing if nothing changes. If I give up now, she would *never* forgive me.

I run through visions and scenarios of the future. What must happen next. Who it happens to, and who makes it happen. A list of families I know from Amondo, and people I have met along the journey to the south and from the outlying areas tally in my head. If I add that to the people Enid and Jonah can gather, we have a start. We need to know the numbers and locations of the Guardian legions, their advantages and weapons, as well as the number of prison inmates. Many of the prisoners may be useful and willing. But I know some won't be released, ever.

Emmie knows the passageways throughout the wall and tower. Toby would know most of the ins and outs of the prison system, and Saraya has a direct connection with him and lives in the vicinity of the prison. We can disable the dune buggies with Uncle Christopher's knowledge; that would even out the playing field in that regard. But everything would need to be in place to roll out simultaneously. All of this needs to happen in different places at the same time to send the Guardians scrambling and spread them thin.

We divide, then we conquer, just like in the books Father and me used to read.

Now I see why we did.

The wall and the tower and getting to Arthur will be the hardest parts. Maybe Nirri would help, but it would have to be her choice. We will need a second option for that, in case she refuses. A line of communication with Emmie and Nirri will need to be established, sharing the barest of details with them, so they can be prepared and not in the line of fire, but also in case they want to offer assistance to the rebels from their location.

I roll back onto the grass and stare at the stone ceiling. At least now I have a small plan to start with. Details and tactics will have to be talked through with Jonah and Enid. Passages from the old books my father had on tactics and strategies for war emerge through the tirade of musings that steal my attention. The element of surprise. Dual assaults on different locations. Inside help. Double agents. Outweighing numbers. Forcing your opponent's ranks apart. I crave a pencil and paper now, itching to plot out all the possibilities we can rain down, one after the other, on the Guardian Regime, and on Arthur.

Shuffling footsteps cut through the images of warfare in my head. Enid appears at the entrance. She stands silently, leaning against the wall. I wonder how long she has been in the passageway, not wanting to intrude. She pushes off the wall and walks over to where I lie. Soft groans escape as she lowers herself to the grass-covered ground beside me. She lies next to me and stares at the ceiling, imitating my position. A laugh escapes, and she smiles at me, tears pooling in her eyes, but her expression is one of happiness, not sorrow.

"This place is such a wonder. Charlie should have been ever so proud of what he achieved," she says.

I agree with a mumble.

"What are you in here thinking about, Harm?"

I recall the last couple of hours before I look over at her.

"Imani." Drawing in a breath, I try to stave off another wave of agony. "And the rebellion."

"We have all waited a long time for you." She pauses with a quick inhale. "Forgive Jonah for his harsh words. Imani was like a daughter to him. He has lost so much, and she was the last good thing in his life."

I blink, quelling the prickling of tears.

"We have all lost so much, and we've been waiting for hope for decades," she says.

Heaviness stirs in my chest. "If I have the ability, do you?"

"No, it was your grandfather's, and your mother's."

My eyes light up, and I sit up, staring down at her. "My mother had it?"

"Yes, but her father—your grandfather—forbade her from using it. He was terrified that she would be killed."

"So, you waited for my mother to have a child, and you were willing to wait, to risk a child?" Bitterness laces every word, and Enid's face tightens as she sits up.

"A lot happened in a short period of time, and it was too dangerous for her to try while Arthur had every Guardian hunting for people with the ability. Waiting was the safest and surest option." She looks back at the ceiling, and her eyes are somewhere far away. "Then she became pregnant with you. That complicated matters, and we sent her away. Every step north broke my heart. To send her away when she needed her mother the most... That no-good father of yours—Barlow, not Andrew—would sooner have turned her in than let her bear his child. So, I took her north, where we had old connections, and then she was Blended with your father, Andrew."

"Did he know about our ability?" I ask, inhaling.

"Yes, he knew it all. He was the kindest man I had ever met. I knew he would look after her and you. And on my way back to the south, I said a little prayer that they would live a normal and uneventful life—even if it meant leaving things the way they were for longer, with the sands and the oppression. I loved your mother so very much, and I just wanted her to have the life and the love she deserved."

"She did, she had that kind of love," I whisper.

Enid's face is a cascade of tears now, her trembling hands sitting in her lap. I grab them, and they fit inside mine easily. I squeeze them briefly and look at her sorrow-filled face.

"My mother was loved dearly by my father. They were inseparable. You made a good choice," I choke.

Enid smiles at me, and taking her hands from mine, she grasps my face. "You are so much like your grandfather, Harm. He would have been so immensely proud of you. And of his daughter." She pulls me into a tight hug. We help each other up and stand in the oasis for a time, admiring the serenity without speaking before heading back to the passageway.

"Barlow had the ability also, you know," I say.

Enid nods.

She already knew.

"He made a bargain with the Guardians," I tell her. "They let him live in the outlying villages, if he agreed to turn me in if I ever came looking for him."

"That two-faced coward. Figures." Shaking her head, she leads the way with her small lantern. The passageway is dank and cold compared to the sun-filled cavern we were just in, and we don't dawdle.

Jonah sits by the meek fire, crafting something from a stick with his knife—a wooden dagger of sorts. He looks up as we enter the space, brows lowered, mouth stretched into a thin line.

"I have a scrap of a plan, but I'm going to need your help," I say, holding Jonah's gaze.

He pushes up from his spot and walks over. I inspect his handiwork with the small piece of wood, chuckling at his attempt at whittling, and he slaps me on the back. "Let's hear it, then." He forces a wobbly smile before wandering back to the fire.

CHAPTER 10
IMANI

I run for hours, not entirely sure whether I am running from the village of Tabara or from myself. Those monsters deserved every inch of that blade. Trindari filth... I would do it again without hesitation. But they were the first unarmed men I have ever killed, and it feels different, almost wrong. Nevertheless, Gwyn's girls are safe now, as are the rest of the village girls. I repeat the words with every footfall. The robe I took from Gwyn is a comfort compared to the thin tunic I was wearing when stranded in the desert.

By the time the moon has started its descent to the horizon, I'm back to a walk. I head east, hoping to get to Indori and find some word of Jonah.

The stars hang in the ever-paling sky as I walk through the dregs of the night. The rush coursing through my veins has long since vanished, but the thoughts of taking the law into my own hands have kept me company for most of the night. I remember my father talking about vigilantes. I remember his words, laced with hate, telling me they were criminals. I huff a dry laugh at the thought of me being a notorious criminal. So be it.

The piercing howls of the night walkers of this desert echo across the sands and over the dunes in front of me. It has been an age since I ever feared an animal, and now that I'm armed with these knives and my bolstered sense of hate, if they attacked, they wouldn't be breathing for long. The sunrise coaxes yawn after yawn from me, and I search for a safe place to rest, for a few hours anyway. I need to sort out my exact location and figure out where on this ruined patch of sand I am going to find Jonah without getting caught.

A small cave-like space created by four closely situated rocks beckons to me, and I stumble my way to the ground just under their protection before my legs give out on me. The dirt is cold, but my heart is warm from running, and from the knowledge that this vigilante just did some good.

I am up before the sun appears over the horizon, vaguely aware of tossing and turning in the cold wee hours of the night. I've slept for a day and a night. I don't know which needed the rest more: my body, or my soul. With a long stick, I break off the arm of a nearby cactus and scoop out the flesh for a watery breakfast, washed down with a drink from my canteen. With the sun at my back, I head to the next village on the outskirts, hoping to find Jonah there.

It takes me around three hours of plowing through the dunes before I slide down the last mountain of sand at the edge of the village. Hood up and wrap safely in place, I make my way to the village center and find a tavern. It is a risk, asking around for Jonah, but I am out of options. The wooden doors give way easily, and I step inside the poorly lit room under the gaze of the man standing behind the counter. I remove the hood and pull down my wrap, hoping the dim light doesn't give away my identity, at least not immediately, in case anyone here is interested in earning a kickback from the Guardians for handing me in.

The wooden counter comes up to my chest, and I glance

around before meeting the proprietor's eyes. A friendly smile cracks his face. "What can I get you, lass?" His hands are drying a glass with a cotton towel.

"I'm looking for my father."

He raises an eyebrow, and a smirk blooms across his face. "Oh, and did you think you would find him in here?"

"Not exactly. He's a traveler. I thought maybe you had seen him pass through?"

"In that case, you'll have to give me a little more to go off. Many men come and go in this establishment."

I describe Jonah, and Enid, on the off chance that she is with him too.

"He was here, a couple of weeks ago. But they left for the wall, south of the prison. Not the Etonia one; the tower side." He leans toward me. "Apparently, they were to pick up precious cargo. That's what the woman called it, this Enid you described. I haven't seen them back here since then. Perhaps they're still there."

The wall... What tower? Is that the prison that Harm was in? That precious cargo could have been Harm.

It is three days' journey to get to the wall. I will need supplies and better weapons; kitchen knives are not exactly suitable for every application. Not that I haven't been able to get the job done with them, but I much prefer fighting knives.

"Where can I get supplies for a journey to the wall, then?"

He raises a brow. "What did you say your name was?"

"I didn't. It's Imani F—" The word catches in my throat. "...from Perendi."

He grunts, casting a cautious eye over his establishment, and his face softens. "Two doors down to the right. Still has a collection of the essentials out back. Tell him I sent you; he'll help you out."

He turns back to the wall of glasses behind him as I push my way out of the tavern and head two doors down.

The small building looks boarded-up, but I push on the door and enter under the sound of a small bell. The front room looks like a small shop with only the basics. Flour, grains, small pelts from a handful of unfortunate desert animals, dried herbs, and other bags with no labels line the walls and the front of the counter. I stand there assessing what I will need for three days. Dried meat, bread or grains, knives... That about covers it. But the only items I have to barter with are Gwyn's two kitchen knives and the name of the man from the tavern.

I check that my hair and face are still wrapped up before shuffling over to take a closer look at the unlabeled bags. Leaning down to smell the burlap, I try to discern the contents, resting a hand on the top one. A pungent acid smell burns my nose. I withdraw my hand, wiping it on my robe.

"I doubt you would need any of that, lassie," a gruff voice says from behind me. I stand and turn to face him. The short, rotund man waddles back behind the counter before looking me up and down.

"What's in the bags?"

"Just a means to an end, nothing you need to be bothered with."

"I need some supplies for a three-day journey."

He nods.

"Bread, dried meat, and..." I hesitate, wondering if he will ask questions. "... a pair of fighting knives."

He raises a brow and slumps over the counter, supported by his elbows while he considers my request. "What have you brought to barter with?" he says, letting out a sigh, as if I am boring him already.

"I only have these kitchen knives. They're sharp and useful for preparing meals, slicing meat," I say, remembering how easily they had whipped through those two boys' throats.

He cocks his head sideways, as if contemplating their value. "I can't give you three days' supply of dried meat and bread for just two knives. And I don't have weapons here, girl."

"The man at the tavern told me to tell you he sent me," I say desperately, searching for any spark of recognition.

He stands and looks at me for an age. I shove my hands deep into the pockets of my robe to hide my fidgeting. He turns and walks away from the counter, stopping at the door at the back of the shop. His hand raised to the wood, he looks back at me and gestures with his head for me to follow. For a few moments, I stand fast, hesitating. When he realizes I'm not following, he pokes his head back in, hissing for me to hurry up.

The small room is lined with row after row of knives, bows and arrows, long daggers, and pairs of fighting knives. The colorful feathers of the arrows make an elegant display, deeply contrasting with the angry metal of the knives and daggers around the room. He plants his feet slightly apart in the center of the room and raises both arms, gesturing for me to take my pick. I am not sure why the mere mention of the tavern owner grants me access to this secret room, and part of me doesn't want to know.

I scan the selection of fighting knives, picking up a pair with a golden metal band on the end. But they are heavy in my hands, and they feel off. I set them back down. Next, I run a hand along the shelf under the pairs of knives, stopping abruptly at a pair with ebony handles. I scoop them up and toss them around in my hands. They sit just right, with the right amount of weight between the handle and the blade. I look up at the shop owner, who is watching me.

"They are yours, if you wish," he says.

"They're beautiful. Are you sure?"

"They are yours. They will serve you well." He ushers me back to the front of the shop and grabs a cotton satchel from under his counter, loading it up with dried meat and small loaves of bread, one for each day of travel. My robe hits the floor, and I grab the satchel from the counter, swinging it over my head and shoulders before donning my robe again. I hand him the kitchen knives in exchange for the satchel.

"Can I ask…" I shift from foot to foot. "… why you're both helping me?"

The man pulls his shirt to the side, revealing a tattoo of a small bird in flight, similar to Harm's birthmark. None the wiser but grateful for his help, I nod, offering a smile.

"You'll see, lass, all in good time. Now you must be off; they'll be wanting to see you," he utters.

"They?" Enid and Jonah? That is the only connection I have to the people in this village. Hope ricochets around inside me like a harried jackrabbit. He simply nods.

"Wait… Where is the tower prison?"

"Just beyond the wall. The entry is in the wall itself, a day's walk south from Etonia, or three from here." He nods to the door, as if urging me to leave. I bid him farewell and thank him for the kindness and the knives before throwing up my hood and securing my wrap. I start walking in the direction of the tower and the wall, praying under my breath that these folk have not just sent me on a pointless errand.

Crouched under a less-than-helpful desert bush, I scan the section of the wall that runs to the left of the tower. I've never been this far south before, and I have no idea what lies on the other side, or who. More desert and hordes of Guardians training, most likely. I search for a break in the wall, any opening that would allow me to get past it and into the heart of enemy territory, so I can find Harm—if they have even kept him alive all this time.

I have seen no sign of Jonah or Enid, and nothing to suggest a caravan passing through, or talk of a healer's work. The last group of travelers I encountered only told me of the two ways to breach the wall, then warned against it, saying that if I managed to get through it, I would never return. But there is no going back now. I think back to the small bird tattoo. I know I have seen it some-where before. I was standing with Harm when I saw it; that much I can remember.

With the sun already easing into afternoon, I move swiftly to the wall itself. Running my hands over every surface, I try to find evidence of an opening. Southbound, I trot down the wall with one hand brushing the stone as I go, past the clumps of bushes that move with the desert winds. There is nothing for many strides; every inch feels like the one before it.

My gaze is on the thick sand under me when the stone under my fingers disappears. I slide to a halt and step back several paces to find the gap. It runs high above my head. I slide my fingers into the small vertical crack in front of me. Darting a glance sideways, I search for another crack identical to this one. Sure enough, six paces along, another one runs up from the sand to three-quarters up the wall. Over my head lies the horizontal crack that joins the two vertical ones.

A door.

There must be some type of mechanism that works this massive stone door. I dust the sand from the surface of the stone next to the crack, but nothing obvious appears. I skip to the oppo-site crack and dust away the sand. Nothing. My hands tremble from the toll of the last four days, and a wash of fatigue claims me down to my bones. The ache in my chest grows and spreads, forcing tears into my eyes. I rest my head on the stone in front of me, palms pressed on the dusty wall on either side of the seam of the door. How am I ever going to find him? I can't even get in!

I push my weight off the stone wall—and the block under my right hand depresses. Sand drifts down from the vertical line above me. The door moves slowly under its own enormous weight. In an instant, a rush of hope sparks through my veins like lightning. The small trees behind me sway in the desert's playful winds as I grab the strap of my satchel and lean forward to step into the dark space.

Without warning, cold metal touches my throat. My breath stops, my body frozen. The smell of tree sap and leaves encloses me from behind. I loose a breath and close my eyes.

I remember Enid. The bird in flight—it was on Enid's wrist. My hand tightens on the satchel strap, my other brushing past my hip, hunting for my knives. But I am no longer wearing my knife belt, so they sit at the bottom of my satchel, under the food, useless.

A woman's body presses against my back, her free hand grabbing my wandering wrist. Her breath flutters past my ear as the sharp edge of her blade digs into my neck. "Don't move."

CHAPTER II
HARM

It has been two days since we left Charlie's cave. My face is still swollen in places, but the damage to my wrists and ankles has mostly faded away. We travel by foot, not risking the caravan this time. Enid and Jonah are taking me to a village far to the south, Indori. They were there just over two weeks ago. Upon entering the village, it appears much the same as every other place I have been. But the air feels different somehow—or maybe my head wounds have muddled my senses good and proper this time.

"We're only a few days' travel from the very southern section of the wall here. The air is different, and the people are a rare find," Jonah offers, as if my thoughts are written on my face for all to see.

"It does feel different," I say.

"That's the moisture in the air. The central desert villages don't have it. This is where it starts," Enid says.

I throw her a curious look; her knowledge of this place seems deep.

"We should get home before the sun sets. I need to get some things before supper," she says.

She has a home here? I walk beside Jonah as he walks a few steps behind Enid.

"Your grandmother is a woman of many assets. I for one am glad to spend the night in a bunk instead of on the ground." He smiles playfully and slaps me on the back.

When we reach the house, my surprise is evident. It is a medium-sized home, with a chimney and a side yard, albeit overgrown with desert weeds. We step inside, and the place instantly reminds me of Enid's house, where I first met her. It's the same layout, with similar items placed around the front room, as if this home is the replica of her first one, or perhaps the original. She lights candles and gives me a brief tour, and I realize that Jonah has been here before. He makes himself at home on the worn couch in the front room and stretches out the days of traveling, one muscle at a time.

Before I have a chance to comment on the home, Enid rushes back out the door to get supplies for supper. I settle down next to Jonah on a chair. The pile of books on the small side table grabs my attention, and I stretch out also before picking up the top one and flipping through it. But the words on the pages don't hold my attention, and my gaze returns to Jonah, who clearly feels very at home.

"What is this place?"

He looks up from his book, much like my father used to. "Your grandmother's maternal home. She's kept it all this time, waiting for someone to need it. Now she does."

"Won't the Guardians also know this is her home and find her here easily?"

"Nope, the ties are long forgotten. They all died out when she was a young woman. It was occupied up until ten years ago by another family. They left too. It's a better place to hide out than a cave."

I return to the book, but my attention is scattered. I put the book down and wander down the hall. I wonder if she built her home north of here as a replica of this one, to remind her of her childhood.

Heading out the back door, I am greeted by a similar stone patio, only this one has no plants or benches, just stone and sand. A short fence, barely standing, despite sections of it being laid over, separates her home from the home behind it. Enid's home to the north backed up to the desert, the last of the homes before the endless sands.

Voices inside pique my interest, and I head back in. Enid is organizing a handful of supplies on the kitchen table and starts preparing a meal. Jonah pushes up from his seat in the living room, wandering to the kitchen, offering to help. She chops the roots as Jonah starts a fire in the iron cooker. They work in sync for a while, leaving me with nothing to do but get in the way, so I amble down the hall and inspect the rooms.

"Yours is the first door on the left," Enid calls out behind me.

I head into that room and plonk down on the bunk. The room is stuffy and warm. I walk to the window and shove the worn frame open. It groans against its glass pane inserts, but a swirling breeze greets me like a long-lost friend. The smell of the moisture on the sands hits me again, carrying a pine scent, just like the forest below that bridge. I make a mental note to ask Enid about that tonight.

An old wardrobe sits against the wall, and I open it. It is all but empty, but a small vertical mirror is attached inside the left-hand door. It is the first time in ages that I have seen my face. A small sound escapes my mouth, and my hand reaches up to touch the damaged places. My nose has shifted slightly to the left, and under both eyes are the purple-green remnants of bruising. A handful of scabbed-over cuts mar my cheekbones and my jawline. But there is no pain anymore. Enid has done a marvelous job of saving my face.

Memories of Fletcher's fists and cane pummeling my face play over and over in my mind. I swallow back bile and steady myself against the wardrobe. I take in deep breaths and remind myself that I got out. Emmie and Nirri got me out.

Jonah's call whips me back to reality. I pad down the hall and seat myself at the head of the table, with Jonah and Enid on either side, waiting to start. Enid grabs my hand and holds her other one out for Jonah's. He takes it before offering me his other hand, and I take it. Enid squeezes her fingers around mine.

"To every small victory, every person we love, and the hope that has finally found us," Jonah says.

Enid nods and smiles at me, tears in her eyes.

"Let's eat," Jonah says. Releasing my hand, he picks up his spoon and digs into his bowl.

Enid's cooking always leaves me satisfied. I finish every mouthful. Jonah then collects the dishes and washes up while Enid and I settle down in the living room. She is fidgeting, watching me as I comb through the small selection of abandoned books coated with dust and sand. I pull out what looks like a novel about a forest people, but on closer inspection, I see that it's more like a field journal. Everything is written in elegant handwriting, filling every line of the page. Some pages have sketches, and one of them looks like a drawing of the wall itself.

I look up at Enid. She is still now, watching me.

"What is this?" I ask.

"My journal, from years ago. I took it everywhere with me." She holds my gaze.

"*You* wrote all this? And did the sketches too?" I flip through the pages.

"Yes, on one of my treks to find healing plants and such. It was a long time ago. That particular journal was filled over several months."

"But these drawings look like the forest beyond the wall." My mouth goes dry. She has been there before.

"That's because they are. You'll also find smaller flora and some insects and so on from the forest floor in there."

"I didn't even know it existed until they took me over that bridge to the tower. How did you get in there and not get caught?"

"There's an entire race of forest dwellers that live beyond the wall. They never cross the wall, just as we don't. While we battle the desert and the sands, they battle the torrential rains and all the diseases that go with it. At least, that was what was happening at the time I was there. I learned a great deal from them. I was there for just under two months before they helped me back across the wall."

Jonah has come to sit with us and is reading my face for a reaction to Enid's words.

"So, you've known about the wall and the two different sides for most of your life?" I ask.

"For around three decades now."

I look at Jonah. "You knew too?"

"In theory. I've never been there."

I close my eyes and pinch the bridge of my nose. I draw a breath before looking back up at them. "So, what part do the forest dwellers play in the rebellion? Are they part of it too?"

"They are aware that it exists. Whether they will be a part of it remains to be seen. Their priorities with the Chancellor are different than ours. When I was there, they were hoping for change, as we were. But it has been many years since it was discussed."

"We could pay them a visit," Jonah says. "It's been a long time since they saw you, but it could be well worth it. There's risk for Harm though. The Guardians are heaviest around the wall."

Enid gestures for the journal, and I hand it to her. She turns it over in her lap before opening it and skimming through the pages. She is looking for something. We wait.

"What prevents the weather from breaching the wall, then, if the forest dwellers are stuck with all the rain?" I ask.

"Some kind of magnetic field," Jonah replies. "Nobody knows for sure; I doubt Arthur even knows that. He's too busy taking advantage of it to bother understanding it."

Pages flip, and Enid scans each one with her fingers.

"Here, here it is! The list of the tribes and their locations," she says, handing me the book. There are at least a dozen tribes on the page, dotted throughout the forest, with one central tribe, its dot bigger than the rest.

"What's that one?" I ask, holding the book up to Enid.

"That's the main tribe. Their leader was who I was first brought to. She would be as old as me, if she's still alive. Once they realized I was harmless enough, they were most accommodating. I had a few desert plants and powders from dried desert bush roots that I gave them, and they taught me the flora of the forest in return. That small plant that lines Charlie's cave is one they have also. It puts you to sleep, if you remember."

"I never saw any evidence of people living in the forest from the tower or the bridge," I say.

"You wouldn't. They keep to themselves, and the forest is vast. It spans an area much bigger than our desert side."

"If we could somehow convince the forest dwellers to join us, that would be a surprise the Guardians wouldn't see coming, and it would give us the numbers," I say.

"Perhaps. But they have long believed that Arthur put up the wall to protect them from us—a tale he spun them from the very start, or so Hanola told me. She was their chief in the central village." She points to the largest dot on the map.

"So, we go to them and ask for their help, show them we're

willing to work and live beside them." My voice raises with the prospect of hope.

"They are not always welcoming of guests. Others have gone over the wall to their forest and never returned," Enid says, brows drawn down.

"We should at least try," I plead.

"Perhaps we should think about it for a few days and see what plan we can come up with that benefits both sides, before we run into their forest too eagerly," Jonah interjects.

"That's a risk I'm willing to take." I think back to the days I spent in Amondo, desperate to escape and to travel. Maybe, just maybe, those who went to the forest side never *wanted* to return.

CHAPTER 12

IMANI

The steel of her blade digs into my throat. I steady my breaths and wait for her to make the next move. If I try to go for my knives, that will be the last thing I do with her at my back. Knowing I let my guard down in the first place brings heat to my cheeks.

"Turn around, girl."

I start to move, but her hand grips my arm.

"With your hands away from your body."

I raise my arms over my head and slowly turn. A woman a few years older than me stands planted in the sand. Her thin, muscular frame is wrapped tight in a cloth of grey and green, her legs covered by tight pants. Covering her torso and chest is a vest of similar material. Resting over her breasts is a weapons sheath, and knives and a long dagger sit firmly in their casings. Her back holds a bow and quiver of arrows. Her wrists are wrapped in the same cloth, and her hair, blonde and straight, sticks out beneath her wrap. From her stance, I can tell she carries the role of a warrior or protector of some sort. In my mind, I see her taking on the Guardians and bringing them to their knees.

Her questions interrupt my thoughts. Mouth slightly agape, I compose myself and meet her gaze.

"Where do you think you're going?" Her green eyes drill into mine, hands now resting on the recently sheathed knife and her long dagger.

"I need to get to the tower on the other side of the wall." Honesty seems like the safest option right now.

"Why would you want to go there?" she retorts, clearly annoyed at my statement.

"I'm trying to find someone."

She raises a brow. "Why are they in the tower?"

"They were a prisoner. I got word that they may have escaped. I need to find out for sure and track them down." I lift my chin slightly higher, feeling less than confident standing in front of her. I need to get to that tower and find out where Harm went.

"First, you will have to come with me. Anyone who breaches the wall comes with me." She raises a hand and points to the open stone door. Something twists in my gut, but I nod, throw back my hood, and step into the dark, narrow space. I have no idea what to expect on the other side of the wall. Going with her feels like a good move. I can scope out what is over this wall while she is leading me to wherever she takes intruders. Maybe it's the prison? If I need to escape, I will. She follows close behind, and the stone door slides shut behind us. I wait for my eyes to adjust to the pitch black. They don't.

She moves around me, keeping a hand on my shoulder. Her other hand brushes across the stone, like mine did before. A dull thud echoes, and the stone door in front of us slowly opens.

Squinting, I gasp. Covering my mouth, I blink a few times trying to make sure what lies outside the stone doorway is real. The smell of moisture and trees reaches me first.

Green.

Everywhere.

The woman steps onto the damp ground, lush grass like in Charlie's cave under her feet. I follow. In front of me are trees so dizzyingly high that they dwarf us instantly, rising tall to meet the sun, like nothing I have ever seen before. Melodious birdsong shrills back and forth from the highest branches as birds of all sizes and varieties chatter away. It is a moment before I realize she is walking into the forest. I jog to catch up, entranced by this place that surrounds me with verdant green life. It is everything the desert on our side of the wall is not.

Her voice pulls me forward. "Keep up, I'm not going to track you down amongst the trees if you get lost," she calls over her shoulder.

I jog ahead again. A breeze carrying the smells of the forest ruffles my hair, and for a moment, I wish it were long again. But it will be several weeks before then, if not months. It's just past my shoulders now, but I have it tied up with the blue scarf from Harm. Briefly, I wonder how Gwyn is getting on, hoping her life is a little easier now she doesn't have to constantly worry about her two little girls staying safe. I fall in beside the forest woman.

"My name is Catori," she offers, and a small smile grows on her face. Her words are kind.

"Nice name," I offer, not returning the smile.

"It means 'spirit'." She tries again, her smile widening into a grin, face lit up with kindness. "You have a name too, I presume?"

"Imani. I have no idea what it means."

Catori laughs, and it echoes through the trees. A smile cracks over my face and I chuckle, warmed by her openness. The knot in my gut all but disappears and every feeling I am getting from her is so genuine.

"It will take us a day or so to get to the village. We'll have to camp overnight. There's a clearing up ahead. It's safe, just gets cold and wet is all."

"Village? But I need to get to the prison in the tower," I say, annoyance lacing my words.

"You will, but everyone who makes it over that wall sees Hanola first. She is the leader of the forest people. If anyone can help you, she can. Plus, technically, it's on the way. Relax, desert girl."

I nod and follow her lead, relaxing somewhat, finally some help. Just before the sun dips over the horizon, we reach a small clearing tucked behind a crest. Catori pulls long strips of bark from a pale tree and makes up two sleeping mats. I start hunting for firewood. I wander a little way into the trees and gather anything that looks dry and useful. Before long, I have an armful of wood and head back to the clearing. Catori has started the makings of a fire, and I dump the wood beside it.

"I'll find us some food. You stay here." She walks away, then looks back. "I mean it—you'll get lost in the dark amongst the trees and become disoriented in an instant. I'll be back in a little while. Keep the fire going."

I plop down next to the fire in agreement and warm my hands. The air cools fast without the rays of the sun. The flames whip and crackle in front of me. The heaviness of sleep calls to me, but I need to eat. I remove my robe and pull off the satchel. Quickly sliding my robe back on, I stave off the cold temporarily, returning my hands to the fire. Once they're warm, I hunt around in my bag for the bread and dried meat.

Catori returns and sits next to me at the fire. She starts working on the morsels she found in the forest, clearly not threatened by me. Amused by how absurd that thought is when she has so many weapons strapped to her body, I let out a small laugh. She looks up, a quizzical look on her face. She has gathered grubs of some sort, a pile of leaves and berries, and a chunk of what looks like tree flesh, piled on two large leaves. My bread and meat look more appealing. She hands me a leaf of food. I nod, silently thanking her before exploring the things on my leaf cautiously. She notices my bread and dried meat, and her eyes are almost pleading. I break the roll and the meat into chunks and give her half of what I have, just like Harm did for me in the outpost the day we met. I breathe through the ache in my chest. We eat in silence.

I leave the grubs until last, popping one in my mouth cautiously. I gag and immediately spit it out, and she roars with laughter.

"I have to admit, your meat tastes better than mine," she says, ripping into the last of the bread I gave her. I spit out the remnants of the revolting grub and wash away the vile taste with water from my canteen. Catori stifles her laughter. I shiver in the cool, damp air that hangs around us like smoke and tighten my robe around my shoulders.

"You desert dwellers really feel the cold. Take a spot as close to the fire as you can. It will get damper and colder as the night draws down on us." Catori points to the sleeping mat of soft grey bark situated closest to the fire.

"Thank you. I guess that means you forest dwellers feel the heat," I quip, and she huffs a laugh.

She studies me. "Guess so—not that I've stayed in the desert for longer than a handful of hours. Horrid place."

I lie down on the bark and huddle my legs to my chest. Licks of heat from the fire find me, and the shivering almost subsides. Catori stretches out on her mat behind me, sighing softly. Exhausted and wrapped in my robe, with the fire warming my bones as sleep throws its weight over me, I drift off.

The calls of the birds high in the canopy wake me. Catori is still sound asleep on her mat, curled up, as I was all night. The fire is all but out, the meager embers struggling to stay alight. I rifle through my satchel and tear off some bread, pulling out my canteen as well. The bread tastes bland compared to the feast we shared last night. I close my eyes and pretend it is something else—perhaps the berries or the chunk of sweet bark Catori gave me.

A crack sounds from beyond the tree line, only a few yards away, followed by another. I freeze and search for movement amongst the trees. Plunging my hand into my rucksack, I hold the cold ebony handle of one of my knives out of sight in the bag. More steps, more cracks, closer and closer. Whatever it is, it's heavy. I have no idea what kinds of large animals wander this forest. My breath catches as I glimpse movement from behind the nearest tree.

A young man comes to a standstill behind Catori, daggers slung across his chest, and twin sword hilts poke up over his broad shoulders. His messy blond hair is ruffled. He drops his blue eyes to where Catori lies. Pulling the knife from my satchel, I stand in one fluid motion and move closer to her. He gives me a curious look, cocking his head to the side.

"Friend or foe?" I demand. But heat flushes my face as I realize his clothes are similar to Catori's.

"Friend," Catori says, and I startle. "Callian, I heard you coming three miles back. Imani, this is my not-so-subtle little brother, Callian." She opens her eyes and pushes herself up, sitting on her mat, stretching her arms above her head and yawning. I lower my knife and sit back on my mat, eyes glued to my breakfast, hoping the heat in my face goes unnoticed.

"Hanola was getting worried. You were supposed to return yesterday," Callian says.

"Well, I have a companion, as you can see. She didn't look like the vine-swinging type, so it's taking a little longer to get home." She stands and throws the bark pieces that made up her sleeping mat into the embers of the fire. It smokes before catching. I sit and eat, watching Catori and Callian.

I quickly finish my bread and wash it down before shoving the canteen back into the satchel. Moving off my mat, I throw my bark pieces onto the fire also. Catori gives me a nod and slaps her brother playfully on the arm before turning back to me.

"We should reach home before the day is done, but you'll have to keep up with us," she says, hands automatically checking her weapons one by one as she looks me over.

"We're running?" I ask.

"Yep. And you might want to do something with that robe. It will slow you down and overheat your body in the humidity after the sun reaches its peak." She waves her arm at my desert robe. Callian raises an eyebrow and grins before she slaps him again.

"I can put it in the satchel when I get too hot." I wrap it around my waist, despite her warning.

Catori holds a finger up to the wind, nodding in the direction of travel as she starts walking westward. Callian's hands fall on my shoulders, and he moves me into place behind her before stepping behind me. Catori takes off running. It takes me a few heartbeats to catch up to her loping gait. Callian remains behind me.

We run.

Fire spreads through every inch of my lungs, and my legs drop like lead weights with every step. The heavy footfalls of Callian behind me slow, and he whistles to Catori. I pull back to a walk, my hands pressing tightly into my sides, trying to temper the ache in my sides. We don't run in the desert; it is too taxing on your body and dehydrates you too quickly. I walk in small circles, and Catori stands waiting, hands on her hips, breathing rhythmically.

"We're not even halfway there yet," she says.

"I'll carry her," Callian offers, not talking to me.

"Do it."

Before I can object, he is in my space, and two corded arms sweep me up. He takes off after his sister. I strain against the humiliation of being carried and try to look anywhere but his face. The path cutting through the forest winds and narrows from time to time. I hold my head back, and the bursts of golden sunlight through the green dappled green canopy rushing by are stunning.

"First time in the forest, Imani?"

I lift my head and school my face into a less embarrassed expression. After a few breaths, waiting for my heart to stop racing, I drum up an answer. "Yep. First time in the forest, first time beyond the wall," I say, thanking the heavens I didn't add "first time being carried by some kind of forest warrior."

Callian smiles back, but his gaze returns to the path in front of him, jaw set and breathing steady.

"I can try running again, if I'm too heavy," I plead, desperate to be put down. Being this close to him makes me uncomfortable. His square face and blue eyes make him easy to look at, and his mouth splits into a wide grin as he shakes his head, looking at me briefly. Memories of Harm curled around me to keep me warm in the middle of the sands run through my mind. The smell of Callian, his body warm with exertion, is overpowering, and I flinch away from his hold. With that thought, I tug at his arm and insist on being let down. Feeling like a small child, I can feel my face burn, and I hit the ground running, if only to put distance between us.

The warmth from his hold still covers my arms, and my heart sinks. Tears burn their way down my face. It feels wrong in every way to be close to Callian. I swallow down the queasiness and focus on each stride, breathing in and out. One arm is across my chest, grasping the strap of my satchel, and the other is powering back and forth, pushing my stride forward.

When the sun reaches its midpoint, Catori signals for us to stop. She walks in slow circles, winding between the trees edging a small clearing, as if doing a perimeter check. Before Callian and I reach the clearing, she winds her way to the ground, legs crossed, and rips her canteen from her side, gulping down every drop. I slump to the ground and sit there, breath heaving for an age before I steady myself enough to drink. The ache in my side has returned, and I clamp my hand over it tightly.

"You should walk in small circles until that cramp subsides," Catori says, whipping her chin up, encouraging me to get up again. I push up on shaking arms, my legs threatening to fold under me any second. I pace slowly around the clearing, hand still clamped to my side, face twisted. Callian walks into the forest, I assume to relieve himself or find food. Eyes to the ground, pacing every breath, I continue until the cramp subsides before plopping down beside Catori.

"You run everywhere?" I ask between breaths.

"Pretty much. It's the only way to travel in the forest. Slow travelers make for good bear food."

My eyes widen. "Really? I'm not sure what that is, but it doesn't sound good."

"Really. But you'll be safe. Callian will be picked off first; he's our back runner." She snorts out a laugh that echoes through the forest around us.

Gradually, I notice hissing and gushing sounds tangling toward us through the trees. "What's that sound?" I ask.

"The waterfall at the swimming hole. Usually I would stop there, but this trip, I'm short on time."

I realize for the first time since I have been on this side of the wall that these people seem so happy, not worn down and angry like the desert dwellers, as Catori calls us. They are also far more trusting than we are. On our side of the wall, that knife to my throat would have been just the first of many threats. Instead, she has helped me and protected me, even though she doesn't know me. A strange feeling washes over me—something good.

CHAPTER 13
HARM

Jonah and I set off to do the rounds with the village people. A rally or meeting would be too dangerous, so we walk from home to home, talking with every household, gauging their willingness to join the rebellion. Of course, we don't call it that. We use words like "gathering," "congregation," and "a movement for the people." These are less conspicuous words if tongues wag, Jonah says. He has thought his sermon through thoroughly. It is not forceful or condescending, and every household that joins us does so by choice.

Later today, my uncle, Christopher, is to arrive. He has been back in Amondo since the gallows. I am looking forward to seeing his beaming smile and hearing of Maryanne. Part of me misses Amondo, but most of me never wants to set foot in that village again. The last memories I have of it are my family being executed. The screams of my mother, the pleading from my little sister, the helpless agony caging my father as he knelt in the sand, tears sliding down his contorted face as he watched his family die. I swallow back the swelling emotions that tug at me.

Jonah walks ahead as we approach another home. He knocks

three times. A small man opens the door, with a leather strap in hand, his face reddened and covered in sweat.

"What?" he grunts.

Jonah asks him politely if we can come in.

"No, you cannot," he spits. "Take your self-righteous speech somewhere else." He slams the door.

Jonah stands there, clearly hoping the door will reopen, but a woman's pleading from inside follows instead, then the crack of the leather strap. Fury lights up Jonah's face, and he collides with the door before storming over the threshold. The man yells. I move to the window and watch as Jonah grabs his raised arm and rips the leather strap from the vicious little man's hand. The terror in his wife's eyes is replaced by a blank expression as she watches Jonah stand over her husband.

"You will never lay another finger on this woman!" Jonah grinds out.

Tears fall from her face, and she straightens her skirts and top, backing away from her husband and toward Jonah. The man shoots Jonah a foul look before ripping his arm from the larger man's grip. "What happens between my wife and me is none of your business."

The woman pales slightly at his words and fumbles with her skirt. Jonah smiles, but it is laced with hatred, and the man swallows hard.

"Never again—or you will suffer the same fate as her, or worse." Jonah nods to the woman. "But by my hands. Understand?"

"You keep to your business, traitor, and I keep to mine. It would be very easy for me to tell the wrong person that you're traipsing around the village, with talk of a rebellion." His face turns to a sneer.

Jonah steps closer to him. "Your secret for mine. You think the Guardians are going to let you get away with abuse?"

The angry man withers under Jonah's taller stature and scuffles backward. "Fine. Now get out of my house," he splutters.

Jonah stalks back through the front door, leaving it wide open before moving to the next home.

"What was that all about?" I ask once we are far enough to be out of earshot and I have caught up with his furious gait.

"I will not tolerate husbands hitting their wives. It makes my blood boil. Bloody cowards."

"What if he runs to the Guardians about us visiting the houses in the village?"

"He won't."

We walk up to the next home, and Jonah raises his hand to knock. But he hesitates.

"You know what? Perhaps we should eat before we cover the rest of these houses." He is clearly still shaken by what he saw, and we walk back past the man's house as we return home. It's quiet; nobody stirs when I peer through the window as Jonah walks on. Maybe the man got the message. I hope for his wife's sake that it got through.

Jonah barrels through Enid's front door and stalks down the hall. The back door opens and slams before Enid has a chance to cross the kitchen from where she is preparing the midday meal.

"What happened?" she asks.

"A man was beating his wife with a leather strap at one of the homes. Jonah stepped in. I've never seen him so furious."

"I see," she says quietly, hands gripping the bench.

"Enid?"

"Let's eat some lunch. Here, take this to Jonah. I'll set the table for you and me."

I carry a small tin tray with leftovers from last night, accompanied by a tin cup of water. I step backward into the door, and it opens as I turn to pass through it, tray in hand. I find Jonah seated on a wooden stool out near the broken fence, his hands covering his head, which is almost between his knees. He does not look up as I stand in front of him, so I set the tray at his feet and return to the kitchen. My spot at the table has a plate of leftovers and a tin mug of water also. Enid has already started, and she points to my plate with her fork. I sit, and we eat in silence.

"Jonah's sister was beaten badly by her husband. You may have met her once. She used to travel with Jonah and the gypsies." She pauses, waiting for my realization.

I remember an older woman with Indie. They were in the caravan together when Imani was hurt, and I hid from the Guardians under her bunk. I shove in another mouthful, and she continues.

"She was a brilliant girl, bright, always so happy, or so Jonah tells me. But her husband left her broken, physically and mentally. She never fully recovered from the trauma of it. She hardly speaks now, and Jonah grieves for her still."

I remember a quiet woman in the gypsy camp. She was crying after Imani had come back injured with my rucksack. That must have been her. The blood and damage to Imani's body must have triggered her own trauma. My food gets stuck in my throat, and my stomach rises to meet it. I drop my fork.

"How do you know all this?" I ask.

"Jonah and I have been working and traveling together since the night you and Imani left to find Barlow. We've shared many stories."

"Just traveling together?" I raise a brow, fighting the smile that is trying to bloom across my face.

"I may be six years older than Jonah, Harm. But when you get to be our age, those things hardly matter." She winks at me, happiness spreading over her face.

The gruff sound of Jonah clearing his throat silences the thoughts that play in my head. He places his tray on the table and joins us, his mouth drawn into a thin line. Enid pats his hand.

"Any more thoughts on the forest dwellers, you two?" she asks. I shake my head, as if her changing the subject has removed my previous thoughts, and I spear some meat onto my fork.

"We're going to need them for numbers. But I'm not sure they'll have a reason to help us," Jonah says, his voice raw.

"Could I travel to their villages and ask for their help?" I ask.

Enid plays with the food on her plate, moving it around piece by piece. Jonah is shoveling food into his mouth, obviously too hungry to reply.

"I can go, if you tell me how to get there. You're both needed here to gather the village people."

Jonah and Enid exchange glances, but nobody speaks.

"Or we can all go," I venture, waving a hand between the three of us.

"I'll think about it," Jonah says.

I dip my chin in acknowledgment and tuck back into my food.

"Christopher should be here before sundown," Enid says.

Jonah grunts, and I grip my fork hard. "Good. I'm looking forward to seeing him." It's the truth, despite the tension that runs between him and Jonah.

"Why do you dislike Christopher?"

Jonah stops chewing. Enid cuts her food before taking another bite, her gaze swinging between Jonah and me.

"Who said I don't like Christopher?"

"Every time you two are near each other, it's like someone has thrown you in the sparring ring."

Jonah swallows his food and stares at the center of the table before answering. "He doesn't like Imani, and he has made that very clear. It doesn't sit well with me."

I chew, mulling over the words. Jonah is like Imani's father; obviously, that would cause tension. Why did I not see this before?

"I would be dead if it weren't for Christopher," I say flatly.

"I know that, Harm. But he still rubs me the wrong way. Imani has done nothing wrong. And what's worse is that he's had run-ins with Fletcher. It's as if he likes that Guardian more than Imani. It gets me riled up."

"Evidently," Enid teases, patting his arm, and a crooked smile eventually cracks over Jonah's face.

"Why doesn't he like Imani?" I ask.

"You would have to ask him," Jonah says.

Enid stands to clear our plates. I let the conversation fizzle out. But part of me wonders what Christopher knows that we don't that makes him favor Fletcher over Imani. There must be a story behind this. Christopher is not an unkind man—not at all. Something doesn't make sense.

After another three hours of going door-to-door, we take a respite from traipsing around the village while the sun covers the sands with waves of heat in a full-on assault. Returning home, we slump into the chairs in the living room. Fanning her face with a book, Enid sits on her chair. Jonah closes his eyes, and I do the same.

The front door flings open, and the three of us jolt, half asleep in our chairs. Jonah bolts toward the ruckus garnering a concerned look from Enid.

Standing by the front door is a robed man, sand settled on his shoulders, face concealed by a wrap. Sand tracks inside with his boots, and he grunts, unshouldering a satchel, letting it hit the floor with a thud. Jonah stands motionless, waiting, arms crossed.

The man's large hand sweeps his hood back and tugs the wrap from his face. Planted inches from Jonah is Christopher, exhausted. Enid jumps up from her chair, motioning for him to step back outside to relieve himself of the sands covering him. She dusts him off, fussing over him, getting a raised eyebrow from Jonah. His traveling robe and wrap are shaken out before being thrown on the hook beside the door, and Jonah collects his satchel from the floor, following as Enid shows Christopher to his room.

She comes directly back to the front room and plops herself back in her chair, resuming the reading she was enjoying before sleep claimed her. Jonah takes up a spot in the chair next to Enid and pretends to read something as Christopher walks into the room and finds a seat next to me. He stretches out, his hands behind his head, complaining about his sore feet.

Jonah puts his book down and stands. "I'll chop the rest of the wood," he says, leaving without looking at any of us.

"What's got his goat?" Christopher says, leaning his head back.

"Never you mind. How's Maryanne?" Enid asks.

"Good. Busy. Her kindness to others is running her ragged these days. I wish she would slow down a little."

"It's good to hear she's doing well," I say, the words falling short of what I feel I owe both of them.

"She asks about you. She would be here in a heartbeat if it weren't for the people she tends to every day." He closes his eyes. After a brief reprieve, he opens them again. "What progress have you made with the village people?"

"Most of them are willing, when the time comes," I reply.

Enid nods in confirmation.

"Good, but it still won't be enough. I've been doing some scouting of my own. There are over five hundred and twenty

Guardians, if you count all the legions, and they're trained and fit. Most village men don't compare in size or strength," Christopher says.

"Yourself and Jonah don't fall into the weak-and-helpless category, I take it." Enid chuckles, and Christopher winks before releasing a hearty laugh. She smiles, shaking her head before returning to her book.

Watching them reminds me of Imani's sarcasm, the way she would dangle the fun and games between us with words that sounded like one thing but meant another. It made our days together interesting.

I get up from my chair and go to help Jonah. My memories of Imani make it hard to breathe, and I don't want to have to explain myself to Christopher.

The crack of the axe drifts through the back door, and I shove it open to find a hot and bothered Jonah chopping wood. The axe finds its mark, and the timber splinters in half. For an older man, he still has the skill and strength to easily get through each piece in one blow. He stops when he hears the door bang, axe swinging beside him, his corded arms covered in sweat. He wipes his brow with the other hand before tossing the axe to me.

I catch it with one hand just below the axe-head, and he gives me a mischievous grin, stepping back to make room for me to chop the last of the wood. It takes me mere minutes to finish off the remaining wood, and we drop to the ground and steady our breath. He grabs the axe from me and starts splitting a quarter piece for kindling. I throw each piece into a pile beside the split logs as he works.

"I miss her, you know," Jonah says.

I know he is talking about Imani.

"I know. I do too—so much," I utter, the words wobbling their way out.

"Losing Luca to the regime was..." He pauses, wiping sweat from his brow again, and sucks in a slow breath. "Imani had been with me for over five years. She was more like my daughter than a niece. I guess I was like a father to her. At least, I hope I was."

"You were, Jonah." I rest a hand on his arm. He wraps his arm around me in a brief hug. "She looked for you for weeks when you escaped the prison. She was terrified to tell you that Fletcher was her father. She carried so much hurt with that, with what he did. That's why she ran away from home in the first place. She disowned him. And when she finally returned to us after her trip to Amondo, she was with you," Jonah says. "I have no doubt that he treated you worse than he should have because she was with you, but it was never going to be pleasant regardless. In Fletcher's mind, you should have been executed, not running around with his estranged daughter."

I sit in silence for what feels like an age. "Is this supposed to get better—this hole in my chest? Because it just tears me up more every day."

Jonah breathes out before pushing up to his feet. He offers a hand, and I let him help me up. We stand there, assessing the wood pile for a time.

"It gets better, very slowly." Jonah looks at me now, and the silver that lines his eyes takes the last of my breath. "But nothing ever replaces what you've lost."

The ache starts up in my chest again as we wander inside to find Christopher and Enid. That's what I figured.

CHAPTER 14
IMANI

On our last stretch before we reach the village, we circle up briefly for a break. My hands automatically clench my sides to suppress the stabbing pains that still materialize, no matter how many miles I try to outrun them. Callian is leaning over, stretching his back, hands below his knees.

I hear the roar before I make out movement. Catori's head whips around, her eyes hunting through every space between the trees. Callian scans the perimeter.

An enormous black beast crashes through the tree line, claws out and muzzle dripping with froth. It stands even taller than Callian. I stagger backward, heart lurching and blood thundering.

"Run!" Catori yells. She whirls around and heads in the direction of the village, shooting an urgent look at her brother. Fear prickles through every inch of me, and I bolt after her. Callian thunders up behind me, and I push my legs faster. He comes up beside me, grabs my hand, and propels me forward. I look back to see the creature gaining on us.

"Just keep running!" he yells.

I force my legs to move faster. With every erratic breath, stars fade in and out of the sides of my vision. Callian's hand is firmly holding mine as we fly around a group of trees and up a slope. The steep ascent burns every fiber of my legs. The thunderous loping gait of the animal behind us is so close that it feels like any second, it will reach out and tear at my back, shredding it with its hideous claws. Panic steals my ability to breathe, and I choke on every parcel of air I pull in.

The village appears, encircled by a ring of large trees. Wind whips past my back. The creature is swiping at us. Nausea rises, and I swallow it back. Callian's hand drops from mine.

"Just keep running," he says before slowing his pace. I turn my head to see him rip both daggers from his chest sheath, heading away from me, running closer to the circle of trees. The creature follows him, an easier target as he slows down. I slide to a halt. It takes everything I have not to scream out to him. The animal makes another strike, only inches from his head.

My chest heaves.

Catori yells from the village perimeter for me to hurry up.

I can't move.

Callian defends with his daggers, the animal almost on top of him.

A piercing woosh sails toward it and Callian.The creature jolts and staggers backward. An arrow. Then another. Then another. The creature slumps to the ground, multiple arrows sticking out of its motionless body. Callian is doubled over panting, but he manages to point to the trees above him, where I see archers, their bows discharged. There is one in every tree as far as I can see; the circle of trees goes all the way around the village. That's why Callian drew the creature away from me.

Composure regained, Callian walks back to Catori and me, grinning like a fool. "Had that bear just where I wanted it." He slaps me on the back.

I look at him incredulously. He has obviously done this before. "That was a bear?" I stammer, in awe of its size.

Callian nods.

Catori's face is stern, her arms crossed over her chest. "You cut it too close, brother. Every time, you get more reckless, warrior or not. You're of no use to us dead."

He laughs, sheathing his daggers. Catori rolls her eyes before walking on, leading us through a village not much bigger than ours on the desert side. The homes are made of timber, but where our roofs are mostly flat and thatched, theirs are woven and slanted. The homes are laid out in a circular pattern, as are ours in the dunes, protecting them from the full frontal of Mother Nature's vengeance. What exactly that looks like here, I can't imagine.

The forest people go about their daily chores on the damp earth. I attract a few looks from people as we pass by, but they offer smiles and small waves. Callian brings up the tail of our traveling trio, chatting to people as we wander past. His hearty laugh brings smiles to their faces. After passing many homes, we come to a large, round home in the center of the village. Smoke billows out from two chimneys, clouding the air. Every one of the village people wears similar colors to Catori and Callian, but their clothing is clearly made for ease of working, not hunting or fighting, like the siblings' more fitted clothing.

We stop at the entrance of the large home. Catori signals for me to wait. Callian stands beside me. He seems bigger now after taking on the bear. Then a voice from inside calls us both in. Callian takes my satchel before I walk in, hanging it on a rack with other miscellaneous items.

The home is one large room, sectioned off by curtains that indicate a sleeping area, an eating area, and a communal area, judging by the furniture that sits casually around the brightly lit space. A woman is preparing a meal in the kitchen area. Two children play on a woven mat in front of the fire below the chimney. An old lady sits on cushions on the floor in the center of what looks like their living room. Catori kneels in front of her, speaking softly. We are then summoned over, and Callian drops to his knees, the same as Catori. I follow his lead, landing on a brightly colored, tattered cushion.

The lines of the woman's weathered face strike me, like ripples in stone. Her blue eyes, much like mine, are lit with happiness and curiosity. Her long grey hair is down, skirting her shoulders, a little wild, with colorful thread plaited through a small portion on each side. A smile comes over her face, and she reaches for my hand, grabbing it with both of hers. Her smile widens to show her teeth, and her hands are warm, much like her expression. "This is Imani, Grandmother," Catori says.

"Hello, Imani. My name is Hanola. You have come from the sands on the other side of the wall," she states.

"Yes."

"That's a long and arduous journey for one your age, and all by yourself?"

"Yes. I'm looking for someone."

"Ah, yes. The only time someone ventures over that wall is to find something they lost—or to take something that doesn't belong to them. My heart tells me you're in the former category." She smiles, and the weathered lines illuminate her face. She squeezes my hand, and I return the smile. "You should rest tonight. We can talk about what you're looking for in the morning, child."

With that, Catori stands and offers me her hand. Exhausted from running, I take it. Callian follows us out, bidding us goodbye as he wanders off into the village center. Following behind, I walk through the village until we reach a smaller home: Catori's. It is well lit, like Hanola's, but much simpler. She points to a sleeping mat at the back wall, and I walk over to it, removing my satchel and robe. She removes her weapons, the metal thudding on the table near her bed.

"You can borrow some of my clothes. The ones you're wearing will give you a rash in about three hours here."

"Thank you."

She walks over, carrying a pile of clothing and pointing toward a curtained area. In moments, I have stripped off, assessing the condition of my skin after what feels like months of not seeing it. Some of the muscle I lost in Mason's cage has returned with all the traveling and better food. I release my hair from the white ties and let it fall, taking note of its length. It's gotten a little longer. I pull on the pants and tie the strips around my waist. The fitted tunic all but covers my torso, and I feel even more naked than I did with the rag of a tunic Mason had me in. But it is so easy to move in, so soft and comfortable. The foreign humidity caresses my skin. I pull on my boots and leave my hair down this time; it has been so long since it was loose. I step out of the changing area and roll my old clothes into a bundle, pushing them into my satchel, and I double-check that my fighting knives are still there. Maybe Catori will lend me a chest strap to sheathe them in if I am to stay here for a short while.

Catori has started a small fire in her hearth and is poking at the logs with an iron as I come into the living space. She drops back onto a large woven cushion and throws me one. I grab it, placing opposite hers, and sit. She throws a piece of fruit to me and rips into hers, gazing into the fire. With the first bite, the juices explode in my mouth. It's so sweet! I put a hand over my mouth to stop myself from dribbling, and Catori snorts at my ridiculous face. I try not to laugh and spill the juices on her floor. She throws me another piece, and we eat the remaining fruit.

The sun is almost down, and the cold air of the forest village chills me to the bone. I hurry to my satchel and grab my robe, putting it on. Catori stands and moves to the door. "Come on, dinner time," she says.

"But we just ate."

"Hardly," she scoffs.

I trail behind her, wrapping my robe tightly over my body, leaving my hair and hood down. We walk back to the center of the village. Long tables are laden with food, women and men busying themselves with the meal. Children run around squealing. We sit down on one of the long bench seats. Catori hands me a plate, piling food onto it. A woman passes by, filling my wooden cup with drink. Catori plonks back into her seat after shoveling food onto her own plate, and we eat. Nobody stares or leers at me; they only give smiles and polite hellos. Every bench is full. The entire village must be here.

"Well, you look a little better than you did a couple of hours ago." Callian greets me with a wide smile. I try to respond with a mouthful of food, eyes wide, and he bellows out a laugh. It's as if happiness is the only emotion these people know. He takes a seat across from me and looks at me again. This time, his eyes stall on my hair. A flicker of something besides amusement flashes through his gaze, and I let mine fall to my plate before shoving more food in my mouth. He plucks food from the offerings and starts devouring his own meal. We eat in silence.

"Do you always eat as an entire village?" I ask on the way back to Catori's home.

"Yep, the entire village eats as one, every meal. Grandmother says it's how you stay as united as a people. I believe she's right."

"You're all so..." I hesitate; I don't want to offend her, but I can't stop my words. "You're all so *happy*."

She grins. "You say that like it's a bad thing."

"No, it's not a bad thing at all. It's just... I've never known anything like this. On our side of the wall, it's not like this. Nothing like this."

She stops and raises an eyebrow. "You mean nobody smiles on the other side of the wall?"

"That's not what I mean. They smile, of course, but happiness is not so abundant there. There's so much struggle, it makes life hard. I don't know if I'm explaining it right."

"Happiness is a choice, Imani, not a consequence of place, time, or action."

She feels so much older than me right now. "How old are you?"

"Nineteen," she says, "and Callian is a year younger than me, if you were wondering." She prods me playfully.

I swallow down the embarrassment, but sorrow laces my next words. "My heart already belongs to someone else—at least, I hope it still does. I'm looking for him. I was told he's dead, but I don't believe that—not for a second."

She stops in her tracks, studying my face as if witnessing pain for the first time. "I hope you find him, Imani." She offers a tiny smile of pity and leads me through her door.

We settle down for the night. I brush my hair with Catori's brush, for the first time in months, and it takes an age to get it detangled. I return the brush to her and she is wrapping her hair for sleep. She looks less like a huntress, and more like an older sister now.

"Thank you for everything you've done for me in such a short time." The words choke their way out.

"No problem, desert girl," she quips and ties off her wrap.

"Night."

"Night, Imani."

I lower myself onto my sleeping mat and stretch out. My legs are sore from all the running, and I tense each muscle and release it before raising my arms above my head and closing my eyes.

"What's his name?" Catori's voice carries through the dimly lit space.

"Harm. Harmen Travesci." A weight settles over my heart, and I force the breath from my lungs.

"See you in the morning," she says. Her bed shifts as she rolls over. The night animals and birds are the only sounds in between the constant crackles of the fire.

Sunrise wakes me before Catori. For a moment, I startle at the woven ceiling above me. The sounds of something hitting the roof over and over makes me sit up. The constant pitter-patter increases in speed, getting louder by the second. An earthy, watery smell hangs in the room. I jump up and grab my robe, along with a knife from my satchel, and stalk to the front door. Expecting to see chaos on the other side, I pull the door open.

A hazy wall of mist wafts by beyond the door. Looking down, I see tiny rivulets gush past.

"It's rain, desert dweller." Catori chuckles where she lies, her eyes closed, just like the time her brother crept up on us in the forest.

Oh. Rain.

It's really rain!

I hold one arm out just beyond the door. My fingers tremble, waiting for some horrible sensation, waiting for the pinprick of each tiny drop. Instead, wetness lands with hundreds of tiny splatters on my hand. It feels wonderful. I step forward and plunge my arm into it.

Howls of laughter come from Catori behind me. A moment later, she is standing behind me, arranging her weapons sheath across her chest. She has put her hair up. She slips her boots on while watching me playing with the rain. I wave my arms around, and the cool water runs down and into my armpit, tickling its way down my side. With a gasp, I look back at her, the wonder in my eyes reflected in hers.

"We have to eat breakfast with Hanola this morning," she tells me. "She wants to hear your story."

"We walk through this?" I ask, pointing at the rain.

She snorts. "Yes, we walk through it. I suggest leaving your robe here, or it will get saturated and take days to dry out. There's a fire you can warm yourself by at the main house." She steps out into the rain. It immediately drenches her hair, running off her face, coursing over her clothes. She doesn't seem to notice. I throw my robe onto my sleeping mat, then hold my breath before stepping out into the rain. It hits me everywhere at once. I feel like I should be gasping, but I can breathe easily. Catori gives me an encouraging look and starts toward the main house.

I follow, palms upturned in front of me, feeling every drop.

CHAPTER 15
HARM

Before the sun has a chance to appear over the horizon, Jonah and Enid have left to visit the remaining villages in our county to rally men for the rebellion. Christopher and I eat in silence over a meager breakfast before we clean up and sit on the floor of the living room to discuss Guardian numbers, our advantages, and the strategies we need to use. Before the day is out, we have maps, lists, and a timeline of what we can pull off to overcome the forces on this side of the wall. But it's not nearly enough.

"By my calculation, we need at least another two hundred men on our side just to match what the Guardians have," Christopher says.

My hope falls when I see his concerned expression beneath the glasses that sit low on the bridge of his nose. "Hopefully, Enid and Jonah can wrangle some on their trip around the county?"

"Maybe," he utters.

"What about the forest dwellers?"

"That's just a fairy tale. They don't exist, Harm."

"They do. Enid has been over the wall. She has lived with them. It was a long time ago, but they do exist."

He removes his glasses and studies my face. "Really?"

"Yes. Here." I shuffle over to the shelf, pull her old journal out, and hand it to him. "This is her field journal. She was hunting for medicinal plants and such when she discovered the forest people. She lived with them for nearly two months."

His eyes flick from the book back up to me, then back to the journal. He flips through the pages. Annoyance drifts through his eyes as his brows lower, most likely because she hasn't shared this information with him.

"She only told me the day before last," I assure him. "I think she only wanted to mention them if we really needed them. They were her friends." I hope that last part is accurate.

Christopher grunts. "I'll never understand women, but hey, at least now we may just have the element of surprise." A small smile pulls up one side of his face. Clearly, my uncle thinks the way I do, like my father did.

We pack away our day of planning, rolled up, tied with twine, and placed in a small wooden box. It will be safer in the box than scattered around the house. We wander to the kitchen to find food before Christopher mentions going out for supplies.

Once he leaves, I amble back down the hallway to my room and lie on my bed. Imani meets me there—her laugh and smile, her pain-filled eyes at the gallows, and Jonah's words, "You are the only one who is a match for that girl." I turn over on my side, thinking of the Blending ceremony. I imagine what ours would have been like, Imani's and mine.

I sit up. I am a dead man, a traitor. There is a part of me that believes she is still alive. But even if she were, me being Blended with Imani would only bring her harm. I slam my eyes shut. It's too late now, anyway. A crushing weight rips the breath from my chest, and I sit on the bunk, pulling at the thin blanket, screaming her name. The pain is so fierce, I pray my heart will stop beating.

It is hours before Christopher returns. He has been dealing with the local merchants, securing weapons and maps. At least, that's what he says he was doing.

I stand in the sand outside the back door, just staring. He came to talk to me, but left when I didn't respond. I have no words left. No part of me cares any longer. I have tried every day of my life to be what people need. And now I stand in the sands that trap us like animals, and I have lost everyone I ever loved. I have no tears left. My heart is an endless pit of nothing.

The door slams behind me, and I turn to see a tray of food set down outside the door, followed by the muffled sounds of Christopher milling about inside. I walk over and pick up the tray. Returning to the sands, I sit and eat. It will be two more weeks before Enid and Jonah return. They never seem to leave me by myself; one of them is always with me. Company is better than the misery of being alone with my own thoughts. They are protecting me, or protecting their chance to change their world. I swallow the last of the food and stand to head inside.

"Need to talk about it?" Christopher's voice startles me from behind, his arms hanging by his sides and worry creasing his face.

"I don't know how." I'm being honest. Nothing I do, nor talking to people about it, seems to help this pain in my chest. If anything, it just makes it worse.

"Come inside before the sun goes down," he says and goes back inside.

I stand holding the tray in one hand. Just as the last rays of the sun recede behind the dunes, I turn and head inside. Everything within me is numb. I pad down the hallway and see the massive array of weapons Christopher has lined up on the floor of the living room. He watches me as I look over the collection. Knives, daggers, bows and arrows, and small, square brown packages are stacked in a neat pile.

"What are those square ones?" I ask.

"Explosives. Very good for taking out multiple targets, or as a diversion," he explains.

"I've never seen them before."

He smiles and makes a wide, dramatic gesture with his arms, mimicking the sound of an explosion.

The rough timber digs into my arms as I bundle up piece upon piece of wood to take inside. I fumble for the back door latch with a free finger and push it open with my foot. The door slams behind me, and sand falls from my boots with every step toward the kitchen.

Christopher is poring over maps and numbers again. The light has faded, and I gather three of Enid's bigger candles. They land with a clunk on the table, and I light them so he can keep working. A grunt of acknowledgment escapes his preoccupied expression.

With the split logs and leftover kindling from yesterday, I coax the last of the embers in the stove back to life, fanning it with one of Christopher's books. Small flickers spring to life before being swallowed by bigger flames. I shut the iron door, sliding the vent fully open to let the fire get going. A pot of stew sits on the warm stovetop. Enid's canister of wooden spoons sits to the right. Plucking one from its home, I stir the stew back and forth, making ripples and waves. The smell wafts from the pot and fills the room. Christopher groans in anticipation.

I hunt for the bowls, finding a small collection behind a curtain under the sink. I fill two with stew and remove the pot from the heat, pushing it to the back of the stove for later. With two spoons I grab en route, I place the bowls on the table. Christopher puts down his papers and thanks me for the food. We eat in silence. Between mouthfuls, he looks at me, contemplative. I eat my stew without a word. The food reaches my mouth, passes my lips, but I don't taste the flavors anymore, and I don't feel it fill my stomach.

"Harm?"

I raise my eyes to meet his. The pain that has been eating me from the inside for months is now reflected in his eyes. I don't answer him.

"You should talk about it, before it eats you alive, son," he says softly.

I try to ignore his words, but the pain spurs back to life in my gut. I concentrate on keeping my breathing even. He notices.

"I can't help you unless you tell me what's killing you."

"I..." My voice chokes on the thickness in my throat. "I... can't." It's true, especially not with him, given the way he feels about Imani.

"Well, if not with me, then talk to Jonah," he says.

A tear slides down my cheek, and I wipe it away before it drips on the table for him to witness. I suck in a breath and figure it will come out sooner or later. Better that he hears it from me.

"Imani," I whisper—and the sound of her name cuts me into pieces all over again.

"Imani," he echoes, his eyes wider than before.

"Yes," is all I can say, my eyes fixed on my stew, hand gripping the spoon, like if I let go, I will plummet into the depths of devastation again.

"Oh, I see." No tirade about her or how I shouldn't care about her—nothing.

I look up. His eyes are calm, but sadness brings his brows down, and he has stopped eating.

"I didn't realize you two were..."

I force a sad smile, but it fades instantly. "You didn't like her. Jonah told me. We don't have to talk about it."

"'Didn't'?" he repeats, stilling completely. He does not know what happened after the gallows either. "I mean, it's a long story, but what do you mean, 'didn't'?" He stares at me, brows lowered.

"Tell me, please. I want to know what happened to make you hate her," I whisper.

He frowns, but slowly sets his spoon on the table. "I don't hate her. But some of the choices she made had consequences that affected us all." His words are soft.

I hesitate to respond. "Tell me."

He shifts in his seat. "Fletcher and I were in a sandstorm once. He had arrested me, but when he refused to take shelter, he became trapped in the sand. I dug him out, and we walked most of the way back to Amondo together," he starts.

I watch and wait for the rest of the story.

"He was a different man back then. A lot of the Guardians were. This was around thirteen years ago. Imani would have been about four or five then. All he spoke about on the return trip was his daughter. A little about his wife, but mostly about his daughter. He had become a Guardian to make sure her world was a better place. Funny as it seems, it was that way once. Then when Imani was twelve or so, she ran away from home. Which isn't that big of a deal, but she ran from him—from her father.

"It broke his heart, Harm," he continues. "He has never been the same. His wife vanished into some other place in her mind and was never the same either—at least, that's what I heard through the grapevine. Although, Petria appeared to be in control of her faculties at the gallows. Never believe everything you hear." He pauses, searching my face. "Fletcher thought Imani was dead for the first six months. I've never seen a man transform for the worse the way I witnessed with Fletcher. She refused to ever claim him as her father again, and that was it. Now, he's the cruel, rigid man you know him as, and they've been at war with each other ever since."

"That sounds like Imani. But no, that's not a version of Fletcher I know. I only know the man he is now," I say.

"A lot of people would have been spared if she had stayed with her family and accepted them for who they are."

"You cannot seriously be blaming Imani for the actions of her father."

"Think what you like, but when people hurt us, others pay the price."

Heat flies up my neck, flooding my face in seconds. I push up from my chair, almost knocking over my bowl. I drop the spoon on the table and storm down the hall. The back door relents quickly under the force of my hand, banging shut behind me. I stalk in circles in the sand. The muscles in my arms quiver as I ball my hands into fists and uncurl them over and over.

Arthur's actions. Fletcher's actions. Imani's actions. Even my own catalogue in my mind, with images of the consequences attached—everything is connected. Only a fool would think otherwise. Wisps of cool air rolling off the dunes nearest the village float through the small yard, but I'm sweating.

The back door slams again, and the thud of boots on sand make their way over to where I stand with my back to the house. Christopher draws up beside me, hands in his pockets.

"Nobody is perfect, Harm. I'm sorry for what you lost, before you even had a chance to make a life together. I can't imagine what that feels like."

My eyes stay fixed on the run-down fence, and I swallow hard. I don't know what to say to the man who saved my life, probably many times now. We stand watching the stars pop from the growing darkness, handfuls at a time. When the heat in my body dies away, I look at Christopher. His face is covered in lines of worry. Being away from his life and Maryanne no doubt has taken a large toll on him.

"You really think we have a chance to win this fight?" I ask.

"We have to. Once we start, there's no going back." He hangs his arm over my shoulders and tugs me toward the house. I follow, glad for the company and the understanding, regardless.

I wander back down the hall to my room and drop onto the bunk. Christopher goes back to the kitchen. Quiet curses come from the half-lit room, and the scratch of a fresh match breathes new light into the kitchen, pouring down the hallway and dancing past my room. I close my eyes to rest a bit before I wash up. I take in deep breaths, trying to relax my body.

A commotion at the front door startles me to my feet in seconds. I fly out of the room and lope down the hallway. Two robed figures stand bent over inside the doorway, sand falling to the floor from their dusty robes. Christopher stands waiting, arms crossed over his chest. The moments slip past slowly, until the smaller of the two stands and removes the robe and sand veil. Enid's weary and twisted face turns directly to Christopher.

"It's Maryanne. She is very sick," she rasps, trying to steady her ragged breaths. "We returned as fast as we could. You need to go to her." Enid places a hand on Christopher's shoulder. "Now."

Jonah stands holding his side. They have been running. Both of them, decades older than me, have been running hard through the desert, most likely through the day and night.

"It was too dangerous and too slow to send word by letter. We couldn't risk them finding Harm, so we ran," Jonah pants. "For two days, we ran. Go."

He gestures to the door, and Christopher is already robing up, grabbing water, and shoving bread into a rucksack. His tortured face meets mine, and I try to say something that would help, but I don't have the words. Instead, I lunge at him and wrap my arms around his big frame, hoping he understands. He hugs me back. Breaking from my grip he slips into the night. Jonah shuts the door behind him.

CHAPTER 16
HARM

I pour water for Enid and Jonah as they sink into the kitchen chairs. The worry in their faces sends nervous bolts through me, and I hope Christopher makes it home in time. I return the stew to the stove and heat up food for them. Neither of them speaks. I shove another log into the cooker and latch the iron door shut. With two bowls of stew in hand, I return to the table, setting them down and taking my spot at the table. Jonah plunges his spoon into the stew, but does not lift it again. Enid sips from her spoon slowly.

"What happened?" I ask.

"It's bad, Harm. Many of the village wells have been poisoned. They're trying to flush people out." He looks up from his spoon, and worry reaches every part of his face.

"Why?" I ask, half knowing the answer already, but not willing to say it.

"To flush you out," Enid utters.

"They would kill hundreds of villagers just to get to me?"

"Seems that way," Jonah says gravely.

"Dammit, those bloody mongrels!" I slam a hand down on the

table and stand, fire racing through my core. A consequence of my escape.

I need some air.

Jonah and Enid are eating as I walk away. I drop into the chair in the living room and plant my head in my hands. I should have just died when I was supposed to. Then Imani would be safe, and the villages would be safe. Charlie would be alive. My *family* would be alive. I should have just died on that hanging pole and saved everyone a lot of heartbreak.

I scream into my hands, no longer caring who hears me. I stand and move to the bookshelf, both hands on the shelf in front of my face, and I grip it with all the strength I have. I shake the shelf so hard that the whole bookcase shudders, books falling from their places, hitting the floor. Whipping around, I almost plow into Enid, who is standing behind me.

"Who is doing it?" I demand.

She stands tall, arms crossed, concern narrowing her eyes. "Fletcher." Her face strains under a new wave of grief.

"Of course he is." I stride back into the kitchen, where Jonah is washing the bowls.

"Okay. So, I turn myself in, and you find some other way to change things. Find someone else they don't know about, or blow it up altogether." I gesture to the piles of weapons and stock Christopher has been gathering.

"I know things are getting bad, but we expected they would once they found out," Jonah says, his tone meeting mine. "If you quit now, nothing changes. They win. We will get through this. The people will recover."

"No! Not one more person dies over this! No more village people suffer because of this," I grind out.

"There are always casualties in war, Harm. This is no different. This is the price we pay to change our world for the better."

"Then find yourself some other mug with the ability to join your crusade. I'm done!" I yell and stalk down the hallway, out the back door, and into the sands.

This house feels smaller than ever right now. I want to scream, to hit things, to strangle the last filthy breath out of Fletcher and every last Guardian. My knees hit the sand, and I release a scream so loud that I'm sure the dead can hear me. Each poisoned, dead villager... because of me.

Families.

Fathers.

Mothers.

Daughters.

Sons.

Sisters.

Brothers.

Tears flood down my cheeks as my fists hit the sand, and I scream with every breath, my head hanging between my arms. Neither Enid nor Jonah comes out to me this time. I crash into the sand and lie motionless until the sobbing stops.

The faces of the people of Amondo haunt me during the fitful wee hours of the morning. I rise from my bed, so exhausted from the last two days that I have no idea how I got back to my bunk. I grab a mug of water and stand at the window of the kitchen as the first of the sun's rays dance over the dunes. The first swallow feels like gravel in my throat.

My next steps are clear. As soon as Jonah wakes, I will tell him my plan, then I leave. My life means a lot less now that others are paying such a huge price. He will not stop me.

"Harm." The gentle voice of my grandmother breaks the morning silence. I turn to face her. She walks up to me and holds my face with her bony, soft hands. Tears well in her eyes, and her chin trembles before she sucks in a breath. "This is hard, but you're strong—stronger than you know, and much more valued than I suspect you realize." She rubs her thumbs over my cheeks. "I'm saying this as the leader of the rebellion for over three decades, not as your grandmother." She studies my eyes, as if she can see past them and into my heart.

"You're their leader?" I choke out.

"You bet, my boy." Her words full of cheek, but her eyes are lined with fire.

"What about Jonah and Christopher?" I ask.

"They're important too. But they answer to me. There is a reason I am hard to find." She pats my face before letting her hands fall to her sides.

"You're the leader because you were married to my grandfather, who had the ability too?"

"No. Because I was the only one who dared to defy the regime."

"There are no other people with the ability left, are there?"

"No. You are the last one."

Blood thunders through my veins. My next move feels selfish and risky now. Nevertheless, I'm doing it.

"I'm going back to the villages, to help those who are left and see the damage for myself."

Her eyes meet mine. "Spoken like a true leader," she whispers, then hands me a rucksack from the pile of sandy items they carried upon their return.

"My rucksack! Where did you find it?"

She throws her hands up and gives me a humorous smile. I have not seen this bag or its contents since the gallows. I rip it open and toss it upside down on the table. The clatter of items makes my heart soar. I run a hand across the pile, tossing the rucksack onto the floor. My mother's journal, the compass my father gave me, a few bits of decaying food—I toss them out the window.

Then my fingers find smooth, cold metal, fine and elegant, and I lift it up.

Imani's pendant hangs from the tips of my fingers. Enid's eyes widen, recognizing the piece of jewelry, her daughter's. The brilliant blue stone in the center disperses the morning sun's piercing rays gracefully around the room, touching the wooden boards of the walls where it lands. My heart clenches up, and I hold in my breath and swallow the pain.

Enid takes the pendant from my grasp, but my hand stays frozen in the air. She looks at the pendant and back to me. From the sadness in her expression, she has figured out who the pendant was for. Imani. Her hand rubs my back. This time, I refuse to let the tide of agony take me under, and I force a smile in return. More tears from Enid. My pain is her pain. So much of my mother lives in her.

"So, what is your plan for helping the village people?" she asks, clearing her throat.

"Not sure. There will be much to be done, I suspect. We'll need to source them clean water first, and take up the slack for those who perished or are too sick from the poisoning to work. Every little bit helps."

"Sounds like you've done something like this before." She bumps into my shoulder playfully. I guess Christopher filled her in about that too, me hiding the boys from the Guardians and getting the entire village punished.

"Once, our village was prohibited from trading. It was a hard time for our people, and I did whatever I could. But it still wasn't enough for some families. And worst of all, it was my fault—as it is now."

She watches the sadness in my expression. "Not everything is your fault, Harm. Sometimes bad things happen to good people. Life isn't always fair. We make the best of what we're dealt. And sometimes, we fight." She squeezes my arm as I return the items to my rucksack—even the knife Imani insisted I carry.

"We will leave tonight," Enid says.

"Let me explain it to Jonah."

Moments after we arrive in the closest village to the north, the screaming starts. Robes on and hoods drawn down, we watch from the shadows as the Guardians gather the people. The pale and drawn faces of each person standing in the dawn light reminds me of the morning of my family's execution. And standing before the crowd that is slowly forming, ushering in Guardians coming out of homes all over the village, is Fletcher.

Mason is not amongst the officers.

I scan the villagers who huddle together, waiting for the vicious words of the commander to rain down. Whispers and sobs are met with canes from the surrounding Guardians. The look of disdain on their faces only brings more sorrow to the filthy, malnourished faces of the people they herd together. Finally, the gruff shouts of Fletcher carry on the cool morning winds, and a line of boys, age fourteen, forms in front of the crowd.

Nine boys stand before Fletcher, some shaking, some immobile but sobbing. To be selected is to be transformed from a wholesome village child into a soulless monster, executing families for the very circumstances the Guardians put them in. Poverty. Inability to pay taxes. This time, one of Fletcher's subordinates walks the line of boys, inspecting each one. I don't recognize him. He makes a second pass before tapping a boy with curly brown hair on the shoulder. The boy flinches, and the Guardian stands taller, towering over him, in his space.

"Turn," he orders, violence lacing his words.

Instantly, memories of Arlo, my best friend, lying in the red sand fly into my mind. My heart thunders in my chest, and I can't look away. The boy turns, his trembling hands visible even from our secluded spot in between the buildings. A woman cries out, and the whip of the cane cuts through the air. Gasps, and then silence.

"Stand with the Guardians, boy," the officer orders.

The boy obeys, and the rest of the line is dismissed. Next, Fletcher steps forward, and the crowd waits, still huddling with their families, terrified of what he will say next.

"For failure to pay taxes for the last two quarters, the Reed family is hereby sentenced to execution by drowning."

The boy standing with the Guardians goes stark white and sinks to his knees in the sands.

"That must be his family," Jonah whispers.

Enid lets out a curse word and a low breath. "That poor boy."

"They're going to make him watch his own family's execution." My voice is nothing more than a rasp, and Jonah shoots me a warning look before Enid grabs my arm.

Wailing infiltrates every space between the buildings, echoing around the village center. I stand motionless as I watch the Guardian who selected the boy throw his siblings into the well, one after the other, two sisters and a younger brother. His parents, their gazes are almost vacant, are dragged by their arms through the sand. His father has passed out and is tossed over the stone wall like a sack of grain by two Guardians. The boy's mother looks back at her son, now held down by the remaining Guardians. He screams something to her before she too is sent into the well. He remains staring at the well, his breath so ragged that I doubt he is getting any air at all.

"I've seen enough," Enid says.

I abruptly realize that she has just witnessed the fate of her own daughter, and my stomach twists into knots when my eyes reach hers. Tears stream down her face. Jonah wipes them away with his hands and turns us both away from the village center. We make our way to the well on the outskirts of their village, determined to find the cause of the poisoning.

"I may be able to identify the toxin and provide the village people with an antidote before too many fall sick," Enid murmurs through a shaky breath.

The rotten smell hits us before we even reach the stone wall of the well, so overpowering that it burns my eyes. How can the people of this village drink this without perishing? Enid lowers a small tin mug with a rope she prepared before we left and dips in into the waters of the well. Jonah and I stand with our backs to her, hoods down, facing the village. The smooth pull of the rope over stone signals that she has retrieved her sample, and we head back the way we came, hoping to reach the rocky outcrop to the west before the Guardians have a chance to fly past in their dune buggy.

It isn't long before Enid ushers Jonah and me into the craggy aisles of the rocky outcrop. We sit in their shade and remove our hoods, drinking from our canteens.

"I don't think we can risk going around to every village, Harm. That was too close for comfort. The Guardians are everywhere now," Jonah says.

I don't reply. The dull drumming of the dune buggy engine reverberates closer, and we remain silent, listening, hoping it doesn't slow down. It doesn't. Throwing my hood back up, I kneel behind one of the lower rocks and watch them as they speed past, leaving a wake of sand behind them. The boy who was selected sits on the back of the buggy, alone, facing the village he just left. He sways from side to side, eyes glazed over, face wet. The Guardians are talking loudly over the engine, but I can't make out their words. Then they hit a rough patch of sand and laugh loudly as they hold onto the bars of the buggy, but the boy topples over the back. He lands with almost no sound, rolling to a stop, covered in sand. He lays unmoving on the hot ground.

The buggy plows on through the sands, the Guardians unaware that they have just lost their cargo. I wait for one of them to realize, but not one of them looks back. Once they are a speck on the horizon, I fly from my concealed spot behind the rock, through the thick sands, and drop down beside the boy. He is breathing, but he's out cold. Seconds later, the footsteps of Jonah arrive behind me. He helps me lift the boy up, and we return to our secluded position behind the rocks, carrying him between us.

Enid's hands work over him fast, looking for injury. He seems fine. She rolls him onto his side and slides her rucksack under his head. The sun is ascending fast in the sky, and Jonah looks more and more set to take off as the minutes pass. The boy stirs, and Enid shakes him awake. Startled eyes meet ours before he starts to howl. Enid tucks him in close and comforts him. He responds to her kindness, wails petering out into whimpers.

She pulls back and wipes the tears from his face. Straightening his ruffled hair and fixing his twisted shirt, she looks at him before speaking.

"My name is Enid. Can you tell me your name?"

"Marshall."

He sobs uncontrollably again.

CHAPTER 17

IMANI

Hanola sits patiently while I try to find the words to tell my story. The amount of sorrow that it entails makes me hesitant to tarnish her happy existence with it. She notes my hesitation and studies the sadness in my eyes. Catori sits on the woven mat closest to the fire, the rain drumming down outside.

"All you must do, Imani, is tell your truth as you know it. Don't worry about our sensitivities. I have lived a long life and seen many things. I will listen to every part of your story and help you the best I can."

"Okay, I'll start with the part of my life that's relevant to the person I'm looking for, then." I close my eyes, hoping that the less I see of my audience, the easier it will be to tell my story. No one makes a sound as they wait patiently.

"I am the daughter of the commander of the Guardian Regime that enforces the laws on the other side of the wall, in the desert. His name is Fletcher. I ran away from home to sever the connection between me and him. Every family he hurt was one I couldn't save. So, I joined the gypsies that travel the sands, with my uncle, Jonah. I wandered the desert, interfering with the regime's orders, trying to save anyone I could. As I got older, I heard more and more stories of the things Fletcher was doing, the innocent people he executed in the name of the law and taxes. Months ago, I followed him to the village of Amondo, where I saw him execute a family. But this time, one of them survived. I saw this as my chance to try and fix at least a small part of what he had broken. Harm was so helpless out in the desert; I couldn't leave him to go off by himself. So, I traveled south to find the last of his mother's family. I was just trying to keep him out of the reach of the Guardians." I let out a shaky breath. "I was only meant to help him get as far away from my father as possible, and to find his family. I wasn't... I didn't mean to..." My words splutter out, and I sit with my eyes closed, focusing on my breathing for a few heartbeats.

"Go on, child." Hanola's hand falls on mine. I open my eyes, and her gaze is fixed on my face.

"During my time with the gypsies, I heard the stories of the dial that alters the weather—the one that keeps our side of the wall in desolate conditions. I heard that it can only be manipulated by people who have a special ability." I pause and look up to see if any recognition shows on Hanola's face. She exchanges a glance with Catori.

"After traveling around to find his long-lost family, Harm—Harmen, I mean; his name is Harmen... He found out he was one of the people who has the ability. Jonah, my uncle I lived with for over five years, had known this, or at least figured it out along the way. Long story, but in the end, I was taken as bait to bring Harm in, and he turned himself in to save me in a heartbeat." My breathing is beyond my control now, and I can't stop the tears that cascade down my face.

Catori gets up without a word and leaves. Hanola's gaze follows her for a moment before returning to me. "Our hearts choose who we love for great reason. I have no doubt that your heart chose this boy because he was what your soul needed. Please go on, Imani. What happened next?"

"I was held captive by one of the officers under the command of my father. He told me that Harm was executed. I don't believe him. I escaped and fled to the next village, then the next. I was trying to lay low, but a merchant told me of a couple who had gone to collect precious cargo somewhere near the tower prison. I had a feeling that it might be him, so I fled to the wall to try and access the tower prison. And that's when Catori found me."

"She told me that you were wanting to get to the tower. But I haven't heard or seen any travelers on our side of the wall."

"The prison in the tower was where he was held, according to the merchant," I say.

"You were going to the prison in the tower?"

"You know of it?"

"Yes, everyone on this side of the wall is well acquainted with the tower and its occupants."

I lean toward her, intent on what comes next.

"You would go to the tower for Harmen?" she asks.

"A million times over," I reply softly.

"You are very brave, Imani. Your bond with him must be strong."

Words are beyond me now, so I nod.

"We will help you in any way we can, but please know that what you propose to do, assuming he's still there, is dangerous."

"Have you heard of the stories of the dial and the weather changing?"

"Yes, we know of it. That's what has kept us permanently

damp through the decades. But the rain on our side also carries with it diseases that are sometimes fatal. I once met a woman from the other side of the wall. She was a healer, and she taught our people many remedies for ailments and some of the more common diseases. I believe both sides of the wall would benefit from the dial being changed back to the way it was before my generation's time. But with only your young man left to do it, I hope it's not too late."

"Me too," I utter.

I look up as Catori returns and plops back down on her mat, wiping away the rain that has wet her face and hair again. Her expression is unreadable to me, but Hanola passes a look to her that I recognize as a thank you.

"You should get some rest, recover from your hard journey yesterday. I need to speak with my granddaughter now," Hanola says.

I push up and make my way back out into the rain. The sensation takes me by surprise again, but I settle into its rhythmic deluge and wander back to Catori's home, collapsing onto my mat. It's not long before a careful knock rattles the front door. I roll over and sit up. Reliving my story with Hanola drained every ounce of energy from me. I fix my clothes and walk to the front door, feeling a little strange answering a door that is not mine. I pull it open to see the grinning face of Callian, his wet, shaggy blond hair matted to his square face. I can't help but smile back. His happiness is infectious, and I laugh at the ridiculousness of his grin.

"Catori isn't here," I say.

"I know. She's off running some errand Hanola just sent her on. She asked me to look after you today."

"Oh, I won't get in your way?"

"Nope, you're coming to training with me. Since you have

those fighting knives, we figured you'd like to learn how to use them properly. Plus, Hanola will insist you rest every moment of every day, if you don't find something else to keep yourself occupied." He runs a hand up and down the weapons belt that hugs his chest, his other hand behind his back.

"Okay, just let me put my hair up and get my knives."

He waits as I pull my knives from the satchel. I dump them on the small wooden table Catori uses for her weapons and then grab my hair, bunching it up before tying it off with my blue scarf. Returning to the door, I find Callian holding out a weapons belt, smaller than the large one over his bulky chest. He signals for me to turn around, and I do so slowly, realizing he intends to put it around me and fasten it. The belt drops down over my head, and I point my left arm up so he can drop it down one side. He plays with the buckles at the nape of my neck, fitting it to size before pulling it around, so the buckle sits between my shoulder blades.

"Okay, let's see what the front looks like," he says.

I snort a laugh and raise an eyebrow as my eyes meet his. He looks flustered this time, so I school my expression back to seriousness. The sheaths that will hold my two fighting knives sit with one below my right collarbone and one below my left breast. He hands me my knives, and I slide them into the sheaths. Perfect, and so accessible—much better than hanging from my hip or down my boot.

"Great, that looks about right. We should go before they start without us," he rasps, walking off.

I follow just behind through the light mist, all that is left of the rain shower. I run my hands over the smooth and fitted clothing, which is much better attire for fighting than pants and a robe. I feel so light and much nimbler.

We round the last home to find a clearing, where ten other village people around our age are gathered, all dressed like Callian.

Warriors. Half are women, half are men. They are standing in a circle, and we join them. A woman a little older than Catori stands in the center, waiting for everyone to settle in and focus. Her long brown hair is tied up, and her blue eyes wander over the group, hands on her hips. She holds her hand up, and the silence is immediate.

"Today, you will be working on strength and accuracy—two very different but useful traits for any warrior. In groups of four, you will rotate around the stations we have set up for you. This is not a competition; just try to be better than your last attempt. We'll be coming around to each group, so if you're unsure, just wait until we get to you. Most of these exercises you have done before." She gestures for us to start and walks over to Callian and me. Two more young women join us, and we make our way to the closest station.

Our exercise is a round target with various distances marked from it. Knife throwing. We stand just behind the closest line, and Callian has a couple of practice shots while we wait. The girl next to me is the same size as me, her light brown hair just brushing her shoulders, and she has kind hazel eyes. The leader moves next to me, her blue eyes squinting above her freckled cheeks as she concentrates on the task in front of us. Callian finishes his practice throws.

"Do you want to go next?" she asks.

I nod and take small steps up to the line. I pull out the knife from under my breast with my right hand and hold it the way Callian held his, arm slightly above horizontal. I stand with my feet apart and hold my knife by the blade. Then I pull back and throw it. It misses, bouncing off the target and onto to the ground. I grimace with a frown and walk over to collect the knife. The others are chatting playfully amongst themselves, and I'm thankful that they don't seem to be watching me. I try again, but this time I put my force into my arm during the throw. I get the same result, and I grunt in annoyance.

Callian appears by my side, as if summoned by my irritation. "You're holding your hand wrong, and you don't need so much force in your throw. Take your time. If you rush, your opponent will just end up with your weapon, because you missed. Try again."

I stand again before the line, feet apart. I hold the blade and raise my arm. It comes down in one fluid motion that is precise and not rushed. And I miss.

"Let the blade slide through your fingers on its own momentum. Don't flick your wrist; keep it locked in place. It doesn't move; your knife does." He nods for me to go again.

I do as he says. Feet apart and breathing in, I pull my arm back, and breathing out, I bring my arm down in one hard, short motion, my wrist locked. The knife flings from my fingers and lands in the target. It's near the edge, but it stuck! I can't keep the joy from my face, and he chuckles at my delight.

"Nice work, Imani." His wide smile lights up his face.

I step back, and the others have their turn. They're good. It makes me even more determined to practice.

A drum beats three times, and we are moved on to our next activity: strength. The bodies of the people who stand in the clearing with me far outweigh mine. Their bodies are fit and toned, and every limb is lined with the muscles they are now flexing, warming up for their tasks.

Callian and the other girls that make up our group are already at the next station when I jog to catch up. A long line of white powder stretches to the tree line and back. In front of our feet are four large, full sacks. We are to run with these to the tree line and back as many times as possible before our strength gives out. I kick the sack at my feet. It doesn't budge. The woman beside me flings one over her shoulder and takes off running, followed by Callian.

Our leader gives me a wink before taking off after the two in front of her. I pick up the bag. It's so heavy that I almost drop it before I can haul it onto my shoulder.

I start a slow jog with it, and the weight presses into my shoulder something fierce. I let out an annoyed groan at my useless body. About a quarter of the way, my legs find a rhythm, and I sort out my breathing. I might actually be able to get there and back. But by the time I reach the tree line, my breath is coming hard. The soles of my feet burn under the weight of the extra load. I awkwardly come to a halt and turn to go back the way I came. But the bag has its own momentum and falls from my shoulder, pulling me down with it. I hit the ground, and the wind flies from my lungs. I lie still for a moment, gasping.

A hand drops down. I look up into the hazel eyes of the brunette woman. She motions for me to get up. "Keep going. It's the only way you'll get better." She offers me a swift smile as my hand lands in hers, and she pulls me up in one quick move. On my feet, I stretch out my arms and legs and bend to pick up the bag. "No, bend your knees, never your back," she says.

I bend my knees and lift the bag onto my shoulder, pushing up on wobbling legs, and she takes off back to the start. I follow at a pace just faster than a jog. At the halfway point, my legs are screaming at me, and each step feels like it is weighted with iron. I push through the last three steps to the start. The others are finished, having done multiple runs, and they walk in small circles to steady their breathing. I bend over, trying to breathe. Nausea finds me, and I stand upright, trying to swallow back the rising bile.

"Okay, cool down for now. We'll have another session this afternoon for those who are up to it," she says.

I collapse onto my bag, close my eyes, and let out a groan. Three bouts of laughter explode next to me. I open my eyes to see Callian flanked by the leader and another smaller woman, each holding out a hand. I take them, and they yank me up, grins on their faces. Callian waves and wanders off to talk with another warrior. The two women walk with me back to the village center.

"I'm Miya," the brown-haired, freckle-faced woman who was running the training session offers.

"And I'm Jeselle," the other says. She sways into Miya's side, giving her a loving look.

"Imani," I say, still too winded to offer any other information.

"You did pretty good for a first timer. Most don't make it past the first station," Miya says, adjusting her weapons belt around her hips and the one across her chest.

"You have more weapons than the others," I observe, scanning Miya's body.

Jeselle rolls her eyes and laughs. "Yes, she does. Don't remind her."

"I am the leader of the warrior clan in this village, and Jeselle is head of the archers," Miya says.

"Oh, wow. I mean, that's incredible! The only position women in the desert are allowed is to be head of a household, and even then, it's not really that even; the men are the true head of the family." I feel like a barbaric outsider from some pitiful place.

"Not here, Imani. Never here," Jeselle says. She wraps an arm around me, and we head toward the eating area. Her arm is so heavily, but I don't want to offend her, and I am so grateful to be part of their day that I just walk on in silence. We find Catori and sit down at her table.

"Hey, how did you do?" she asks, her eyes lighting up.

"Terrible." I huff an annoyed chuckle, and her concerned look drifts to Miya.

"She did just fine for her first time," Miya says, and the concern on Catori's face washes away.

"Grandmother—I mean, Hanola—wants to see you later. She has something for you," Catori says.

"Thanks. Should I visit her after lunch?"

"I'll go with you, at sundown. I'll find you then. While you wait, perhaps you can help me with my rounds?"

Even when I am a burden, their kindness never falters.

CHAPTER 18
HARM

The journey home with Marshall is slow. He is thin, and tires easily. The poverty his village has endured is worse than most, and it shows in his sunken face. Jonah and I prop him up for the last part of the slog through the sands just before the outlying village we now call home.

The day is well into twilight when we cross the threshold of Enid's home and lower Marshall into one of the lounge chairs, and she fetches some water and stew for him. He doesn't protest, completely still now. I know that vacant stare; he is back at the well, watching his family die before his eyes, helpless to stop it. Just like I was. I wonder briefly if that's what Christopher, Maryanne, and Imani saw in me after my family was executed and I lived. Most likely.

Enid comes with supper and a blanket. Despite being hot and worn out from desert travel, Marshall is shaking all over. "Shock," Enid says. She wraps him in the blanket, anticipating his temperature plummeting. He holds the stew in his hands, but does not lift the spoon to eat. Enid offers to feed him, but nothing registers on his face. A hole the size of Jonah's big hands spreads through my aching chest as I relive slivers of what Marshall must be feeling right now.

Jonah leaves the room, and I hear the scraping sound of one of the bunks being moved. Through the dim hallway, Jonah is dragging his bunk into my room, for Marshall. A few moments later, he appears back in the living room.

"Now there's only one bed in Enid's room," I point out, raising an eyebrow.

"We'll make do. Marshall needs a bed." He gives me a wink and trails into to the kitchen to help Enid.

I glance one more time at Marshall before heading to the washroom to clean up. The sound of the water pouring into the bath relaxes my tired and tense muscles, and I load in several buckets full. I strip and examine my face in the mirror. It has been over a year since I was in Marshall's position. My face has changed a little since then, the lines harder, my face squarer and in need of a shave. I pour a small portion of water into the sink and lather up Jonah's soap on my face. With his old razor, I shave lines down my face and over my chin and neck, removing the miniature forest that has sprung to life over the last couple of weeks. A knock on the door makes the blade jump, and I steady my hand at Enid's voice.

"Hot water, Harm," she says, and her footsteps fade away.

I wrap the thin, worn towel around my waist and open the door. I haul the steaming bucket up and throw the heated water in with the cold, replacing the bucket in the hall and shutting the door. Releasing the towel to the floor, I climb into the bath. The water pulls me in, enveloping my body. I lie back, breathing heavily, cupping my hands to gather the warm water. I splash my face and slide beneath it, fingers rifling through my filthy hair, and exhale, sending bubbles to the surface.

Pushing up out of the water, I grab the small bar of soap and lather every aching muscle before washing my hair and face with it.

Small nicks on my face from shaving burn to life, and I groan, the tiny pains reminding me that I am still alive. For a moment, when I was standing in front of Marshall's vacant face, I thought I could have easily died after my family did, just willed myself to stop breathing. And right now, in Enid's home, with her and Jonah with me every step of the way, I'm glad to still be here... until the thoughts of Imani find me, at least. A rap on the door means I've been in here too long.

"Dinner is ready," Jonah says.

I dunk myself one last time and climb out of the tub. Drying off, I find my pile of clothes in the small cupboard. Clean clothes feel so opulent. The soft and light cotton shirt slides over my chest, and I do the buttons up to the last three. I pull on pants and fasten them before making my way to the kitchen.

Enid and Jonah sit in their usual spots. Marshall has been moved to the table also. He sits there just staring at the food, as if it is foreign to him. I plant myself on my chair and pick up the cutlery. Enid holds out her hands for us to take. We all join hands. Marshall recognizes the gesture and takes my hand and Enid's too.

"To hope. May we live in its presence always," she says, dropping our hands and digging into her stew.

I break my bread, dipping it into my stew before biting off the end. Marshall's trembling hands follow my actions. His first bite is tentative, and his eyes widen when the flavor fills his every sense. He rips into the bread again and shovels into the stew with his other hand. I watch him, remembering that I have forgotten what hunger is.

"You can slow down, there's plenty more," I say, giving him a kind smile that lights up my eyes.

He nods slowly and makes a point of chewing his food. Enid pushes a cup of water toward his plate, and then one to mine. We eat in silence, devouring every last morsel. Then Jonah gathers our plates and heads for the sink. Marshall's eyelids are lowering, and Enid signals for me to show him to our room to sleep. I help him out of his chair, making sure the blanket around him stays over his shoulders.

We reach our room, and I sit him on his bed. I take off the blanket and lay him down on his side. He brings his knees to his chest and closes his eyes. I drape the blanket over him and leave him to sleep, hoping his dreams won't haunt him, but knowing from experience that they probably will.

Enid, Jonah, and I sit in the living room reading for an hour or so before the screaming starts. Jonah pushes out of his chair and rushes down the hall. Enid and I follow.

Marshall is cowering in the corner of the room, his eyes wide, his hands on the sides of his face. Jonah kneels in front of him, talking softly. Enid lights the candles on the dresser and brings one over so he can see better. His stricken face is pale, and he is sweating profusely. Enid starts instructing Marshall to feel the stone under his feet, the warmth on his skin. She tells him to look at the flicker of the candle's flame, and the eyes of the man in front of him. She talks about the sounds of the animals outside, the calls of the night birds and the scurrying of the small desert rodents outside our window.

Marshall's eyes relax, and she tells him to count in between his breaths, but he shakes his head. So, Enid counts for him, trying to get him back to the here and now. His stiffened body starts to soften. Jonah sits beside him and wraps an arm around him. The boy rests his head on Jonah's arm, and then the tears flow. He sucks in breaths between sobs. Enid gets up to leave him with Jonah, and I follow her back to the living room. She settles back down in her chair with a ragged sigh, the pain on her face straining the weathered lines. She is silent for a time before speaking.

"Is this what you went through after…" Her voice trails off, too shaky to finish.

"Similar. I was older, but it was similar."

"I saw you after we brought you back from the prison. I saw what you were like after losing Imani. It was the same as Marshall, Harm."

I just stare at her. I don't remember some of it.

"You called out for her in your sleep. You screamed her name so many times, and I thought Jonah was going to fall apart every time. You cried like you couldn't stop—all while you were sedated. I've never seen anything like it."

I just stare at her. I don't know what to say. I felt every word once I woke from being sedated, but didn't realize she had heard them.

"Was losing Imani worse than losing your family?" Her words are kind, despite the nature of the question.

I look away from her. Comparing the two sends hundreds of small rips through my chest, a reminder of how much I have lost in such a short period of time.

"It was different." I breathe out, forcing back the prickling tears. "A different emotion." She doesn't press the issue, but I don't want to her to dismiss the way I felt about losing any of them. "Losing my parents and Amaya broke my heart, and it was hard to breathe every day after." Now I am sucking in air and holding the arms of the chairs with white knuckles. "But losing Imani was like being smashed to pieces while being suffocated." The words come out in splutters. Instantly, I need air. I jump up from the chair and stalk down the hallway, slamming the back door, angry at Enid for making me relive even a fragment of that pain again.

She doesn't follow me, and the only sounds are the soft words of Jonah that drift out the bedroom window as he talks with Marshall. I sink to the ground, legs crossed under me. I gather handfuls of sand and throw them into the wind, watching them drift and spread before they plummet down back to rejoin the rest. I lie back and stretch my legs out, my arms under my head. The stars shimmer, as if dancing on the spot upon their dark satin blanket.

The house is quiet by the time I wake in the sands, and I get up and dust myself off before heading inside. I ease onto my bunk, not wanting to wake Marshall, the steady rhythm of his breathing the only sound in our room. Hopefully, he will sleep until daybreak now. Lying in the same room as him and having seen his raw devastation reminds me how far I have come, how many times I wanted to give up, but didn't. I close my eyes, and sleep finds me easily this time.

The feeling of someone watching me makes me crack one eye open. Looking down at me is the devastated face of Marshall. He fiddles with the corner of his blanket, but seems to be examining every inch of my face, looking for something. I smile at him briefly before sitting up. He shuffles a little and clears his throat. I raise an eyebrow and wait.

"You're okay now?" he asks.

"Morning, Marshall. What do you mean?"

"After my nightmare last night, Jonah told me your story... about how you lost your family," he says, and his meaning dawns on me.

"Yes, I am okay now," I offer and run a hand through my hair. Some sand from last night sprinkles down onto the bunk.

His sadness wanes a little, and I offer him what I know. "Here is what I can tell you. It's one of the most painful things you'll ever go through. But it gets a little easier with time. It's been over a year since I lost my family. But Marshall, it will never go away. Just when you think you're better, and the memories can't hurt you anymore, they do. But you just keep living, just keep going. There isn't another alternative—not one that's worth it, anyway." I try not to sound completely despondent as he sits absorbing every word.

"Can I stay with you and your grandparents?" he asks.

I snort out a laugh, and he cracks a small smile.

"What?" he whispers.

"Enid is my grandmother, but Jonah is not my grandfather." His eyes widen, and he looks back through the door, as if he will be able to see them together.

"Enid was a widow for a long time before Jonah found her. But," I say, getting up and stretching, "that's a story for another day. Jonah is part of my story—mine and..." I stop, feeling like every beat of my heart can be seen from the outside. "Never mind; another day. Let's eat breakfast." I head down the hall.

Before I reach the kitchen, I realize something is amiss. It's too quiet, no noise from the kitchen, no chatter between Jonah and Enid. Only a few steps in front of me stands Jonah, his back to me, facing the front door, which is closed. He is motionless. Enid walks silently out of the living room and grabs my hand before grabbing Marshall's. She shushes us with an almost inaudible sound. The shape of her lips and the terror in her eyes speak volumes. We pad toward the back door, and she ushers us out, holding it still to prevent it from creaking. She points to the back fence. I grab Marshall's hand, and we jog to the fence, followed closely by Enid.

Scaling the lowest point of the broken-down fence, we round the building on the other side. Enid helps Marshall through the window of the empty neighboring house. I let her climb up on my knee before handing her through the window to Marshall. I pull myself through the window, and we crouch down between a cupboard and the wall.

"Jonah is about to open the door for Fletcher,"Enid whispers.

Every drop of blood drains from my face, and my hands start to tremble. She grabs them both and holds them tight. I slam my eyes shut, forcing breath in and out, hoping that will be enough to stave off the terror rising in my body. Marshall puts a hand on my shoulder. Judging by his perplexed reaction, he must have no idea that the man responsible for executing his family is just next door.

"Who's Fletcher?" he asks. Obviously, Fletcher has not paraded his name around Marshall's village the way he did in Amondo.

"Nobody good," is all Enid says. I open my eyes and stare at the floor. My hands are cramping up, and I stretch them, trying to loosen up the pain. "He must be looking for you, Harm. He must be desperate, coming into the outlying villages past his jurisdiction. You cannot stay here."

"Then where do I go?" I ask. What part of the desert doesn't contain Guardians?

"Marshall and I will travel together and go north to the next outlying village. Surely, they won't bother to venture that far. Harm, I need you to go in a different direction."

"Where?"

She looks at me for a moment, as if she's contemplating telling me something she has been thinking for days.

"Over the wall, into the forest. It's the only place he won't find you. You're too important."

The shock must have registered on my face, because Enid is rubbing my hands now.

"Once they retire for the night, you leave." Her decision is final. I nod, but my body is numb.

"Yes, okay," is all I can say. Traveling through the desert to the wall, making it over, and then finding the tribes swallows my mind and fills it with something like dread. But logic tells me that staying here is a death sentence. I have to go.

We walk back to the house after hearing Jonah's signal. No one speaks. As day turns to evening shadows, Enid goes about gathering food for me. Tears flow down her face the entire time. Marshall watches on, sadness and fear twisting over his face. Jonah is packing my rucksack while I stand there, trying to think my way through the best route to the wall.

"All you need to do is go directly south," Enid directs me. "That will get you to the furthest part of the wall. There's a concealed stone entrance. Push on the stones that surround it. It opens like the one you went through to meet Saraya; it's the same mechanism to get to the other side when you're inside the wall. Once you're on the forest side, head toward the center to find Hanola. Keep southwest. Take my field journal with you; she will recognize it, if she's still alive. If not, her children should."

Jonah is dressing me: robe and sand veil, rucksack and boots.

"You must make it to the forest, Harm. I will see you again, my precious grandson." She rests a trembling hand on my cheek. I place my hand over hers. Jonah grabs me in a tight hug before checking outside for movement.

"How will I know when the rebels are ready?" I ask.

"Someone will come for you, Harm. Or I will send word." She ushers me to the door. Marshall gives me a lost look, as if me leaving is another blow.

I slip out the door and into the shadows before winding my way through the buildings of the village. Within moments, I am encompassed by the darkness of the desert night, leaving my only remaining family behind. Alone again. With every step into the darkness, the ache in my chest spreads.

To keep from screaming, I run.

Fast.

CHAPTER 19

IMANI

Smoke engulfs the large area inside Hanola's home. Catori waves her hands in front of her, tracking a path to the cushions on the floor in the living room, where Hanola sits. She is cross-legged, her hands in her lap, eyes closed. Catori points to the cushion directly in front of her grandmother, and I drop down onto it, arranging my body to mirror hers. I close my eyes and wait. The smoke I have been waving away upon entering now finds its way through my mouth and nose, curling in tendrils that send my head aloft.

Catori's footsteps fade, and Hanola starts humming, four notes only. She repeats the melody, and her soft, warm hands fall over mine. Every breath takes me further from the grasp of this world. My body sways slightly, in time with her repetitions. Her grasp is constant, grounding me. I feel safe with her. An incantation cuts through the smoke in a language I don't understand. Her hands slide from mine. Everything surrounding us falls away.

"Mother Earth, hear our words. We must travel beyond the veil just once. We search for someone, a soul of worth, a soul of your goodness." Her humming begins again. She places an object in my hands and wraps my fingers around it. "If he is to be found on this mortal ground, let it be known." Humming again. My swaying body stills, and a tingling starts in my fingers and floats over my arms and toward my chest.

"Can you feel him, Imani?"

I wait to see if the tingling changes.

Nothing.

Her humming starts again, louder and faster, and I grasp the object she has given me, sending every thought, every memory I have of Harm into the space between Hanola and me. I don't know what else to do, and this feels right. The tingling turns into a fiercer sensation before burying its way into my chest. The ache spreads and then peters out. Wetness slides down my cheeks, and a splash of water hits my hands.

"Open your heart, sweet girl. If he is there, you will find him."

I push out the dearest memories I hold of him: his arms around me in the cold desert night, his lips on mine, his eyes burning into mine with need, over and over. The smoke stings where tears slide down my burning face. I see his face—so many times, so many memories. I touch his face. The moment his eyes meet mine at the gallows, the memory freezes in place. I search, discovering every part of his face. An ache in my chest grows and tightens. My body trembles, every breath comes too fast.

"Imani, open your eyes," Hanola says.

I can't.

I can't take my eyes from his face, terrified that he will disappear. Hanola's hands hold onto mine now, my lifeline back to this time and place. I feel every part of my body, and it feels like I'm running—running hard, like that day in the forest. It's hard to breathe, but I can't stop. Hanola's hands are shaking mine, but I can't leave; I won't leave him again. His face is twisted with agony and fear. I will not leave him.

Hanola's kind face beams when my eyes finally open, and she pats my shoulder. I am lying down, the cushion I was sitting on now supporting my head. I push to sit up. A sharp ache hits my head, and I sink back onto the cushion, taking a deep breath. My body feels like lead as I roll onto my side. Hanola rubs my back and whispers something about a distance traveled by the mind. She keeps rubbing my back for a few moments before returning to her cushion. Her eyes are lively. What happened while we were chanting?

"Imani, did you see your Harmen?"

I nod, but I'm not sure if I saw him or just remembered him.

"Did you feel anything in your body when you saw him?"

I try to sit up again, not wanting to be lying down for this. I hold my head with my hands once I am up and move around on the cushion to get comfortable. The throbbing in my head feels like it will split me open any second.

"I don't know if I saw him, or just remembered him. My hands were tingling at the start."

"What happened after the tingling?"

"I went through every memory I have of him that means something to me. But I got stuck on one—the last time I saw him. I could see what he was feeling. It was like time stopped."

Hanola's smile widens. "Then what happened?"

"Then the tingling went up my arms and into my chest. But it disappeared just before I noticed I was crying." I shift on the cushion and press my palm to my aching forehead. "After that, I couldn't leave him, the image of him—like if I did, he would stop existing. It was hard to breathe. Then it felt like every muscle and bone in my body had the feeling of running. After that, I must have fallen asleep?"

"I've only seen this a handful of times. You feel so exhausted because you traveled from here. You left your body and fell into his.

The connection between you two must be strong. It's not something that happens to many people, and there is a certain magic that entwines lovers that cannot be broken by distance or time; it exists between you both like a silver thread. This silver thread is so unbreakable that nothing and no one—not even Mother Earth herself—can destroy it. That is the reason you were able to leave your soul and combine with his for a short time."

"But what does that mean? He's still alive?"

"Yes. If he were no longer alive, you would have felt nothing. His soul would have moved on, and you could only rejoin him in the next life, should you both believe."

He's alive.

I knew it.

My breath turns to sobs, but my lips curve into a trembling smile. "Why did I feel like I was running?"

"It was not you who was running, Imani; *he* is running. Your body was within his, and you could feel every movement he made." She clasps our hands together. The excitement on her face is overwhelming.

"Oh," I utter, tears tracking down my cheeks again. My heart flutters around like a bird in a sandstorm. I try to control my breathing. Harm is alive. He is running.

He's alive!

And if he's running, he's not in the prison. My hand flies to my mouth, stifling a strangled cry that is the start of something much bigger. I suck it back down, and my eyes meet Hanola's.

"Thank you," is all I can get out.

She smiles back. Her eyes are weary, and Catori appears at her side. The smoke is all but gone, the doors and windows open. Catori extends her hand to me, and I pull myself up. My head thumps and feels like it still sways above my shoulders. My legs falter a little with the first step, with me still thinking they have run for miles. I wave another gesture of thanks to Hanola, and Catori walks with me back to her home.

"She'll be asleep for the rest of the day, so any questions you think of will need to wait until tomorrow," Catori says.

I can't find the words to describe what she has given me. "Your grandmother is incredible. I wouldn't want her to be burdened with my troubles."

"She's not the chief of the forest people for nothing, Imani." Catori winks.

We settle down in front of the hearth, and she hands me a plate of food.

"Lunch already? How long was I out for?"

"A couple of hours. She said you traveled far and didn't seem to want to return. It took her over an hour to get you back." Catori shoves a bite into her mouth.

I follow her lead. The rich flavor of the food brings me back to the plate in front of me.

"If he's traveling, how do I track him down?" I ask, pushing the food around on my plate.

"We've sent word out. If he's in the forest sector, we'll know within a few days' time," Catori says.

Gratefulness overwhelms me, clogging my throat. I hold her gaze, trying to find a way to thank her for all they have done for me in this short amount of time. But my words can't budge past the rock in my throat. For the first time in such a long time, I glimpse something like hope.

"You can go to training this afternoon if you're up to it. Otherwise, Callian can collect you on his way tomorrow."

"I think I'll pass this afternoon. My legs are shattered, and my head feels like it's ready to split in half."

She nods and continues eating.

I pick pieces of food from my plate before asking my next question. "Where are your parents?" I hold my breath, in case I have offended her.

"They live another village over. We see them every month. We used to come here all the time as kids to visit Grandmother, and for every party she ever threw. Callian and I came here to train once we were of age. Why do you ask?"

"I don't know. I kind of guessed you didn't have any." I feel silly as soon as the words leave my mouth.

She laughs through her mouthful of food. "Oh, no, Callian and I definitely have parents. Our mother is Hanola's daughter and is chief of her village. But they don't have training for warriors or hunters there, so we came here. All the children who volunteer for either role do. Most return after their training. I stayed here for my grandmother, plus, our home village has plenty of warriors and hunters. I like it here."

"I can see why. It's such a peaceful place."

"All forest villages are, Imani. We train for training's sake, mostly. Warriors do accompany hunters in the forests for protection, mostly from bears. We hope we never have to use force, but one day, the time may come when we need to protect ourselves, or others."

Does she mean the desert side? "Does Hanola decide for everyone, then?"

"Pretty much. She sees things, visions. She saw you coming."

My eyes widen, and I swallow the morsel of food lingering in my mouth. "Is that why you were at the wall?"

"No, she only saw you after I found you. Or perhaps I should say, she felt you once you crossed the wall. That's why Callian turned up the next morning, just in case you had one over on me." She winks, and I laugh. As if I could best Catori.

"She really is an extraordinary woman. Does your mother share her abilities?"

"To a certain extent. But she hasn't been honing hers for as many decades as Grandmother has. Hanola's abilities will pass to the next leader of our forest clans when she passes into the next life." Catori leaves the house after the meal to tend to her rounds of some sort before heading into the forest to hunt until dark. Callian and one of the other warriors are going with her. Part of me wishes I could go with them, but my body is wrecked from this morning, so I wander around the village instead. The people are all friendly and stop their work to chat whenever I come near. I pass the home of a woman who makes the clothing for the village warriors and hunters, like I'm wearing. She is busy fitting a young man with a new shirt and holds a length of string around his waist as she looks up at me. A brief smile touches her lips before she returns her glance to her patron.

Further along, I find a blacksmith. The reverberating echo of metal on metal drifts though the wide doorway, and I wander in. Curious to see where their weapons are made, I walk around the front room of the building, which is almost like a merchant's stall. The front room is lined with shelves, much like the secret room of the merchant I traded with for the fighting knives. I see long daggers like those Callian wields on the shelf, as well as a longer blade like a sword, and small fighting knives like mine. The blacksmith is bent over a forge in a workspace off the back of the building, pounding a blade flatter and longer with each swing. I turn and run a finger across the cold steel of a fighting knife with a dark handle.

"Fine knives, those," a deep voice offers.

I spin around and meet his gaze. The friendly face of the blacksmith I was just watching belt into steel looks back at me. He walks over to the shelf and picks the knives up, then hands them to me. They are so light and well balanced that they seem to float above my palms.

"They're magnificent." I return them to the shelf.

"You're one of the new trainees for the warrior and hunting division?" he asks, taking in my attire.

"Not exactly."

He raises an eyebrow.

"I'm from over the wall. From the sands."

"Oh. What brings you over the wall?"

"I'm looking for someone. Someone who was in the prison."

"You're looking for a convicted criminal?" His expression turns jovial, and he looks me over again.

"He's not a criminal. Well, not in the horrible sense, at least. But he's someone dear to me, nonetheless."

"Does he have a name?"

I hesitate, but remember that I have told everyone else here his name, and I wait a heartbeat before speaking. I have nothing left to hide now.

"Harmen Travesci. A week ago, I heard he was in the prison at the tower."

"Wait here. Have a look around. I'll be back shortly." He walks out through the back of the room. I wander around, running a light hand over his immaculate work. Every blade and handle is perfect. I have never seen such an admirable collection of weapons.

Minutes later, he returns with a woman. By the way he ushers her with a hand on the small of her back, I gather that this is his wife. She is not much taller than me, and well rounded. Her grey tunic and long, dark skirt are covered by an apron dusted in flour. Her wiry dark hair is tied up, and wisps of flour cover her ruddy cheeks. She wipes her hands on her apron and then over her cheeks before her dark eyes meet mine.

"This young lady is looking for a Harmen Travesci," he says to his wife.

She takes a quick, sharp breath before grabbing my hands in

hers. "My name is Carol. I work in the kitchens at the tower for a week once a month. We supply meals and such to the prison, but we also supply all of the people in the tower—including the Chancellor, the Guardians, and *every* prisoner."

My eyes meet hers now, and I mostly understand what she is saying.

"I don't take the food to the prisoners, but some of the other servants there do, and we all talk amongst ourselves. I know who you're looking for. But he isn't there anymore. He escaped somehow." Carol squeezes my hands, but her eyes have gone dark— glazed over, almost—and her face twists in sorrow.

My breath stops.

"You must know, he was in a bad way. Our girls who deliver the prisoners' food told us how badly he was beaten. It was like he was not of this world anymore—like his mind had gone on him. He screamed a name, over and over, for days on end. Toby, one of the Etonia prison workers, was eventually assigned to him because of it. It was scaring the servants, seeing how sorrow that deep could exist without killing a person." Her breath turns ragged, flushing her face, and her husband sits her down. I step forward, still in her grip.

She looks up at me. "Imani. He kept screaming for a girl called Imani, like a man possessed."

I flinch in her hold and draw back. Her eyes widen as she realizes who I must be. My chest cracks, tearing my heart apart. I wipe my face dry and thank her, hurrying for the door.

"Wait!"

I hesitate in the doorway, holding myself up on the frame. "He got out, lass. Someone got him out. He's not here and not in the prison. Wherever he is, he'll be looking for her—for you. Of that I am certain."

I run.

I run from the village toward the training clearing. I didn't think I had any emotions left after this morning, but they pour out of me as my knees hit the short grass. I scream, one agonized scream after another. My hands fly over my heart, as if that will stop it from cracking in half. But he is alive. I knew this. Images form in my mind of him in pain, in some rotten, filthy cell, calling for me—and I didn't hear a single word. I cry on the grass until I have no tears left to give.

A warm hand lands on my back, and I hear the soft words of Callian, followed by Miya's. Callian lifts me up and hugs me to his chest, one arm around my back, one under my legs. Numb, I close my eyes, laying my head on his chest.

Moments later, I am lowered onto my mat in Catori's home. An hour later, food is left beside my sleeping mat. Catori's soft voice coaxes for me to eat something, but I only curl up tighter. No one asks me what happened, and I don't bother eating. The darkness swallows me whole, and I fall into the never-ending chasm of sleep.

CHAPTER 20
HARM

It has taken two days of running off and on for me to reach the southernmost part of the wall. There is nothing here but a handful of spindly trees and miles of stone wall that stretch out on either side of me. As per Enid's instructions, I start the hunt for a seam or groove that marks the door, for a stone that I can depress to open the door in the wall. It could be anywhere on this massive stretch. The sand and heat burn my fingers, and I alternate hands. I hunt for any sign of a door for well over an hour before stopping for water. The last of my supply sloshes around in the bottom of my canteen. I need to breach this wall sooner rather than later.

The winds at my feet stir the sand into a flurry. Looking back the way I came, I see the first signs of a sandstorm stirring. I *really* need to get through this wall. I head further north, thinking I have gone too far south to find the opening. As I walk along, I run one hand over the stone. The sandstorm builds at a rapid rate, mere miles to the east. If it closes in, I will be buried. I pick up the pace.

Come on, come on...

The winds whip around me, blasting sand against my face.

Now I wish I hadn't stowed my wrap in my rucksack an hour ago. Small drifts of sand build miniature dunes along the wall. The storm growls, swallowing the air around me. My heart flings against my ribs, and I hurry along the wall fast, the sands trying to swallow my feet. My hand, almost numb from the rough surface I have held it against for hours, trembles.

A sudden squall of wind throws me against the wall, and I raise my hands to protect my head. The sides of my robe flap around wildly, slapping me hard over and over. I crouch down, trying to avoid the worst of the winds. I press my hand against the wall to steady myself, fingers inching along the stone. The hard surface finally relents under my hand, and the grinding of stone is barely audible over the howling winds. I lift a hand to protect my eyes, staring at the stone brick that has just retracted under my touch.

The sands at my feet start to move, and the first crack in the wall appears.

Found it!

The door opens painfully slowly. I retreat from the reach of the raging storm behind me as soon as I can squeeze myself through. I pace to the opposite side and start hunting for the next stone to press, hands flying over the stone in panicked movements. The door closes, and I am left in the pitch black. My left hand finds the stone, and it sinks beneath my touch just as the first door slides shut. Seconds of darkness menace me, before brilliant rays from the other side burst through the small crack, gold and green. Splinters of light dance around, growing larger as the door slides open to my left. Fragrant scents of pine and earth hit me first, followed by moist air.

Gasping, I forget to exhale.

CHAPTER 21

IMANI

Another night of pouring rain has the ground underfoot slippery and the air cold. I shiver, waiting for Callian to swing by, so we can train together. I need the distraction while I pass the time, waiting to hear word about Harm from the other forest villages. Miya and Jeselle are still in our group, the four of us now a more formidable team, my skill having improved significantly in most areas.

We walk to the training grounds, and Callian chatters about the weather. He has been somewhat reserved since he carried me back from the training grounds like a rag doll. The awkwardness I don't mind so much, but I would love to know why he is this way with me now. The laughing Callian that I'm used to, I liked much better, when he didn't seem distracted. He isn't himself.

Miya's energetic instructions fill the damp air. She barks out the skills and exercises for today's round before making her way to our group. Miya and Jeselle greet me; no awkwardness from them. We start out climbing tall posts set with sparse iron pegs. Each post, as we move along the line, has fewer and fewer pegs, forcing us to use strategy to get to the next peg.

Jeselle, the lightest member of our team, whips up the posts like a spider and leaps between the sparse iron pegs, grinning all the way. Her muscled legs and small frame help her immensely—a skill she no doubt uses to scale the trees that surround the village, where the archers position themselves. I may be small, but I lack the leg muscles that she carries.

I reach the first post, grasping the iron peg in my right hand, testing to see how it responds underhand. After the first four pegs I have a pattern down and reach the top in no time. Miya lets out a whoop, and I throw her a grin and wave, scaling back down. Callian is two posts over. He is concentrating, as his bigger, heavier body makes his job harder, but he reaches the top and scales halfway down before dropping to the ground, landing with knees bent, and a brief grin stretches over his face.

I make my way to the next post and start the climb. This time, there are only half the iron pegs than the last. It makes me stretch to the point where I feel like I will fall before getting to the next peg. I use my feet and legs to spring up, and my fingers curl around the peg above me. Instantly, I tighten my grip. My body swings off the peg that was holding me in midair, and I panic that I will fall.

"Find your next peg, Imani! Check your breathing, maintain your control," Miya instructs below me.

Oh, good—at least she might have a chance at catching me. I grunt out a breath before wrapping my legs around the pole. With my weight mostly taken off of my one hand, I hunt for the next peg. It's just out of reach, but my position is strong as I stay wrapped around the pole. I let go of the peg and grab the pole above me with both hands and shimmy up until the peg is in comfortable reach. I grip it with my left hand and look down as I place my right foot on the previous peg. Using this new pattern, I move to the top.

Once I am wrapped around the swaying pole at the very top,

exhilaration rushes through my entire body. Larger warriors than me have climbed this pole, and yet it feels set to topple at any minute. I hear Miya and Jeselle from below, their voices concerned, but I am not afraid. I take in the mass of trees that make up the continuous forest around us. Above the canopy, birds flit in out and of the greenery, calling to one another.

Callian's voice snaps me back to reality. He is calling me down, his face tight with concern. I wave him off and start my descent. It is slow—painfully slow—and by the time I jump off the last peg and hit the ground, my legs are wobbling.

"What were you doing up there?" he asks. The annoyance in his voice pangs through my chest. His face is so serious, and his eyes remain fiercely on mine.

"I was just looking around. It's stunning." I wipe my hands on my pants, breaking eye contact, trying to dismiss the conversation.

"Why didn't you come straight back down? You could panic at that height and fall!" he snaps, standing with his arms slack by his sides, his chest rising and falling fast.

"Did I look like I was panicking, Callian?" I throw back, shoving my hands onto my hips.

"You should have come straight back down." His words are softer now, and the look on his face has turned to hurt.

"Whatever." I storm past him. Training is over for the day. He grabs my arm. I tear it out of his grip and stalk my way back to the house. I slam my knives onto the small table and go behind the makeshift wall to change. My clothes are sweaty and dirty. I pull a cream tunic from the pile of clothes I have in this small room and slip it over my head, and I put on training pants again. Their fitted form feels good on my body, and they're comfortable. I pull my hair out and let it swing down, just past my shoulders now. The waves of it bounce around.

The better food, training, and overall living conditions of the forest have helped my body and mind. In the small mirror in the changing area, I inspect the now elegant curves of my body, and my muscled arms. I lift the tunic and lay a hand on my flat and hardened stomach.

A knock startles me. I drop my shirt and fix my clothing before stepping out of the changing space and opening the door. Callian stands in the doorway, hands clasped in front of him, gaze on the threshold. I stand in front of him, arms across my chest. I can feel the heat from him. He raises his blue eyes to meet mine. Sorrow lines them, and my fire disappears.

"I just came to apologize. You are perfectly capable of climbing a post and perching on the top. I had no right to chastise you for it." His eyes search mine. I don't know for sure what he's searching for, but with the look on his face right now, I can guess what's going through his head. It has been there since the day he carried me home.

"Don't worry about it. No harm, no foul." I try to lighten the mood, but he remains staring back at me, his face unchanged. I should be apologizing, not Callian. I open my mouth to speak, but he raises a hand.

"Imani, I had no idea what Harmen means to you. I guess I should have figured that out, since you've traveled half the world looking for him. The other day, when I carried you home—it's bothering me. Not the carrying you part..." He shifts on his feet. "The part where you were hurting so bad, and none of us could do a damn thing to help you."

"Oh." I stand motionless, waiting for his next words. I have only been here a short time, but these people feel like family.

My eyes are trained on his, and he pulls me into a hug so tight that I almost choke. I let out a smothered cough, and he releases me, stepping back. He cracks a smile and runs a hand through his blond hair with a muscular arm. I throw a punch into his chest, and he chuckles, the tightness draining from his face.

"So, do you want me to stay away from you? Would that be easier?" I ask, the words paining me as they leave me.

"No, that's not what I meant at all. We'll help you find him, Imani. I promise."

In the space of a heartbeat, I realize that the sadness and suffering we are so accustomed to on the desert side is almost foreign to the people of the forest. I see the effect it has on Callian, and my overwhelming need to protect him and Catori, Hanola, Miya, and all the forest people from what we endure on our side of the wall knocks the air from my lungs. I pull in a handful of deep breaths.

Somewhat recovered, I nudge his arm with my elbow. "Come on, let's eat. I'm starving."

We walk in silence to the eating area and sit at one end of the table before a woman comes over with a jug of drink and places a platter of food in front of us. I rip at the bread with my teeth. Catori sits next to me and elbows me with a smile. "What's with my brother?" She is loud enough for him to hear.

"Nothing much. Did you get to training today?"

"Nope, I was out on the perimeter all day. Hanola felt something there. I went out to check, but I didn't see anything. But that doesn't mean no one's there. I'll go back out this afternoon, to the southern parts. You and Callian are welcome to tag along if you like, but it'll take us a night and day." Her eyes stay fixed on her brother's gaze.

"I will. I could use a run," Callian says, his expression full of mirth.

"Me too; that would be nice," I say. "Plus, I haven't been in the forest much since I got here. I would love to see it again."

"Well, that settles it, then. I'll tell Hanola the three of us are going. Callian, can you gather some supplies?"

He nods, and I offer to help. He smiles at me. I ruffle his hair with my free hand, although he sits higher than me, and he laughs at my attempt at roughing him up. Catori gives me a quizzical look before grabbing her last mouthful, then taking off to Hanola's home.

An hour later, Catori, Callian, and I are running through the forest with our packs. I have a stick that I used in combat training, plus my two knives. Catori's chest is lined with fighting knives and daggers, and both thighs carry a long dagger. Callian has a broadsword across his back, tucked in next to his bow and quiver. The three of us look like we're hunting something, with the glint of the weapons reflecting off all three of us. We pass through the streams of sunlight that break through the canopy and hit the soft, mossy green ground.

By the next morning, the clouds that hang above the canopy grumble as we fly through the forest. The last time I was here, I could hardly keep up with the siblings. Now I keep pace and enjoy every stride, despite the load on my back and the weapons on my chest. My hair flows behind me. The soft cloth of my tunic whips around my ribs, eddying with the motion of my gait and the gusts of air from the storm developing overhead.

When we finish this trip, I want to start making my way to the tower. I need to find Harm. If they get word of where he is, I'll hear on my way back through. After this trip, my next destination is that tower. As much as I would love to stay with the forest people, I am restless without him. Who knows what chaos is going on back in the desert sector? How many more people are suffering? We need to change things. Out of sight is not out of mind for me. Once we're back, I will talk to Catori and tell her I'm leaving.

We reach the top of the rise that makes a brief summit before the gradual descent through the rows of trees. There is a clear path through them, and I now know it winds through the forest to reach the wall with another day of running. I look at Catori, and her eyes scan the depths of the forest, ascertaining if it's safe for the three of us to step onto the narrow sunlit path between the trees. Her face hardens, and she hesitates, hands hovering over the hilts at her hips.

She freezes.

CHAPTER 22
IMANI

Catori and Callian on either side of me, we search the spaces between the trees for any movement. Wind tunnels through the trees and bustles around my feet, whipping up leaves like children playing. Even though I want to explore the forest, I hesitate to take the journey through the trees, having only known open spaces my whole life. The ground is layered in leaves from seasons past. Trees tower over my head, reminding me of my insignificance, with birds frolicking from branch to branch.

A step lands with a crunch that echoes through the trees in the distance. I freeze before moving into a defensive position. Callian pulls out his bow and one arrow from its quiver. Catori draws her fighting knives from her chest.

A figure stands a few hundred feet down the path, still as stone. It is a man; I can tell that from the stance and shape. I concentrate my efforts on scoping him out. He carries no weapons that I can see. He wears a cotton shirt and brown pants, under a desert robe.

I take a few steps closer, as if that will help me see him better. He moves after I do, getting closer, but a large distance still lies between us. I halt and hold my position, my hair playing around my shoulders, as if losing patience in the stillness, wanting to be like the wind. Catori and Callian move in beside me, a step behind, my second line of defense. They have trained for years, and for a moment, I doubt my position. But Catori nods, her face all-knowing as she throws a look to Callian in a sibling communication that I don't understand. Catori's hands tug at the buckles on the weapons strapped over my chest. She flings the leather straps off my shoulders and places the weapon holder in Callian's waiting hand. A soft smile lights up his face.

"What are you doing?" I ask.

"You won't be needing these for the moment, Imani," he says. I hand my stick to him. He dumps everything on the ground. Catori grabs my shoulders and turns me to face the robed figure in the trees.

He walks a few steps closer, his demeanor as guarded as mine. "Hello?" he calls.

His voice.

My heart races.

Eyes wide, I strain to see him standing on the sun-dappled path. He waves and tilts his head, as if getting a better look. He calls again. The forest around me disappears, and my breathing turns ragged.

"Hello!" I shout back. Dropping my arms to my sides, I force every breath. I glance at Catori, who now stands next to Callian. Both of their faces are stretched with smiles.

Callian nods toward the man standing in the trees. "Go on."

I pull my gaze from theirs and track my way through the space between me and the robed figure.

Please be him. Please, please be Harm.

Halfway through the tunnel of trees, I make out his face.

Harm.

A strangled sob leaves my chest, and I burst into a run. My rucksack bangs against my back, and I claw it from my shoulders as I run, tossing it on the ground. His name leaves my lips in breathy sobs. I fly at him as fast as my body will go. The sounds around me fade, replaced by my pounding heart. My breaths come in waves of sobs. I try to call out to him, but my voice shakes so much that I can't form the words anymore.

In another few strides, he recognizes me. His eyes widen, and he bends over, grabbing his knees. His chest heaves. I stop dead, mere feet away from him. He looks up at me, his deep brown eyes full of pain and disbelief, and stands back up. In three more steps, I fling myself at him, jumping up onto his hips and throwing my arms around his shoulders. He teeters back a little, but straightens, wrapping his arms around my waist. I bury my head in his neck, surrounding him with my untamed hair. He groans and holds me tight. Sobs rack both our bodies as we cling to each other.

"Imani."

The sound of my name melts my heart, sealing all of its shattered pieces back together as one again. I gasp for breath through uncontrollable sobs. I push back and grip his face with my hands. With trembling fingers, I trace every inch of his jaw, his cheeks, running a thumb over his lips. Every breath too quick, I alternate between sobs and small huffed laughs.

"Imani."

I meet his gaze. Rivers of tears cover his face, and his brown eyes hold a rugged stare, penetrating mine. I place my hands on either side of his face again, tracing his cheekbones and lips with my fingers, making sure he is real. I run my hands through his hair, and he softens underneath me.

"Imani."

His hands grip my waist, and his gaze wanders over me, inch by inch. He utters my name over and over now, as if in a dream. His gaze turns vacant.

Something flips in my stomach. I release my legs and stand in front of him. He falls to his knees, eyes still unseeing. I drop to mine, tangling my hands in his shirt.

"Harm?" I choke out. My hands shake, clutched around the opening of his shirt. The warmth of his chest I have longed for since our last night in the desert outside Etonia, builds a burning behind my eyes. Tears sting their way down my cheeks again.

"Imani," he breathes, and his hand slides behind my neck and into my hair. A whimper leaves my mouth, and I press my forehead to his. He mumbles my name over and over. Something isn't right. His words are too vague, like he's dreaming. What happened? What happened to him while I was not there? I swallow back the pain thundering up through my chest.

"I'm here. I'm here, Harm." I make sure the words come out clear and solid. I wrap my fingers around his face and raise his head, lifting his gaze to mine. "Hey, look at me. I'm here. I am really here."

He doesn't respond for a moment, and my heart breaks. Air rushes out of my lungs like flame. I swallow past the lump in my throat and press my lips to his briefly. He looses a painful moan. I lean back, searching his face.

His breathing is erratic. "I thought you were dead. They... they all told me you were gone." His hands wander over my face, while his own contorts in agony and relief.

I place a finger over his lips and press my body into his, so he can feel that I am real. I thrust my lips onto his and kiss every part of his mouth. He responds, gentle and loving, needing me as much as I need him. We run out of breath and slowly part, Harm's eyes locked on mine. I rest my head on his chest and listen to his heart beating, fast and strong, in time with his breathing.

"I thought you were dead." He lifts my head up with his hand. His voice is steadier, but tears cascade down his jaw.

I take in a deep breath, trying to control myself before I speak. I want my first words to him to be good ones. "I've been searching for you for months. All I knew was that Fletcher took you after the gallows. I couldn't believe you were dead, so I started looking for you after I escaped."

"Escaped? From where?"

"Mason."

His eyes search mine for my meaning, but I will not ruin this moment with those memories. Finally, he stands and holds out a hand. I slide mine into his and rise. We walk back to Catori and Callian. Harm is holding my hand tightly, like if he lets go, I will disappear.

"Your hair is shorter," he says just before we reach the siblings.

I throw him a wry look that results in a shade of horror on his face; perhaps he is remembering how it got short to begin with. The torture, the execution day. He schools his face before Catori speaks.

"You must be Harm," Catori says, her face lit up with excitement. "I'm Catori."

Harm looks from me back to the siblings, their faces beaming.

"Yes, nice to meet you." His gaze falls back to me, still studying every inch of me, as if making sure I am real.

Heat flushes my face and I lean into Harm. "I don't greet just anyone like that."

Callian stands, arms crossed, with a smile softening his face. "And, this is my brother, Callian."

Callian extends a hand, and Harm shakes it.

"We should keep moving. It isn't wise to stand around for too long in the trees, unless you're planning on being a bear's dinner," Callian quips.

Catori scans the trees as we go, looking to see if anyone else lingers in her territory. We make the midway clearing before dark. Callian wanders off into the trees to find food, taking Harm with him, while Catori and I set up a fire. She stares at me as I stack the firewood I gathered from the forest floor, her hands busy laying out the sleeping mats from our packs.

"What's up?" I ask, meeting her stare.

"Nothing." But her hands freeze on the mat.

"Obviously it's not nothing."

She sighs and rolls out the last mat. "Hanola saw him coming." Her voice is soft, and her green eyes meet mine. Then I remember the look she gave Callian before Harm called out to us, and my mouth gapes. I knew there was something in that look. "Why didn't you tell me?"

"She told me not to. She didn't want to get your hopes up if he had come with ill intentions."

"What? Why would Harm have ill intentions toward me?"

"I don't know; it didn't make sense to me. But she said there was a dark shadow with him. She said to keep you close and stay alert. That's why Callian's here."

Heat rises in my face, and I swallow hard. "Callian knows this too?"

"Yes. I'm sorry Imani, but something wasn't right. Hanola is rarely wrong about these things. But time will tell." She forces a smile.

Harm and Callian return, and we all share a plate of sweet bark, berries, and some sort of pale worm that I refuse to eat. Callian shoots me a grin while biting into one, and I squirm. That makes him laugh. Harm sits next to me, his body touching mine, and he eats the food on his leaf. He's too quiet. My chest aches with all I want to tell him—like that there is nothing between me and Callian, who is like a big brother to me. That everyone told me he was dead, but I refused to believe them. That I have been searching for him for weeks. The things Mason did to me, how he was so angry when I escaped, and that I know it's not over. Instead, I sit next to him, chewing on the sweet bark I have come to love as much as the people the who share it with me.

Harm drops his leaf and pushes up from the ground. We all stop chewing and watch him as he walks off into the dark forest. Callian makes to rise, but Catori places a hand on his shoulder. I get up and head into the darkness after him.

"Don't let him go too deep," Catori calls from behind.

I nod and pick up the pace to reach Harm. The darkness swallows me quickly once I am away from the fire. I try to adjust my eyes, slamming them shut for a handful of heartbeats before flinging them open. I can see a little better, but I can't see Harm.

"Harm?"

No response.

I walk further into the darkness, despite my body telling me to turn back. After another few steps, I see him sitting on the ground, his back against a tree, his head in his hands and resting on his knees. Pain flows all around him. My heart falters. I drop to my knees at his feet. He doesn't look up. Motionless, I remain in front of him, just breathing, trying to find what to say. When no words come, I run my hand through his hair and down the back of his neck. He looks up, and his eyes are pain itself. I place my hands on his cheeks. "Tell me what hurts." The words choke their way out.

He sucks in a breath and puts his hands on top of mine. Thousands of thoughts flicker through his gaze—all the things he wants to say, but hasn't found the words for yet.

"Everywhere, Imani."

What has he been through since the gallows? I try to imagine what took place. Fear and sadness claw at me, but I shake my head and dislodge their grip. I turn my body and sit next to him up against the tree. I wrap my arm through his, and his fingers curl around mine when I slide my hand into his. "Tell me just one thing."

"I thought you were dead," he whispers.

"But you're here?" If he thought I was dead, why did he cross the wall?

"Enid sent me over the wall. I can't go back. Fletcher is looking for me everywhere."

I jerk at the sound of my father's name. It's as if, with me being on this side of the wall, he stopped existing, and hearing his name again is a slap to the face, a reminder of all that he is and everything he has done. The healer Hanola spoke of...

"She's been here before?"

"Yes." He is looking at me now. "I thought you were dead, Imani. I wanted my heart to stop beating."

Panic and the heavy ache that grips my heart strangle me. I look at the ground, and the weeks I spent in Mason's cage, being told he was dead, come flooding back. The night I cried until the sun came up. Every time I wished I was dead too, if only to see his face one more time. Tears burst the dam lining my blurry vision and fall onto the moss underneath me.

His hand touches my cheek, and I meet his gaze.

"Mason told me you were dead—that Fletcher killed you," I breathe. "He shut me up in a cage in his house. He would only let me out if I gave him what doesn't belong to him."

His eyes scan my face, and he swallows hard. "You."

I nod, and he puts his other hand on my face, caressing my cheeks before his fingers find my hair and the back of my neck. His warm hand on my skin creates sparks in my body. His eyes have changed. Where there was pain, now there is adoration and desire.

"Finally, after weeks, I found a way to escape. I have so many things to tell you—all the things that happened while we were apart."

He nods, moving his body in front of me and resting his forehead on mine. "Me too." He kisses my cheek, over and over, one hand in my hair, the other holding my face to his. Harm puts his legs around me and pulls me into his chest. His familiar scent that I have longed for for months makes my breath catch, and I swallow to push back tears, this time from overwhelming relief. He strokes my hair while he hugs me tight. We stay embraced tightly, listening to the night sounds of the forest.

A thunderous crack is only preempted by the blinding flash of lightning, and Harm jumps to his feet, pulling me up with him. Seconds later, a deluge of rain pelts down through the trees. I smile and look up—but he is shaking, gasping for air, as if he's drowning. The rain hammers down around him. I realize this is his first time in the rain. I grab his shocked face with both hands.

"Harm, it's rain. Just breathe. You won't drown." I know that means something entirely different to him than it does for most people.

His eyes track to mine, and I offer up a smile, holding one hand out with my palm up, so he can see the drops bouncing off. He watches, his face melting from fear into wonder. It takes him a few moments before he meekly holds out his own palm, imitating me. His breathing returns to normal. I run a hand through his wet hair, brushing it backward. He looks different in the rain; his eyes shine. I like it. We stand there, feeling every drop that falls on our skin, watching the way it cascades down the trunks of the ancient trees before gushing and swirling across the mossy forest floor, trying to find its end.

The silhouette of Catori wades through the rain toward us. She is drenched as well, and her gear is on her back. Looks like we're moving out. I take Harm's hand and lead him back through the trees to the now-smoldering fire. Callian hands me my pack and weapons. I organize myself, and Harm grabs his belongings. Catori gives the signal, and we move out from the clearing at a run. Catori heads up the line, followed by Harm, then me, and lastly Callian. I catch his gaze before we slip into our set pace. His eyes are kind, but concerned.

After a couple of hours, the moon is high above us, and the steam from our heated bodies wafts off us in the cold, damp air. Harm bends over to catch his breath, and the rest of us walk slowly in circles before Catori motions for us to move out again.

"Wait," Callian breathes as we turn to run on.

We all freeze.

His hand is held up, his eyes scanning the dark forest. Catori pulls her blades and follows his eyes through the trees. Nothing stirs for the next couple of minutes. Whatever Callian thought he saw, it's gone now. Catori grunts and sheathes her blades before taking off at a run. We fall in behind her, and Callian trails us, a little further behind this time.

Someone is following us.

CHAPTER 23

HARM

Two days have passed since I arrived at the forest village where Hanola lives. I've met her once, and she spoke of Enid fondly. There is still some kind of suspicion hanging over my arrival, even though I have told Hanola all I know, and that Enid sent me here seeking refuge. The people of the village are friendly, and Imani's friends are clearly fond of her, especially Callian, Catori, and Miya. I sit at the long communal table in the village center and eat a plentiful supper as the three women Imani sits with banter about something I don't really hear. They laugh and eat while I sit next to Callian. He watches on too, also not saying anything.

Imani looks perfect. She has been here for weeks now, and her body is not drawn and thin like it was in the sands. Her face glows with the pink that health and good food brings. The stars dance above the long stretch of table, only outshone by the happiness of the people around me. The stark contrast of this place with my own home does not escape my notice.

Somewhere in the village, music starts up, and the steady beat, with people's hands on the table keeping time, reverberates through my body. A smile spreads across my face. Callian jumps up to jig around, followed by the hysterics of the four women in front of us. I can't help but let out a chuckle and clap along in time to his ridiculous dance. Spinning around, he almost topples over, pounding his chest before Catori yells at him to sit down through fits of laughter.

Imani is like I've never seen her before, so happy and free. Her eyes connect with mine, as if she just read my thoughts. I smile at her, hoping she can see me the way she sees her new friends.

The revelry dies down after dinner is done, and Callian and I make our way back to his home. I have a sleeping mat on one side of his house, and he sleeps on the opposite side in a bed. The fire in the center keeps the space dry and warm as the temperature plummets during the night. Being here has relaxed my ever-alert body into something that resembles calm, and the soft snores of an exhausted Callian lull my eyes closed. It's not long before sleep takes me down.

My body jerks awake, and my eyes fly open before my mind registers the scream.

Imani.

Within seconds, both Callian and I are out the door. He carries two knives, racing toward Catori's home. We burst through the door to find Catori standing there, armed and waiting. Imani is kneeling over someone on the ground, and her hands are shaking. She holds a knife to their throat, the other knife drawn back and marking her target, the chest of the person under her.

Callian walks over to the fire and lights two lamps, handing one to Catori. I move closer to Imani. Her breathing is erratic. Lying on her sleeping mat is a male figure, with worn and ripped dark grey pants. I track up the length of his body to the light grey shirt that hangs from his heaving chest. My stomach plummets, and fear rises, prickling its way across my skin. Now I understand why Imani is shaking. I send a look to Callian that I hope he interprets as a warning.

Mason.

"Imani," Catori says. Her words are soft but firm.

Imani's knife presses into his throat, and a trickle of blood runs to the floor. "How did you find me?"

"Imani," Callian warns.

I move to her side and look down at Mason. Face twisted with his usual facade of hate, he's not afraid, although he should be.

"I have come to take what's mine," he says to her, not breaking his piercing glare.

"There is nothing here for you, Mason," I grind out.

The second the words leave my mouth, I know it was a bad idea. But it's too late to creep back into the shadows now, and I will not leave Imani's side, ever again.

"Get your knife off my throat, Fletcher."

Imani's eyes go wild. Her blade plummets toward his chest, but Callian grabs her arm, the point of the blade inches from Mason's ribs. She spins to face the warrior, a mix of shock and betrayal on her face as she stares at him. She rips her arm from his grip before stumbling back from Mason. He clambers to his feet and takes a swing at me. I meet his arm with a defensive strike, but fall a step backward. Callian shoves him against the wall in one swift move and holds him by the throat with his forearm, as if his patience has just run out. Mason flails around under Callian's arm. He chokes, but Callian keeps pressure on him.

"Take him to the cells. I will not wake Hanola in the middle of the night for this," Catori snaps.

Callian tugs Mason off the wall, shoving him out the door, a firm grip around one arm. Despite Mason's apparent strength over me, he is no match for Callian.

I turn back to comfort Imani, but she's gone. I rush out of the doorway and search for her. Catori appears by my side, and her worried glance confirms my thoughts. Mason being here is bad. "She's probably in the training area. I'll take you."

She leads me through the village until we reach the training area. Sure enough, a small figure sits in the center of the grassy clearing. Catori offers a small smile and leaves me. I stand on the edge of the clearing, wondering what Mason has done to Imani, every scenario I run through in my head worse than the last. Finally, I walk over to where she sits and drop down beside her.

"You okay?" I choke out.

"I'm fine." Her words are thin, vague at best.

"Callian has locked him up."

"Good." She pulls at the grass, ripping it from the earth.

"What happened?" It's tearing me apart to not know.

"I woke up, and his hand was over my mouth. I kicked him squarely, then outmaneuvered him until I had my knife on his throat."

"That's not what I meant."

She stays silent for a long while. "He told me he would wait until I gave in to him. I didn't. Then I escaped, and he trashed the village." Her words are clipped. More grass flies from the earth under her hands.

"None of that is your fault, Imani."

"But this is. He's here because of me—and now all these wonderful, happy, free people are in danger because of me. He said he would find me, Harm. It's my fault he's here." Her chin wobbles.

"Callian is not going to let him hurt anyone. And I'll kill him myself if he lays another finger on you." The words are loaded with emotion, choking their way out.

Her blue eyes, lit up by the moonlight, meet mine. She knows I mean it. And I do. If that filth lays one finger on her ever again, it will be the last thing he ever does.

I will make sure of it.

Callian's gaze meets Imani's over breakfast as she stares at her plate, not eating. She pushes her food around with her fork. I rest a hand on her shoulder, and she responds with a brief look, her brows pushing down as she lets out a sigh and drops her fork. Catori sits down across the table with her plate of food and offers her morning greeting. She must have been gone before Imani woke.

"You were gone early?" I ask.

"I've been with Hanola since dawn," Catori says, stuffing food into her mouth.

"She knows about Mason, then?"

"Yes, and she wants to see you this morning. Imani and I will go out to the training grounds." She nods toward them. Imani mumbles in agreement, and I finish off my food. I wander over to the ladies working in the large communal kitchen, and they take my plate. A particularly ruddy woman with dark hair tied up and an apron covering most of her grey tunic and dark skirt rounds her work bench, holding my hand with a squeeze before ushering me away from their workspace. I return to Imani and plant a kiss on her forehead, the way my father used to do for my mother. She looks up and puts her hand on my chest before resting her forehead below her hand. I wrap a hand behind her neck, and she releases a long sigh.

Her eyes raise to meet mine, and her face is relaxed. She pats my chest. "You shouldn't keep Hanola waiting."

Her hand slides from my body, and I bend down to peck her cheek. An amused scoff comes from Catori, and I turn and make my way to Hanola's home. So many questions float around my mind for Hanola—about the way things are, about her knowledge of the dial, about Enid, and even about Arthur.

Warmth emanates through the half-open doorway of Hanola's home, and before I have the chance to knock, her voice calls me inside.

She sits on her living room floor. I realize I haven't seen her anywhere else, and I wonder if she ever leaves her home.

"Sit, Harmen." She points to the cushion in front of her. I lower myself onto it, and she greets me with a wide smile.

"Good morning, Hanola."

"Catori was here earlier. She told me what happened last night." She straightens on her cushion. "This tells me two things. Firstly, the shadow I saw around you did not belong to you. Secondly, the Guardians will now feel free to infiltrate our forest and our villages if this is not dealt with immediately. But it is complicated, for a few reasons. We have spent the better part of forty years left alone in exchange for food supplies and services, and I intend for it to remain that way. However, in saying that, there has always been a plan sitting in wait to overthrow the Chancellor, when the time was right. The young man who arrived last night is part of that also. I have foreseen it."

I open my mouth to object, and she raises a hand. But how can Mason be part of the solution, when he's an officer for the problem? The fact that this entire plot is so much bigger than just me and a dial takes me by surprise. Hanola must be the most omniscient person I have ever encountered. I stare in awe at her calm demeanor as we discuss the epic task that lies at our feet.

"Tomorrow, we will have guests. It has been some months since their last visit. But these two women are crucial in keeping my people safe, and we have a long-lived understanding. I am hoping that with their help, we can contain the incident with that Guardian. I need you to tell them who you are. Our relationship with them has always been based on honesty. I am certain they would know you exist, but we must be up front with them, so they have all the knowledge they need and can work to keep my people safe. This safety also extends to you and Imani while you reside in our territories." She closes her eyes.

I want to say something reassuring, that I will do anything she asks of me, but I am not sure what is appropriate and whether it is my turn to talk. Before I can put together a response, she opens her eyes, and her face softens.

"Now, it is my turn to share some knowledge with you," she says, turning to the space behind her pillow and picking up a book. It looks just like Enid's field journal. My eyes widen, and as she notices my reaction, something like amusement washes over her features.

"You've seen something similar to this journal before, I assume?"

"Yes, my grandmother gave me her version of it before I left for the wall." My recognition of the timing dawns on my face, and Hanola raises an eyebrow.

"Your grandmother?"

"Yes."

We sit there in silence for a handful of heartbeats, staring at each other.

"This is the twin journal to that of a woman who crossed the wall decades ago. She came searching for a few things, and to deliver a message," Hanola says.

"I knew Enid had been over the wall before, but I didn't know much beyond that."

The mention of her name lights up Hanola's eyes, and the wrinkled edges tighten. She opens her book and hands it to me, and the handwriting on the page she chose strikes me: Enid's.

"All of her knowledge about the plants she brought with her on that visit is in here." She points to the writing quickly before flipping the pages until she reaches a section near the back. "Here, however, is a topic of a different nature. You will recognize some of the names in this diagram. This is your family tree. Enid and her husband, then your mother and your father, and then this symbol under their names is you. Your mother was pregnant with you. As both of your parents held the ability, your ability to manipulate the dial is like none before—even greater than that of its current controller."

Her eyes are steady on my face as she waits for my reaction. I stare back at her, blood flowing faster through my veins as she takes in my understanding. Why doesn't anybody ever tell me the whole story? I grind my teeth and pinch the bridge of my nose, closing my eyes.

"You were the message she was delivering: the news of your imminent birth. She also said there had been a complication, but she never elaborated, only asked us to wait and sit on this information until the time was right."

I open my eyes. Her gaze, trained on my face, never falters.

"Was," I choke out and clear my throat. "*Was* my father. He's dead now. They killed him."

Her brows raise, but she remains silent, waiting for the story to unravel from me. I tell her about my mother leaving her family, about the man who raised and loved me as my real father. I tell her about Barlow's intentions, and the day he was hanged for not turning me in. I tell her about Arthur and Charlie. I tell her about everything that has happened since the day I lost my family. I tell her about Imani. I tell her about my hope of changing the dial and recreating the counties for the better for all. I talk. She listens to every word.

"For one so young, you have lived through so much already," she says and places a hand on each shoulder. "I cannot tell you it will be easy, but what I can tell you is that it's almost time. We've been waiting for you for so long..." Her voice falters. "And I know you will do this; you will be the one to make what is wrong right again. You are the last star to align." She grasps my shoulders and closes her eyes. I close mine, feeling like that is the right thing to do. She starts to hum, a repetitive melody, over and over. After a minute, her hands fall from my shoulders, and I open my eyes. Her hands are in her lap, and her wide eyes stare into mine.

"What do I need to do?" I ask.

"The people must be blended together, on both sides of the wall. We change the dial, then take the tower. That is the order in which it must be done."

"My people will need to be apprised of the details, and we'll need to plan together to make this happen," I say. "My grandmother is the leader of the rebels. She'll need to have as much information as possible to coordinate on our side. Weapons and explosives have been stockpiled to aid us in taking the wall. But without knowing the exact number of Guardians and their locations, we're going in somewhat blind."

"We can discuss those details at another time," she says, hands wandering over the floor for her stick. "For now, I need you to train with Callian, and prepare mentally and physically for when the time comes to put our plan into action. We've waited decades. Waiting another few months for you to build strength and come of age won't make a difference."

She gestures for me to stand. I jump up from the cushion and lower my hands to help her up. Her thin, wrinkled hands grasp mine, and she pulls herself to her feet, leaning on her stick. I stand in front of her, as if waiting to be dismissed. She is still holding my hands and looks up to meet my eyes.

"You will be the salvation so many have hoped for, Harmen. Go now, and make our world the place you have always wished it to be." She drops my hands.

I bow my head to her.

She chuckles at my formality, and I smile before taking my leave. The inside of her home feels too warm now. I walk out the door and suck in a breath. The heaviness in my shoulders transfers to my stomach as I look around at this peaceful village that is home to so many happy people. I think of every village in the sands, home to folks who suffer and barely survive, and the many who don't.

My mother's words echo through my mind. She knew, from the moment I was conceived, what I was to do. *"You take after me, you know. I would have done the same thing. It's in our blood, Harmen."*

I just wish she could have been here to see it.

CHAPTER 24
HARM

Callian stands before me. His large frame bears a belt of knives, and he holds a wooden sword at arm's length. I wield the same piece, but mine sags, my arms burning under the weight of it. He lunges one more time, and I stumble backward, tripping over my own feet. An annoyed grunt comes from Miya, who waits on the boundary of the sparring ring with Imani, Catori, and Jeselle. I drop the wooden sword to the ground and suck air into my heaving chest. I don't have the strength to both attack and spend all my time on the defense—which, I have been told, is how you lose a fight, not win it.

I have been at this for a week, but I am no better. My drive to attack another human is less than nothing. I know I need to be able to fight, but I never imagined weapons.

"Mid-battle is no time to feel bad for your opponent," Miya snaps, and I grapple my sword from the grass and raise it with shaking arms. Imani watches on, her face wrapped in concern as she chews her nails and shifts from foot to foot. She could take me down in minutes. Her training and fire for a fight far outweigh mine as I stand now, opposite Callian, sweat running down my arms, chest, and back. We've trained through the heat and the rain and under the stars, and only a week has passed.

"This is useless. He has no motivation," Catori says.

"Just give him more time to adjust to the weight and put on some bulk," Callian offers in my defense.

"No, we're not waiting. Callian, come here. Harm, take a break," Miya barks.

Callian tosses the wooden sword on the grass at my feet and jogs over to Miya. She whispers something in his ear, and he jerks backward. Tilting her head, she lowers her eyebrows. "Do it."

Callian hesitates before jogging back to the village. I sit on the grass, trying to catch my breath. Imani speaks with Catori, her words short. The irritation in her voice is obvious, and heat rises in my neck and face. I'm thankful that my entire body is already red from exertion; I couldn't bear further humiliation. The grass relents under my back as I lie down and focus on my breathing, stretching my arms to try to relieve the burning. Miya says something to Jeselle before I hear the jogging steps of Callian returning. I lie with my eyes closed, hoping for just a few more minutes before they make me get up.

"Up, filth!" Callian barks.

My eyes fly open, and I rise into a sitting position before I see him properly. He stands over me now, and I gawk up and down at his muscled frame. He is dressed from head to toe in a Guardian uniform, ragged, torn, and dirty.

Mason's uniform.

He kicks my ribs and barks at me again. Heat rises, this time from deep in my gut. My fists ball up. Within seconds, I am standing in front of him, my weapon before me. Every breath burns, but the rest of my body is numb.

He takes a step forward, and I freeze. Blood thunders through my head. Every scream I have ever heard rushes through me. But still, I stay standing, waiting to defend. As if disappointed, Callian braces his shoulders and whips a brief look at where the others are standing. In my peripheral vision, I see Miya swing an arm in front of Imani, holding her back.

"Give me Imani," Callian growls.

Everything goes still, blurring into nothing. Callian's face morphs to Mason's, his voice just as corrosive. My hands clench and unclench around the hard wooden sword, and I grind my jaw tight. The air in my lungs escapes and does not return. The horrendous noise pulsating through my ears barely drowns out the roar that leaves me. Callian flinches, but he says her name over and over.

I draw back the weapon in my hand and carve a path toward his chest. He blocks, the grey shirt shifting over his flexing arms. Every movement of the uniform sends me flashes of the men who wear it. Every encounter that has seen me come off second best to them. Every second Mason held Imani, and I was powerless to stop him. At the gallows, dragging her away from me...

I step sideways and attack with a blow that lands on the grey uniform, sending a shudder down my arm. A grunt comes from the man before me. He lunges again, and I step into his space, connecting my weapon with his. I hold him there before he shoves me aside with one move.

"She doesn't belong to you, filth. She will be mine, whether that's her choice or not."

The moment the words leave his mouth, ringing starts in my ears. I rain down on him with hit after hit, landing every blow with such force that my arms shake against the weapon, which threatens to splinter under my white-knuckled hand every time. Blow after blow, I charge at him. He is on the defensive now. He stumbles backward, and just before I connect with his face, he falls to the grass a couple of steps away. I raise my weapon as I close the gap.

Far-off voices call my name. Ignoring them, I calculate the best place to strike.

Imani's face eclipses the view of his prone body on the grass, so close to mine. The voices are louder. Something warm and soft touches my face—a hand, then another. Sweat runs down my face. My arms lower to my sides, and the cramped hand relaxes, the sword thudding to the ground.

"Harm, stop," she whispers, her eyes pleading.

I search her face, checking for myself if she is okay. My legs sway underneath me, and I drop to my knees. Breath heaves from my chest, and I rest my head on her stomach. I reach up and cling to her shirt.

Behind her, the body moans and rises to its feet. I slam my eyes shut, remembering it's only Callian, not Mason. A heavy hand grasps my shoulder. I pull up to my feet, and every set of eyes is on me.

"I think we just found what motivates Harm," Miya says, winking at Imani and me.

A blush creeps up Imani's face, and she turns to face Miya, stepping backward into my space, arms across her chest. She stands between them and me, protective, as if they have found an open wound and intend to exploit it. Imani's tortured gaze tracks over Mason's tattered uniform, taking in every stain and rip, before she locks eyes with Callian.

"Take that ridiculous uniform off before Harm kills someone," Jeselle utters, her sorrowful gaze fixed on Callian, who as far as I know has never lost a fight.

"I'm sorry," I say to Callian, who starts for the village.

He spins back. "Don't be. She's worth it." There is a flicker of guilt just visible in his gaze. He turns again and makes his way back to the village.

"He'll live." Miya rolls her eyes. "Now that we know what

you're capable of, you can expect harder training." She slaps me on the back. "You can thank me later."

Hanola appears at the edge of the training grounds, waving Catori over. She jogs to her and returns a minute later.

"Hanola wants you to take her to the cells to see Mason. Something to do with a vision she had," she says to Miya, with a raised eyebrow.

Miya wanders toward Hanola. Catori offers to help Jeselle, and they walk off, laughing about something. Imani and I pack up the sparring ring in silence.

The tables are laid out before us like nothing I have ever seen before. Whoever Hanola's guests will be, they are surely welcome. We are all washed and dressed. The women all wear simple dresses, and most of them have their hair down. The men are shaved and wearing their best clothes. The communal space is lit up with lanterns that burn all around the tables, with some hanging from the trees that surround us, like a low blanket of stars just for us. Melodies from the musicians who sit at one end of the gathering drift through the air. Callian and I head to the smaller of the two tables to grab a drink of what he calls forest wine. It's nothing I've ever drunk before, and he waggles his eyebrows and hands me a cup.

It burns all the way down. I am sure this is payback for me flogging him earlier. He laughs as I choke on the last mouthful. His hospitality has been unending since I arrived, and I feel guilty for what happened in the sparring ring. But at least when things happen, I know I am capable of fighting. He drains his cup and gets another. I take another tentative sip. It burns all the way down again, and I put my cup back on the table. Callian shakes his head at me. "You don't have wine over the wall?"

"Is it that obvious?" I scrunch up my face and scan the table for some water. He chuckles before his face straightens and he nods, gesturing behind me.

I turn to see Imani and Catori. Imani wears a light blue dress with a silver-threaded belt. Her hair is down, falling over her chest, meeting the silver trim of the bust of her dress. Her hands hang beside her elegant, curved waist. Catori falls in beside Callian, adjusting his clothes like a mother. Imani's eyes meet mine, and I feel her all the way down to the very center of me. We haven't spoken since the sparring ring. I open my mouth to say something, but nothing comes out.

She steps into my space, and her chest touches mine. I look down, and the depths of her blue eyes swallow me whole. Her face is soft, and the corner of her mouth creeps up. She puts her arms around my neck, and I slide my hand under her hair, holding her. With my free hand, I pull her closer still and hold her there by the small of her back. Her breathing is heavy now, like there is no one else around but the two of us.

"You might want to save that for later," Catori murmurs.

Our attention is drawn to her long enough for us to see a small group of people entering the common area. Leading them is Hanola. She moves steadily to the end of one of the tables. Before anyone speaks, Hanola motions for everyone to find a spot at the tables. Imani and I file in next to Callian, Catori, Miya, and Jeselle, but we remain standing, as the rest of the village does. Hanola's guests stand beside her, hoods over their faces, and for a moment, an anxious wave sweeps over me. I grab Imani's hand. Hanola motions for us all to be seated.

"Tonight, we enjoy the food our lands provide and revel in the company of some of our dearest and oldest friends." She gestures for the food to be brought over and sits. Following her lead, her guests sit before removing their hoods.

I recognize the golden hair first, then the kind eyes of her companion. Nirri and Emmie sit on either side of Hanola. Next to each of them is a Guardian-type officer, but their uniform is different. An older officer with short grey-flecked hair sits by Emmie, smiling and talking across the table. A young man with dark hair and piercing blue eyes sits quietly beside Nirri, studying every person she speaks with. Instead of the light-and-dark grey combination, they wear white-and-grey uniforms, and their shoulders bear no epaulets. Despite their size, their demeanor is not offensive or overbearing. Nirri and Emmie speak to them occasionally, the same way they would to any other person here. I sit, staring at them both, my mouth agape.

I am unaware that Catori is watching me until she speaks. "You've met our guests before, Harm?"

"You could say that. They helped me escape from the prison." I drag my gaze back to her. She smiles and starts piling food onto her plate. I find some for mine. Imani is picking at a small portion of bread while Callian watches Nirri, letting out a long breath.

"Emmie is the Chancellor's wife, and the girl with her is their granddaughter, Nirri," Catori says.

"I didn't know he had a family, let alone a granddaughter," Imani scoffs, still staring at her plate.

Callian tenses, gaze drifting between Imani and me.

"She's much more than that. You're looking at the next Chancellor," Miya adds.

"If there is a next one," I growl.

"Stop talking about her like she's the enemy," Callian grinds out, all amusement now drained from his face.

"My brother has had a thing for Nirri since they were kids," Catori says. "They used to play together every time Emmie would visit. Then they got older, and things changed. Still waiting for you to make your move, little brother."

He tosses a chunk of food at Catori as crimson flushes his face. Imani glances at Callian briefly before tracking back to Nirri.

"You okay?" I ask, leaning into Imani. She looks at her plate before loading more onto it. I wait, my shoulder touching hers, before she turns to me and shoves a bite into her mouth. She holds me there with her gaze before swallowing.

"I'm fine, Harm." She returns to the food in front of her.

I look back at Callian, and he shrugs before digging into his food. We eat in silence. It isn't until Hanola thumps her cup on the table and slowly stands that we bother straying from our plates. The chatter ebbs into silence, and the cutlery stills.

"Tonight, we are blessed to have our two special guests from the tower: Emmaline..." Hanola waves to Emmie. "... and her granddaughter, Nirri," she says, waving a hand in Nirri's direction. "Our bond has been strong for decades, and tonight, we have another reason to celebrate our connection and our people."

Before she says another word, my entire body seizes up.

"We have discovered hope, and it will not be long before all of the peoples on either side of the wall shall have the freedom and the lives we have waited so long for," she says before sitting down.

My gut flips. She's talking about me. Forcing out a long breath, with heat rising in my neck, I shove another mouthful in to try to distract myself.

Emmie stands this time, her cup in hand. "To the people everywhere who have lived under this reign." She lifts her cup, and the folks at the tables follow her lead. Clinking builds like a wave before reaching us. We lift our cups and clink them with one another's. Imani meets my eye when our cups connect. Her gaze is distant, and I can't read her face. She lowers her cup and downs the contents. Slamming it down, she pushes up and stalks away.

Callian's foot connects with my shin, and I wince. He nods his head sideways after Imani, and I rise to follow her. This time, she marches to Catori's house. The door slams behind her. I pull up just short of it.

Without knocking, I shove the door open, slowly. The lanterns are lit, their shimmering lights flickering around the small house. The fire burns low in the hearth. Imani stands with her back to the door, her hands on her hips. The light plays with her curves, reflecting off the blue-and-silver accents of her dress. Her shoulders heave up and down. I pad over to her and stand behind her. Her scent fills my senses, and my body responds to her being so close. This time though, no one is here to interrupt us. I rest my hands on her arms and turn her around.

She looks at the floor. I put my hand under her chin and raise it. Wetness shimmers on her cheeks, and pain shines through her eyes. I wipe away her tears with my thumb, one side and then the other. I trace my finger over her lips. They tremble under my touch, and a fresh cascade of tears runs down her cheeks. I pull her into my arms. She sobs between breaths, grabbing my shirt and balling it up in her fists. I hold her close, wrapping my arms around her. Her smell intoxicates me, a heady feeling in my chest, and my body responds to her against me.

She is breathing into my chest, both hands gripping my shirt. My face is buried in her hair, every exhale building like a rising tide. She moves her hands down my torso and presses her chest to mine. Her heartbeat thumps against my chest. I feel every beat until she releases me and pushes back. Her face is calmer now, but my face is reflected in the tears that still pool in her eyes. She slides a hand behind my neck and runs the tips of her fingers through my hair. Her mouth opens, but nothing comes out.

"What is it, Imani?"

"I just thought..." Her breath hitches, and her chin trembles.

"... you recognized her from..." She pauses again, closing her eyes. "... while we were apart."

Her breath stops.

"They broke me out of the tower prison. Nothing else," I assure her.

Imani searches my face, pulling in a breath.

I cup her face in my hands. "I don't want to talk about them now."

Her gaze intensifies. My hand runs down her neck, tracing the contours of her collarbone, then down her breastbone, only stopping at the bustline of her dress. Her hand slides inside my shirt, the other grabs my collar, and she walks backward until she hits the wall. I keep going until I cover her body with mine. This time her hands run behind my neck, and she pulls my face toward her before covering my mouth with hers. I kiss her back, softly, then harder as I lose the last bit of control I possess. Every part of me aches for her. I am torn between trying to restrain myself and doing what feels so right.

The rap on the door is almost inaudible over the heaviness of our breathing. Imani freezes against me, her hands tightening around my neck. The knock sounds again.

I create space between us, and her hands slide to my chest. Her eyes are locked on mine, chest still racked with impatient breath. She closes her eyes to regain control before releasing me. She steps around me and heads for the door. I bide my time, waiting for my body to deescalate. Light spills into the room as she opens the door to Catori on the other side.

"Hanola needs you both to come back. The dinner is done, but she must speak with you and our guests before she retires for the night." Catori keeps her gaze on Imani. I walk over to where they stand and nod in acknowledgment. Catori walks away, heading for

Hanola's house. Imani looks back at me, her face a mix of desire and concern.

By the time we reach Hanola's, I have my head on straight, filled with thoughts of plans, resources, coordinating two peoples, and so on. We enter the home, and like always, she sits on the living room floor, this time with her two guests. They rise as we enter. I stand beside Imani, waiting for Hanola's instructions. Emmie and Nirri's eyes widen as both of their gazes reach my face.

CHAPTER 25
IMANI

Nirri throws her knife and hits the bullseye before returning to stand beside me. A year younger than me, she is swifter, kinder, and taller. I watch as she makes the task seem easy and effortless. My mind is elsewhere today. All I can think about is Mason being here. Why would he risk his post with the regime to come here? Something doesn't make sense about it all. And why would my father task him with holding me, if that is what he was doing? With every passing thought, I grow more restless.

"Your turn, Imani," Nirri says, bringing me back to earth.

"Yep."

She raises an eyebrow, but falls in behind me. I throw the knife with every mixed, horrible, confused feeling I have for my father and Mason. It misses by a mile, and someone yards away shouts at me. I storm back to the line, and Nirri takes another knife from the rack. She positions her feet and rolls her shoulders back. The wind tosses her perfect blonde curls around her neck, and she takes a breath before releasing the knife with swift force. Bullseye. I groan silently and rip a knife from the rack. I try to copy her process, feet apart, shoulders back, breathing in. The knife flies madly toward the target and clips the edge before falling onto the grass. I let out a growl and stalk past Nirri. I'm done for the day.

"Imani, wait up!" Nirri calls, her footsteps quickening before she falls in beside me. "What's up? You've been doing this longer than me. Callian said you're usually so great at the knives."

"Nothing," I say, hoping she won't press the issue.

"No." She grabs my arm in an elegant hold, and I stop, spinning on my heel to look at her. I can't control the grief in my eyes now.

"It's not nothing," she says, her voice soft, like her grasp on my arm. Even her annoyance is gentle.

"I can't stand it," I hiss, tearing my arm from her loose grip. I feel ridiculous, but nothing can stop this feeling. "Mason, here, locked in the prison. I should be happy he's caged, like he did to me. But I..."

"But you're not?" she finishes my thought.

"No." I search the ground for some kind of logic in my overwhelming empathy for Mason. "I'm not."

"Did you feel that way when you had your blade to his throat?"

Stunned, I meet her gaze, mouth agape.

"Callian told me."

"Yes. No..." I close my eyes and release a low groan. "I don't know." Maybe the dampness of this place has seeped into my brain. Or more likely, it's the kindness.

"Oh," she says. Her hands go to her chest, and she grasps the knife belt that lies across it. "Do you want to see him? I know a thing or two about the regime. Maybe he didn't have a choice either, Imani." Her gaze wanders back to the sparring ring, where Callian and Harm pace around each other.

The fire in me flickers to embers, but heat flushes my face.

"You know, when Harm told my grandmother his story last

night, I felt off. I'm not a desert dweller, and I don't claim to know what it feels like to live the way your people do. And I feel…" She hesitates. "… guilt. I feel guilty for all that Harm and others have gone through, because of my grandfather. Some of us are helpless against this regime, and others have no choice."

I frown and shift on my feet. She's talking about the Guardians. "Did I mention that I'm not a fan of your grandfather?"

Nirri huffs through a laugh. "Not many people are. And not many people are welcoming enough to let us visit, but Hanola and my grandmother have been good friends for decades."

"Will you come with me?" I ask. There are things I want to say to Mason, and I could never take Harm with me to the cells. Catori doesn't think me visiting is a good idea.

She nods, but pulls out a thin piece of cloth and wraps it around her face before wrapping up her hair. "So he doesn't recognize me," she explains, then gestures for me to lead the way.

The cells in the forest village are no more than wooden cages sitting on the permanently slimy mud floor under one roof. The smell hits us before anything else, moldy wood and stale human waste almost making my stomach fly out of my throat. All prisons, I realize in that moment, are much the same: they only exist for human suffering, no matter what side you're on. The green-and-grey-clad guard waves us in, but stands in the doorway behind us as a precaution. We pick our way through the narrow passageway to the last cell. The poor light is accompanied only by the trickling sounds of water and the moaning of the few inmates that inhabit the place. I wait for my eyes to adjust.

The outline of Mason's naked body stops my breathing. It never occurred to me when Callian took his clothes that he wouldn't return them. Or maybe Mason refused to take the uniform back; who would know? I step up to the bars of his cell. He sits on a small wooden stool at the back of the cage. His head hangs low, like he has fallen asleep reading a book. Nirri falls in beside me and lets out a low breath. Mason looks up, and his face is drawn and grey. His once muscular and overpowering body has thinned, his ribs showing. His sandy hair hangs in his face, and he shivers in the damp air.

"Have you seen enough?" Nirri whispers.

"One more minute." I try to remember what I wanted to tell him. But I am torn between hatred, guilt, and shame. Hatred for the face that tormented me, guilt for his current state, and shame for being here without telling Harm. "Okay, let's go."

We walk away from the cell back through the damp, dimly lit forest prison.

"Imani." His voice is weak.

I stop dead in my tracks. Nirri grabs my hand, holding me to the spot. I turn and stare. He stands holding the bars with both hands, legs trembling in the cold with no clothing. I edge closer to his cell until I am standing face to face with him. His light blue eyes, which held such ferocity when I was imprisoned in his home, scaring me to death for days, are now sunken and defeated. Sadness is the only emotion they let through now.

My body trembles, both from the hard memories that hold those same eyes, and from the shock of seeing another human's deterioration in front of me, knowing I've played a significant part in it. His gaze searches mine, his mouth open. No words leave his lips. I swallow, gripping the hem of my tunic in both hands as my heart races alongside my mind.

"We should go," Nirri says softly behind me.

I turn and continue walking toward the exit.

"Imani, please let me explain!" Mason's strained calls follow every step I make.

I stride into the sunshine outside, and Nirri encloses me in a firm hug before ordering one of the forest guards away on errand.

Minutes later, she hands me over to a warm and familiar body that hugs me tight before sweeping me up into his arms. I lay my head on Harm's chest and command myself to regain my composure before we reach wherever it is that he's taking me.

This time, the house that we return to is not Catori's; it's Callian's. Once we are through the door, everything is similar to Catori's, but with less furniture, and clothes hang over the changing screen instead of in neat piles. Small bunks sit on either side of the space. They must have replaced Harm's sleeping mat.

Harm lays me on one and lowers himself to the floor beside me. I lie on my side, trying to tell him why I was there. I inhale and try to form the string of words before closing my mouth and eyes. Everything I wanted to scream at Mason now seems insignificant under the tide of things I want to tell Harm to explain why I was there, the things that crash through my mind every time someone brings up how badly he was hurt in the prison. He slips his hand around mine and rests his head on the bunk beside me. I put my hand around his neck and run my fingers through his hair. He moans softly, and I fight back the ragged breath that threatens to tear me to pieces just being this close to him.

"I'm sorry you had to go there by yourself," Harm says. "I should have taken you days ago, but I didn't want you anywhere near Rayner."

"Nirri went with me," I choke out. "I just wanted to say something to him, but when I saw him, I couldn't get the words out. I wanted to tell him he would never be free again, and how he would go to his grave having never touched me the way he wants to."

Harm lifts his head, eyes burning with fury. "He knows that, Imani," he says, his voice raw. My heart flutters in my chest; I'm scared that I have upset him.

"Why are we in Callian's house?"

"Catori told us not to let you near Mason. Now I understand why. I didn't want her finding out you went there."

I pull my hands away from him and wrap my arms around my chest.

"Mason can be dangerous," he goes on. "Unless he defects properly, I doubt Hanola will ever let him leave that cell."

Part of me doesn't believe that anymore—not after what I just saw.

"What happened that made you want to go in there?"

"Nirri was telling me about when she found you. I wanted to scream at someone. Mason is just as responsible as Fletcher for you being there. I thought he deserved it. But I..." I pull in a breath. "I didn't expect to see him like that."

"Prison is not a pleasant place for anyone. It might be best to stay away from Mason. I will see that he gets some clothes." He gets up, and I push up and stand next to the bunk.

"Harm," I call as he goes to leave. He comes back to me, standing just short of close enough, and I grab his hands in mine. My heart races as the words form in my mind. "If Hanola would Blend us, would you want to be Blended?"

He studies my face before speaking. "Considering that I'm not able to exist without you, we should probably do that." He grins and kisses my forehead, then one cheek, then the other. A soft kiss lands on my nose, and my body wakes up with his touch. Finally, his mouth meets mine. The breath between us turns ragged, and I grab his shirt and ball it up with both fists. I pull him around to the bunk and push him backward. He sits on the bunk and looks up at me. The flickering light from the fire beside us throws shadows over his face, and I step between his legs. His head rests on my stomach, and he grabs my hips with both hands. He lets out a long breath, and I force back a giggle. After a minute, he looks back up at me.

"Well, if you want to do things properly, we can ask Hanola to Blend us. Then we can finish this conversation," he says, his eyes never leaving mine, a smile growing over his gorgeous face. I grab his hands and pull him up and close to me. He wraps both arms around me and sinks his face into my hair. "I've waited a lifetime for you, Imani. When I take my last breath, I will still be yours."

"And I yours. Where you go, I go," I whisper.

He groans and lifts me onto his hips, one hand under my bottom and one hand around my shoulder, kissing my neck and mouth. I have to fight the urge to rip his shirt from his chest. He nips my ear and drops me to the ground. I land on my feet, and he spins me around to face the door. Stepping around me, he presses a kiss to my forehead before leading me outside by the hand. It takes me a few moments to catch my breath and realize we're heading back to the training ground. This will be the last of our training for the day, and then supper.

CHAPTER 26
HARM

Callian and I have been standing around this old wooden table longer than we should have. Imani, Nirri, and Miya are mulling over one strategy after another. So far, the only thing we have come up with that has unanimous agreement is that the easy part is manipulating the dial itself. That task, of course, falls to me. I have found the old notes in my grandfather's workbook from my workshop in Amondo. The drawings that I found long ago, dog-earing the pages, turned out to be the cradle the dial itself rests in. Emmie identified it immediately, revealing the story of its making and my grandfather's skill in designing and creating it—long before anyone suspected its use would result in the oppression of the people.

Emmie sketched out the layout of the prison near Etonia—the entire length of the wall, the wall prison, the tower, and prisons—before retiring to bed. Her help and Nirri's knowledge of the Guardians' numbers and locations help more than they know. This information must be relayed to Jonah and Enid. Miya yawns, and we agree to reconvene after training tomorrow afternoon.

"One last thing before you all go," Hanola starts. "I have

decided that the best course of action for the young Guardian we are currently holding is that of rehabilitation. He will start integrating into the village as of tomorrow, during the day, then he'll go back into confinement at night until I decide he has made sufficient progress. Catori, you will be overseeing his movements and schedule. If we are to create a new world from all of this, we start now: we start with the first person we can help. If anyone has a problem with my decision, I suggest you find it in yourself to understand life from his perspective, and what is best for everyone moving forward." She searches the faces before her, finding some stunned, some indifferent. Mine is twisted between the two, as I'm torn between needing things to change and wanting to keep Imani safe.

"Harm, can you deliver the message to him, please?" Hanola's gaze catches mine.

I know it is not a request; Hanola calls the shots around here. So, I suck in a long, ragged breath and nod. She offers me a small smile before turning and walking further into her home toward the fire.

Great. Just great.

The guard opens the door for me, and I stop in front of Rayner's cell. He is curled up in the corner on a bunk far too small for his frame, eyes closed, breaths steady. He's asleep. I temper the annoyance rising in my core.

"Rayner, wake up."

He cracks an eye, sitting up and lets his head fall backward onto the wall, gaze finding mine. His face is blank. Maybe he thinks he's dreaming.

"Hanola has a message for you."

"Whatever you've come to say, I'm not interested, Travesci. If you haven't noticed, I'm the bad guy."

I want to tell him it is the choices he's made that landed him here, but we both know that's not the case. Hanola's wisdom replays in my mind: none of us ever had a choice.

"Whatever you say, Mason." I think about turning and leaving him here to rot, but Hanola gave me an order, so I push my shoulders back and drag in a lungful of air.

"You are to be rehabilitated as a civilian. Hanola's orders. That was her message."

He stares at me as if I have just offered him the moon, mouth agape.

I step closer, until I am all but touching the filthy bars of his cell. "Don't screw this up, Rayner."

He gets out of bed and pads over to the bars. He stands at the same height as me, and for the first time in our lives, he isn't bigger than me. My training has bulked me up, and I surpass his pitiful state right now.

"About holding Imani..." he starts.

I hold a hand up and shake my head. He closes his mouth, but stands there waiting for me to respond. Instead, I turn on my heel and stalk toward the door.

"It's not what you think, Travesci."

His words trail off as I slam the prison door behind me. Too tired to spend another minute on Rayner, I wander home with Callian, and my eyes are closed before my head hits the pillow.

Our days have been spent in training. My clothes that once hung off my lean frame are now tight over the bulk of new muscle.

Callian tosses me some new clothes, and to my surprise, they are the same as my old ones, just slightly larger and newer.

"My father isn't a warrior; he's a lumber smith. This ought to fit you," he says.

"Thank you. These are getting a bit tight." I pull my shirt off over my head and throw the new one on. The cotton cloth sits comfortably over my bulkier frame, and I tug the trousers up and fasten them with my old belt. My boots look shabby and old under the newer clothes.

We pad over to breakfast, where Catori and Imani wait for us, ready in their training clothes. I pile food onto my plate. Part of me will never get used to a surplus of food. Once our bellies are full and everyone is fully awake, we make our way to the training grounds.

Today our rotation has us running with sacks of sand, all weighted equally, and our laps increase as we progress down the line. Callian takes off with his sack over his shoulder and makes it back from his first lap before I set off on mine. The sack sits heavily but comfortably over my right shoulder, and I run hard to reach the end and come back. Imani and Miya are sparring in the ring with knives. I take a moment to catch my breath and watch them dance around each other with intense agility. Callian grunts, back from his second round, bringing me back to the sack on the ground in front of me. I haul it onto my left shoulder and take off for the two laps on the second run. By the time I return, I'm breathing hard. The next run takes four laps. On the last lap, my legs begin to burn, turning to lead with every step closer to the line. Breathless, I let the sack fall and plonk myself on top of it before my legs fail me completely.

Callian returns from his last run and does the same. "She's a good fighter, Imani. She has quick feet and an even quicker mind," he says.

We both sit there, watching her dance around Miya with her knives out. Her lean body works smoothly under her clothes. Her hair is wrapped up in the blue scarf I gave her, tied under her hair at the back.

"She's always been fiery." I chuckle.

Callian laughs from deep in his chest. After a moment, the grin falls from his face, and he shifts on his seat. "You're lucky, Harm. Not all of us get what we want." His last words are a mere whisper.

I look down, scuffing my feet in the grass beneath me.

"Some of us wait years for what you two have and don't find it, or simply can't have it," he says.

"Nirri?"

He hangs his head, nodding. He sucks in a breath. How that might happen between Callian and the Chancellor's granddaughter, I have no idea.

Callian stands, and I follow his lead. All I know is that I am grateful for Imani and the friends we have found.

The lunch break was short, the air damp around us. We hover around the table in Hanola's home, plotting what movements to make and when. We are elbow deep in maps when I feel a tap on the shoulder. I turn to look behind me and Hanola stands there, supported by one of her many walking sticks, beckoning for me to follow her. The others continue to talk tactics as I follow her to the living room floor. As always, I sit in front of her and wait for what she needs to tell me.

"I've been watching you and Imani. I know your history, and the great lengths both of you have gone to for each other," she starts. I put my hands in my lap, wondering where she is going with this. "I am aware that on your side of the wall, two people can be Blended at the age of eighteen," she says.

I nod in agreement, now knowing where this is going. I have been meaning to approach Hanola for days, but training and war talks have taken up most of my time.

"On our side of the wall, we have a similar practice," she says, one eyebrow raised. "So, I would like to offer up our village for you to hold a ceremony, if you're both ready—and a home, for as long as you remain here." She takes my hands and holds them, waiting for me to respond.

I have to remember to breathe. Memories of my parents' home and their life together circle through my mind, and all the occasions when my mother spoke to me about being Blended. I think of the dreams I used to have of the girl in the trees, who was and always has been Imani. I realize I haven't responded, and I suck in a breath.

"I will talk with Imani and see what she wants to do," she says.

I already know what her response will be. Hanola keeps my hands in hers, and her face straightens out.

"It is far from my place to tell you what to do. But if you'll take some advice from an old lady, it's better that you have your day and enjoy each other before you go to battle with Arthur. You won't be in the same mindset or have time for something as special as this once things are set in motion." Her eyes communicate something resembling regret, and she releases my hands with a pat. I nod and rise from the cushions, returning to the table.

The chatter still revolves around what, when, and where, but my mind is elsewhere now. My gaze lingers on Imani as she talks with Miya. The breath halts in my chest. My stomach plummets. I need air.

I stride through the door and suck in air like I'm drowning. I bend over, gripping my knees. The possibility of only having limited time left with Imani suffocates me.

After moments of panic and forcing every breath in and out of my chest, I return to the table. Standing beside Imani, I slide my hand into hers, and she leans into me while she talks to Miya about who should go in what group for the siege of the tower. My gaze falls to the map. Callian and Catori have made red marks on all the positions that have Guardians. Then it hits me, in their moments of discussion of taking out officers of the Guardian Regime, that Imani may come up against her father. I have no doubt that she hates him to the core—but asking her to kill him, should it come to that, would be too much.

I swallow down the bitter thought and listen to the tactics Catori is spelling out to Callian. He, the trained warrior, stands with his arms folded over his chest as his older sister barks out orders. Even though she is a huntress and he a warrior of this village, as second-in-command under Hanola, she holds authority over all the forest people in this home. The evidence of its success lies all around us—a forest territory filled with happy, prosperous, and free people. Such a concept would never be allowed on our side of the wall, and I wonder what life would have been like if the women were at the helm instead. In that moment, I vow that when things change, the person who has the suitable skill and knowledge is to be appointed to a given vocation, regardless of their gender. Plans are made and tasks delegated before we all retire to bed.

Callian and I have a journey to make.

The fire in Imani's eyes is like nothing I have seen before. "No way! You can't do this!"

"I don't have a choice. We need everyone to be on the same

page. Nobody apart from me and you knows their way around on the other side of the wall, and you sure as hell are not going!" I match her tone.

"You self-absorbed ass! I'm not the one with a price on my head!" she spits. "And don't you ever, for even a second, think you control what I do!" She stalks through the open door of Catori's home and slams it behind her. The murmurs of the village folk who had stopped what they're doing to watch us peter out, and they return to their tasks.

I run my hands through my hair and pace back to Callian's house. I knew she wouldn't be happy, but it's not like I have a choice. I don't want to leave, but Callian won't be safe on his own over the wall, nor will he know where to go or who to connect with. I rip out my rucksack from under the bunk, mindlessly stuffing a handful of items in for the journey.

Hanola has promised a Blending ceremony for Imani and me when I return. I was hoping Imani would be too excited about that to worry about my short trip over the wall, and I feel guilty for underestimating her. She has been ordered to stay here to train and help organize the ceremony. A small house on the edge of the village is empty, and Catori is taking Imani there today to clean it up and start getting it ready for the night of the ceremony. I would much rather do that than go back over the wall.

"You ready?" Callian says from the doorway.

"Yeah, nearly." I consider whether to go see Imani before I

go. I don't want to be in her space if she doesn't want me there, but I don't want to leave without saying goodbye either. I shove my knives in the belt across my chest and slide a longer one into my waist belt. The rucksack thumps my back when I toss it over my shoulder. The traveling robe I came in hangs across the changing screen, and I rip it down and shove it under one arm, noting the wrap still rolled up in it. I head for the door, where Callian stands loaded up with weapons and a rucksack of his own. A traveling robe is rolled up and tied up under his rucksack.

We head through the village in silence. Catori's home is only a few houses away. Callian looks at me before looking toward Catori's place, and he hangs back, letting me go ahead. I look back at him before taking tentative steps up to the door. I push it open. "Imani?"

Something shatters as it connects with the door with a loud crash. I push the door all the way open. A ceramic jar lies in pieces on the floor. Imani sits on her sleeping mat, silent, her head in her hands, but her body is trembling. I drop my rucksack at the threshold and walk over to her, kneeling in front of her. She doesn't look up, doesn't move. I put my hands around her head and lift her face.

Pain controls every single inch of her face. My heart races faster by the second, threatening to splinter at any moment. Wiping away the tears on her face, I kiss her forehead, both her cheeks, and then her mouth. She sobs under my touch. Tears leave my own face now and splash on her cheeks beneath mine.

"I will come back to you, Imani," I whisper, choking on her name before I release her face and rise. I walk to the door. Heart hammering in my chest, breaths too shallow, I pick up my rucksack and close the door behind me. I know it is a risk going over the wall, and being apart again wasn't the plan. I replay the pain on Imani's face, and a weight pushes down on my chest.

Callian waits by the next house over, and I catch up. I wipe my face dry with my sleeve, taking in deep breaths. He shoots me a reassuring look as we near the edge of the village. I look back briefly before we break into a run to travel through the forest.

After two days and nights of traveling through the forest, we reach the wall. I search for the right stone to press, finding it much easier than before. The bulky door slowly slides to one side, and I hunt for the second stone before the light around us disappears. Callian stands behind me, his breathing the only other audible sound in the small, dark space. My hands caress the wall and finally locate the stone as it recedes under the weight of my hand. A crack of burning light materializes in front of us, and I throw an arm up to protect my eyes. The desert sun hasn't invaded my gaze for weeks, and I wait for my eyes to readjust to the intense brightness.

"Harsh sun, brother," Callian says.

I chuckle at his words and step into the sands, and something sentimental finds me. The grains of sand glitter under my boots as we trudge through the dense body of dunes around us. We are heading for the outlying village where Enid and Jonah are living. Last time I traveled this stretch, I ran most of the way, at night. Running during the day would be unwise, so we plan to find a place to hide and wait it out until night falls.

In the distance, just before the northern horizon, stands a Guardian outpost. We keep southwest of it and don't stop until we reach a rocky outcrop that encompasses a small cavern surrounded by sparse clumps of desert flowers. I head into the relatively cooler space and check for recent activity before gesturing for Callian to follow me inside. We flop to the cool ground and remove our traveling robes. Chugging water, Callian lays his head back and rubs his temple with his free hand.

"You okay?" I ask.

"I think I'm dehydrated already. My head is throbbing."

"Lie down and rest. I'll wake you up when the sun goes down."

He pulls off his rucksack and positions his large frame within the limited shade of the overhanging rock. I pull out Enid's field journal and flip through the pages before pulling out Hanola's field journal and turning through its pages. It occurs to me that these two women have been planning this for decades, communicating only when necessary, their ideals the same, their people their main focus. I flip through both journals, noting the identical information they took down. The journals note all the small ways they could both help their people without drawing attention, biding their time until they were ready to reverse the effects of the dial.

Biding their time until I came along.

CHAPTER 27
IMANI

Mason sits next to Catori, eyes fixed on the colorful cushion beneath him. He is wearing new clothes, the same as Harm's button-up collared shirt and pants, and they fit a little loose over his thinner frame. He has had a shave, and his hair is combed. His light blue eyes are prominent now that he has cleaned up. Hanola's gaze takes in all three of us as she sips her tea from a ceramic mug, chipped from years of use. She seems to consider the three of us before she moves on her cushion, sitting taller.

"If we have any chance of taking control of the dial, Harm needs the parchments that detail how to control it. That information is vital to his success," Hanola says.

I study her face, and her eyes bore into mine. Mason glances at Catori for the hundredth time since we sat down. I can't tell if he's scared of her or fascinated by her. She gives him a bored sideways look.

"I will do whatever it takes to help Harm," I say, my words soft. I know the weight that statement can hold.

"Good, I was counting on that. Mason, you'll need to cooperate fully with this new plan. And I expect, in exchange for your freedom and our support, you will commit yourself to this role and help Imani."

Mason nods. "I'll help in any way I can."

"Good, good. A good start to a new life, young man." She winks at him.

Gratitude fills his eyes, and his mouth wobbles slightly. It is a softer side of Mason that I doubt anyone else could have found but Hanola. Catori holds her grandmother's gaze for a moment before shifting it to me. If she has a problem with Mason being out of prison, she isn't letting on. Harm was reluctant at first, but I can see Hanola's point. As much as I hate the Guardians, they have about as much control over their lives as the desert dwellers do.

"So, just to confirm, you want Mason and I to carry out this task when Harm goes into the tower? Shouldn't we get the parchments before that?" I ask.

"Maybe, but that would mean a preliminary visit to the tower. Every time we enter, we risk discovery or worse. One visit with you all there. If he can change the dial without the parchments, excellent. But you will be obtaining them while he gets a preliminary look at the dial. That way, if he cannot alter it, you will come home with the parchments for him to study so he can try again. And we will have the upper hand with the dial."

"But what if we're caught?" Mason asks.

"Then you use the prior arrangement you had with your commanding officer to your advantage, young man," Hanola says. They exchange a look, and Mason agrees. What is Hanola talking about?

"What prior arrangement?" Catori asks, echoing my concern.

"That's for another time my girl. And this conversation stays between the four of us. Do you understand?"

We all agree, but Catori's eyes are fixed on Hanola's. Her brows lower. Hanola raises a hand, and Catori sighs, dropping her gaze.

"That will be all for now." Hanola indicates that she wants to rise, and Catori jumps up, helping her to her feet.

Mason and I walk out the front door and wait for Catori. What isn't she telling us? She stalks past us and grabs Mason's arm roughly. He follows her for a moment before planting his feet. She spins to face him. "What are you doing?"

"I need a moment with Imani."

Alternating my gaze between Mason and Catori, I stay rooted to the spot. Finally, I nod.

She drops her hand from his arm. "Fine, I'll be a couple houses down. Behave."

Mason's lips crack into a crooked smile, and I swear Catori's face reddens, if only for a second. We both watch as she wanders two houses down and leans against the wood, plucking a dagger from her chest belt to clean her nails. Her focus is split between her knife and her charge, Mason. I doubt she can hear us from there. Even ex-Guardians get respect here. Trust and respect are earned and kept, and everything is smothered in kindness. I wish the desert side could be like this one day.

Mason turns to face me, and I brace for whatever he's going to come out with next.

"About the arrangement I had with your..." He shoves his hands in his pockets. "... with the commander."

"What about it? Why does it include me?"

He dips his head with a breathy laugh. "Back in Etonia, when you were at my house, I—"

"That? Do you always follow orders to the letter, Mason?"

"Not all of us have the luxury of disobeying your father, Imani. And there was more to it than just holding you out of sight." He shifts on his feet, but holds my gaze, pausing for a moment. "What do you think about Hanola's plan?"

"The part where we work together?" I roll my eyes at him and track my gaze to something else—anything other than Mason's face. I am having trouble processing this softer, more humane side of him.

"Imani?"

"I'll do whatever I have to for Harm and for our people," I say, closing my eyes and pinching the bridge of my nose.

"Good, I guess," he says, his words timid.

"You *guess*?" I snap my head up.

"I mean, I won't let you down. Believe it or not, we want the same things."

I huff a sadistic laugh and meet his gaze. The fire in mine makes him fidget.

"Actions before words, Mason." My hand touches my cheek as the memory of his hand slapping my skin pulses to life. His gaze hits the ground.

He opens his mouth to speak, and I raise a hand.

"Don't."

I turn on my heel before I say something I regret. We need to get past our differences if we're going to have any chance of making this assignment of Hanola's work.

"I'm sorry, Imani." His voice echoes behind me, his words strong and true.

"Yeah, right," I mutter under my breath and walk away.

"Imani." My name is almost a plea.

I stop, staring at the grassy ground beneath my feet.

"For what it's worth, I thought I was doing you a service, helping you stay alive," Mason says.

I stalk back to where he stands. He leans back a little as I broach his space. "Oh, really? Well, what was all that talk about submitting to you or never seeing the light of day?"

He shifts on his feet, pushing his hands through his sandy hair. His composure breaks, his throat working before he clears it. "I said I was trying to help, not that I'm a saint." Breathing out a chuckle, his light blue eyes study my face, as if he's considering it now. I shake my head at him, and he steps back, shoving his hands in his pockets. "Lucky for you, you're not my type," he mutters, his gaze wandering to where Catori stands.

"See that it stays that way." I spin and stalk off, but pause a few steps away, turning back. "While we're shooting the breeze..." I cross my arms over my chest. "Why did you come here, then? Why not just let me leave?"

"I was afraid that if Fletcher found out I let you escape, we'd both end up on the wrong end of the Chancellor's rope."

I hold his gaze as his jaw clenches.

"The Chancellor ordered your execution, Imani. But it was conditional. Only if we couldn't..." The words trail off.

"Couldn't what?"

Mason tilts his head, face twisting with something like disgust. "If we couldn't contain you."

The fire in my belly peters out.

"Fine. Do not screw this up, Mason."

He salutes me and smiles, the first cheekiness I have seen from him since we were twelve. Something odd twists in my chest—a sliver of compassion for him, maybe.

I roll my eyes at him and storm home.

CHAPTER 28

HARM

A familiar face opens the door after the third knock. His expression takes no time to form and is a mixture of delight and concern. Without a word, Jonah pulls me in for a hug, disregarding the pack on my back and my companion to my left. My body aches from running through the night, and the small, warm rays of the dawn light produce a new wave of sweat. My robe clings to me as I peel it from the saturated clothes underneath. Callian removes his robe as well, including his wrap, and Jonah studies him carefully, gaze instantly moving to the fitted warrior clothing.

"Harmen, you look like a good wash wouldn't go astray. It's good to see you, my boy. Who's your friend?" He beams, holding me at arm's length.

"Jonah, this is Callian, from one of the forest villages over the wall. He's a warrior and a grandson to Hanola, who you already know of." Pride swells as the words come.

Jonah ushers us both in, scanning beyond the door before shutting it, most likely checking if we were followed.

"It's nice to meet you, Jonah. Imani speaks of you very fondly and often," Callian says with a wide smile.

Jonah's eyes widen, and he walks to the kitchen table and grabs it with both hands, half bent over. His stunned gaze finds mine. I probably should have started with the fact that Imani is alive and well. His eyes bore into me.

"Imani is in the village we came from. She would have come with us, but she has other duties at the moment," I say.

Jonah's eyebrow raises at that.

"She's training with Callian's sister," I offer, holding back the part about our Blending ceremony, realizing this is something I should have talked to Jonah about before agreeing to Hanola's offer.

"I see. And you've come to see your grandmother? She isn't here. Christopher and Maryanne are out back though. You ought to see them." He pads down the hall, and Callian and I follow.

"I'm sorry I didn't send word about Imani. I didn't know how."

Eyes laced with hurt, he turns back to look at me. "Don't worry about it. I figured if she was alive, you would find her."

"She found me, actually." I offer a meek smile.

"Of course she did," he murmurs and walks ahead. He reaches the door and stops, his hand on the handle, pausing. He turns back, meeting my gaze, face tight, brows lowered. "There's something you should know before we step outside."

"Oh?"

Callian stands quietly beside me, taking in Jonah and the home around him.

"The poisoning of the wells has gotten bad. The entire village of Amondo is gone—all of them except a few, that is." Wistfully, he turns back to the door, pushing through it.

I stand frozen, my breath gone.

Arlo's family, gone.

Felicity and Enora, gone.

My father's friends, gone.

All the boys I helped that selection day, gone.

Mason's family, gone.

Callian's heavy hand touches my shoulder. Dozens of men we had counted on for the rebellion are also gone. I swallow. We push through the door, following Jonah. He moves slowly over to where Christopher and Maryanne sit in two weathered wooden chairs. The sun glints through Maryanne's thinning hair. She sits beside her husband, book in hand, covered in a light blanket, despite the rising heat from the morning sun.

Christopher pushes up from his chair and hugs me close, but my eyes are fixed on the pale and drawn face of Maryanne. Her thin hands set the book down, eyes almost vacant. I force myself to breathe. Christopher releases me, and I move to kneel in front of Maryanne. She grabs my hands. Hers feel so light and frail.

"What happened?" I ask Christopher.

"Poison. The well was contaminated, and the people didn't realize. I got Maryanne out before it got too bad, but the poison has wrecked her body. She's improved a little, but the healer here says this is as good as we can expect. Most of the others didn't survive." His voice is so soft, trembling on every word.

"Who contaminated the well?" Callian asks, gaze swinging between Christopher and Jonah.

"Guardians," I reply.

I get to my feet and walk back inside. Jonah and Callian follow, and we sit in the living room. I hang my head between my knees and clasp my hands behind my head.

"We came to coordinate the movement of both sides of the wall, to put an end to all this," I say softly from between my knees.

"Good," Jonah says.

"We just need to gather your side, and the forest dwellers will be ready to go in a couple months." I rise, putting my shoulders back.

"We've been gathering men since you left. We have around five hundred from various villages, not including the men we lost in Amondo," Jonah says. This is encouraging.

"We strike in two months," I say. "That gives everyone time to organize themselves around the plans and strategies we've devised."

"You sound like Christopher now. Good thing; I don't think he'll be able to leave Maryanne now," Jonah says.

"No word from Enid?" I ask, thinking he must be missing her with all that has been happening around him.

"Nothing, but she'll be safe. She isn't the leader of the rebels for nothing, son," he quips, forcing a smile. I chuckle a little, trying to lighten the mood.

Jonah gets up to put together breakfast, while I show Callian to my room to view the stockpile of weapons that Christopher has hauled in from various merchants over the last six months. His eyebrows raise at the sight of the explosives. They have been stored away for decades; I pray they still work after all this time.

We shut the door to the spare room, which was once mine, and join Jonah in the kitchen for bread and stew. Callian chews politely, but I can only imagine his struggle to swallow this after the food he's used to.

"There's something else I need to talk to you about, Jonah," I say, and he looks up from his bowl. Callian meets my gaze and suppresses a smile, then grabs his food and heads to the living room. I smile meekly at his back. Jonah spoons another mouthful in. "When I return to the village over the wall, there's going to be a ceremony."

Immediately, I regret my choice of words, knowing I should

have been asking, not telling. Jonah stares back at me, chewing on the pasty grains. Waiting, he nods.

"For Imani and me." My breath catches, and the spoon in my hand suddenly feels heavy between my fingers. I wait, trying to gauge his reaction.

He takes his time, swallowing his food. I shift in my seat. My face is frozen, and my mouth goes dry. Then Jonah hits the table with his fist and bursts out laughing, his hearty chuckle echoing through the house. "About time, son!" He slides his hand over the table between us, like a handshake of sorts. I reach out and connect my hand with his. For the first time, my hands look more like a man's and less like a boy's next to Jonah's. I breathe out, and he laughs again.

"I have a request for you though," I say.

He squeezes my hand before going back to his food. "What is it?" he asks between mouthfuls.

"I want you there, for Imani. She would want you there."

He stops chewing. His nostrils flare, and moisture fills his eyes. "Wouldn't miss it for the world, Harm."

Clearing his throat, he scrapes up the dregs of his bowl. I shovel food into my mouth before my chest explodes, breathing my way through the last of my stew. I stand and collect the bowls, dump them in the sink, and set to washing them for the next meal.

A hand clamping on my shoulder makes me turn my head. Jonah stands beside me, silver lining his hazel eyes. He nods before walking into the living room.

The rest of the day and most of the next, we sit around maps and talk strategy with Jonah and sometimes Christopher. His attention is mostly on Maryanne, and my heart breaks every time he walks her to and from their room.

"Any updates on Fletcher?" I ask Jonah.

"Nothing out of the ordinary, just his usual behavior, and the situation with the wells. He seems to have busied himself with tormenting those who are still here. But I doubt he's given up looking for you, Harm."

"Who's Fletcher? And why does that name sound familiar?" Callian asks.

"Imani's father," I murmur.

Recognition lights up his face, and it takes a few moments for him to respond. "Oh."

"Mason is—well, *was* his first officer."

"And now he's our prisoner." Callian's face is triumphant.

"Not exactly a prisoner," I mutter.

Jonah shakes his head. "How the tables have turned."

With all the plans laid out and Jonah and Christopher up to speed with the numbers and order of events, it's time for the three of us to return to the forest. The trip will be slower this time, walking instead of running. We pack enough food for four days and fill our canteens. Christopher is to send word if Enid returns. Jonah is anxious without her, especially now that he won't be here when she comes home. We wait for the sun to fall and the stars to rise before throwing our robes on, hoods over our heads. We start out toward the darkest veil of the sky, keeping south until we reach the wall.

The crackle of leaves underfoot produces an unfamiliar spring in Jonah's step. He has walked for three days now and doesn't show any signs of stopping. I can only imagine the emotions he's feeling, waiting to see Imani. Callian takes the lead, and I follow up in the rear of our trio as we traipse through the trees that tower above us. Every now and then, Callian calls for us to catch up, noticing that

Jonah has stopped, his head turning on his shoulders as his awe of the forest hits him time and again.

We stop momentarily for a mouthful of water, the three of us scanning the trees. Callian and I are looking for predators, but Jonah just stares in wonder. A few more hours, and we can set up camp. I hope the rain stays in the clouds above us for the rest of the journey.

By the time we reach the first camp clearing, Jonah is struggling, his gait slightly awkward and getting slower by the mile. We stop and start setting up camp. He sits on the grass, watching Callian and I make a fire and roll out our sleeping mats. I head into the forest, searching for the bark Imani told me about that Catori used for her sleeping mat her first night in the forest.

It doesn't take long to find a tree that is wrapped in layers of drooping bark. I pull off long lengths of it and throw them over my shoulder. Arranging them next to the fire for Jonah, I explain the night air with its cold moisture to him. The fire roars to life as soon as the flames reach the dry leaves Callian swept up.

Callian disappears into the trees, and I know he will be finding food, probably desperate for something other than the bland offerings he's had these past days on the desert side of the wall. It isn't long before he returns, arms full of pickings from the generous forest around us. We sit and eat the portions he dishes out.

Jonah makes a few odd faces as he tries every type of food Callian gives him. I chuckle at the face he pulls at the pale grubs and toss mine into the fire. We settle in for the night, lying on our sleeping mats under the grand canopy of the forest. The calls and sounds of the night birds and small animals keep time with Jonah's snoring on his mat beside me, lulling me to sleep.

Hissing wakes me. Callian stands above me, dousing the fire, packed and ready to go. I sit up, running a hand through my scruffy hair. The stubble on my face reminds me how many days I've been away. Jonah is awake, sitting on his mat, eating a handful of dried meat from his rucksack. I eat a handful of leftover food from last night and wash it down with my canteen. Packing up the rest of our things, we head off through the forest again. One more night under the stars before I can hold Imani, burying my face in the dark waves of her hair. One more night until I can breathe again.

I trail behind Jonah, the same as the day before, the knives on my chest my best defense should a bear find us. I had listened with my mouth gaping open as Imani told me of the bear they'd encountered and how Callian had diverted its attention, protecting Catori and herself. His selflessness makes him a true warrior, and I couldn't be more grateful to him for keeping her safe. The walk is slower today, as the traveling is taking a toll on Jonah. We hardly break a sweat, but he doesn't have the muscle mass we do.

As the sun slips over the last rise before home, we make camp again. It's the same routine as last night, and we turn in earlier this time—me in anticipation of tomorrow, Jonah out of pure fatigue. Dreams only just find me before my shoulder starts shaking. Coarse whispers startle me awake. Callian is crouched beside me, knife in hand, his hand still roughly shaking me. I bolt upright and pull both of my knives from my chest belt. In the dark light of the night forest, I see the fear on his face.

"Bear," he whispers.

My stomach flips, and I lean over to wake Jonah. He sits up with a startle, and I press a finger to my lips. Callian creeps to his rucksack, bent over. We grab our belongings, leaving the sleeping mats behind. Hauling Jonah to his feet, we jog through the forest, making sure to stay downwind of the predator. I am trailing again, acutely aware that if the bear bursts through the trees at us, I am to defend. I run through every part of my training in my head while I tail Jonah, working through a basic plan in case it attacks. After half an hour of jogging, we slow to a walk, giving Jonah a break. His hands press to his sides, and he doubles over. Callian monitors every single movement in the trees.

"Sit just for a moment," Callian offers to Jonah.

He almost falls onto a log nearby.

I scan the tree line again before sheathing my knives and reaching for my canteen. "We can't stay still too long."

As I shake the last drop of water from my canteen into my mouth, the color drains from Jonah's face. I turn and track to where his gaze falls behind me. Emerging from the trees stands the biggest black animal I have ever seen. My heart flies into a frenzy as the canteen drops from my hand. The steel of Callian's blade whines as he draws it. I pull in a deep breath and rip both knives from my chest. The roar from the bear is deafening. A low growl leaves Callian as the bear closes the space between us.

"Jonah, run!" Callian barks.

Jonah pushes up and runs unsteadily down the dim forest path. Callian moves, blocking the path between the bear and Jonah, weapons ready. Another roar leaves the swiveling head of the bear, its claws sweeping at the air in front of it. It lunges toward me. I step under its black arm, spinning back to face it as it swings around. Callian shouts my name, but I plunge my knife into its side before it can come at me again.

The bear's low scream rips through the trees as it towers over me. Both knives wait ready in my hands. It swipes, and the sharp sting of its claws on my arm sends me stumbling backward. Callian is yelling my name. I catch a glimpse of him, bow taut, arrow marking its point. I step around, bringing the bear with me. The arrow flies, and the bear drops with a thud, sending birds scattering from their nests.

"You really like to do things the hard way." Callian shoots me an amused look before ripping the arrow from the bear's eye socket.

We gather our belongings and start off running to find Jonah. Only a half a mile down the track, we find him sitting on the ground, leaning against a tree.

"You missed all the fun," Callian says, pointing to my arm that now has blood trickling down it, soaking my sleeve.

Jonah jumps to his feet. "What happened?!"

"Harm wanted to dance with the bear, but it came off second best." Callian slaps my good arm and takes the lead. I rip my sleeve the rest of the way and tie it around the wound, using my teeth to keep the end taut while I make the knot.

We walk as fast as Jonah's pace allows, the cool air driving us forward. After hours of walking, the first light of dawn creeps over the horizon, lighting the path in front of us like a river of gold and brown between the trees.

Within minutes, I see it.

Home.

CHAPTER 29
IMANI

Miya leaves nothing behind as her blade connects with one of mine. Her wavy brown hair bounces around her shoulders; she always wears it down when she fights. Apart from Harm, she is my favorite person. Her belief in me never wavers, and she is constantly challenging me to be better, like an older sister. I grit my teeth against her steely downward force and push back, the burning in my legs making it harder than usual. But she doesn't let up—and I don't want her to.

The last words I said to Harm play over and over in my head, like a bird that exists just to torture me with its mocking call. Through the blades in my hands, I funnel the anger I've felt with myself since his last words to me: *"I will come back to you, Imani."*

Another strike from the side, and my other blade meets hers, nowhere near as powerful. I deflect it, hoping it stays away. No luck; she comes at me again, and I fling my raised blade down and spin out of range, preparing to defend, knowing all too well that she will just wear me down. I sidestep her next lunge.

My breath burns with every cycle in and out of my lungs. Sweat runs down my arms and through the valley between my breasts, trickling down my hard stomach. Wisps of hair that have escaped my blue wrap fly around my face, flipping up and falling back down with every labored breath. Miya lines me up for one last strike. I am exhausted; all I can do is skip around her and hope I don't trip over my own feet. Her muscular arm rises above me, and her eyes drill down to my face, a flicker of hope passing through them as she sees me lift to defend.

The whistle reaches us before her blade starts its descent. She loses her focus and turns to see Jeselle motioning for us to stop. With our hands by our side, we watch, chests heaving, as three figures approach the sparring ring. Miya lets out a chuckle and grins at me.

I make out his clothes first. My feet are planted on the ground, and I try to steady my breath and get my legs to move. Miya takes the knives from my hands. His eyes meet mine, and happiness chokes its way out of me. I sprint toward Harm.

He drops his gear, and his brown eyes search my face. With a flying leap, I jump up onto his hips and cup his face in my hands. His arms wrap around my waist, supporting me. His face is warm as I lay kiss after kiss on every inch of his smiling face.

"I'm sorry," I whisper, pushing back, studying his face.

He chuckles softly. "Me too. I missed you something fierce."

I shove my hands in his hair and kiss his cheeks, his nose, and his forehead, holding my lips there. I close my eyes, slamming my mouth over his.

A chuckle from behind Harm drifts past. I know that voice. I push back and stare at Harm. He smiles at me, and his jaw clenches. He lets me down and takes my hands in his. "A Blending gift, from me to you."

I step sideways, gripping his hands tight. Staring back at me is Jonah.

My heart stops.

My breath stops.

Tears run down Jonah's face, his wide grin wobbling, his arms stretched toward me. I propel myself forward, eliminating the space between us and flying into his embrace, letting the sobs rack my shaking body. His strong, familiar arms hold me tight. The last time I saw his face in the crowd at the gallows plays over in my mind. All the air escapes me; I can't breathe. My legs sway under the heady feeling. Jonah lowers me to the grass and kneels, holding me. His hands stroke my hair.

"My girl," he whispers.

I chug through another round of sobs before lifting my eyes to study his face. Every line and angle is so familiar. I press my hand to his cheek, and his chin trembles.

"I missed you," I breathe.

"Likewise," he whispers, pulling me in tighter.

Harm offers a hand to each of us after my last sob has ebbed. I grab his hand and let him pull me into his chest. I wipe my face on his shirt before extending my hand to Jonah as well. The man who has been a father to me for the past five years slowly pulls up to his feet. He fixes his shirt and dusts off his knees. Callian offers to show him the village, and he accepts, with a last look at Harm and me. I beam a smile at him so big that my face hurts. Harm's arm around me tightens.

"We need to introduce Jonah to Hanola before the ceremony. She's going to want to talk to him," Harm says.

I nod and lay my head against his chest. His heartbeat calms me, and I close my eyes, wanting to stay in this moment forever.

Jonah spends the better part of three hours after lunch with Hanola, including a visit to the cells that takes an entire hour.

While Harm and I prepare for the ceremony tomorrow, somehow Catori, Miya, and Jeselle have managed to turn the communal area into a stage, set for something positively magical, or so they tell me. I am banned from seeing it, so I eat my dinner on my mat in Catori's house tonight.

Harm is sanctioned to Callian's home as well. They all find it amusing that we're apart for one last night. In every spare moment I've had outside of training, I have spent the last two days scrubbing and preparing the small house we will call our home in this village. Finally, it's just as I had imagined a home of my own would be when I was a little girl. Everyone in the village has offered up something either useful or beautiful, and the house is made up perfectly, simple but welcoming.

Best of all, it's ours.

The cup of cold tea stares back at me as Hanola watches me size it up. The brew she has made comes directly from Enid's book of herbal remedies, and this one in particular is for preventing two people from creating new life. I agree that it's necessary, and I am happy to take it, but I have never given it any thought before now. Hanola encourages me to drink. I raise the cup to my lips, close my eyes, and drain it in a matter of seconds. She nods and smiles, handing me a small container of the dried herbs that are supposed to last me a few months. I thank her and make my way back to Catori's house.

Thoughts of my own mother flippantly wash through my mind. I haven't thought about her for years, but it bothers me—more than I would like it to. Especially now.

My dress for our Blending ceremony hangs over the changing

screen. I brush my hair before filling up the small bath at the back of Catori's home. Steam floats off the cascading water as I pour it in. I peel off my clothes, running my hands over the curves of my body. Fragrant petals sit in a jar beside the bath. Scooping out a handful, I sprinkle them over the bath. Their sweet smell fills the air the second they hit the warm water.

I slide into the bath. The water covers my body, rising higher the lower I sink into its welcoming, steamy warmth. Catori has a jug sitting next to the bath, and I submerge it in the water and pour it over my head. Water flows through the waves of my hair. The small pieces of soap stuck to the sides of the bath make a good lather as I slide them over my skin and into my hair. Lathered up, I lie back and close my eyes, breathing in the luxury of the bath.

A knock rattles the door. I jerk away from the side of the bath a little.

"Just a minute." I submerge back into the water, washing out the soap in my hair roughly with my fingers. Bubbles ascend as I let out a breath. I break through the water and rise from the bath in one fluid motion. Water flows over my curves as I wrap a large cloth around myself, drying off as I step away from the bath. Conscious of the translucent barrier around my wet and naked body, I make for the changing area. I pull on a pair of pants and my old tunic, leaving my wet hair hanging over my shoulders. I skip to the door and tear it open.

The patient face of Miya greets me. "You ready to make that gift for Harm?" she asks, tilting her head, and her eyes wander over my wet hair.

"Yes, sorry. Just let me find my shoes and wrap." I wander back to my mat, pull on my shoes, and pluck my blue scarf from the changing screen. I wrap up my hair as I follow Miya out the door. We head to Hanola's first, to collect sketches that Enid gave her decades ago. The old parchment feels frail in my hands, and I turn it over to check the back before admiring the woman in the sketch. Her face is just like Harm's, her hair waves of blonde, blue eyes staring up at me. She would have been around my age. Her hands cradle her swollen stomach—a token of a better future that Enid brought with her to show Hanola all those decades ago when she crossed the wall.

For Harm, it is the last physical memory of his mother, whom he treasured, along with his father and sister, more than anything else. Looking into the eyes of his mother, my heart breaks for her son, threatening to burst my chest open into hundreds of pieces. Hanola has insisted that Harm should have it, and I want him to have this last piece of her. It is one of the only gifts I can give him right now.

Miya and I amble to the small house that will be mine and Harm's. We set to work with our knives, hulling some sweet-smelling wood, shaping each piece until we have enough for an ornate frame for the sketch. The warm tree sap she collected earlier fastens the pieces together, and we weigh it down with rocks and wait for the frame to cure.

"You excited about getting a home of your own?" Miya asks, a grin plastered across her pretty, freckled face.

"Yes." I hesitate. "A little nervous too."

She nods and smiles. "You'll do just fine, Imani." She winks at me and wraps an arm around me. I rest my head on her shoulder and loose a sigh.

"You and Jess..." I suck in a breath. "You weren't nervous on your first night together?"

She removes her arm and takes my hands in hers. "Everybody is on their first night, no exceptions. But you and Harm are each other's world. You two will be more than okay."

I nod, releasing a wobbly breath, then rise, shuffling around the little home, making sure everything is in place. A small table and two matching chairs sit to the left of the entrance, covered by a thin cream cloth, a gift from one of the village people. The hearth is lit and stocked with more wood than we need. The bunk, wider than a single bed, is adorned with soft blankets and two cushions from Hanola's home, her gift to us. A tall changing screen and a bath like Catori's sit against the back wall in the right-hand corner. Lastly is a small dresser, where I plan to display the sketch of Harm's mother. The light is starting to fade.

"We should get back to Catori's and get you ready," Miya says.

I agree and take a last look at the home that Catori and I have put together over the last few days. Warmth spreads through my chest. I pull in a long deep breath before turning on my heel and heading out the front door. I haven't seen Harm since yesterday, and already it feels like a week.

We round the corner before Catori's house, and the laughter finds us before we open the door. Catori and Jeselle sit on the floor in the center of the house, threading a needle through fresh flowers that lie scattered on the floor in front of them. Their hands weave the petite blooms into rows along the fine strings.

"Time to change, girl." Miya ushers me toward the changing screen.

"Already?" Time seems to be evaporating, but somehow also dragging, each moment building up my nerves and my excitement. At the same time, I have never felt so grounded and sure about anything as I do now. I pull off the clothes I wear, and once I am down to my bottoms, a hand holds my dress over the flimsy wall between us.

"Uh, I don't have any supports on yet," I say, looking down at my full bare chest, the peaks hardening in the cooler air on this side of the room.

"You won't need them, Imani, trust me." Miya laughs, and heat crawls up my neck into my cheeks. I'm glad she can't see my face. I step into the dress and slide it over my soft, clean skin. I run a hand down the ivory fabric, over the elegant stitching at my hips. The bust is lined with the smoothest ribbon I have ever felt and the long skirts pool at my feet, the layers making my figure appear so feminine. Miya's hands tug at the laces on my back. She's right; the bust is tight enough to hold me in place. My face reddens again.

"Just breathe. You have both waited a lifetime for this. He's probably just as terrified as you," she says, spinning me around. Her kind face meets mine, carrying a smile that lights up her eyes. The multitude of days I have spent with Miya have given me something I never thought I would ever have: something like an older sister. Her and Catori both are. I smile back at her and breathe out a long breath. Catori and Jeselle stand hovering around me, while Miya ducks behind the screen to change.

Flowers now adorn my dark waves, and the three women wear them around their waists and on their wrists. My chest stays bare for the Blending stone that hangs in a cradle of woven gold on the necklace Harm has carried with him since the day he fled Amondo. I hadn't even thought about the rituals that usually go with the ceremony until now. In my mind, I see the two tall glass urns of sand, one from each household, blended into a new vase, signifying the Blending of the betrothed. I guess we won't have that, being in the forest.

"Ready, Imani?" Jeselle asks.

"Yes." I bunch up my skirts and slip on some shoes Catori lent me. Miya takes my hand, and we walk to the center of the village with Catori and Jeselle in the lead, looking elegant with their hair down around their shoulders. Murmurs rise from the village people who are gathered. My heart hammers in my chest, my hands turning clammy. We reach the edge of the communal area, and the wonder of the transformed space takes what's left of my breath.

Light from hundreds of lanterns illuminates the large area, dangling from the trees above us. The tables have been moved to make a path from one end of the eating area to the small ceremony space, and benches line every step between Harm and me, filled with happily chatting people. Music is playing somewhere, almost drowned out by the whispers of the women and men who stand upon seeing me.

I swallow back a sob and breathe out. Miya squeezes my hand before flanking me with Catori, and Jeselle leads. Every voice goes silent.

Searching for Jonah, I scan the crowd erratically. As Miya and Catori step ahead of me, a familiar silhouette appears at my side, his arm hooking through mine. Jonah's beaming face looks down at me, his eyes lined with silver as he pats the hand he is now holding. We pause briefly as his gaze strays from mine to the end of the row of lanterns and smiling faces.

Harm.

With Callian by his side, Harm stands, hands clasped in front of him. Warmth and longing rise in my chest as butterflies take flight deep in my core. I grab Jonah's arm, and he rubs his thumb over my trembling hand.

"You look beautiful, Imani," he whispers as he walks me toward Harm.

The music grows louder. The kind, smiling faces of the forest people who have welcomed me from the minute I crossed the wall brighten as I reach them, resting their right hands over their hearts as I pass by, holding them there. Ahead, with a smile stretched over his face, Callian sways into Harm's shoulder and whispers something to him. Harm huffs out a small laugh, then he looks at me, and his jaw clenches, his Adam's apple bobbing. The last few steps don't even register.

Now, I stand staring at Harm's face. His eyes watch my every breath. Jonah kisses my cheek before leaving to stand with Catori, Miya, and Jeselle. I notice for the first time that Hanola stands in front of a small wooden table adorned with candles and three glass vases, with sand in two—one on my side, containing the golden sands of Perendi, and one on Harm's side, with the reddish sands of Amondo.

I turn to Jonah, and he winks, one of the happiest smiles I have ever seen on his broad face. On a soft cloth in front of the vases lies a blue stone set in intricately woven gold, suspended from a golden chain. The pendant Harm has carried with him, always. I look back at Harm, and his smile encompasses his entire face as he holds my trembling hands in his. His chest rises and falls deeply, his jaw flexing as he studies my face.

"Hey," he whispers.

I squeeze his hands and blow out a breath. "Hey, yourself." I chuckle through a wobbly breath, smiling up at him. He shuffles closer, silver lining his eyes. His clean cream-colored shirt and dark pants mirror the colors of my dress and hair. His warm hands steady my body with just the touch that binds us together as we join hands.

Love and admiration light up Hanola's face. She is dressed in long, flowing robes, with a colorful long necklace made of twine, a large metal amulet suspended from the end. It must be her ceremonial dress. She clears her throat, and we turn to look at her. "You two ready?"

We nod simultaneously, and she tilts her head with a smile.

"On this day, two sands become one, Blended for eternity. May they be carried by the wind, but never separated. These two people are now and forever entwined like the sands of the dunes, bending to no other, forever loyal, and holding strong through the storms that weather them, now and always." She raises her hands, fingers laced into a peak above her head.

"Now and always!" the people behind us chant, patting their hands over their hearts twice, like a heartbeat.

"Okay, don't keep us waiting, you two." Hanola winks.

Harm releases my hands and slides one around the small of my back, pulling me closer. His other hand runs behind my neck, and his mouth closes over mine. I put my hands on his hips and tug him closer to me. Hanola's voice chants a rhythmic sound as the sand falling from our two vases hiss into the one, and we stay in the embrace until she has poured every last grain together. A small sound from Hanola signals that the sand is blended, and we pull apart.

My chest heaves as Harm picks up the stone and opens the delicate clasp. He drapes it over my head and fumbles with the fine metal clasp for a moment with shaking hands before running both hands down the chain and tracing a finger over the stone. He looks up from the brilliant blue stone and smiles when our gazes meet. This time, tears spill down his cheeks. I take his hands and hold them steady while he sucks in a long breath. His jawline glistens, and I run my hands over his face, thumbing the tears away.

Hanola chants once more, and the crowd echoes with "Now and always." We turn back to the beaming faces of Jonah, Miya, Callian, Catori, and Jeselle. As if from some invisible cue, folks start lining up at the tables. And with a subtle gesture from Hanola, they sit as one. Food appears, carried by the women of the kitchen and the village children. We follow Jonah to a nearby table reserved for us and our friends,and we sit,so close that nearly every part of us touches.

Harm is holding my hand tight, looking at Callian, who is rambling on about something he isn't listening to. Catori, Miya, and Jeselle file in around us. Miya winks at me and starts piling food onto Jeselle's plate before filling her own. I nuzzle Harm's neck before kissing it. A kiss lands on my head, and I straighten up and declare that I am starving. Miya laughs at my sudden discovery of starvation, and we eat and laugh until the moon is high in the sky.

CHAPTER 30
HARM

The last of the revelers have left, and Imani and I sit holding onto each other, neither of us wanting to let go. She looks up at me, and her blue eyes light up with excitement. "I have something for you," she says, jumping up from the seat, leading me through the village. Her hand is warm in mine, and her scent drifts behind her, waking up parts of me that I have been trying to suppress for weeks.

The door to our small home is covered in well wishes in the form of ribbons and dried herbs and flowers. She pushes the door open, and I stop before the threshold, pulling her back to me. With a swift swoop of my arm under her legs, she rests in my arms, and her mouth finds mine, her eyes closing. We cross over the threshold together. Her hands wind around my neck, her fingers sliding through my hair, and I smile against her mouth. Her eyes open, and I set her down in the living room of our home.

Her fingers slip from mine, and she takes a frame from the small side table and hands it to me. Before I can look at it properly, she grabs a lantern and holds it above the image. My mouth gaping, my heart skips a beat. Inside a neat wooden frame made of many smaller pieces sits an image of my mother, her features sketched to perfection, her arms low and cradling her stomach—with me in it, I imagine.

"I know how much you loved your mother, and I wanted to give you something to last, better than the memories in our minds that fade over time," Imani whispers, her face close to mine as she takes in the image. I shift my gaze from the portrait of my mother and keep a firm gaze on Imani, swallowing past the lump in my throat.

"Miya helped me make it for you—the frame, that is. Hanola had this image of your mother. She said Enid gave it to her a long time ago." Her hand slips into mine. I just stare at her, my heart pounding in my chest.

"There's one more thing," she says and places the frame on the kitchen table before pulling me closer to the bunk—our oversized bunk, layered with blankets and two pillows. The flickering lantern light and the fire in the hearth dance over her elegant features, and I follow where she leads me.

"I've wanted to give this to you for so, so long, Harm." Barely a whisper, her voice falters. She lifts my hand and places it over her heart. With both of her hands behind her back she unties the ribbons that hold her dress around her curves. She slides the dress from one shoulder, then the other. Blood thunders in my veins. Her eyes are soft, their dark centers dilated as she watches me watching her.

The soft ivory fabric falls from her bust and over her waist and hips, hitting the floor. Heat flushes her face. I glide my hand down from her heart to her round, velvety breast. The breath leaves my chest and doesn't return. I step closer to her, sinking my mouth into hers. Her hands guide my shirt up and over my head. We break apart for a heartbeat to tug my shirt off. Her hands work around my pants fastener while I trail kisses down her neck and onto her shoulder.

"Harm…" she whispers.

"Imani," I whisper back and place a hand over her heart. Wrapping the other behind her neck, I press my forehead to hers.

"I love you more than anything in this world," she says. I find her gaze. Her eyes are wide and dark. "I want all of you, Harm."

My pants fall to the floor. She glances down, her heart thundering in her chest under my hand. Mine races in time with hers. I press up against her soft body and pick her up, lifting her onto my hips. Her mouth covers mine, and I hold her for as long as I can bear before lowering her onto the layers of blankets.

Imani looks up at me, her trembling hand running over my cheek and behind my neck, and she pulls me down to meet her. I plunge into her mouth with every part of me that I have been holding back for weeks. Her legs wrap around me, cradling my hips. She looks at me expectantly, studying my face.

"I love you more than anything in this world too. Let me love every inch of you first," I whisper and trail kisses down her neck. My lips reach her breasts, and she lets out a soft, low groan. The ache in my body doubles. I plant more kisses over each round, velvety mound before kissing their peaks, one after the other.

Imani squirms beneath me, and a gruff rumble falls from my throat, my lips stretching to a smile. The throbbing in my body is almost unbearable now. I continue placing kisses down her stomach, over her hips, the insides of her thighs. A small cry follows, and I track my way back up to her face, planting feather-soft kisses one at a time as I go.

Imani pulls me back up over her body. "Harm," she growls. I move her legs apart with my knees and press myself against her. Her back arches, her chest pressing into mine before she returns to the soft bunk. She pulls my mouth to hers as I sink into her. She whimpers, and I pull back, needing to see her face. She grabs my shoulders and pulls me back down, her mouth on my neck, fingers through my hair.

The steady cadence of our joined bodies elevates the sensation between us. Imani starts to tremble. I pull her up to me and lean back to rest on my heels, so she sits above me. Now she takes up the rhythm. I run kisses over her chest, resting my lips around one peak, supporting her with my hands on her back.

Her breath catches. "Harm…" My name is a plea.

We lose ourselves, the steady rhythm between us becoming desperate. She leans back, and the sweetest moan cascades from her lips, her face twisting with tortured bliss. Immediately, the ache in my core shatters into a thousand brilliant pieces as I follow her over the edge. The throbbing eases, and tingling starts in my centre as the relief fades.

Chest heaving, I kiss her mouth and trace my hands up her neck, cupping her face. Her palms rest on my chest. Releasing her face, I press my forehead to her chest, and her face lowers to nuzzle my neck. We hold on, wrapped in each other's arms, until our breathing settles and sleep claims us.

Imani's soft body is pushed against mine, and I wake to my body already responding to hers. With one hand, I sweep the hair from the side of her face and plant kisses on her cheek and down her neck. She moans and grabs my hand before rolling over and covering my mouth with hers. The space between us closes, and every inch of our bodies touches.

She presses her hands onto my chest and trails a finger down my stomach. My heart thunders, accelerating with every inch that her hand descends. I trace a finger around her velvet peaks, moving in time with her rapid breaths. Every part of me aches for her again. I pull my mouth from hers and watch her elegant face change with the movement of my hand over her body.

I almost don't hear the impatient rap on the door over the blood thundering through my head. Imani and I stare at each other, waiting for the knock to either sound again or retreat. Another comes, this time harsher and more urgent. I kiss her mouth and flip us over, pinning her under me. She grins, dotting kisses on my chest. Reluctantly, I climb out of the bunk to find my pants. I fasten them and plant a kiss on her forehead, pulling the blanket over her and padding to the door.

A flushed and irritated Catori stands across the threshold. The heat rises in my cheeks as I remember, too late, that I don't have a shirt on.

"Hanola needs to see you—now." She looks past me. "Both of you."

"Just let us get dressed. We'll be there shortly," I say and shut the door. I help Imani off the bed, and we dress in our training gear as fast as our hands will allow. We make quick time to Hanola's. Inside, Jonah, Catori, Miya, and Jeselle are already waiting. This time, Hanola is not sitting on her living room floor. She stands with her stick, facing Jonah, her expression serious.

"What's going on?" I ask.

"There is a rumor of mass killings on our side of the wall, at the hand of the Guardians, in the village of Etonia," Jonah says. "Fletcher is executing dozens of people. I'm not sure if it's connected to the rebels, but we need to find out, and fast, before they run with the idea and snuff out the rebellion before it even begins." His face is grave as he looks between Imani and me.

"That's the village next to the prison. What can we do?" I ask.

"You'll have to assess the situation once you get there, but you can either create enough of a diversion to stop the slaughter of innocent people, or you can assassinate Fletcher himself," Hanola says.

All eyes are on Imani now. She doesn't flinch, her jaw set in fierce determination, like he's just another hideous enemy that needs to be done away with.

"We can leave now," I say. "I just have one errand to run; it's important. Then we pack up and leave for the wall."

Jonah nods, but his eyes are still surveying Imani.

"You, Jonah, and Imani will go. We will make final preparations for infiltrating the tower upon your return," Hanola says and waves us away, as if every second we stand in front of her is too long.

I grab Imani's hand and lead her out of Hanola's house. In the lane outside, I turn her toward me, checking her over, as if the mere words had damaged her.

Her gaze remains fierce. "I'll pack for us both while you run your errand," she says flatly. Her calm composure sparks worry deep inside me, but I head for the prison cells regardless. I look back and watch her walking to our home, her gait quick, her fists balled. Her fire is ignited. I almost feel bad for Fletcher.

Almost.

The guards at the prison wave me in. Dim light surrounds the last cell at the end of the passageway. Sitting in one corner is Mason. In this moment, I feel the tinge of something I recognize as sympathy for him, knowing what I came here to tell him. He sees me and moves to face the wall. I stop a step before the bars of his cell.

"Mason." I try to add kindness to my voice, despite all the history between us.

"Leave me alone, Travesci," he rasps. His physical self is a shadow of the muscle-bound Guardian he was.

"I need to talk to you. I have some news." I talk as if what I have come to say won't destroy him.

He stays motionless for a moment before pushing his thin frame up from the filthy floor. At least this time he has clothes on. "What could you possibly have to say to me?" He almost resembles a mangy animal beaten down by a cruel owner.

"A few days ago, I was back over the wall, on our side." I don't know how to say the next part. "I was in one of the outlying villages, and there was news... of Amondo."

I watch his reaction in the half light. He shifts from one foot to the other, as if the emaciated bit of weight he carries is still too heavy.

"The village was poisoned, by the Guardians. There were no survivors." My words are quiet, and I wonder if he heard me. "I'm sorry."

He looses a low growl. "I don't believe you."

"Almost every person in the village was killed, Mason."

It takes a few moments for him to realize what I am telling him. His parents, his sister, Marla—gone. His hands grasp the bars with white knuckles as his face contorts in pain. He slides down the bars and hits the grimy floor with his knees. Agonizing sobs rack his chest. I step back and watch his face.

The pain that twists it ignites in me as memories of my own family being executed sends stabbing pains through my chest, followed by an ache in my heart. I breathe out, watching him come undone with every painful groan. Guilt seeps into my bones. I have known about this for days, and I only just told him.

I turn and retreat through the prison door. The wails from his cell follow every step I take. Tears burn in my eyes, and I drag in a long breath. Regardless of the things he has done to me and Imani, I can't hate him right now.

I find Imani sitting on our bed, two rucksacks and our traveling gear ready to go. Her face is less stonelike now, but I sit next to her and wrap an arm around her. The agony of Mason's cries still lingers in my consciousness, and I can't find the words to console her, knowing how much she hates the things her father commands and does. She gets up and dons her gear before throwing me a hard look. I realize it's not about me, but Fletcher. I rise and put my gear on, following her over the threshold of our home, ready to take on any fight she sees fit to fight at her side, from this day forward.

Jonah meets us under the line of trees that surround the forest village. He is ready for the journey. I hope he is fitter this time, having a few decent meals under his belt; I don't need another bear encounter on this trip. Of course, with the mindset Imani is in, she could probably take one down by herself.

We have barely reached the forest edge when Jonah speaks. "This could very well be a trap for you, Harm. Fletcher is good at getting you to come to him. Both of you."

"Possibly, but what alternative do we have?"

Imani walks ahead of us, lost in her own thoughts.

"What do you think she'll do if she meets him face to face?" Jonah mutters.

"I don't know. It's not likely to be anything pleasant," I say, remembering the training Imani has endured for months now with Miya and Callian.

"Last time she encountered him, she was fiery but mostly incapable. This time, she could kill him with one fluid motion," Jonah notes, as if I had forgotten.

I raise an eyebrow at him, and he laughs. "I, for one, am not going to stop her from doing that."

Jonah frowns, but says nothing.

We walk in silence for an hour before we reach the first clearing. Another two days of traveling takes us to Etonia, the village at the prison wall. We find Saraya in her merchant stall, undercover, like the last time we were here. She looks surprised to see me, but ushers the three of us from her stall to her small home on the other side of the village, opposite the prison, shutting the doors and windows before turning to face us.

I take down my robe, revealing my face.

"Harmen," she says, her voice faltering, "you should not have come here."

CHAPTER 31
HARM

Imani removes her robe next to me, and Saraya's eyes widen. A look of regret and pain creases her face when she catches a glimpse of Imani's blue stone pendant dangling over her shirt. Jonah throws a look between Imani and Saraya, but says nothing. Saraya moves to her small living space and drops into a chair, her hands cradling her head in despair. Then her head snaps up.

"Enid. Enid is here too, with a young boy that she has taken in. I saw her two days ago when she visited my stall." She pauses and rocks back and forth. I have never seen her so unsettled. I kneel in front of her and pull her hands from her face.

"What did she come to you for?" I ask.

Jonah and Imani stand behind me now.

"Just to make certain I hadn't seen you. She seemed to think the random executions were Fletcher's way of drawing you out." She looks up at Imani briefly before looking back at me.

I wish she hadn't done that. My body goes rigid, ready to make a grab for Imani if she gets it in her mind to storm off after Fletcher. She did it once before at Enid's house.

"We mostly came to gather information," I lie, patting her hands and standing up to face Jonah and a stone-faced Imani. It is hard to believe this was the face that was so full of love and desire only hours ago. I have always known Imani has a strong personality, but now, she is pure fire.

"There is to be another execution this afternoon—two men who were suspected of joining the rebel cause," Saraya says, clearly unsure if the information is correct.

Jonah shoots me a look. Two birds with one stone, as always with Fletcher.

"When?" I ask.

"In about two hours." She pulls back a curtain and glances at the sun.

"Okay, we'll watch from the shadows. Hopefully, Enid is nowhere to be seen either," I say. The pull I have in my heart to see my grandmother is outweighed right now by the desire to keep Imani safe, but an ache starts regardless.

After hugs from Saraya, who studies Imani carefully, the three of us head toward the small door in the side of the prison wall. I pray we don't run into Guardians en route, and that our small hiding spot from last time is empty. We weave our way through the homes of the village, robes on, hoods down, wraps over our faces. Jonah halts at every corner of every house, checking the path is clear. It takes us twice an age to reach the last house before the wall.

Jonah's hand flies up, and we freeze behind him. Voices round the corner, and Imani pulls me down and against the house. Jonah holds his breath. Two Guardians walk past our spot, arguing about something, not noticing the three figures in the shadow of the house. Imani's eyes are closed. I squeeze her hand, and she looks up at me. Her blue eyes pierce mine, worry etched into her beautiful face.

The small door opens easily under Jonah's hand. I step

through, tailed by Imani, whose fingers rest on her knives the entire way. She spins to close the door. The last of the light disappears, when something cracks behind me. Imani gasps, and I spin back. Her body slackens, and I catch her before she hits the ground. Jonah scrambles to start a light in the dark space. I fold myself around Imani protectively, anticipating another blow. It doesn't come. Jonah's flame flickers to life, brightening the mortified face of Marshall.

I rip the wrap from my face. His hand slaps over his mouth as he recognizes me. Jonah removes his garb. Marshall drops his lump of wood to the ground and throws himself at Jonah, sobbing. I sit with my legs underneath me and cradle Imani in my lap. I stroke her hair, waiting for her to regain consciousness, fully expecting her to come up swinging. With my free hand, I push back her hood and pull her wrap from around her face and

hair.As if she read my mind, her eyes flutter open. Her fist flings upward, and I grab her wrist. A low growl rumbles from her chest, her arms straining against mine before she recognizes my face.

"Hello, beautiful." I chuckle, and she rolls her eyes at me. I release her, and immediately she touches the back of her head and winces. Planting a kiss on her forehead and then her cheek, I help her sit up and remove the rest of her robe and her rucksack.

There are one too many voices in the dim space. I stop what I'm doing, hands freezing over my rucksack. A throat clears behind me. I look back at Jonah, who is holding Enid's hand. Her face is lit up with a smile, her eyes lined with silver. Jonah squeezes her hand before letting go, and we meet in the middle. Her arms fly around my neck, pulling me down into a tight hug.

"You found her!" Enid cries. "Heavens, you found her, my boy!" Her body trembles in my hold as she cradles my head to her shoulder.

"I did," I choke out past the lump in my throat.

"Hello, Enid," Imani says, her voice soft.

"He did more than that, Enid." Jonah laughs.

Enid pushes out of my embrace, holding me at arm's length. Her mouth falls open, and her eyes widen. Imani stands on wobbly feet and ambles over beside me. Enid pulls her in for a hug that threatens to take her off her unsure feet. Then she holds her at arm's length and looks at her, as if checking to make certain she is alive. Her gaze falls to the pendant on Imani's chest, and she looks up at me in wonder before looking back to Imani.

"That makes this old woman very happy." She hugs us both before holding us both back, taking one last look. Her face falls. "But you shouldn't have come, Harm." She straightens. "Especially not now."

"We know what's happening. Is there any way to stop it?" I ask.

She shakes her head. "No good can come of you being here. It's too easy for things to turn bad for you, and for Imani." She looks between us again, and I take a step closer.

"We can't just let those men die!"

"If you're captured again, we have nothing left. No way to alter the dial. No hope of changing things for the better. This is much bigger than just two men," she says, her tone final.

"But how can we just walk away? There must be something we can do...?"

Her face turns hard, much like the stony expression Imani has worn most of the day. "No, Harm, there's not. Go back to the forest, stay safe, and when the time is right in a matter of weeks, you'll be able to do the most important task yet."

I turn my pleading look to Jonah. He shakes his head. Enid is right. We shouldn't have come.

"What if I stay and do something? Harm can go back over the wall, but I can help you," Imani offers to Enid.

My heart races and my hands start to tremble at the thought of being apart from Imani again. Enid turns back to her, as if considering it.

"No! That is not happening!" I rasp, the fear and pain in my words obvious to every person here.

"I don't think that's a good idea either," Jonah starts. "We can't have either of you distracted. Both of you need to be able to focus. Where Harm goes, Imani goes. And on another note, I don't think that's a fair proposition, Imani. Fletcher may just as well kill you as he would Harm. Or he might use you to get to him, like he has before. That is not an option."

Enid examines Jonah's face and agrees. I turn to Imani, and her eyes meet mine. They are as pained as my own.

"I'm sorry, Harm, I didn't think that through. I need to sit down." She wobbles to the ground with her hand out to support herself on the musty wall. I kneel in front of her, searching for something to say.

"I feel so guilty about what Fletcher's doing. It's my fault." Her whispers turn to sobs. "I would never leave you, and I definitely don't want us to be apart again. But I have to do something. Someone needs to start doing something. This has to stop!"

Jonah and Enid watch as I console her. I cup her face in my hands and rest my forehead on hers. "None of this is your fault, Imani. Fletcher makes his own choices." I wipe away the never-ending stream of tears from her soft cheeks. My heart breaks with every whimper that leaves her throat. How could she possibly blame herself for the atrocities that man has committed? Her hands reach for me, and I move closer. She grabs my shirt and buries her head in my chest, trying to steady her breath. I rest my chin on her hair.

"We will end this, together. When all the pieces are aligned and everyone is ready, when we have the best chance possible. Then it will be over," I say, trying to sound as confident as Enid.

Imani breathes deeply. With a sigh, she untangles herself from my arms. Her face has returned to the stony look from earlier, but this time she lets me in. I hold her gaze, and she traces my cheek with her hand, forcing a small smile.

Muted echoes of people gathering at the call of a Guardian drift past the closed door. Jonah moves first, cracking it open to peer through.

"People are gathering in front of the gallows," he says, turning back to us before shutting the door.

Enid fusses over Marshall, helping him with his robe before donning her own. Imani and I robe up too, wrapping our faces, and Jonah follows our lead. Checking that a direct path to the back of the crowd is clear of Guardians, we slip through the door and amble out to mix with the crowd of onlookers. The tang of old blood and human filth hits me like a fist to the face. Instantly, memories of the last time I was here rob my lungs of air. I grab Imani's hand and hold onto it like it is life itself. Once in the center of the crowd, I slam my eyes shut and force breath in and out of my lungs.

Imani grips my arm, her body warm against mine. "Breathe," she whispers.

In the darkness of my mind, I see her beaten face and mutilated hair, the filth she was covered in, barely hidden by the worn slip she wore, and it crushes my chest, the weight of the images sending blinding pains through me. Breath quickens around my racing heart.

"Look at me, Harm," Imani says, her voice kind but unbending.

After a heartbeat, I open my eyes and turn to look at her face.

Her brilliant eyes hold mine, and fierce determination swirls through them, accompanied now by adoration.

"The last time we were here..." I choke out whispered words.

She moves into my space and holds my face with both hands. "It's over. We leave as soon as this is done." Her forehead presses to mine. She traces her fingers over my lips through the wrap, then returns to standing beside me.

We wait.

Soon, Guardians haul two shaking men to the stand of the gallows.

"I don't recognize them," Enid whispers.

"No, they're not part of the rebellion. He's executing random people. This is a trap. We move out when the ruckus starts." Jonah's words are like a blade. Enid was right: we should not have come.

When the last of the stragglers reach the crowd, doors on either side of the gallows open. A line of Guardians spill from each and start surrounding the crowd from both sides.

"Now. You need to go now—both of you," Jonah hisses.

I spin back, and Imani follows, still holding my hand. We weave through the crowd as fast as we can without drawing attention to ourselves. The sound of Jonah swearing above the shuffling crowd pushes me faster, and I shoulder my way past people, Imani right behind me. We cannot get caught here—not again. I glance to the side of the crowd. The line of Guardians is halfway around the mass of people. My thundering heart makes it hard to focus on anything but getting out.

"Hurry, Harm!" Imani cries.

I push past the last of the crowd. The Guardians have surely spotted our movements by now. We have no choice but to run, and I am glad of the months of training and running in the forest. Imani and I fly across the sand, faster than anyone has ever gone on foot. Yelling behind us pushes us faster, but the robes we wear slow us down.

An engine roars to life, and my stomach plummets. Imani throws me a wild look, and we burn through the sand, heading for the rocky outcrops. We need to lose them, and fast. The droning call of the dune buggy's motor waxes and wanes as it courses through the sand, closing in on us. We are only a hundred feet from the rocky outcrops when the buggy swings around us. The two officers on board hold smug expressions. Imani and I slow to a halt, standing our ground. In unison, we fling our robes off, freeing our hands and weapons.

The Guardians jump down from the buggy, sauntering over to where we stand. One holds a cane, and the other nothing. They grin and bear down on us like predators, unaware of the true nature of their prey. The Guardian with the cane lunges for me. In an instant, I rip the long daggers from my hips, my blades crossed over each other, and I meet his wooden weapon with more force than he anticipates. The second officer dances warily around Imani. Her expression has turned to one of amusement; she is playing with him.

A brief wisp of shock washes over the face of the officer in front of me before he regains his composure and strikes again. I sidestep him, slicing through his sleeve and spilling his blood on the sand. An agonized grunt leaves his mouth as he grips his arm with his free hand. I stand my ground, motionless, waiting for him to decide whether he will fight or run. Beside me, Imani holds her fighting knives ready to intercept either officer.

The cane rises again, and this time he lunges toward Imani. I turn to block him. His hand leaves his wound, and he shoves past me, homing in on Imani. She sidesteps him, and he spins to face her. I step behind him and rest my blades against his throat. The eyes of his companion widen, and he steps backward on trembling legs.

"I suggest you leave us be," I hiss into his ear.

He stiffens as I press the blades more tightly to his throat, and he tries to nod. I release the blades and shove him into the sand. Scrambling to his feet, he turns on us and growls, charging for me. A heartbeat later, Imani's blade leaves her hand, sinking into his chest, and he drops to the sand with a thud. I sigh and roll him over with my foot. The terrified officer standing next to the dune buggy flies into the driver's seat, thrusting the machine into gear before roaring away from us. Imani retrieves her knife.

The drone of another buggy catches both of our attention, and we turn as one. Fletcher jumps from the vehicle. My gut sinks like a stone. Our wraps are off, hoods down, and Imani stands frozen in the sand as he stalks his way toward us. The knife, dripping with his officer's blood, dangles between her fingers. I step forward, putting myself between them. Fletcher chuckles a sadistic laugh before stopping inches away from me. His face is hard to read— somewhere between annoyance, hate, and grief. He glances at Imani and grabs my arm.

"You're with me, boy," he growls.

Imani shoves past me, pressing the knife to his sweaty, sand-covered throat. His Adam's apple bobs before he meets her gaze. She holds his stare, fire consuming her eyes.

"Let him go," she snarls.

"Not this time, Imani. Travesci's time is up."

I stiffen at the thought of returning to the prison—or worse. Imani twists the knife into his neck, and a small line of crimson streaks toward his crisp grey collar. "I said let him go, Fletcher."

"Is that any way to talk to your own father?" he chokes out in a huff, nodding at the knife in her hand.

"Last I heard, you have no daughter." Her words are laced with fire.

He holds her gaze for a moment and his body softens slightly. He glances at me, hand still tight around my upper arm, before tilting his head back. He sighs, then grabs Imani's wrist with one swift move. She wavers only slightly and stands her ground. I spin from his grip while he is focused on her, and he pulls her hand from his neck, squeezing her wrist until the knife hits the sand. Imani groans softly, but holds his gaze, mouth twisted with venom.

"And you wonder why I left. This regime has turned you into a monster," she breathes.

His jaw clenches, and he opens his mouth to respond, but closes it again. "You're supposed to be with Rayner, staying out of trouble," he growls.

Imani rolls her eyes at him. "Who says I'm not? But you can't trap me like an animal in a cage, Father. I can assure you, I am doing my part."

He glances at me, then back to her.

What the hell is that all about? Mason was supposed to hide her or something? Is he talking about after the gallows? Pushing down the thoughts I can't afford to comprehend right now, I slide my sword from my back, cringing as it makes the smallest of whines. I step around, watching every movement Fletcher makes, but he seems to be entirely focused on Imani, his face working through pain, regret, and grief before his eyes eventually glaze over.

We only have seconds now. I slam the hilt of my sword into the back of his head, and he collapses to the ground at Imani's feet. She stares down at him, chin wobbling. It is the first time I have seen anything but her hatred for him. Her stunned gaze meets mine, and I pull her into a hug. We stand for a heartbeat, shaking. The realization that he will wake up pushes me to move, and I release her.

"We need to get out of here," I say, thumbing away the tears from her sandy cheeks.

She nods and sheathes her blade. We shrug on our robes, not bothering with the wraps, and run as fast as we can through the thick sand, toward the wall. We cannot stay here. Every minute on this side of the wall has been a mistake—even more so now that a Guardian is dead by our hands. I pray Enid, Marshall, and Jonah made it out of Etonia unrecognized.

CHAPTER 32
IMANI

The green side of the wall has never felt so welcoming. As the stone door closes behind us with a dull clunk, it hits me: Harm and I can never go back. Until all this is over, we can't risk being on the desert side. Guilt creeps over me briefly as I wonder if we could have handled the situation with the Guardians better. I pray Hanola doesn't need us to go back there again.

Harm walks in front of me, a few paces ahead. He finds a fallen tree and sinks down to rest on it. I sit down beside him and remove my robe. He pulls his off too, shoving it into his rucksack. I roll mine up and tie it under mine. We sit in silence for a moment, listening to the life chattering in the canopy high above us. I pull my canteen out and guzzle mouthfuls. The dry desert sands have left me parched now that I'm no longer used to it. I pass the water to Harm. He swallows a few mouthfuls before handing it back.

"We should get moving. No need to be bear food today," I quip, giving him a nudge. He smiles tentatively back at me, his gaze falling back to the forest floor. Something is eating at him.

"You okay?" I say softly, standing.

"Yep." He stands, checking his knives.

"Okay." I raise a brow at him before starting off the run in the lead, leaving Harm to be the tail.

Moments before the last rays of sunlight disappear behind the wooded horizon, we reach the first clearing. It feels like we have been here so many times over the last few months, but this is the first time Harm and I have been here alone. The peaceful tranquility hums around us as we walk in circles, blowing out deep breaths. I scan the forest floor for small pieces of wood to use as kindling.

Before long, I have an armful and place it near the fire and sit. Harm appears with a selection of larger logs to keep us warm overnight. I watch his face as he builds the fire before sinking onto the grass beside me. The worry in his eyes spills out onto his gorgeous face. He looks up, aware that I am staring at him. For a moment, I worry that he's annoyed with me for throwing my knife into that Guardian. I should have let him handle it.

"Can you tell me what's wrong?"

His gaze remains trained on the flickering fire. "I don't know if I can do this."

My breath stops, and I rock back to sit on my heels, stomach flipping over. "Which part?"

"Be what everyone expects me to be. I don't think I'm strong enough."

The pain in his eyes twists through my heart. I move closer, sitting so our sides are touching. "You're plenty strong enough. The fact that you care so much only proves that."

"I don't know... Seeing you fighting that Guardian, after it was over, I..." He groans, low and soft. "I can't bear the fact that you were in danger, let alone me being the reason." He studies his trembling hands, and I wrap mine around them.

"I can look after myself. I don't need you or Mason to keep me safe," I whisper, placing a hand on his cheek. "You remember the day we met in that run-down Guardian outpost?"

He chokes out a laugh, but his eyes don't meet mine. "How could I forget?"

"Did you think I needed protecting then?"

"Definitely not." He smiles and holds my gaze.

"Well, it's no different now. I'm the same person. Making me yours doesn't make me weaker; if anything, it makes me stronger, because now I have more reason to stay alive. And as for Rayner, my father's plan was stupid. There was no way I was staying in that cage."

His hands take my face, searching for something. "There's something I never told you."

"Oh?"

"Before I met you, back before the outpost near Amondo..." He hesitates, swallowing. My hands fall to his chest, and he looks at his lap for a moment before looking back at me. "You're not allowed to laugh, okay?"

"I won't," I whisper.

He drops his hands, wrapping them around mine still on his chest. "I used to dream about you, long before I met you, long before I knew your name. You just appeared in my dreams over and over, standing in the sand, your hair dancing in the wind."

His fingers twirl the escaped lock of hair from my wrap next to my neck. My heart hammers in my chest.

"But there was one dream that felt more real than all the others," he says through ragged breaths. "I was here, not far from the wall—and in the distance, near the tree line, you stood there, as if you were waiting for me. Do you know when I'm talking about?"

I shove my head in my hands. It's the day we found Harm, when Hanola sent Catori, Callian, and I to the wall. I thought my heart would shatter the moment his body met mine. I try to steady my breathing, blowing out long breaths. I wipe my face and look back at him. "You dreamed that before you even knew who I was?" My voice is almost inaudible, my heart set to burst.

"Yes," he whispers.

His arms wrap around me, his soul around mine. I kiss his neck, and he nuzzles mine, his breathing heavy. He lifts his head up and cups my face in his hands. A wobbly smile cracks over my face, and he returns it before kissing my mouth briefly. I chuckle and push away from him. He gives me an intrigued look. I stand and move closer to the fire. With one hand, I take off my knife belts, one at a time.

His face blooms into a wide smile. He watches as I remove my tunic, then the fighting pants. I throw them next to the fire and turn back. His face is serious now, his breathing fast. My undergarments fall to the ground, and he closes his eyes briefly. When he opens them, they're laced with fire. My heart thunders in my chest as I move close to where Harm sits looking up at me.

"Come here," he rasps, low and desperate.

I kneel in front of him. Harm rises to his knees to meet me. His hands reach behind my head, and with a few quick tugs, my hair falls around my shoulders. His hand slides behind my neck, and he pulls me closer. I cover his mouth with mine. My need for him burns. I tug at his shirt and pull it over his head, tossing it to the ground. He stands and makes short work of the rest of his clothes. His body is covered in muscle after months of training as he returns to kneeling in front of me.

I run a hand down his chest, with my other on his cheek. He sits on the ground, and I straddle his lap, my bare knees sinking into the damp earth on either side of him. Our skin touches as he lifts me into position, so close to him. His warmth throbs against my stomach, waiting. He traces the roundness of my breast with his hand and kisses the peak. A small cry leaves my lips, and he lifts me again. This time, the tip of him finds my center. He looks at me, waiting for permission.

"I want all of you, Harm," I whisper.

He lets me fall into his lap, and the full length of him fills me. He lets out the sweetest low groan, and my chest aches, stealing the last of my breath. I cover his face in kisses and nuzzle his neck, moving my mouth over every part of him. Together we move through our cadence, fire rising with every movement. He bites down on my peak, his hands cradling each breast. I slide my fingers through his hair. His face lifts to meet mine, and I plunge into his mouth, wanting every part of us entwined.

"Imani."

I breathe out a ragged sound, too far gone to talk.

He returns to my chest, and I moan softly as his tongue caresses the peak he has clamped between his teeth. His hands move my hips in a strong and steady rhythm. I hold against him, slowing us down. He moans my name, and the sound vibrates through my chest. Warmth accelerates through my core, and then release finds me. He finds my mouth and covers it, kissing me through every wave of beautiful agony. He smiles against my mouth and lowers me onto the grass. I move to take him in.

He grips my wrists and places them above my head on the grass, holding them there. His mouth finds my neck as he continues the dance between us, his movements deliberate and strong. The warmth grows in my core again. I cry out breathlessly, unable to control the spiral of warmth building again. Harm raises his eyes to mine briefly. He returns to my breasts with a few nips to each before kissing his way up my neck, reaching my face. My chest arches for him to return.

"Where do you want me Imani?" He releases my wrists, and I pull him back down to my neck. Pleasure rips through me again, this time more forceful, and I meet his hips with mine for every wave that corresponds with his rhythm. He lets out a long, emotional groan that thunders through my chest and into my heart. Both of our souls are now firmly wrapped around each other's. He lies covering me while I kiss every inch of his face. We remain in place, breathless for moments, every part of us tingling.

Harm kisses my forehead before moving to put his clothes back on. He moves closer to the fire and sits on the grass. I sit beside him, resting my head on his shoulder, and he wraps his robe around me.

We watch the fire dance before us for an hour before he reaches for me again. He plays with my hair. The warmth of his fingers on my neck sparks a pool of warmth low in my belly, and I turn and kiss his mouth, just as hungry as before. A heartbeat later, our clothes lie beside the fire again.

This time, we don't wait. I spread my knees on either side of his lap and lower onto him, both of our bodies throbbing in time to our pounding hearts. His mouth finds my breasts, my peaks with his teeth, his lips, his tongue. Every touch, every tiny movement he makes sends lightning through my body.

The wind shifts slightly, and a low grumble resounds from above. The first drop of rain lands and runs down his shoulder. He chuckles and returns his mouth to my chest. Fat raindrops splatter onto our hot skin. I moan long and hard, tilting my head back as the rain starts pouring down.

I look down at Harm, his hair saturated around his face. He holds my hips and raises me from him. I groan, and he lets me fall. Again, he lifts me and lets me fall, and I feel the full length and shape of him every time. He lifts me one more time, but this time he places me on the wet grass, pushes my knees apart, and buries his head in my center. I run my hands through his hair. A gasp leaves my chest as his mouth finds the apex of my center.

The warmth of his mouth pulls a wave of ecstasy through me with every stroke and suckle. I grip the soft, clumpy grass with both hands, crying out, breath so shallow that my chest feels set to explode. His hand finds my center, and he slides two fingers into my burning core. I tighten around him, and he moans. He teases me with small movements, flicking his tongue over the bundle of nerves at my apex. Every caress of his mouth and tongue rips tingling currents through my center. I tighten around his fingers again, and he looks up at my desperate face with a cheeky smile.

I grab his shoulders and motion for him to sit up. With one more short round of his mouth and tongue on my throbbing apex, he sits up, and I move onto his lap again. He plunges me downward with his hands on my hips. I moan so loudly that it echoes in my chest. His movements are desperate, his chest heaving. I nip his earlobe and kiss his neck, running my hands through his saturated hair.

My core lit up, I teeter on the edge, set to spill over. Every breath that heaves its way out of my chest drags with it a small cry. I pause with his full length inside me, feeling every inch of him throbbing in time with his heart. I hold his shoulders, wanting this to last as long as possible for both of us. My throbbing apex is set to betray me any second, rubbing against his hard stomach.

"Harm," I whimper.

"Imani." His voice is nothing more than a hoarse whisper.

"Where do you want me?"

"Right where you are," he breathes.

I lengthen the height of my rise and fall, encompassing the bell of him with every stroke. His breath leaves his chest ragged and uneven. Hands gripping my hips tighter, his face changes with the beautiful agony as he rides the waves of his climax. Mine cascades after his, and I slow my movements to a shallower, gentler stroke before resting in his lap, letting the last of our waves ebb from our trembling bodies. Still deep inside me, he rests his head on my chest, his breath labored, his whole body shaking. I wrap myself around him.

"I will never spend another day without you," he whispers into my chest.

Warmth spills into me, and I draw in a wobbly breath. "You'd better not," I choke past the lump in my throat, lifting his exhausted head up to mine. His face is full of happiness and lingering traces of pleasure. I dot kisses over his face and neck. I move from his lap, and he shudders as we part. He is wrecked, in the best way possible.

I dress and wander into the trees to find some food. A few moments later, I return. Clothed and close to the smoldering fire the rain has dampened, Harm is asleep on the grass. I untie my robe from my rucksack and lay it over his spent body. I grab his robe and sit next to him, pulling it over myself. His smell lingers in the material. I smile and press my body into his, as if I still haven't had enough of him. I eat my handful of berries and sweet bark leaning against him, his robe over my tired body. The night birds call out around us as my eyes slide shut, my body weary, my mind content.

CHAPTER 33
HARM

The trip back to the village was quick with just the two of us. My mind was replaying the hours Imani and I spent tangled together, which did not help me concentrate on my surroundings. Luckily, no bears or other predators could be bothered to wander across our path this time. We now stand outside Hanola's home, and I hesitate briefly before I push through the door, Imani beside me.

Catori and Callian are both sitting on the living room floor with Hanola. We lower down next to her, close to each other.

She smiles at us both. "What did you find out?" she asks calmly.

I look at Imani. She is still, staring at Hanola, so I offer the information. "Fletcher is executing random innocent men as bait to draw me out."

Her gaze turns briefly to Imani before returning to me. "So, these men were not rebels?"

"No, Jonah and Enid didn't recognize them. The crowd was gathered like any other time, but this time, Guardians were sent to surround the crowd—dozens of them. It was a trap. We got out, but not without spilling the blood of a Guardian."

"I see." She closes her eyes and taps her fingers together for a moment. Opening her eyes, she looks directly at Imani. "Did you see your father?"

I hold my breath, fire growing in my chest at Hanola's pointed question.

"Yes," Imani replies softly.

"Good." Hanola moves her attention back to her grandchildren. I control the urge to react to Hanola. They remain staring at each other for a period before Hanola dismisses all of us but Imani. I get up and leave with Callian and Catori.

Once outside Hanola's house, Callian slaps me on the back and raises an eyebrow.

"What?" I say.

Callian's eyes are fixed on the stains on my clothes. I hold back the part about having none on when we were doing what he thinks we were.

"Oh, you know what," he chuckles.

I try to stop the heat from rising to my face, but fail. He laughs out loud at me as we walk to the village center to eat. I hook into a plate of food, having missed the variety and volume of food you get in the forest. It feels like we've been gone a lot longer than only a couple of days. My mind wanders back to last night as I eat. Callian cleans up his food and waits for me to finish.

"What do you think Hanola wants to talk to Imani about?" I ask Callian.

"No idea. Hanola doesn't share unless you need to know. Guess we don't."

I finish off the last of my food, and we return our plates to the ladies in the kitchen, who take them and offer beaming smiles.

"I have to see Mason before we start. I'll catch up with you," I say.

"I think he's back in the cells while Catori is out on patrol," Callian says and nods, jogging off to the training clearing.

I walk across the village to the prison. The guards wave me inside like last time, and I walk with determination to the last cell. Mason sits on the floor, staring at nothing.

"Mason."

"Go away, Travesci," he mutters.

I move a step closer. His state has deteriorated even in the last couple of days after I told him about his family. He looks at me now, but remains on the floor. "I said, go away." His voice cracks on the last word.

"Stand up," I snap.

He tries to laugh, but chokes.

I make my way back to the guard and request the keys. With a raised eyebrow, he relents, moving to cover the doorway as I return to Mason's cell. I unlock the cell door and walk over to Mason.

"Get up, Mason." My tone is kinder this time.

"No, just leave me here to die," he whispers. Tears float down his filthy, unkempt face, leaving a shimmering trail in the dirt. I bend down and grab him under the arm. He shoots me a confused look.

"Get up!" This time it's an order.

"Fine," he chokes, scrambling to his feet, his thinned body swaying with the movement. Beside my muscled frame, his emaciated state appears even worse.

"I have a deal to offer you."

He meets my eyes this time. His are sunken and grey, the fire and obnoxiousness that were once there extinguished. "What could you possibly offer me that I would want, Harm?"

I keep my eyes on his. "Purpose."

"I have no desire to be a part of your games. I lost my family for it. I'm done with sides." He sits back down.

"Suit yourself. If you would rather rot in a cell than redeem yourself, that's fine by me." I slam the door. Turning the key in the lock, I tear it out and walk back down the passageway.

"Wait. What's the deal?" he calls.

I stop dead. "Freedom. Complete freedom, in exchange for your help."

It's a risk; I know that. But I won't see him rot in a cell if there is another way. Fletcher's words come back to me: Imani was supposed to stay with Rayner and out of trouble. Was Mason trying to protect her all along? But the gallows... Nothing makes much sense.

But on the off chance that Mason is willing to keep that order and help me protect Imani from the Chancellor, I'll take the risk. Hanola's plan is taking too long. If he is going to be of any use to us and be able to help me protect Imani, he needs to train. But his freedom comes with a condition.

"What about Hanola's rehabilitation plans?" he asks.

"You continue those. But if you lay a finger on Imani, Rayner, or upset her even the slightest bit, I won't bother bringing you back to these cozy cells. I will end you—and that is a promise."

"Why would you offer me this, after all I've done to you and Imani?"

I stand there, trying to squash the anger that has risen in my veins, mentally tallying the losses both Mason and I have suffered. I turn slowly. "Because I know what it's like to lose your entire family and have nothing left. And because I'm nothing like Fletcher. This is your chance to make a difference, to be part of the right side of this fight for once."

I leave, handing the keys to the guard as I storm out into the sunshine. I run to training and meet Callian in the sparring ring.

Anger still coursing through my veins, I snatch up the sword he throws at my feet. Every cell of my body funnels fire down my sword, and Callian needs quick work and a strong arm to hold me off. The training session flies past, and we're heading back to the village center in no time.

I walk through the doorway of our little home to see Imani pacing, hands clasped in front of her. She sees me and stops, frozen.

"What is it?" A bolt of worry rips through me as I take in her pained, twisted face.

As if I wasn't supposed to see it, she composes herself and forces a smile. "Nothing, I just need to take a walk," she says as she slips past me and walks out the door into the sinking afternoon sun, heading for the tree line on the outskirts. I want to follow her, but I know better.

So instead, I light the hearth and take a bath. It's nightfall before she returns. Her demeanor is normal, as if I had just imagined our last encounter.

"I'm starving. You want to go eat?" I ask.

"I need a bath first. You want to help me out of these clothes?" Imani gestures to her tunic.

I move over to her space and take off her tunic. Next, I remove her undergarments. Her full breasts meet my hands, and my body aches for her. She kisses my mouth lightly, but walks to the bath by herself, leaving me standing with a throbbing ache for her. In no time, I hear the water swelling around her. I try to distract myself with reshuffling the logs on the fire, but nothing helps.

A muffled sob echoes from behind the screen before the water gurgles as she submerges herself in it. Worry bunches my chest tighter with each sob she looses. I wait for her to resurface before I round the screen. My brow is low and tight. Her face is trained to neutrality as her eyes meet mine, and she gestures for me to hand her the soap. She lathers up her body, and mine responds to her a little more. She ducks below the waterline, washing away the soap before holding out a hand for me to help her out.

I take her hand, and she stands. Water courses down her body, over her shoulders, rolling over her full, heaving breasts and down her hips, past her center. I place my hands under her arms and lift her out of the bath. Her legs wrap around my waist before I have a chance to lower her to the ground. Her mouth slams into mine. I kiss her back. Her skin is warm and wet in my hands as I hold her, hands clasped under her bottom.

With three long strides, we reach the bunk. I lower her down, sitting her on the edge, and kneel. Running hands up her arms and over her neck, I cup her face.

"Imani, what's going on?" I'm desperate to know, trying like hell to ignore the fire building in my body right now.

"Nothing," she breathes.

My face doesn't change.

Her brow lowers. "Hanola wanted to talk about Fletcher. It upset me, that's all." Her hand has slid into my shirt now, her fingers tracing the muscles of my chest.

"You know you can tell me anything, Imani. I'll always be here to listen to you, to protect you, and to love you." My hands leave her face, one finger running slowly down her chest through her heaving breasts, past her belly button, halting a hair's breadth away from her throbbing bundled apex. She takes two deep breaths before removing her hands from my body, lacing her fingers through mine.

"I know, Harm." Tears slide down her cheeks.

I rise and sit beside her, wrapping my arms around her, holding her tight. Her chest heaves as she cries. The fire in my body for her wanes as her shaking body wilts. We stay like this for over an hour, Imani crying, me holding her. Only when I realize she's gone from shaking to shivering do I unwrap my arms and help her dress. Her blue eyes scan my face, and her chin trembles again as I hold my hand out to take her to supper. I pull her close and walk her to the village center. We eat surrounded by our friends, but Imani is quiet, fresh pain in her eyes as laughter and conversation drift around us.

I lie awake into the small hours of the night, scenarios playing out in my mind—anything that could make Imani that upset. With her soft body pressed up against mine, her steady breath and heartbeat comfort me, and eventually I fall asleep.

Imani grabs her weapons before rummaging through the top drawer of our small dresser to find another long piece of cloth to wrap her hair up. She is still turning over the contents of the drawer when I place my hand on hers and turn her toward me. Her eyes meet mine, and she plays with my hand with her fingers.

"Imani, can you tell me what happened?" I whisper, pulling her closer with my free hand.

She looks to the floor as her breath catches. A knot twists in my stomach, and I draw a lungful of air, steadying myself. My thoughts spiral into the darkness of everything that could possibly be causing her pain. With a sigh, she pushes back from me, her gaze meeting mine again. She's smiling, but the joy doesn't reach her eyes.

"Nothing, Harm. I just had a bad day, that's all. Not a big deal. My emotions are a little all over the place these days. Maybe it's the tea Hanola has me drinking," she explains.

I stare at her face that is in stark contrast to last night. Deciding to drop it, I release her back to the drawer. I pull on my weapons, readying for the day's training. "We can go and grab some breakfast, if you want."

"Sure, I'm famished after this morning." She wraps her hair in her blue scarf, highlighting her brilliant blue eyes.

Without another word, we head toward the village center for

food. We find Callian sitting at the table, eating a pile of food that looks like it could feed three men. Letting out a chuckle, Imani plonks down beside him and grabs a plate from the center of the laden table. I sit next to her, piling food onto my plate. My stomach growls, and I bite into the fruit I chose.

"Harm, I had a chat with Mason before breakfast. He wants to take your deal and help us." Callian's face is lit up with amusement as he chews his food.

"My offer to Mason still stands. Hanola is on board with it, as is Catori. I guess I should talk to Hanola about it again, see if she's okay with Mason training with us."

"Probably a good idea. Although, he's been no trouble—surprisingly, for an ex-Guardian—so she most likely hasn't changed her mind about him. And it helps that he could come in handy." Callian waves as he departs, leaving his words hanging between Imani and me.

"Does Hanola trust Mason to help us, if it comes down to it?" Imani asks eventually.

"I don't think she would trust him; that would be foolish. But she may have a use for him. He knows more about the Guardians and what goes on in that tower than anyone else here."

I finish off my food. Imani eats slowly, studying her plate. Is the tea she drinks to manage her rhythms affecting her more than she lets on? I make a mental note to see Hanola about it. If it has side effects, I want to know what they are. I won't let Imani suffer just so I can find release, no matter how much I crave her every minute I'm awake.

CHAPTER 34
IMANI

Four weeks have gone by since Mason started training with us, and I'm still not used to him being around. Every afternoon, he sits with Hanola and Catori while Callian stands guard outside the elder's home. Nobody speaks of what Hanola and Catori do or say with him, but since the deal he made with Harm, he has visited with the leader every afternoon.

He has been assigned to Catori for training, which is almost fun to watch. She is hard on him—really hard. But he keeps getting back up, keeps coming back. Metal clashes together as we watch Catori swing into Mason again and again. He wasn't started on a wooden weapon like the rest of us. Possibly they assumed he didn't need it, being a Guardian, or maybe they don't care if he bleeds. Either way, he has earned some nasty cuts from being too slow under Catori's relentless offense, but he's never fazed. He's different than he used to be on our side of the wall. His arrogance is gone.

Nobody speaks when he falls to the ground, weapon held over his head, his shaking arms over his face. In less than a heartbeat, Catori stands over him, weapon raised, chest heaving. Harm has gone still, his breath held, fixing a stare on the pair in front of him. He hasn't said anything to any of us, but it's obvious he doesn't hate Mason the way he once did, even though he keeps him at arm's length, and I wonder if that is for my benefit. The compassion he shows everyone is automatic. I should have realized he would be no different with Mason after he lost his family and his purpose; Harm has been there himself.

"Not bad, Guardian. Next time, don't let me in your close zone, and you may have a chance of staying alive." Catori takes away his weapon before pulling him to his feet. He grunts in return, wiping the sweat from his face and neck with a cloth from his pants pocket. Once he beats Catori, he is promised a new set of clothes, but that hasn't happened yet. He stalks back to Callian's side, not looking at any of us as he passes where we sit.

Harm stands and plants a kiss on my forehead before jumping into the sparring ring with Miya. She pulls her hair loose, letting it fall around her shoulders. A grin stretches over her face, and she winks at me before turning back to Harm. This ought to be good.

He draws his two long blades from his sides and takes up an offensive stance. She circles him, not breaking eye contact. He throws her a wide smile, and she lunges at him head on. Her broadsword lands in the center of his crossed daggers, and she presses toward him. He stands his ground before flinging her backward. My breath stops as Harm spins to her side, plunging his dagger at her ribs before she ducks out of his range. Without a pause, he repeats the maneuver, arriving beside her again, and she spins away from him.

He stalks over to her position, wielding both daggers in a pattern before him. Damp air hangs around us, and sweat runs down his face and arms already. Miya lunges with an offensive move that he anticipates before their blades collide. Throwing her off again, he spins and rounds her like a vulture circling its prey.

She lays into him with swing after swing of her weapon, which he meets effortlessly. His corded arms make the effort it takes to hold Miya at bay seem like a child's game. She regroups and comes at him again.

This time, Harm sidesteps her and lets her pass him before turning to come up behind her, his right blade landing in front of her throat, his left pointed into her ribs. With her free hand, she pushes out against the arm holding the blade to her throat and spins away. Before she has a chance to meet him with her broadsword, he is in her space, one blade in her side, one resting against her throat. This time they face each other. A wide smile appears on her face, and she lets out a chuckle.

"With your combination of speed and the ability to anticipate your opponent's moves, paired with the natural strength you now possess, I'd say you're ready, Harm. Well done."

He lowers his blades from her body, sheathing them.

"Just remember, take no prisoners. You're going to have to curb that compassionate part of you when it comes down to the wire, or you'll end up on the wrong end of a blade, brother," she finishes and slaps him on the shoulder. He stares back at her, sweat running down his face, neck, and arms.

"Will do." He grabs a cloth to wipe away the sweat before sitting down.

Miya motions for me to join her next, and I stand and walk into the sparring ring. As soon as my feet cross the threshold, my body automatically gears up, and my senses tune into every sound and movement Miya makes. This time, she replaces the sword with daggers, matching my own fighting knives. She stands inches taller than me, but what I lack in height, I make up for in speed and intention, so she has told me.

I waste no time assuming the offense and fly into her with both blades. She counters each move with force, her size proving to be an advantage at this point in the fight. Circling cautiously, she lunges to one side of me, trying to catch me off guard. I spin out and try my own attack. Miya blocks me with one blade and swipes the other toward my abdomen, which I meet with my own. Our arms are suspended in a tangle, and she holds me to my position. This is the moment I can use my speed against her.

I retract and duck to her side before she moves into the defensive, the first sign of a losing mindset. One more sharp sideways step, and I have both blades digging into the sides of her neck. With a flick of my wrists, I could sever both of the veins pulsing under the soft skin of her throat. Her only move now is backward, or else my blades would slit her open. She lunges back.

I release the hold I have on her, but her stance is now lower than mine. I drop my right-hand blade—a risk, but I have her on the back foot, literally. Stepping up beside her, I shove the heel of my palm into her chest, forcing her to the ground. With my left hand following my right instantly, my blade now rests along her glistening throat as she lies on the ground beneath me in less than a heartbeat.

"Nicely played, Imani," she breathes under my knife.

I back up and offer a hand to help her up. She grabs it, pulling herself to her feet.

"One thing I want you to remember: never underestimate your opponent," she says. "Looks can be deceiving. They may underestimate you, since you're slightly smaller than most, but don't let that fool you either. And never..." She wipes her face and hands with her cloth. "... never lose that fierceness you have. It's your best asset and keeps you in the game. You too are ready."

She throws me a cloth. I wipe the sweat from my face and neck and wait for my breathing to return to a normal pace.

Harm walks over, and we pack up the sparring ring. His hand lands across my fingers as we grab the same weapon to put away.

His deep brown eyes meet mine, and his expression is almost pleading. I know I've been off, but after my meeting with Hanola, I find it so hard to level out my emotions. And Harm is suffering for it.

I force a smile and touch his face. His warm smile stops my breath. He leans down, softly kissing my lips, and I suck back a sob before slamming my mouth onto his. His hands find the back of my neck, and I melt under his warm touch—the touch I had to wait so long for.

By the time we pull apart, the others have all left, and we walk home in silence. Harm holds my hand, speculating about Mason's visits to Hanola. I comment whenever he pauses for too long, but my mind is a million miles away.

"Imani," he says, stopping me with the hand he's still holding.

"It's nothing. I told you, I just feel a little off." It's the truth, after all. I have to deal with this myself, and I have to get through the next few weeks myself; no one else can do it for me. I've done hard things before; I can do what Hanola asks of me if it helps Harm. I would do anything for him—anything. That includes Hanola's new assignment for me, no matter how much it hurts.

"Seeing you like this worries me," he says and pulls me into a tight hug. I pull in a deep breath, taking in his smell, his warmth, and the weight of his arms around me. Home. I will do anything to make sure I don't lose this. I can't keep letting him worry; it's not fair, and it upsets me when he's not happy. I steal a few more moments encapsulated in his hold before I resolve to at least level out my emotions and go back to normality, for Harm's sake. With a pass of my hands over my face to ensure that it's not going to give me away, I push back and hold his gaze properly for the first time in days.

"Please don't worry. I'm okay. We're okay. More than okay." I rise to my tippy-toes to kiss his mouth, one hand running my fingers through his dark hair. The exhilaration catches me, and I pause for a moment, my lips on his, wanting nothing more than to drag him home and lock the door. But before I can give in to my baser needs, Harm pushes me back, his face wrapped in love and concern.

"Alright, but please remember, I'm here. I will do everything I can to take care of you and make you happy. Whatever you need, I'll help you find it. Whatever comes our way, we'll get through it. Together, Imani." His fingers trace my cheeks, the warmth creating sparks along my skin. My heart flutters, and the desire to pull him into me surges again.

"Together. We do this life together," I affirm, and he smiles back at me from the depths of those brown eyes. I pray he remembers that when the time comes.

We walk hand in hand to the eating area, finding Catori and Mason already dining at the table. She casually chats to him about forest life as he eats in silence. He listens, absorbing every word, never taking his gaze from her face. Harm sits down opposite Mason, and I sit close to him, grabbing a plate and loading it up. I am halfway through my food when Mason stops chewing, staring at me as if lost in thought. Harm goes rigid beside me.

"I'm sorry, Imani, for what I did to you," he whispers.

I drop the food back on my plate. Harm relaxes slightly beside me, and his warm hand lands on my leg. I don't know what to say. For months, I hated him, hated all Guardians, but mostly him and my father, and I desperately wanted nothing to do with either of them. But you can't choose your family, any more than you can choose the people you love, or who love you.

"Forget it," I finally say and go back to my food.

"I doubt I ever will," he says.

I look back up at his face, and my gaze flicks between Catori and Mason. Catori sits calmly chewing her food as if we're talking about the weather. Does she know what he did to me, and what he has done as a Guardian? She's no fool; she probably knows the kinds of orders he's carried out during his short career as a Guardian. Her face remains neutral, but mine has twisted in anger at the memories of every moment I've spent with Mason since the gallows. Heat rises through my face, and I grab Harm's hand that rests on my leg, lacing my fingers through his.

He lets out a breath. "Remember my promise to you, Rayner."

Mason snorts and returns to his food. What promise would Harm have made to Mason?

Before anyone else speaks, Catori signals for Mason to rise. He follows her to Hanola's, Callian falling in beside Mason halfway to the house.

"What promise did you make to Mason?" I ask Harm.

"Nothing good."

"Oh?"

"One of the conditions of his freedom was that if he ever caused you grief or laid a hand on you, I would slit his throat." His face is stone.

What the hell?

"You don't think I can look after myself?" I rise from the table.

"No—I mean, of course you can. But if he ever lays a hand on you, after everything that's happened, I will kill him, Imani."

Part of me loves that he is so protective of me, but the other half is insulted that he's insinuating that I wouldn't be able to take care of Mason myself. And if I'm honest, I much smaller part of me is devastated at the thought. I stalk back to our home, hoping he doesn't follow.

I slam the door and rip my weapons from their belts before taking the belts off as well. Surprisingly, I don't feel the need to take revenge on Mason or see him harmed. Seeing him move into Callian's house and the frown on Callian's face was almost enough to make me laugh. Harm's forgiving nature has rubbed off on me.

I am halfway through undressing when our front door opens and Harm steps through. Closing the door behind him, he leans against it with his hands behind his back. His face is serious, but kind. He stands and watches me as I take off the clothing I wore at training.

I slip behind the changing screen and pick out some pants and a top to put on. Still naked, I spin around—and run right into Harm's chest. His hands grab me, lifting me onto the small table in the changing area. The rough wood is cool against my skin, and he tugs me into him as his mouth finds mine. My heart thunders as my body responds to his. The urgency and ache for him in my chest returns so powerfully that I can't breathe.

"You are the most precious thing to me in all this world, Imani. Whatever it is that's eating you, please, let me fix it," he breathes into my hair.

I run my hands under his shirt, wanting his warmth on every part of me. I breathe through the now ragged breaths that have settled in my chest. "I just want you."

"I'm all yours, and I always will be," he growls.

I tug his shirt over his head. He kisses my neck, and his hands play in my hair as I fiddle with the fastener on his pants. Moments later, they hit the floor, and he pulls my hips toward him with the corded arms I have been watching all morning. I close my eyes as his arms envelop me in an embrace, and home finds me. Arching me back, he finds my chest with his lips and teeth. We meld together with one soft motion, and a ragged cry falls from my open mouth as tears blur my vision.

CHAPTER 35
HARM

Every person in Hanola's comfortable home sits restlessly waiting for her to start. She sits on her floor cushion, humming the familiar tune we've all heard at one point or another. Imani sits next to me with her hands in her lap, fingers fiddling with the material of her shirt. Catori and Callian sit on the mat opposite us, one sibling on either side of Mason. His presence reinforces Hanola's words to me this morning.

It dawns on me as we all sit in silence that she most likely has a plan for him. She is the only person I have ever met who has everything thought through beforehand. Hanola would have to be the most strategic person I know. Her strategies always end in the betterment of someone or something though; there is not a cruel bone in her frail old body.

Hanola raises one hand and opens her eyes.The melody stops instantly, but seems to linger in the air around us. Her gaze lands on Mason, and he shifts on his cushion under her stare. Catori stiffens slightly beside him, her gaze holding to her grandmother. Callian focuses on Hanola, hardly noticing his sister or Mason.

"Mason, before we hash out the remainder of our plans for the

"

tower, perhaps you could provide us with some information? It would sure aid our warriors if they were aware of what they're walking into. Anything you deem helpful, I would like to hear it," Hanola requests.

Mason shifts on his cushion again. His hands rest on his crossed legs, and his gaze remains on the weathered forest leader, who offers him an encouraging smile and open-armed gesture.

"Do you want to know about the Guardians who are assigned to the tower?" His voice is hoarse.

"Yes, please—anything that you think would be useful for Catori and Callian." She nods to both of them in turn.

Mason looks at Catori briefly, and something like worry flickers through his eyes. A moment slips past with no response from him before he lets out a long breath.

"The tower where the Chancellor resides is manned by his private guard, along with twenty other Guardians. The private guard are never far away from him, always in the same room or outside in the halls. The twenty men cover the exits and any possible infiltration point, like low windows and such. There are six levels in the tower. The very top—the roof, I guess you would call it—is just an empty space, but it could be used as a lookout. The top level is his meeting room, where he sits in a large wooden chair in the center and collaborates with Fletcher and other senior Guardians." He pauses briefly, eyes drifting to Imani.

"There's also a large table with the latest projects and plans, to the side of his and Emmie's chairs. The dial is up some more stairs, in a back room overlooking the eastern forest. It's locked and not much bigger than Callian's house, and it's manned by two Guardians. The level under that, level five, is the private rooms, bedrooms and such. Below that are the dining and domestic areas, and also a large common room that Nirri spends most of her time in. Level four connects to the bridge that spans across to the wall and the prison. There isn't much on that level, except for quarters for high-ranking Guardians that adjoin the larger barracks and courtyard. Level three is weapons and the armory, but apart from the canes they carry, nothing else is usually disturbed. Level two is the cells. The lowest level is where they keep the information on the dial and anything left over from before the dial was changed—also locked. Two Guardians are on duty there at all times." He waits for Hanola's response.

"That is more than I had hoped for. Thank you Mason," she says and pats his hand as a meek smile appears on his face, lasting only seconds. "Do any of the Guardians in the tower carry weapons?"

"Just their standard-issue canes. The weapons in the armory are old and haven't been used for decades; there was no need. The people have been oppressed for so long that a greater caliber of weapon hasn't been required. Throwing people in the well, along with the hangings, has proven enough to control them. We learned a few things on the history of the regime in our initial training."

Catori shifts on her cushion, and Callian shoots her a sideways glance.

"You have been very helpful, but I have one more request," Hanola says.

Mason nods in response.

"What can you tell us about the forces in the prisons and on the desert side of the wall?"

"A fair bit. There are around fifty Guardians stationed in the prison. It's the largest barracks on the desert side. There are pairs of officers assigned to each functioning outpost. Fletcher is the commander of the Guardian Regime, and he moves between the tower, the prison, and the desert villages as required now. Before I..." He sucks in a breath. "Before I left, I was his second-in-command, because I received a high score on the final training exam. I've been in all the locations many times, accompanying Fletcher. There are also another forty Guardians in training. At least, there were when I left." This time his gaze flicks between me and Hanola, as if worried that his next words are going to do damage. "They amped up the selections when Harm escaped the tower prison, and also because there are plans to create outposts throughout the forest side of the wall."

Hanola stills, her face hardens, and she manages to stifle a gasp. Catori's grip around her cushion tightens, whitening her knuckles. Callian breathes out, long and slow.

"Why would they want to do that? The forest villages have been here without interfering for decades," Imani asks Mason.

"Control. Arthur has long suspected a connection between the villages on either side of the wall, and he thinks it has something to do with the rebels," Mason says.

Imani shoots me a sharp look. He's right; they are connected through the rebels. Which makes me think, there are people willing to betray their own on both sides of the wall.

"There's something else, and this is going to take some process-ing." Mason checks each of our faces. I hold my breath, trying to imagine what could possibly come next. "There is another part of the wall—another section of controlled environment."

Catori's mouth falls open.

"But it's not patrolled, just closed off from the rest. The inhabitants are less than friendly, and Arthur doesn't send Guardians over often, unless there's a threat," he finishes and takes in each of our faces, which are now staring at him in disbelief.

"How is that possible?" Hanola asks. "I've never seen anything other than our side, the forest, and some of your side, the sands."

"Only a handful of high-ranking Guardians are aware of it, and for good reason," Mason says.

"And you know about it because Fletcher told you?" I ask, skeptical of this new information.

"No, I was on patrol in the halls when Arthur and Fletcher were discussing options in regards to controlling the mountain people."

"'Mountain people'?" Imani echoes.

"Yes. Their terrain is nothing like either side of the wall we've been on. It's all high peaks and low valleys. And snow, its this frozen type of rain. A lot of the land is inhospitable, but there are at least three groups of civilization, judging from the maps I got a glimpse of when I was in the meeting hall with two other officers the day before." He pauses. "The day before they brought Harm in with that old man."

"Charlie," I breathe.

"He was some relative of Arthur's, the officers were saying. Anyway, I was supposed to be on duty all day, but I left so I could get back early to..." He stops, and his face brightens with a hue of shame. "... Imani, when I had Imani. I never went back after she left, but I discovered that much, at least." His eyes scan the rug on the floor beneath us.

Heat rises to my face. My heart rate doubles as I realize he's talking about when he held Imani prisoner. My fists clench, and Callian sits up, shooting me a cursory warning look. Hanola's wizened eyes swing between Mason and me while we sit tensely in the awkward silence.

"Okay, so what now?" Imani pipes up, as if we had all been discussing the weather, not her own imprisonment.

"Now, my girl, we have a lot more information than I anticipated—but that's a good thing," Hanola says. "You can never be too prepared for hard things. With all that Mason has volunteered, I think it's best if we infiltrate the tower with stealth, not force. We need a few things to help overturn the Chancellor. The first is to control the dial, and the know-how to do so. That information lies in the basement, I'm sure of it—technical diagrams, an old manual of some sort, perhaps. You and Mason will retrieve that for us." Hanola focuses on Imani intently.

"No, not happening, Hanola. We go as a team, or not at all," I insist, and I receive a look from Catori that lets me know arguing with Hanola is not tolerated.

"Mason and Imani will retrieve the information and anything of use for after we change the dial," Hanola says firmly. "Secondly, Catori, Callian, and yourself will have a preliminary go at the dial and then take after the Chancellor. You'll need the three of you to take out the personal guard, at least. We can use Miya and Jeselle if you think it's warranted, but more people means you're less likely to get in and out undetected. It also means more loss of life, should things go wrong."

"Agreed. A small team will work much better," Catori assents.

"So, that settles it then. We breach the tower together, than split up and get our respective jobs done, then meet back at the entry point and run like hell." Callian's grin makes us all relax a little, despite the tasks that lie ahead of us now.

"That will be all for now; you can go back to your preparations," Hanola says. "Mason, I would like you to stay for a little longer. I have some things to discuss with you." She gestures for the rest of us to leave.

"I will stay, Grandmother," Catori says firmly, her gaze never wavering from Mason.

"That will not be necessary, my child. I'm sure Mason will behave himself." She smiles back at Catori, who nods and leaves with us, her gait stiff as she shoots Callian a worried look before glancing at Mason. Her worry is not for Hanola; it's for Mason, and what goes on in here with him. He sits patiently on his cushion, but his breathing has elevated slightly, gaze fixed on Hanola, his hands gripping his knees tight.

The day's light has started to fade. We file in around the table for the evening meal—all of us except Mason. Catori's attention swings from the conversation at the table to her grandmother's door every few minutes. Mason has been in there for hours. What could take that long? I pop a piece of fruit into my mouth and pour Imani some water. She sits quietly beside me. For days, she has been too quiet; she's not herself. She tells me it's the tea. I know it's not.

"Not hungry?" I ask her.

"Not really." Her eyes flicker to Hanola's door briefly before returning to her plate.

A long moan splits the evening chatter around us. Catori stops eating mid-chew, eyes fixed on Hanola's home. Callian pauses, tracking his gaze to what Imani and Catori are staring at. He drops his food and rises.

"Don't," Catori snaps, her eyes never leaving Hanola's door.

Callian sits and picks at his plate. "I don't know why you're getting all bothered by Hanola working with that Guardian," he utters under his breath.

Catori's gaze snaps to Callian. "Mind your business, little brother."

Then, the air splits with a painful cry from inside Hanola's home—Mason's. Catori and Callian jump to their feet. Every villager looks up, silence filling the eating area instantly.

"Stay here," she growls at her brother before stalking to Hanola's door.

Another cry from Mason. Imani stiffens beside me. My throat

closes up just imagining what is going on inside that house. I put down my food and watch as Catori enters without knocking. Desperation fills Mason's next breakdown. The sharp voice of Catori rings out from the home. A few moments later, the cries die down, and the villagers return to their plates. But neither Catori nor Mason leaves Hanola's.

We finish our food, and I wander from the table to the kitchen to give the ladies our plates. Warm smiles reward my thoughtfulness. Imani sits next to Callian, both of them waiting, staring at Hanola's. I round the table's end and rest my hands on Imani's shoulders. She looks up at me briefly, and I kiss her forehead.

"Should we go and see if everything's okay?" Callian asks, fidgeting where he sits on the bench. His concern for his sister and grandmother has his face scrunched up, his brows lowered.

"Maybe," I say.

Imani rises and heads toward Hanola's. Callian and I follow her lead, a few steps behind.

"Do you know what she's doing to him?" I ask Callian.

His jaw clenches, and he sucks in a breath. "I have an idea."

Nothing pleasant, then. A small part of me twinges, feeling partially responsible. Just before Imani reaches the front door, it opens. Mason and Catori step outside. She is close to him. His face is pale, and he trembles from head to toe. She guides him away from Hanola's home before stopping in front of Callian. Tears stain her cheeks, silver still welling in her eyes.

"Take him home," she says to Callian.

He nods slightly before taking Mason's arm. His mind elsewhere, Mason trails beside Callian, gazing at nothing.

"What happened?" Imani whispers, her breathing fast.

"Hanola was helping him to transition back from his previous training. It's not a pleasant experience to endure," Catori says. She watches as Mason is led back to Callian's home, swallowing before blowing out a long breath.

"You okay?" I ask.

She looks at me, only just tempering her annoyance. "I am not the one who just lived through that, Harm." Shaking her head, she heads home.

With a knock harsher than intended, I stand waiting for Hanola. Moments later, she appears behind the half-open door, her lined face smiling up at me. The fire I carried here ebbs out.

"Yes, Harmen?"

"I need to talk with you about Mason."

Hanola pushes the door back before retreating to her living room floor, beckoning for me to follow. After a minute passes, she has descended to the floor, and I do the same, sitting on a cushion opposite her.

"What do you need to discuss about Mason?"

"You're including him in this mission?"

"Yes, I thought that would be the best option for him," she says. Her face is neutral. She doesn't speak of what was happening to Mason in here earlier.

"After all the atrocities he's carried out, you trust him?"

"I did have some doubts. But that was before."

"Before what?"

"Before he lost both his family and his purpose. You've been there too, as you very well know. If there is any chance that he can be saved from the regime, this is it."

"You think he'll change who he is because you gave him a chance?"

"I believe everyone deserves a second chance, Harmen. Being

selected by the Guardians is not a choice. Carrying out orders as a Guardian, no matter how terrible, is not a choice. The life your people live in the sands is not a choice. But I can give him one now. Do you understand?"

I stare at her blankly, but I do understand. I don't trust Mason, but I know he had no choice in most of the things he has done in this lifetime. None of us do.

For a second, I'm standing back against the well in Amondo, Mason's fist bunched in my shirt, his other hand tight around my arm. *I can't help you, Harm.* His words were soft, but pained, and it was a complete risk with Fletcher only a few feet away. Even then, unwilling to carry out his orders, he had no choice.

"Mason has never been a person I got along with, even as children. If you think this is going to be for the best, I trust you. But..." I hesitate, not wanting to sound disrespectful. "I don't trust him, and I don't know if I ever can, after everything he's done to me and Imani."

"I realize you three have a history, Harmen. But I won't prevent someone from becoming a better person because of their past mistakes, and neither will you," she warns.

No, I won't. I wasn't brought up that way. It could have very easily been the other way around; it could have been me who was chosen for the regime. I push up to leave, and Hanola lays a wrinkled hand on my knee.

"Harmen," she starts, studying my face.

"Yes?"

"Things may get much more difficult before they get better. Whatever happens, you need to keep going. Please remember that." She offers me a small smile, but worry lines her face.

I nod and rise, her hand falling from my knee. She watches me leave as I shut the door behind me, leaning my head against it on the other side. I breathe out a long, slow breath and close my eyes.

So, Mason is part of my village—again. Only this time, he doesn't have the upper hand. Life can be interesting sometimes. I just hope Hanola is right about him.

I wander to the training area. Everyone is silent and watching the sparring ring. Mason and Catori stand motionless, in a standoff of sorts. Sweat runs down both of their faces and arms. I plonk down between Imani and Callian. Miya and Jeselle sit on the opposite side of the ring on the grass, eyes fixed on Catori.

"They've been at it for half an hour already," Callian says, brows lowered as he watches his sister lunge at Mason again. He blocks her with his two blades in the X configuration we have all learned. A low growl resonates from Catori as she whips to his side and lunges once more. He spins and blocks her before stepping back. Another lunge, another block.

For what seems an age, he defends as she comes at him from every angle. Frustrated, she stops and lowers her weapon. Face twisted with anger, she stands, chest heaving, watching Mason watch her. His body is shaking, and he refuses to engage her, other than to block her blows.

"Fight me. All you do is defend!" Catori finally grinds out.

"I don't want to fight you, Catori," Mason rasps through ragged breath, his arms hanging by his sides, hands loose around the hilts of his blades.

"Yes, you will fight me. You will do as you're told, Guardian!" She steps forward and raises her weapon again.

"Don't call me that," Mason says in a low growl.

Imani grabs my arm. It has been a long time since we've seen the fire in Mason. What memories does it bring back for her? I dread the thought.

"Then make me stop," Catori snaps.

"I said I'm not fighting you."

"And I said you are, Guardian!"

"I'm not a Guardian, and I will *not* fight you, Catori." His arms and hands shake below his heaving chest.

"Prove it!" She steps into his space, only inches from his shaking body, hers matching his with a tremble that echoes through her words and weapon. Their eyes stay locked on each other for a handful of heartbeats.

Mason drops his weapons.

He sinks to his knees and rips his shirt open, surrendering his undefended chest to Catori. Breaths choke out of him. He tilts his head back, exposing his throat to her, his veins throbbing. He closes his eyes. She lifts her blade to his throat and grabs his hair with one fist, and he swallows. She rests her gaze on his face as he opens his eyes to meet it. Catori's stare burns into Mason, and the hand holding the blade pressed into his skin trembles.

Seconds later, she composes herself and stands tall. Taking a step back, she sheathes her blade and grunts before stalking toward the village. Mason remains on the ground, knees dug into the grass and dirt.

"Well, that was entertaining," Callian murmurs before walking over to Mason. He extends a hand and helps him up. Mason pulls his shirt around his chest. Callian removes the weapons and escorts him back to the village. We watch them go, and Jeselle and Miya walk over to our side of the ring.

"That's new," Jeselle says.

"I've never seen Catori so strung out in the sparring ring, or in any fight, for that matter. Something has gotten under her skin with this Guardian," Miya says.

"Maybe she's tired of being tethered to him," I say.

"Maybe," Imani says softly, but her eyes are far away.

We walk back to the village center for lunch before we are all expected at Hanola's—another meeting to iron out the details for infiltrating the tower.

Tossing and turning, I flip the pillow over again, searching for a cooler surface. Imani is sleeping like the dead after training hard today—or yesterday, rather. The moon has started its descent.

A long cry winds through the village homes. I sit up. Another cry—and it turns into a scream. Footsteps thud somewhere in the center of the village. I shake Imani awake.

"What is it?" she rasps, pushing her hair from her face.

"Someone's in pain," I utter, tossing the blanket back. I throw on a shirt and lower a hand to Imani. She rises from the bunk, grabbing her robe from by the door as we head into the darkness. Moments later, having followed the continuous moans, we stand in Callian's doorway.

Mason is curled up on the floor, his face contorted, his shaking hands gripping his hair. Catori pushes past me and lowers herself to the floor beside him, her light nightgown barely covered by the wrap she is hugging close to her body.

"Mason," she whispers, and he stills briefly.

Callian sits on his bunk, watching his sister, his face stone.

"I don't want to... Please, I don't want to!" Mason gasps.

Catori sits beside him, resting her hand on his arm. "Wake up, Mason. It's just a dream."

His hands slide from his hair to cover his face. A strangled whimper leaves his heaving chest. Imani grips my arm tight and leans into me. I swallow the lump in my throat, cataloguing every image that could be playing out in his mind right now.

With a jerk, his eyes fly open, and he stares up at Catori.

"There you are," she whispers, forcing a wobbly smile. Mason cycles through ragged breaths and sits up, realizing he is on the ground. Catori stands and offers him her hand. He looks between the three of us watching him and slides his hand into hers. She pulls him to his feet and guides him onto his bunk. Callian lies back down, hands under his head, staring at the ceiling.

Mason sits on his bunk, back to the wall, and his eyes flutter closed. Catori walks toward the door, and he opens his eyes.

"Catori," Mason rasps, his face wrecked by whatever he saw.

"Do you need me to stay?" she asks.

Callian turns his head, brows lowered, trying to catch her gaze. Mason's jaw feathers, and he swallows. Catori walks back over, sitting next to him, her back up against the wall.

"We should go," Imani utters, but doesn't move.

Catori wraps an arm around his shoulders, and he rests his head on hers. She closes her eyes a heartbeat after his close. I turn to leave. But Imani steps into the house.

"What are you doing?" I ask.

She walks over to the bunk, and Callian tracks her movement. Imani lifts the blanket and places it around Catori and Mason. She turns back, briefly glancing at Callian, offering him a sad smile. Her face is almost as wrecked as Mason's. I lose a long, exhausted breath. None of us get out of this easily, no matter who we are.

If I know one thing, it's that things change, always. You can only do the next right thing.

CHAPTER 36
IMANI

The dawn's sharp light slips over the eastern horizon as Harm and I double-check our weapons, waiting for Callian and Mason to meet us at the outskirts of the village. Harm has been on edge since yesterday's meeting with Hanola. I myself can't help thinking about how the day's events are going to play out, how they may change some of us. I say a silent prayer to whoever will listen that we all come back safe and in one piece, tasks carried out without using the alternative plan. The alternate plan Hanola relayed to Mason and me makes my stomach twist. My mind is heavy, and I busy myself with adjusting my weapons.

Callian assures us that we can reach the tower by midday if we run. I am not sure arriving exhausted is our best move, but ending up bear food is not a great option either. Catori has organized a backup team, should we fail to return by dark: Miya's team will move in to rescue us—or whoever is left of us, anyway—should things go wrong. It is not a peaceful way to ensure our return, and I'm sure Hanola would not agree, but Catori is adamant that our return is worth the cost.

"Ready for this?" Harm wraps me in his warm hold as Callian and Mason approach.

"Not really," I murmur into his chest. I can't be any more honest than this. My heart aches at the thought of what may happen today.

"Ready when you are," Callian chirps, hands double-checking every weapon strapped to his muscled body. The three boys are all bulk now, even Mason. Each one of them is adorned with an arsenal of weapons, as are Catori and I. We have head wraps to keep us from being recognized once we breach the tower, but for now, mine is tied around my waist.

"Right. Let's get going. The sooner we get there, the sooner we can come home," Catori says, her words soft but serious.

We take off at a run, Callian in the lead, followed by Mason, then Catori, with me and then Harm in the rear. Halfway there, we stop for water before Callian motions for us to move again. The run keeps my mind from spiraling into panic over what I am about to do. Harm's steady breath falls behind me in time with his footsteps. Part of me wishes we could take off in the opposite direction and go far away, just the two of us. Tears trail down my already flushed cheeks, whipping off my skin and into my wake. I try to focus on Hanola's words, how this is the only way we will ever make things right, for all the people. Without those parchments, Harm won't be able to work with the dial. I say it over and over: this is for him. Pushing the desperation from my mind, I run hard to keep from falling apart.

The ominous grey tower ascends above the five of us, like something dark you would find in your nightmares, its shadows chasing you as your legs fail to move. Only faint forest sounds drift in the air as Callian finds the servants' entrance that the forest people who work here access every morning and night. We secure our head wraps before he pushes the door open. My heart takes off like a frenzied bird, and I suck in deep breaths, hands firmly on my knives. I follow the siblings, Mason, and Harm into the dark passageway of the tower's ground level. After moments pass, our eyes adjust.

"This is where we split up," Catori whispers. "Imani, Mason, you take the descending stairs. Harm and Callian, we take the ascending stairs."

Nods follow.

I grab Harm and pull him toward me in the dim space. I smash my mouth on his and grab his neck, with one hand running through his hair and the other on his chest. I try to breathe, try to get out some words before we're separated, but a rock in my throat wedges them in.

"I'll see you soon, Imani."

I swallow back the half-choked sobs swelling in my chest. "See you soon," I push out.

He squeezes me tight briefly before letting go to follow Catori and Callian. When I turn back, Mason is waiting for me, and we jog down the dim passageway and descend the stairs to the lower level. My aching heart thunders in my chest, and I wipe away the tears that I can't stop with every long stride. We reach the last step, and I compose myself with a long inhale before we round the corner. Drying the moisture from my face with my sleeve, I meet Mason's gaze. He gives me a reassuring look. We rip our weapons from their sheaths and turn the corner.

Six Guardians stand between us and the chamber door—not two. Mason stands beside me, his weapons trembling slightly in his hands. It's the first time he has come up against his own men.

"Breathe. You can do this," I whisper.

He gives me a quick look. In tandem, we launch, wielding our weapons against the six Guardians, their canes held at the ready, their wood against our blades, our skill against their numbers. I slice my way past the first Guardian who reaches me. He falls with one move of my blade against his chest. Every time one falls, the remaining men realize what we are capable of, now anticipating our moves, so we change our tactics, as Miya and Catori taught us.

Three Guardians lie behind us now, and the remaining three charge as one. Mason pauses, sheathing his fighting knives, and rips his broadsword from the scabbard on his back. The whine of metal echoes through the passageway, and they hesitate for only a second. Slashing their canes from side to side, they come at us running. I sidestep one and turning on him with a quick flick of my wrist, I slice his neck open as he propels past me.

The two remaining Guardians have Mason up against the wall. He is keeping them at bay with every motion of his sword, but defense is the fastest way to lose, and that sword is all but useless in close proximity. I toss my knife in my hand, adjusting my grip before I throw it into the neck of the left-hand Guardian. Instantly, he grabs for his neck, ripping the knife from it. Bad move.

Blood spurts from the gurgling wound as he face-plants into the stone floor. The last Guardian steps back, shock on his face as his comrade's life sputters out at his feet. Mason seizes the opportunity to drive his blade straight through the man's gut, and he drops to his knees beside his fallen comrade. Collapsing against the wall behind him, Mason's face is as white as the stone.

Stepping over the bodies, I grab his wrists and tug him off the wall. His bewildered eyes find mine, filled with terror and sorrow. Mason turns back and removes his blade from the man's crumpled body. I throw him a cloth, and he wipes the blood from his blade before sheathing it. He motions for me to continue, bending over and grabbing his knees. I know this scenario. It's the first kill he has actually felt. He staggers to the opposite wall, losing his stomach on the stone floor. I shift from foot to foot. Every minute we waste means less time to get what we need and get out, less chance of us going home.

"Mason, we need to move."

He looks at me, heat rising in his face. "I know. I'm sorry. This has never happened before."

I walk back to him, grabbing his arm. He stands and follows, and I release him.

We make a run for the last door in the passageway, the door to the chamber that holds what Hanola needs. The door before us stands taller than us by half. The arched wooden doorjamb is framed with metal, and the latch is secured with a large lock with three keyholes. It's like nothing I have ever seen before. I let out a low growl.

"We knew it would be locked, but *three* keys?"

"They really don't want people to know what's in here," Mason whispers, finally composed. He makes to move back to the Guardians to search for the keys.

"No, give me your sword, I'll force it open. It'll be quicker." I hold out my hand to receive the weapon. The metallic whine echoes around us, and my heart begins to race as more minutes are wasted. I grab the blade and force it through the arch of the metal lock. Using all my body weight, I pull down on the blade, now up to its hilt in the lock's grasp. The metal bends, but does not break.

Mason's hands land on top of mine. I freeze. The last time he touched me, he left a welt on my face that lasted for days. Every muscle in my body tenses.

"Let me help, Imani."

I swallow back the lump in my throat and nod slightly. "On three." My words are choked up from his hands on mine. I breathe through the panic, eyes closed, and flick through memories of Harm. After a handful of heart beats, I open my eyes.

"One," Mason whispers softly, taking over from me as his gaze burns into my face. His expression registers that I am uncomfortable with him touching me, and he has adjusted his words to compensate.

"Two," I say, as if agreeing with his help. But his hand burns on top of mine.

"Three!" he breathes.

We slam down on the top of the hilt. The lock shatters to the floor, and clanging echoes through the passageway beyond us. I wince, breathing out as I remove the last of the metal hanging from the door's latch. The rust on the latch and cradle groans and splinters before giving way, and I shove the door open.

The breath leaves my chest, and I stand with my mouth agape. Before me are rows and rows of shelves, packed with dust-covered relics. A beam of sunlight shines directly into the center of the vast chamber, landing on a table. A small draft dances around my feet.

Mason clears his throat, and I look back at him, almost having forgotten he is with me. His face looks as shocked as I feel. We take a tentative step toward the metal shelving units rising above us, almost twice our height, but still not reaching the ceiling. Light filters through the rows of tall, nearly opaque windows, with bars just visible behind their grimy surfaces. Nobody gets in here.

Yelling from beyond the doorway snaps me back to reality. Thunderous footsteps follow the voices. Mason grabs my hand, but I pull it back.

"We need to hide," I snap.

"There's no way out of here; they'll find us in minutes. If we run or hide, we can't stick to Hanola's plan," he says urgently.

"I don't want to do this."

"Imani, we have to."

"I don't know if I can."

"I won't let them hurt you."

"How can you? You're a traitor to them, Mason."

He shakes his head, but doesn't explain. "Please, just trust me," he whispers, just as the Guardians fly through the doorway. Mason throws his hands in the air. Hesitating, I follow his lead, hands above my head. Within seconds, we are face down on the hard stone. Mason's eyes are fixed on mine. My heart thunders against my ribs so hard it almost connects with the floor. Breaths shudder from my body as a Guardian pulls my hands behind my back, binding them with rope.

If Mason is lying, I will kill him myself, regardless of Hanola's plans.

Firm hands pull me to my feet and shove me along the passageway. Mason's stare is still burning into me, his hands now bound behind him too as we are escorted side by side. We ascend the stairs and stop at the doorway to the bridge, sunlight filtering in around us.

Standing halfway across is Fletcher.

I let out a low growl, and Mason looks to the middle of the bridge and swallows hard. I stand tall in the grip of the Guardian behind me, heart hammering in my chest. Inhaling slow and deep breaths, I walk when pushed forward.

Mason's face changes to one of arrogance. A flutter in my chest raises a lump in my throat as I glance between Mason and Fletcher. I don't trust Mason, but Hanola does. Whatever plan she has for him, I pray he is about to execute it, or it's all over.

CHAPTER 37
HARM

Blood pounds through my veins after running the whole of the ascending stairs to the top level of the tower—Catori's idea. It is easier to fight your way downstairs than up them, and she wasted no time silently scaling the levels of winding stairs. Around the next corner, if Mason hasn't sold us out, is the door that leads to the dial. It will be guarded by two Guardians.

On the whispered count of three, Callian spins around the corner, blades out. Two thumps follow, one after the other. He's quick; they didn't even have time to call for help.

"Clear," Callian whispers loudly.

"You first, Harm. I'll protect the rear," Catori says.

I step out from behind the corner and over the limp bodies of the Guardians, who are no longer breathing. Stepping up to the door, I handle the lock, small and old. It's not exactly worthy of what it's guarding, which makes me suspicious. Callian breaks the lock with the hilt of his sword.

The door opens easily, and immediately I see the dial sitting atop a wooden pillar—just like the messy sketch my grandfather drew in the notebook from my workspace at home in Amondo. He made this pillar, and the techniques he used on the wood and its joint pieces are the same ones I used for years. I run a finger over a joint, tracing its tail-like shape, accented by a small curve on one tip, his patented design. Difficult to do, but essential for your work to endure.

"Harm, can you change it back?" Catori whispers, her eyes flicking between the dial and the door.

We are essentially trapped up here. If Guardians come, we will have to fight our way out, which is not ideal; we would tire before they would run out of Guardians.

I scan the face of the dial, but I don't recognize anything. Everything on its face is made out in symbols and in another language; I can't even read it.

"We can't stay here much longer," Catori hisses. "Tell me now if you can't do it; we can just go back with the information Imani is getting." Her feet are shifting, her blades turning in her hands.

"No, I can't even read it," I choke, my hands trembling as I brush the face of the dial one last time.

"It's okay. Let's go. At least now we know."

I glance at it one more time, trying to memorize the details before following Callian out the door, followed by Catori, who silently shuts it behind her.

Callian and Catori have flanked me every step of the way, and now we backtrack to the meeting room. Arthur's seat is empty, as is Emmie's. I stand in the spot where I kneeled here last time, watching Charlie die. The wooden floor gleams, like nothing bad ever happened here. Wasting no time, we run to the next level down. A living room. No sign of Nirri or Emmie. The furniture is elegant, wooden, covered in soft fabrics, with brass decor and paintings full of color. The smell of musty timber and old books fills the space, and I linger too long.

"Harm, we have to keep moving," Catori hisses.

Callian leads the way as we run down the next set of stairs. Something isn't right. Why is the place so empty? The tower is bigger than it looks from the outside, and I'm hoping that we've just missed something. If we don't find Arthur first, he is sure to find us, leaving us at a big disadvantage when we lose the element of stealth and surprise.

Shouting from the bridge grabs our attention. Catori signals for us to descend the stairs again. We make a silent but hasty retreat to the doorway that leads to the bridge. Callian stops abruptly, and I run into his back, Catori stumbling to a halt beside me.

"No," Callian rasps, his body rigid.

I walk around him to get a better look. Standing with their hands behind their backs, in the grip of Guardians, are Mason and Imani.

My heart flies into my throat, and my breath stops.

"Imani..."

Callian grips my arm, holding me where I stand. Tendrils of fear snake their way through my body, radiating through my thundering chest. My hands tremble around the grips of my blades, still sheathed.

"Wait," Catori breathes.

"Sir, we found these two downstairs," the Guardian holding Mason reports.

"Forest dwellers. It's been a long time since I've had to deal with your people," Fletcher snarls.

Imani struggles against the grip holding her, and Fletcher unceremoniously slams her across the head with his cane. Two more Guardians step toward Imani, holding their canes ready to strike. A strangled moan leaves my throat, and I strain against Callian's hold before Catori's hand grabs my other arm.

Imani slumps to the bridge, hands bracing herself. I let out a painful whimper, and Callian shoots me a warning look. Rage thunders alongside the fear that fills every part of my body. Every breath is an effort.

"Wait! She's with me!" Mason yells at Fletcher, ripping off his head wrap.

"Rayner! What are you doing here?!" Fletcher demands, confusion puckering his face.

"As ordered, sir, I have successfully infiltrated the forest and desert rebel camps, and I felt it was time to report," Mason says. The Guardian holding him releases his grip and unties his wrists. Mason's calm and arrogant words grate on my raw nerves, and a tide of sickness rolls in my gut.

"No..." Catori's utters. Her face drains of color, but she stays frozen in her position, her grip on me even firmer.

Mason waves a hand, and the Guardians over Imani retreat. "She's with me," he repeats, leaning down to help Imani up. With a swift tug, he removes her ropes. Her small frame next to Mason's makes the fire in my chest rise up my neck, my hands balling into fists.

Fletcher looks from Mason to Imani, not yet realizing who it is, her head wrap still in place. "That wasn't part of your orders, Rayner. You were to act alone," he spits.

Imani moves closer to Mason, brushing herself down and double-checking her weapons.

Mason's face is stone. "I did what you asked, and I took the liberty of ensuring that your half of our bargain was honored."

Fletcher looks between Mason and Imani, his face turning from confusion to understanding. Callian's free hand grips my shoulder. My heart lurches in my chest.

"I did your snooping, and in return, I got what I wanted, Fletcher—and you know very well what I want." Mason's gaze burns into Fletcher's.

The clouds overhead shift in the southerly winds, and sunlight pours down on the bridge. A glint of the gold chain around Imani's neck catches the eye of Fletcher. He steps toward her, hand outstretched to grab it. Imani raises both hands, and her fingers make quick work of her head wrap. Her dark hair falls around her shoulders. My legs lose every inch of strength holding them up.

"Hello, Father," Imani coos, her hands resting on her hips.

Fletcher's eyes widen as he rips the chain from her chest to inspect it. Her Blending pendant glimmers in perfect hues of blue in his hand. Mason steps in beside her, sliding his arm around her waist, tugging her against his side.

Nausea rises, burning my throat. The three of us stand frozen. Small, quick steps hurry down the stairs above us. Seconds later, the flushed face of Nirri meets our stricken stares.

"What are you still doing here?! Arthur's private guard are coming! You need to run!"

When none of us move, she alternates her gaze between our three devastated faces.

"Whatever happened, it's about to get a lot worse if you don't run. Please, Callian, go!" She touches his arm.

He stares at her, then back at me. Briefly, he grabs Nirri's face with both trembling hands, planting his mouth on hers.

"Thank you," he breathes, releasing her face.

She stares at him with wide eyes for a heartbeat before pushing him toward the stairs. Callian grabs my arm on the way past and shoves me down every step toward the exit. Behind us echoes Nirri's gasp. "Oh, no..."

Her words fade in the growing distance between us. The ringing in my ears drowns out the thundering in my head. Within moments, the fresh air of the forest side of the wall hits me. I blink, looking around, praying this is all a bad dream. But Imani is not beside me, and the look on Callian's face cuts through me like a newly forged blade.

"Run, Harm!" Callian chokes.

I fall in behind Catori. Numb, I run, following her. Callian's heavy stride follows mine, matching every step. For hours, we run. The ringing in my ears disappears, then there's only silence, as if the forest has taken away its sounds. We break through the last row of trees framing the village just before the last rays of the sun shrink over the western horizon. Miya and Jeselle are waiting for us.

"Where are Imani and Mason?" Miya says. Jeselle grabs her arm, worry seizing her face as her eyes search the three of us for an answer. Miya's face crinkles in fear. "Catori, where is Imani?"

"They're not with us," Callian breathes.

"Are they behind you?" Jeselle asks.

"No," Catori chokes out.

"Why not? We don't leave our people behind, Catori, you know that!" Miya snaps.

"They are no longer our people, Miya," Callian growls, stalking past her.

Miya's face pales, her body rigid. Her breath stops, her eyes widening.

I hit the muddy ground, knees sinking into the damp soil, wet grass meeting my forehead. As I gasp for breath through the weight crushing my chest, my hands pull through my hair. Jeselle lingers, staring at me before going after Callian. Dazed, Miya releases a curse, throwing an arm around Catori's shoulders and leading her back to the village.

Screams pour out of my chest in a never-ending chain of sorrow.

She is gone.

Standing beside Mason.

What the hell?!

The dial... I couldn't even read it.

I touched it...

Nothing happened.

Imani.

No. Please, no.

Every piece of me rips apart from the inside. Every hope, every dream of a better world, and her in it with me.

Gone.

Imani is gone.

I rise, rocking onto my heel, letting my head fall backward. My screams turn to a thunderous roar.

CONTINUE THE STORY

TAP THE IMAGE TO KEEP READING!

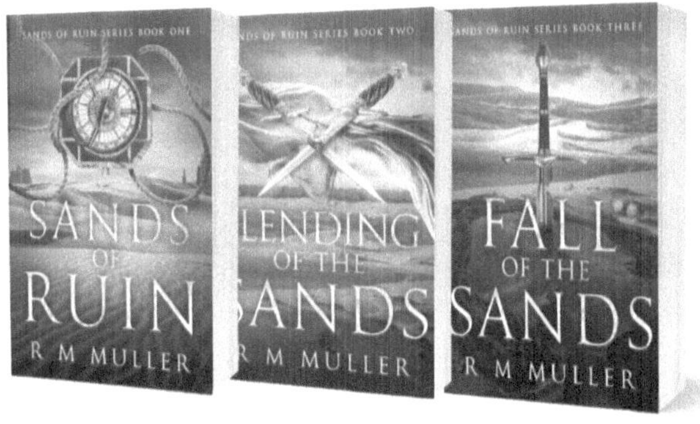

SANDS OF RUIN SERIES BOOK THREE
FALL
OF THE
SANDS
R M MULLER

ACKNOWLEDGMENTS

This series has taken me from dabbling to dedicated! I have so many wonderful people to thank for that, but mostly my readers... And my characters! (I wouldn't be here without either of those.)

Louise, for reading this story and helping me make it its best. Robin, who's editing insight is greatly appreciated. Lindsey, for being my eagle-eye ... Rebecca, for getting all ducks in their rows ... Christian, for your brilliant and creative cover design. To all the writerly friends that have encouraged me through the journey of creating something from nothing, you are absolute legends.

My patient and very grammatically correct mother, who reads every book I write. To my girls, for letting me bounce plot ideas and scenes around with them, and always giving me very honest (read: blunt) feedback, my four mini Imanis.

And to the strong women in my life who refuse to give in, Imani was moulded from each one of your courageous traits!

Thank you to every reader who has found themselves on this page (and perhaps in these pages), you are truly rockstars!! Thank you for journeying alongside Harm and Imani and loving them as much as I have.

About the Author

Perched on a thin limb in a tree that had stood for decades, was a skinny, little farm girl. Her focus was solely on the scrappy notebook and pencil in her hands. Oblivious to the swaying branches around her and the voice of her mother calling her down, she scratched out a story. For the first time her imagination made it to paper, and she was obsessed.

Rose-Marie is a mother to four vivacious daughters, wife to a grazier, sister, daughter, etc. Stories and her little bunch of humans keep her alive and give her purpose every day, and the reason she spends a disturbing amount of time with imaginary people, in imaginary worlds, most days.